Charles Gidley was born in 1938 and was educated at University College School, Hampstead. He joined the Royal Navy as a Dartmouth cadet at 16, qualified as a Fleet Air Arm pilot and flying instructor, and later became a minesweeper captain and the senior pilot of the Royal Navy's Airborne Early Warning squadron. Since leaving the Royal Navy in 1980, he has been writing for a living.

Before becoming a novelist, Charles Gidley wrote extensively for television, contributing to the BBC's drama series *Warship* and *Wings*, and Yorkshire Television's *The Sandbaggers*.

Other novels by Charles Gidley are *The River Running By* (1981), *The Raging of the Sea* (1984), and *Armada* (1987).

He was brought up in the Brethren but broke away on joining the Navy. Later he converted to Roman Catholicism, but after 15 years he left the Church and now prefers not to identify himself with any particular religion.

Available in Fontana by the same author

The River Running By
The Raging of the Sea

CHARLES GIDLEY

The Believer

FONTANA/Collins

First published in Great Britain by
André Deutsch Limited 1986

First published in Fontana Paperbacks 1987

Copyright © 1986 by Charles Gidley Wheeler

Printed and made in Great Britain by
William Collins Sons & Co. Ltd, Glasgow

PREFACE

In his preface to *Father and Son* Edmund Gosse wrote:
'At the present hour, when fiction takes forms so ingenious and so specious, it is perhaps necessary to say that
the following narrative, in all its parts . . . is scrupulously
true.'

While I cannot make the same claim for *The Believer*, I
can say that I have been scrupulously careful, in shaping
this work of fiction, to include nothing which I did not
consider entirely in keeping with the attitudes, behaviour
and beliefs of the early Plymouth Brethren. Also, I would
like to make it clear that I have no argument at all with
spiritual faith, but only those sorts of religiosity which
claim a monopoly of the truth and whose divisive doctrines have wrecked (and continue to wreck) so many lives
and set so many families at variance.

This book should not therefore be regarded as an
historical romance, but rather as a cautionary tale, and
because it has been written as if I had been born in 1838
rather than 1938, the reader should not expect twentieth
century hindsight, a comfortable resolution or any sort of
liberated behaviour from my characters. Such modern
techniques would have been quite out of place in a novel
which is essentially a piece of reproduction furniture, and
if their absence detracts from the enjoyment of the novel,
I apologise.

Charles Gidley, September 1985

PART ONE

Damascus

CHAPTER 1

'And what,' enquired Mr Lethbridge, staring intently up at the young man who stood before his desk, 'is your opinion of public hanging?'

Blair Harvey had been invited into the senior partner's office for an introductory interview, and was anxious to make a good first impression. Lethbridge – a lean, energetic man of fifty – had already quizzed him about his family background, and while Clannaborough, the old clerk, wheezed in and out with documents for signature, Blair had been required to give a summary of his academic achievements, political inclinations and knowledge of the law.

'Public hanging?' he repeated, playing for time.

'Yes, sir. Public hanging.'

Blair put on his intellectual frown. He had already made light of the fact that he had scraped the minimum degree at Oxford, giving the impression that he had been too preoccupied with a consuming interest in ethics and theology to score a brilliant First.

He was just about to suggest that he was inclined against the idea but that, on the other hand, there seemed to be certain advantages in making a public display of justice being done, when Lethbridge leaned quickly forward and whipped off his spectacles. 'Have you ever attended one?'

Blair rocked on his heels, blinking rapidly. 'I must confess, sir, I have not.'

'In that case I think you had better. Dubuis is to be hanged tomorrow, and as we don't hold public executions more than once or twice a year in Exeter, it will be as well if you go along.'

Harvey's mouth opened and shut several times, and he uttered a little croaking sound that was not at all in keeping with the impression of self assurance and manly bearing which he had intended to present.

'What's the matter with you, boy? Are you squeamish?'

'N–not at all, sir.'

'Very well then. Tomorrow at midday precisely. I shall expect a detailed account of the proceedings from you, together with your comments upon the advantages of public execution – or disadvantages as the case may be.'

Blair was both excited and apprehensive about going to see a man hanged, and couldn't help wondering whether his lamented mother would have approved. On leaving Oriel, his tutor had told him that great things were expected of him, and the combination of an adoring parent, a profusion of elder sisters and a generous endowment of good looks had given him that peculiar over-confidence sometimes found among young men of second-rate ability.

The prospect of witnessing a hanging mitigated such self-confidence, however, and he felt a little frightened that the sight of a human being on a gibbet might alter him in some unexpected way.

Striding down Idle Lane to his lodgings that evening, he told himself that such thoughts were ridiculous. He had taken the opportunity to read up the case after his interview with Mr Lethbridge, and had discovered that Dubuis was a French fisherman whose smack had been blown ashore near Exmouth the previous winter, and who had fallen in love with a lady of the city, murdering her in a fit of rage on discovering that she was a prostitute. A petition for clemency had been presented by the French

Ambassador to the Home Secretary on Dubuis' behalf, but this had been rejected. Meanwhile, the editor of the *Flying Post* had taken advantage of the story to thunder about the superiority of the English legal system. 'Dubuis is a whore-master and a murderer' the leading article had declared, 'and the only punishment a just society can allow is that he be hung by the neck until he is dead.'

Harvey had never before encountered the term 'whore-master', and was rather intrigued by it. All in all, he was beginning to think that witnessing the comeuppance of M Dubuis would prove to be an educative experience.

He climbed the narrow stair of Mrs Mudge's house, and entered the garret. A plain deal table stood under a narrow window, and a truckle bed sagged under an oedema of doubtful looking bedding. There was mildew in the press and candlewax on the dresser, but to Blair such inconveniences added to the romance of the place, and he could never enter the room without imagining some day in the future when a brass plate over the door would record that it was in these humble surroundings that the famous Lord Chancellor had made his beginnings.

Peering out of the dormer window, he was rewarded with an unrestricted view of roofs and chimney pots; but if he looked diagonally out to the left, he could see a short stretch of the River Exe, upon whose waters the rays of the setting sun were depositing a blood-red sheen.

He straightened, and after a moment's thought took a sealed letter from an inside pocket. It was addressed to a Dr Brougham, and had been written by Blair's tutor at Oxford. Ever since setting out in the mail coach five days before, Blair had longed to read its contents, for the simple reason that they were concerned with his favourite subject.

He stared down at the black copperplate handwriting until – overcome by temptation – he decided to do a little intelligence work.

Having lit a candle dip, he waved the seal gently over

the flame to soften it, and opening the sheet, read:

Sir,

I commend to you Mr Blair Harvey, who has recently graduated here and who is to take articles to a firm of solicitors in Exeter. Having served as his tutor I know him to be a young gentleman of high moral values and good intention. He will, however, be a stranger to Exeter, and as he is still of tender years and a somewhat impulsive nature, I fear it might be easy for him to fall into bad company; I shall be obliged therefore to you, dear sir, if you will afford him your patronage and, if you would, introduce him to your circle.

Assuring you of my continued respect I remain,
Yours truly
Tobias Watling, D.D.

Post Scriptum: One of the Fellows here – J.H. Newman – asks me to convey to you his warmest regards.

Had Blair lent such close attention to his Latin prose translations as he now gave to this letter, the elusive First would undoubtedly have been his. Pacing up and down so that a loose floor board squeaked repeatedly, he pondered it at some length, seeing it as the first important crossroads of his career.

He had already made some enquiries about Dr Brougham, and had discovered that the gentleman was a wealthy curate with a large house in the cathedral grounds; but the references to his own tender years and impulsive nature irritated him considerably, and he felt even less inclined to present the letter than he had when Dr Watling had given it to him on the morning of his departure from Oxford.

Did he really wish to present himself to this worthy

straight away? Might it not be amusing to enjoy a little anonymity in the city before entering the sort of society Dr Watling or Dr Brougham might deem suitable?

He could imagine how it would be: he would attend at the Divine Doctor's church and present his letter. He would be invited to call at the vicarage for tea, and on the strength of the favourable impression he would make (yes, it would be all too favourable!) other invitations would follow. There would be a whispering Mama, anxious to foster his friendship and marry him off to one of her brood of tittering daughters. He would be surrounded by swooping necklines and fluttering hearts; he would become their 'dear Mr Harvey', 'one of the family' – and before he had time to say Exeter Assizes his bachelor days would be over and he would be condemned to provincial mediocrity for the rest of his life.

He shuddered. Was this the way to start a full and triumphant career? Did one who might end up on the Woolsack go pleading to a twopenny-ha'penny cleric for his patronage and protection?

There – it was done. The letter was torn in two. And four. And eight.

He opened the window and watched the little squares of paper flutter down upon the urchins playing in the back alley, and smiled to himself at the thought that this simple action had in all probability changed the entire course of his life.

Following the advice of his landlady, Blair Harvey made an early start the following morning, and after a hearty breakfast of hot coffee and salamandered bacon, he set out to walk to the county gaol.

He was amazed to find that the streets were already a moving mass of people. They were entering the city in carts and two-horse wagons and on foot; the gin shops were already doing a roaring trade, and by the look of jolly festivity on the faces of these rosy-cheeked Devon people, they might have been coming for the horse races or the county fair.

Striding importantly along and swinging a silver-topped ebony stick left to him by his father (who had died when Blair was six) he fell in with the mob and went with them out to Northernhay, where fields separated the northern wall of the city from the gaol and the military barracks beyond.

He found himself considerably outnumbered by the lower classes in the company he was now obliged to keep, and was struck by the cheerful camaraderie that prevailed. Feeling it his duty to obtain a good view of the proceedings, he elbowed his way closer until he was within feet of the gibbet itself.

It was made of wood and painted black, and had been erected up against a side door. The first sight of it caused a slight shock of excitement which he found strangely disturbing in that it was not entirely unpleasant. Having stared at it for some time with an intensity which sometimes belies an empty mind, he turned his attention to the people around him.

A little way off, a shout of laughter drew his attention. Some ragamuffin children had been playing hopscotch in the prison yard, and an old hag with draggled hair and no teeth had insisted upon joining in. The sight of this old dear hopping and stamping her way up the chalked squares was causing her spectators to double up with mirth, and Blair caught himself laughing at her before he remembered that this was a solemn occasion.

He turned back to the gibbet. One of the prison officers was barking orders, and a moment later a line of chained convicts was led out into the open in order to witness the execution. Their appearance brought forth more hoots and screams – this time from a group of women who stood right up against the scaffold itself, and whom Blair had noticed making saucy suggestions to anything in trousers.

One in particular tickled his fancy: a girl of fourteen or

so with dark eyes and black hair, a red mouth, good teeth and a well-filled bodice. When she saw that she had caught his eye, she raised her eyebrow so invitingly that he experienced sensations he anticipated might be difficult to describe in a letter to his sisters. He looked quickly away. These women, he realised, must be *whores*.

He watched them covertly, thinking that it might be interesting – even educational – to have intercourse with them. However, as the city bells were chiming the quarter before midday, and final preparations for the dropping of M Dubuis seemed to be in hand, he decided that this was neither the time nor the place to do so.

A door opened and a man in a leather jerkin mounted the scaffold. He set a ladder up against the horizontal bar and hooked the rope onto an eyebolt. For some minutes there was a hush, and during this time most eyes were fixed upon the motionless noose. There could be no doubt that minds were concentrated.

A gasp went up: a side door had opened, and Dubuis, his hands bound before him, was led out. A woman standing in front of Blair turned and winked. Her face was reddened with gin. 'That be 'e,' she confided, to which Blair replied that he had already noted the fact for himself.

There was a jostling for a good view now, and Blair jostled as hard as any, telling himself that he was the one person in the crowd with a good reason for doing so.

He saw in Dubuis' face a surprising intelligence, even sensitivity. He looked more of a thinker than a murderer or fisherman, and it seemed that he was quite oblivious of the crowd. His face turned skyward and his lips moved; he made the sign of the cross with his bound hands, then submitted himself to the executioner, who fitted a white stocking over his head, turned him to face away from the city and placed the noose about his neck.

For a few seconds, the hangman whispered in his ear;

Dubuis nodded calmly. Suddenly, the import of what was happening reached Blair Harvey: he wanted to shout, 'No – stop – we have no right –'. But the executioner was already descending the steps to operate the trap; Dubuis stood alone, quite still; there was a squeak and a bang as the trap door opened and a thump and a jolt as the body dropped, jerked and swung; then immediately an anonymous pair of black gloves reached up from below, seized the legs and gave an almighty jerk, so that a sudden foam of blood appeared in the white head covering and a terrible gargling cry came from Dubuis.

The effect this performance had on the crowd was varied. Some shrieked, some wailed, some called upon God and some seemed to achieve a strange sensuous delight. One little girl cried bitterly, rubbing her fists into her eyes and begging her elder sister to take her away from that terrible place. As for Blair Harvey, he experienced a slight queaziness for some time after, but by supper was back to his normal self and able to put away two good helpings of tripe and onions; and that evening he recorded in his journal that the experience had been 'a very instructive lesson in the checks and balances of that most complicated of engines, viz. the law of England,' omitting to comment that the most forcible impression made on him that morning had been the looks of invitation he had received from the women who stood beneath the gibbet.

The witnessing of the hanging had other, more subtle effects upon him. He had never rubbed shoulders with the many-headed in so intimate a way before, and the experience of it had been an eye-opener. The instinctive feelings of injustice aroused by the sight of Dubuis making the sign of the cross and humbly submitting himself for despatch into eternity had disturbed him more than he cared to admit. It seemed to him that the plight of the common people was indeed a miserable one, and he could not help reflecting that it would be a fine thing indeed to be their champion.

He became particularly aware, as he grew to know Exeter better, of the unfortunate plight of women in the city. He watched them haggling over ha'pennies in the fish market and pork butchers, queueing for water at the South Street conduit or gossiping together under the Guildhall arches where miscreants sat in the stocks, and was tempted to believe that they belonged to a lower species. As time passed, his attention focussed increasingly upon the city whores. Having deliberately separated himself from polite society by tearing up Dr Watling's letter, he found that time hung heavy in the evenings, and he began to yearn for female company.

What he would really like to do, he decided, was to have a long, serious talk with one of these ladies in order to discover how they lived and in what way he might improve their lot in life. The thought even occurred to him that he might go down in history as the benefactor who finally rid England's cities of their prostitutes.

A chance to further these ambitions offered itself on a hot Saturday afternoon in August, when the fair came to Southernhay. Blair had gone along with money in his purse and the intention of widening his view of social conditions. A barrel organ piped and clattered out the same tune over and over again; a man with huge moustaches invited brave young men to take on the champion at a bare knuckle contest, and on the far side of the green, beyond the agricultural displays, a contingent from the barracks marched and countermarched to the sound of fife and drum, while sergeants and corporals attempted to persuade bystanding youths to take the King's shilling.

Blair wandered among the stalls, enjoying the noise and the crowds and feeling a sense of rightness in the world: the sun was shining, Napoleon was beaten, and he was present among these good people for the best of all possible motives. What a fine place the world was, he thought, and willingly donated a penny to a gypsy woman who sprawled by the entrance of a refreshment tent with a baby at her breast.

Turning away from this act of charity, he found himself face to face with the young girl who had caught his eye under the gibbet some weeks before.

'Like a bit of fun for a shilling, sir?' she whispered urgently, and touched his hand.

He blinked rapidly and a vein throbbed in his forehead. She was so young and innocent-looking that he could not really regard her as a whore. And might she not make a very pleasant and informative interviewee?

'Come on, love,' she wheedled. 'What's a shilling to a gentleman?'

He wished that she had not approached him in so public a place, and that he had had more time to think. 'Perhaps we could – ah – go for a stroll?' he suggested.

Her eyes widened. 'Oh, yes, sir! I know just the place!' She winked. 'Down by Berry Meadow, sir.'

He very nearly weakened, but then he thought of his mother, and shuddered. No, really he could not do it. He turned abruptly away, and walked off to mingle with the crowd who were laughing at a youth half way up a greasy pole.

He would not normally have volunteered for so degrading a competition as this, but felt driven to prove himself; so he paid his halfpenny to the perspiring butcher who had donated the prize of a piece of beef, and having removed his coat, waistcoat and neckcloth, he proceeded to climb.

Several attempts had already been made on the pole that afternoon, and the sun's heat had melted much of the lard with which the stake had been smeared. He discovered that by wiping the fat off with his sleeve and wrapping the pole tightly between his thighs he was able to achieve a grip and – encouraged by yells and hoots from below – edged his way to the top.

This was an achievement indeed, and having got his

armpit over the top and removed the hunk of beef he felt that the occasion warranted a speech.

'Ladies and gentlemen!' he started, imagining for a moment that he was mayor of Exeter. 'As you can see, I have won the prize of a fine side of English beef.' (It was not fine at all, for several bluebottles were buzzing about, having recently propagated their species upon it.) 'But as you will also observe when I descend, this prize has been achieved only at the cost of soiling my shirt and trousers.'

He was about to rehearse a speech often made to him by various uncles and academics about achievement only being possible at the cost of pain or detriment when he saw the girl again. She was gazing up at him, and from his point of view presented an unusually fine aspect of her most attractive features.

'Therefore I propose,' he said, feeling himself about to slip from the pole and altering the thrust of his speech, 'that any good honest girl who will volunteer to take in my laundry and return it to its original spotless condition shall be rewarded with a handsome portion of this sirloin.' With that he slid down faster than he had expected to, arriving in a heap at the bottom of the pole, to be saluted by the girl, whose more respectable offer he felt happy to accept.

Ignoring a yokel in a smock frock who remarked that she'd be taking in more than his washing, Blair led the way off the fair ground, his heart thumping in anticipation while the girl, bearing the meat, followed a pace or two behind.

She didn't know what all the fuss was about, for sure. She'd made him a decent offer, only a shilling, and now he was going on about taking in his washing. Well, that wasn't the reason she came here with him, they both knew that and she said so straight out to his face as soon as they were in his room and the door shut. 'I'm not washing no clothes,' she said. 'I'm above it.' So he took the meat off her and called downstairs, very snooty, to Mrs Mudge and when she came up he gave it her for a stew, holding the door shut behind him so she wouldn't see into the room. Then he comes back in and tries to get her to go, but she spins him the story about her father being in Princetown for thieving and he changes his mind and tells her to sit down, no, not on the bed on the chair, so she does. He's got a head on him as noble as a lion, and hair that goes straight back in waves and his hands are gentleman's hands like she didn't often see because she'd never done business with gentlemen, not yet any road, not before this one. Then he starts asking her questions, all the usual ones about how old she is which was fourteen but she says sixteen, and how long she's been doing business which was over a year but she says only three weeks and looks soft and innocent, the way they like you to be. And she guessed that he was more than half innocent and all, with his Cupid lips and his eyes like a choirboy's and nice straight legs too; and except for the pig fat on his clothes not at all mucky or greasy like some of the journeymen and farmers that came in on market day and wanted everything twice over for fourpence halfpenny. No, he was better than that lot, he was gentry, and gentry was worth giving a good time because they made regular customers, that's what the girls said. They said one regular gentleman was better than any number of casuals because they got attached to you and gave you presents and if you got into trouble they could be talked into coughing up regular and setting up the little bastard for life and you could end up gentry yourself with little viscounts and marquises for grandchildren. So she asked him how he likes it and he sucks in his cheeks and says 'I'm not contemplating taking advantage of your services my dear, I don't have need of that sort of thing.' 'Oh yes you do, sir,' she says and feels him with her hand to make sure it isn't a rolled up stocking he's got in there, and he smiles his little boy smile again, sort of proud of himself and not knowing where to look and a vein goes pumping down his forehead. He asks her name and she tells him, Molly Burke. 'Irish?' 'Yes,' she says. 'Come over with me dad.' He looks at her very close, his eyeballs jerking from side to side and up and down and his breath sweet and warm in her face, so she unpicks her front and gives him a view of the hills. 'Come on, my lovely,' she whispers. 'I ain't eaten all day,' and he says 'Molly, Molly, Molly, you don't know what you're saying.' 'Don't I sir?' she says, and she takes his hand and stuffs it down her front and his tongue comes out and licks all around his mouth, like as if he's going to have strawberries and cream. He says all right then, help him with his boots and he sits on the bed and she pulls them off and falls over backwards on purpose, so's he can see what he's in for and they turn it into a game: she jumps on him and pushes him back and dangles them right down over his mouth so his eyes look as if they'll pop. 'You ain't never done this before, have you sir?' she says, and he looks up between her arms and says, 'Many a time and oft,' as if he was Lord Byron himself, so she starts undoing his buttons making out he's a little boy and saying what have we here and who's a big boy then and would he like a kiss, and she gets every last stitch off of him too, and there's hardly a hair on his body except for the fuzz round his Thomas O'Reilly, which is up in the air and looking very promising, so she gets out her piece of sponge just to be ready like and he wants to know what it's for, so she tells him it's to keep away the babies. 'Well I never knew that,' he says. 'There's lots of things you don't know,' she says and proceeds to show him, too, and he learns so quick she begins to wonder if it should be she who ought to be paying him a shilling because they do it this way and that way and the other, and he can't seem to get himself a-going until all of a sudden he does, and that's when the fuss sets in because he can't stop himself and he's so tight in there he can't get out either and he starts moaning and gasping and weeping and chopping his teeth, and all of a sudden it's all hands man the pumps and he's got the guilty consciences, calling out to his mother to ask her what he's done, saying he's ruined for life, he's sold his birthright and dallied in Sodom and Gomorrah; he's down on his knees, stark bollocky, beating his head against the bed-post and sobbing like a four-year-old, so she pulls down her skirts and does herself up proper and says what about my shilling then, to which he replies she can take it out of his purse, there on the table – take as much as she likes but just go, so she looks in the purse and finds a sovereign, six shillings, a crown and a few pennies in it. Well, she knew her place and wasn't having him say she robbed him, but he'd had more than twice a shilling's worth so she took two, then four, then put them back and took the crown, then thought that'd be difficult to change so she took the six shillings after all, and when she opens the door there's Ma Mudge down on her knees at the keyhole and she stands up all flustered with her clogs in her hands and her bunions sticking out like Jerusalem artichokes, and some lunatic's banging and screaming on the wall next door; so Molly Burke knows what's good for her and gets out while the going's good.

Anyway, she still didn't see what all the fuss was about, because she gave it him good and he did his stuff with plenty over for seconds all round as they say, and it was a pity he come all over God-forgive-me because she reckoned he'd have made a good regular gentleman and she might have kept herself clean for him if he give her a few shillings a week by way of a retainer. She could have kept herself clean and lived respectable. But that was men for you, all different and all the same, and the best thing to do was get on and forget all about him as quick as possible, which was what she did.

CHAPTER 2

Percival Brougham liked to think of himself as a man of many parts; well rounded in the classics, amusing in conversation, the keeper of a good table, the benefactor to many causes and the admiration of his parishioners.

He lived with his wife Jane and his daughter Susannah in Broad Gate House, a well proportioned building erected during the reign of Queen Anne, which stood opposite the cathedral in Cathedral Close. Lamp-blacked chains were supported by low white posts on either side of the porch, and wistaria clung to the bricked-up window above it. The elevations were of Heavitree stone, and the rows of sash windows nicely spaced. At the rear, there was a walled flower garden, with lawn and sundial, a separate vegetable patch and a few apple trees. To the side were the laundry, the stables and the coach house.

Inside, to left and right of the panelled hall, were a study and the front parlour, with the dining and drawing rooms to the rear and a kitchen and scullery beyond. A square spiral staircase mounted to two upper storeys and a garret (where the servants slept), and the bathroom on the first floor was served with running water, pumped up to a cistern at six o'clock every morning by the boy.

Dr Brougham slept in the bedroom over his study and his wife over the front parlour. Susannah, who was their only surviving child, slept on the second floor and used her room as a study, having recently taken up Greek and Hebrew.

23

It was a well regulated household – too well regulated for Susannah's liking. Her father insisted upon having his meals plentiful and on time, and the days ticked by with the awful precision of the upright clock in the hall.

For all the outward calm this household presented to the world, it contained within itself – like the country at large – its own peculiar turmoil, for there had existed a conflict of belief between Percy and Jane that had its roots in a far older argument: one that had been rumbling through the country for three hundred years. Ever since Susannah could remember (and that went back to the years before Wellington's great victory) her father had been engaged in a war of words, a war that was conducted in the dark confines of his study, where he was more or less continually engaged in the writing of some thesis, treatise or letter. The purpose of his war had at first been to bring about a return to the doctrines and traditions of the early church and to shake Anglicanism out of its lethargy; but more recently it had developed into a more or less open campaign to re-unite England with Rome.

In the early years of her marriage, Jane Brougham had been required by her husband to listen while he read aloud his outpourings, and Susannah had grown accustomed to the sound of her father's voice, buzzing and booming behind the closed study door, and to seeing her mother emerge looking bored and distraught.

Slowly, her husband's leanings towards Rome had soured Jane and had caused a reaction in her: the more she heard of Papist doctrines, the more she came to detest them, until she had finally abandoned even the Anglican Church, choosing instead to attend the assemblies in the dissenters' meeting room at the bottom of South Street, near the city wall.

The disagreement had effectively wrecked relations between husband and wife: it had spilled over into every other aspect of their life together and had inevitably found focus in their only daughter.

24

She was torn between them. She loved and respected her father who, from her earliest years, had encouraged her to study, and had generously put at her disposal the entire contents of his extensive library. At the same time she admired her mother for her selfless work among the poor and for her stout refusal to give up her beliefs. But this split in her loyalties brought about a further conflict, for like so many children of ill-matched parents, she could never quite escape the feeling that she was in some way to blame for the hostility and bitterness that lurked in Broad Gate House.

One day when Susannah was seventeen and already possessed of a certain wistful beauty, Mrs Brougham had a coughing fit while instructing Mrs Roughsedge, the cook, upon the dinner. She came out of the kitchen and stood coughing in the hall so violently that Susannah came down from her room to pat her on the back and enquire if there was anything she could do. Mrs Brougham, unable to speak, shook her grey curls, and putting her hands to her mouth hacked up a vile mess of bloody sputum.

The attack passed, but mother and daughter knew very well what it signalled. The doctor was sent for, and Mrs Brougham – on Susannah's insistence – retired to her fourposter.

That evening, over grilled sole and oyster sauce, Susannah discussed her mother's condition with her father.

Dr Brougham observed that he had half expected his wife to contract some fell disease sooner or later, for Mrs Brougham had been quite irresponsibly reckless in the way she had gone visiting in slums and hospitals.

'We must make her last days as comfortable as we may, Susannah,' he said, 'and pray that she will be spared a lingering end.'

'But Father! Dr Runciman assured me that if Mama is well nursed, she has every chance of making a complete recovery!'

'In that case you will have to nurse her, my dear,' said

Brougham, who had an unusually low opinion of the medical profession. 'And if Dr Runciman ever calls when I am abroad, kindly insist upon obtaining my permission before attempting to leech her.'

Four years of devoted service to her mother began. Mrs Brougham's attacks were nearly always heralded by a succession of gaspings for breath, at which signal Susannah would immediately put down her book or her pen and rush to her mother's bedside. Lifting her forward, she would support her mother while the coughing lasted, holding a pottery bowl beneath her chin.

'If only I could die!' Mrs Brougham would whisper when the attack was over and she was lying back against the pillows. 'If only I could release you from this burden!' – to which Susannah would reply that she must not think such things and that with patience and prayer she would soon be fit and well.

Her optimism was ill-founded. Mrs Brougham slipped on down the inevitable decline, until by the summer of '26, both knew that it was only a matter of weeks before the end came.

One Sunday afternoon when the last anthem was echoing in the cathedral and the people were pouring out onto the greensward in front of Broad Gate House, Mrs Brougham had a talk with her daughter about the future. She told her that when she was gone – 'No, let me continue, Susannah' – she must not feel bound by duty to remain at her father's side for ever.

'Nor should you be in any hurry to marry,' she went on, 'though should you find a gentleman who is both loving and considerate as well as being your equal in matters of intellect, you may take it for granted that you have my blessing. But above all, dearest, whether you marry or no, always try to retain within you that spark, that independence that I have seen in you ever since you were making your first steps, for provided you can do so, you will be blessed with a pure heart and a cheerful countenance.'

Susannah sat on her mother's bed and sighed inwardly. She had heard such lectures before, and found them somewhat tiresome. As an only child of elderly parents, she had long wished to escape the parental home. She considered herself presentable, but not beautiful: her face was untroubled by pock marks, and her neck and shoulders moderately well shaped. Her auburn hair was inclined to be wispy, and behind those gentle blue eyes lay a humour and honesty that enabled her to admit to herself if to no one else that the loving attentions of a suitable gentleman would be very welcome.

'Did you hear what I said, Susannah?'

'Yes, Mama.'

'And will you be sure to remember it when I am gone?'

'Mother! Please let us have a little less talk about something which has not happened yet, and is most unlikely to happen for a very long time!'

Mrs Brougham sighed, and her eyes filled with tears. They remained silent for some time. Holding Susannah's hand, she began to pray silently that her daughter might be blessed with a greater share of happiness than she herself had known, and that if ever she did marry it would be to a man with whom she could be equally yoked. Thinking these things, and remembering the four children she had borne and lost in infancy, brought forth a bitter sob.

'Mama! You should not upset yourself so!'

'It is not *I* who upset *myself*!' Jane whispered.

Reluctant to be drawn yet again into her parents' squabble, Susannah released her mother's hand and went to the window. The cathedral clock was striking four. Looking down upon the Close, she was just in time to see a distinguished looking young man stride up to the house, and a moment later she heard the front door bell ring.

With Jane ill for so long, there had developed among the

well-to-do widows and spinsters of the city a certain hopeful expectancy, for it was becoming clear as day that a fine opportunity to make an excellent match would soon present itself. Percy Brougham was therefore a trifle hen-bound, and understandably pleased when a young gentleman came up after matins at St Petrocks.

'Blair Harvey, sir,' he said very decently. 'I was given your name by my tutor at Oxford, who said I should introduce myself.'

Brougham shook him warmly by the hand, saying with complete sincerity that he was delighted to make his acquaintance. He asked which college Blair had attended, and was told.

'Oriel indeed! Then you must know Mr Newman!'

'I do indeed, sir.'

The curate said well well well and Blair mentioned a few more names for good value: Richard Hurrell Froude, John Keble –

'Keble! I used to lecture Keble at Corpus Christi back in o-eight!'

Blair went pink with reflected glory and Brougham asked what had brought him to Exeter. Having explained, the young man became solemn. 'I – ah – wondered if I might ask a favour, sir. Could I prevail upon you to give me half an hour of your time? It is a spiritual matter, and one of some urgency.'

This was another pleasant surprise, for Percy enjoyed the company of spiritually minded young men. He assured Blair that he would be delighted, and as he was free that afternoon the pleasure of Mr Harvey's company was requested at four, when the Doctor would be entirely at his disposal.

Blair had spent the night in an agony of post-coital remorse that was so intense it was almost enjoyable. He saw himself as having been changed from a young man with an unspotted conscience into a philandering monster who would be dogged to the end of his days by the spectre of a scarlet whore. Brought up in dark blue Anglicanism, he had no hard rock of faith upon which to fall back, no instinctive recourse to repentance and the free forgiveness of sin, but rather thought in terms of bargains. It was for this reason that – at some time a little before dawn – he made God what amounted to a business proposition. He was prepared to make himself known to Dr Brougham and to re-enter the safe stockade of Exeter society on condition that the Lord would preserve him safe from scandal, disease and illegitimate fatherhood. It was on these terms that he rang the bell at Broad Gate House.

He was admitted by the servant known as 'the boy', who was in fact a man in his early fifties whom the parson had recently fitted out in buttons and whose name was Dobbs. He took Blair's black top hat in that reverent way of all good retainers and ushered the young man into the study.

'Sir,' said Blair, when he had accepted a seat and the door was closed, 'I will admit it frankly: since arriving in Exeter I have erred and strayed from my way like a lost sheep.'

Dr Brougham selected a churchwarden from the rack on the mantel and filled it with best Virginia. While he did so, Blair outlined some of his activities since arriving in the city, starting off with an inexactitude about mislaying his letter of introduction and ending with the powerful effect he claimed the hanging of Dubuis had had upon him.

Brougham puffed at his pipe, and the smoke from it rose to the moulded ceiling and spread out like mist on an autumn evening.

'I do not wish to embarrass or offend you, sir,' Blair said, joining his fists, 'but certain of my sins weigh heavy on my mind, and I hope that you will be able to assist me in making amends and conducting myself better in the future.'

Brougham removed the churchwarden from his lips and said solemnly, 'You may tell me as much or as little as you please, sir. I shall treat it in absolute confidence.'

Blair looked at the floor and shook his head. Now that his frolic with Molly was history, he wanted to make the most of it.

'Does it concern women?' the curate asked.

Blair nodded, and his eyes filled deliciously with tears.

Brougham crossed to the fireplace, where he gently tapped out his pipe on the fender before returning it to the rack. He paced about the room, his fingers linked under his coat tails, his eyes first on the Axminster and then on the frieze. An idea had occurred to him that appealed greatly, and he was now at pains to put it to this young man as persuasively as possible.

'There are certain of my cloth who believe – and I with them – that the abandonment of some of the sacraments at the Reformation was a sad mistake upon the part of the Bishops of the newly established Church of England,' he began, and paused to look down upon the glossy waves of hair on Harvey's head. 'It may be that a formal, private, act of confession would benefit you yourself in your present circumstances.'

'Sir?' Blair said, not understanding what the curate was driving at.

Brougham trembled with pleasurable anticipation. 'Do you not feel a need to unburden yourself? To accuse yourself fully and openly before God?'

For the second time in twenty-four hours, the vein in Blair's forehead swelled, though he did not think for a moment that he was now being tempted by a different sort of whore.

'Yes, sir,' he said. 'I believe that is so.'

'In that case, I suggest, if you are agreeable, that you make your confession to me, as an ordained priest. Do you understand what I am saying?'

They were both excited now. Blair licked his lips, and

blinked rapidly. He looked up into the face of Dr Brougham, forcibly conscious that he was in the presence of a superior mind. 'You mean – you mean after the fashion of the Church of Rome, sir?'

'Is that offensive to you?'

It was as if the curate had made a most intimate suggestion.

'I do not know the form of it, sir,' Blair said huskily.

'I will instruct you in it,' replied Brougham.

There was a silence, during which a carriage went by outside, its wheel rims crackling on the cobbles; and inside Percy Brougham's study the atmosphere itself seemed to crackle with its own peculiar electricity, for Blair was himself beginning to be attracted to the idea of recounting what had happened and Brougham was achieving an almost sensual delight in the prospect of hearing his first confession.

Brougham drew the curtains to exclude prying eyes. With his back turned to Blair he said, 'If you would prefer it, Mr Harvey, I would be willing to hear your confession in Latin.'

Blair coughed and tapped his fingers together. 'If it's all one to you, sir, I'd prefer the vernacular.'

The curate moved away from the window and took his seat. 'Kneel here by my chair,' he said softly, 'and make the sign of the cross, thus. Now start – 'Bless me O my father –'

'Bless me O my father –'

'For I have sinned . . .'

'For I have sinned.'

'I accuse myself . . . Go on.'

So Blair continued, with difficulty at first, vaguely, and without detail; but on Brougham's insistence he became more explicit and embellished his story considerably, feeling that a single tumble with a prostitute was hardly worthy of so solemn an occasion. He invented several other escapades therefore, and threw in a little gambling

31

and cock fighting for good measure, so that by the end Dr Brougham was quite shocked that so pure a young man should have been brought to such depths of depravity; but he found the experience deeply satisfying nevertheless, and his only regret, as he stood at his window and watched the young man stride away across the cathedral grounds, was that Mr Harvey had declined to make his confession in Latin.

Jane died on a clear night a few days before Christmas. Susannah found her lying on the floor beneath her window. Soon after her funeral, Brougham made it clear that he intended to be a cheerful widower.

'I am considering the purchase of a summer residence,' he told his daughter in the new year. 'Exeter is all very well, but it would be pleasant to get away for a few weeks in the year, don't you think?'

They were at dinner. He had sold a few bonds, bought a new carriage and restocked his cellar. The household was still in mourning, but there was already in the curate's manner a hint that spring was not far away.

'It seems a very good idea, Papa,' said Susannah who since her mother's death had been at pains to live amicably with her father.

'We could make ourselves a tidy income from it, too,' he went on, 'for we shall not wish to stay in it all summer, and it might be let to tenants.' He replenished his glass. 'I had the thought that we might travel. It is a long time since I was in Italy, and you would benefit greatly from a visit.' He tipped his chair back and looked at the ceiling, remembering a not entirely virtuous youth. 'Venice, Florence, Rome . . . it would do us both no end of good.' He shot her a mischievous glance. 'Just wait, my dear. I shall have you educated yet!'

Zilla, a pale, subservient girl with straight black hair and a squint, crept in to serve the spare ribs. When she had withdrawn, Susannah said that as she found Greek and Hebrew more absorbing than Latin, she would prefer to go to Athens or the Holy Land.

'Pshaw!' went the curate. 'Greece is full of pagan mythology and Jerusalem full of Turks. No, no. Italy's the seat of culture, my dear. Even Byron knew that.'

She knew she should feel grateful to him for taking such a close interest in her education, but could not help reflecting that she would prefer the company of a less learned and younger person with whom to make such a tour.

Dr Brougham had seen the slight change in her expression. 'Now what's the matter? Come come, Susannah, we must put what is behind behind us. Mrs Brougham would not have you mourn so if she were alive today.' He laughed. 'Ha! *Non sequitur*! Humble apologies!'

She put on a smile for him and they discussed where they might have a villa. She suggested Scotland, for she read the novels of Sir Walter Scott as a relaxation. Dr Brougham gave short shrift to that idea, however: 'What we need is a little place near at hand where we can slip away for a day or two whenever we feel inclined.'

His way of including her in his plans made her uneasy. She felt she was already being turned into his permanent companion, or honorary wife. Within a week of her mother's funeral, he had insisted that she move downstairs to the bedroom over the front parlour, saying that as she was now the lady of the house she must have the best room. The move had seemed to her doubly ominous: not only was she taking her mother's place in the household, but she was also becoming trapped as her mother had been trapped: before, she had been able to see over the city wall to fields and the river; now her view was entirely dominated by the cathedral.

She could not help remembering how often her mother had urged her not to feel bound in loyalty to her father, but to go out and find her independence. There seemed fat chance of that now! Her father discussed with her every idea and plan that occurred to him, and had begun to require her to enter his study in order to listen to him reading the latest section of his treatise on the Antinomian heresy. What made the situation so difficult for her was his obvious affection for her – an affection that she could not fully return, however hard she tried.

Within the space of a month, he had unwittingly placed her in the same sort of bondage her mother had suffered and finally rebelled against. She felt him turning her into his chattel, his sounding board, and the sensation was distinctly unpleasant. He discouraged her from attending the literary society meetings held once a month in the city and frowned upon her exchanging visits with the few friends she had in Exeter; he required her to attend matins at St Petrocks when she would have preferred to listen to the sermon at St Davids, and whenever the subject of her private studies arose, Dr Brougham had taken to remarking pointedly that if she was serious about academic achievement she might do a lot worse than act as his personal amanuensis.

His plans for the purchase of a villa went rapidly ahead. Wrapped in a heavy cloak and wearing a fur-lined wide-awake, Dr Brougham drove down to the coast and returned three days later to announce that he had found the ideal place in Teignmouth, which was fast turning from a down at heel trading port into a fashionable resort. 'It is the most attractive of harbours,' he said. 'Why we have never visited there before I cannot imagine.'

There was a sad irony in this, for Jane Brougham had often spoken of Teignmouth and the Den, having herself holidayed there with cousins as a child.

A week later, Mr Lethbridge called on the curate to discuss the legal aspects of the purchase, and at dinner that evening Brougham announced that a deal had been struck and that a contract was being drawn up. 'And what is more, I have decided to make yourself a co-owner, Susannah, so you will become a woman of property.'

34

She was not sure she wanted to be a woman of property under such conditions, for although she might have joint ownership of a villa, she would become even more firmly the property of her father. She foresaw that he would now use her to supervise the decoration and furnishing of the new house and that she would be required to oversee its management in his retirement years. She considered telling him frankly that she wanted no part of it, but felt that such a step would be ungrateful and disloyal. Besides, to look on the bright side, she needed a new interest in life, and the house in Teignmouth might provide a means of temporary escape.

The following Saturday, on returning from a visit to her friend Mary Groves, the sister of a local dentist, Susannah found her father stamping up and down the hall in a froth of impatience.

'Mr Lethbridge has just this moment left, Susannah. He brought the contract to be signed and witnessed, and I had no idea at all where you were. You have kept a gentleman waiting over an hour, and though he maintained a very civil manner I could not help but be aware that he was displeased. I think the least you can do now is go directly to his offices in order to put your signature to the contract so that he may exchange it with the vendor on Monday.'

She turned round at the door without taking off her gloves.

'And I would suggest,' added her father, 'that in future when you wish to go out you should leave word with the servants as to where you have gone and how long you intend to remain abroad.'

She set out along Catherine Street, turning left into Stephen Road and right into the High Street. There had been a light fall of snow the previous day, which was now thawing in the February sunshine. Going along towards the solicitor's office, her thoughts were in a turmoil of rebellion and anger. She was nearly twenty-two and her father was still treating her as if she were fifteen!

A clerk opened the door to her and she was shown into the office of Lethbridge & Wright, where a young man in his shirtsleeves sat copying at a high desk, his back to a blazing log fire.

She recognised him immediately: it was the young man who had called on her father one Sunday afternoon the previous summer. He stepped down from his high stool and bowed.

'Blair Harvey at your service, Ma'am,' he said, and looked at her as if he could see much more of her physical self than was on display.

She was in mourning, yes, but what splendid mourning! Could she possibly know how perfectly plain black and white set off the winter pink in her cheeks and the dark speedwell of her eyes? He was seized by an urge to admire her from every angle, to walk round her as if she had been sculpted in marble; nor was it merely the outward appearance of her that captivated him – not simply the fur-trimmed dress, the gathered waist, the velvet cape, but much more – all that lay within and beyond her physical presence: the spirit, the nobility and the fire.

'I have come to sign a contract,' she said. 'My father – Dr Brougham –' She broke off, and he realised that he had been staring at her too closely.

'Dr Brougham?' he echoed.

'Yes. It is a contract –'

'A contract?'

'Is Mr Lethbridge not arrived back?' She looked round the office, as if the senior partner might be hiding up on a shelf.

'He has already left. He will not be back until Monday.'

She looked dismayed.

'Would you like to sit down, Miss Brougham?'

She collected herself and looked back at him. He saw the firelight reflected in her eyes. 'No – thank you. My father is making a purchase – a villa in Teignmouth. I am to be the joint owner and am required to sign the contract. I understand there is some urgency as the vendor –'

He held up his hand. 'I shall fetch it immediately. It is ready for your signature.'

She smiled (smiled!) her thanks and he left her standing before the fire, with a glow of flames on her face. He went into Lethbridge's office, found the contract in a desk drawer and brought it out. As he emerged from Lethbridge's office it seemed that she had gone and he wondered if she had taken fright at his manner and run away; but she had only moved round to look up at the titles of the law reports and legal manuals on the shelves by the fireplace.

He undid the coloured tape and spread out the contract on a table. 'Yes, your father has already signed, so you must add your signature here above his, Miss Brougham. I shall find you a suitable nib, let's see, is this one too fine? And . . . ink.' He weighted the corners of the document with little judges, wigged and gowned in ornamental brass, and stood back from the table with a sweep of the hand to indicate that all was ready. She took up the pen and glanced back at him, a little amused at his cavalier manner.

As she dipped the pen into the inkwell, he realised that he was making a mistake.

'Wait,' he said. She looked round. They were side by side at the table. 'Your signature must be witnessed, and I should not do it. If you will bear with me a moment, I will find the clerk.'

He went quickly along to fetch Mr Clannaborough, and the old man loped in after him – loping out again to fetch his spectacles on learning what was required of him. When he returned, Susannah put her name to the contract, and Blair noted with admiration the easy flow of her letters and the way she placed a simple little twirl beneath the capital S.

Clannaborough hacked and coughed and signed alongside, and having been pointedly informed that that would be all, winked behind the visitor's back and shambled out. Blair shook sand over the ink and blew it into the fire.

'You have a very fine hand, Miss Brougham.'

She looked about her. 'My glove,' she said.

They saw it at the same moment: it had fallen from the table when Clannaborough had been signing. Blair dived to retrieve it, and Susannah bent at the same time so that for a moment they were unusually close. They straightened; he handed the glove over; their fingers touched. When she thanked him there was a sort of gaiety in her manner. He wanted to swim into her eyes.

'I fear I may have inconvenienced Mr Lethbridge this afternoon,' she said. 'Will you pass on to him my apology?'

He bowed and said he would do so, though he was sure it was unnecessary.

When she put on the glove it seemed that her fingers were beckoning to him. He stared at them and blinked very fast when he saw her looking at him, feeling that she must regard him as very insignificant, but when he showed her out she thanked him warmly and allowed him to shake her hand as if they were already firm friends.

Returning to his office he stood a moment before the blaze hardly able to believe that she had been there with him only minutes before; then, clasping his arms about his shoulders he spun round and round and round, and when he stopped, the bookshelves, the fire, the high desk and his coat hanging behind the door went on whirling, and he staggered from foot to foot whispering, 'Susannah! Susannah! Susannah!

She would not have believed it possible to desire the company of a man so forcibly. On returning to the parsonage, she went straight to her room and paced up and down, reliving each second of the encounter until it was imprinted in her mind. She looked again into his eyes and remembered how he had looked at her as if she had stood naked before him; she recalled the way his mutton-chops had twitched and a vein had enlarged in his forehead. Had she led him on? Well what if she had!

'Blair Harvey,' she whispered aloud, listening to the sound of the name, enjoying the B and the V of it. And I have to admit, she thought, that it was not merely a spiritual attraction, for while we spoke there was a feeling of . . . fullness, as if my body were secreting some fluid into my veins. Am I unique in this? she wondered. She was a little frightened at the strength of the feeling, which was returning even now. Why should her meeting with Mr Harvey make her so suddenly conscious of her woman-hood, and particularly of her bosom? This was strange territory indeed, territory of which she had little know-ledge, though she knew that gentlemen did not content their ladies simply by sitting at the end of their tables and complimenting them on their beauty.

'Blair Harvey,' she whispered again, and wondered suddenly if their meeting had made him as conscious of his bodily self as she was now of hers. That, in turn, caused her to imagine him undressed: she saw him in her mind's eye on a pedestal, like Michaelangelo's David, strong limbed, muscular, the strange, tiny creature nestling at his loins.

She bent and pressed her hands against her face, trying to make the image go away; but after a few moments let her hands drop. Why should she *not* think of him thus? She harmed no one by doing so, and she had always considered the gift of a lively imagination as a blessing. That broke down another barrier – a flood gate – for if she could think of him naked, she could think of herself naked too: she could imagine herself walking to him until her body brushed his. She could imagine the gentle touch of his lips upon her neck and shoulders, and that first, magical contact between his Zeus and her Venus.

Trembling, she walked about the room, laughing and

whispering to herself. 'I am very, very wicked – and he is wicked too, for I saw it in his eye.' She pressed her hands to her bosom, shivering as if at the height of a fever, aware of new, powerful feelings flooding her body in a way that she would never have dreamt possible.

'We shall be wicked together,' she breathed. 'I shall have Papa invite him to call. We shall be married on a windy day in April and live in the country with a large family and very little seriousness.'

Having her father invite him to call was not the simple matter she had presumed. Guided by a lively intuition to tread carefully, she put the idea to him one evening that they might throw a small dinner party in the spring for her friends the Groves: the dentist, his wife and his sister Mary.

'We really should entertain them at some time, Papa,' she said. 'Mr Groves will be leaving Exeter in the autumn. He has decided to sell his practice and train as a missionary. He goes to Dublin to read theology as a fellow commoner in October.'

Brougham was not at all well disposed to the Groves family. They were stalwart anti-papists, and had been friends of Jane.

'I was thinking,' Susannah went on, 'that if we invited them it might be well to invite another gentleman also, so that Mr Groves and yourself will not be outnumbered.'

He looked up from his onion soup and took the bait.

'And what gentleman do you have in mind, Susannah?'

She pretended to think for a few moments, and wished that her mother were alive to do battle on her behalf.

'Is there not a new young gentleman doing his articles with Mr Lethbridge?'

He finished his onion soup. 'Is there?'

'I believe so.'

'Will you ring?'

She took the little brass bell that was kept by her place

setting at meals, and a moment later Zilla slipped in, whispering her excuse-me's as she removed the plates and served the saddle of lamb. When she was gone, Brougham fell upon his food with relish, the subject of dinner parties apparently forgotten.

But Susannah was not ready to let the matter drop: she had inherited her father's obstinacy if nothing else. 'Papa – you have met Mr Harvey, have you not? Did he not call on you last summer?'

He looked up. 'What if he did, Susannah?'

'Then – we are acquainted.'

'We? When did you meet Mr Harvey?'

She touched her throat and coloured, explaining that they had been introduced when she had gone to Lethbridge's to sign the contract.

Dr Brougham said, 'I see,' and snorted pointedly.

'I hope you will not think me ungrateful, Papa, but I do not have much opportunity to mix in society, and I thought –'

'You thought that you would persuade your father into inviting the first young man that catches your eye to dine at this table!'

The lamb was finished, and the Stilton and port-wine fetched from the sideboard.

Susannah decided to try a new approach. 'Dear Papa,' she said demurely, 'you said yourself that Mama would not have us mourn too long, and she often said she wished I could meet more people of my own age. The Groves are good people, and Mary is full of kindness to me since Mama passed on. I thought, as Mr Harvey had already called upon you last summer, that you were well acquainted with him and would have no objection at all to inviting him.' She gave a little nervous laugh. 'And he has not "caught my eye" at all.'

'In which case he has caught something else more dangerous, Susannah, for I have seldom seen you in so high a colour when discussing a mere acquaintance. Mr

41

Harvey may indeed have called upon me last summer, but that does not mean that I am obliged to acknowledge him as a personal acquaintance, or that I should consider him a fit person to put his knees under my mahogany.'

With that, Dr Brougham attacked the Stilton, and the remainder of the meal was conducted in silence.

After the first rapture of meeting Susannah, Blair found himself in a quandary, for he had not achieved the spiritual catharsis he had hoped for from his private confession the previous summer, and had not darkened the doors of St Petrocks – or any other church – since.

Though he had not actually fallen by the wayside with the likes of Molly Burke again, he had in recent weeks felt an increasingly urgent need to repeat what she had taught him so expertly. His six months in Exeter had also developed his personality somewhat: he had taken to spending his evenings philosophising after the fashion of Dr Johnson as did so many young gentlemen of his day; sitting in the front kitchen of the White Lion, he took pleasure in causing a laugh by eyeing the serving girl or putting his hand up her skirts when she least expected it. In this way, he believed, he was cutting a dash and making a reputation for himself as a man of the world.

Now, quite unexpectedly, a woman had turned him upside down all over again, for Susannah's natural grace and very obvious virtue forced him to see his life in a new light. All those late night drinking sessions and arguments about existence now seemed sadly squalid, and he saw with a shock that he had come perilously close to turning into the pseudo-Bohemian and half-baked, prattling cynic he had always promised himself never to be.

Sitting at the deal table, his journal open before him and frost making patterns on the window, he stared into the guttering candle flame and prayed fervently that Susannah might feel in some small measure the fierce longing he now felt for her, and that the Lord would help him overcome the inconvenient obstacle to true love presented by the fact that her father was the one man in Exeter he could not look in the eye.

Soon after Septuagesima Sunday, however, he was required by Mr Lethbridge to take some documents along to the parsonage for Dr Brougham's approval, and he rang the door bell with very mixed feelings indeed.

He was admitted by Dobbs, who bowed obsequiously as he took the young solicitor's hat and stick, and showed him into the study.

'So Mr Harvey,' Brougham said from his armchair. 'We meet again.'

'Yes, sir.'

Brougham looked the young man up and down. He had been angered that Harvey had never condescended to return to his church, having expected their original encounter to be the beginning of an acquaintance as between patron and protegé; but as the young man was now here in a quite different capacity, he felt that any comment on their previous meeting would be inappropriate.

Blair cleared his throat. 'I have brought the report on the searches in respect of the rights of way beneath your property in Teignmouth, sir,' he said. 'Mr Lethbridge sends you his compliments and apologises for not attending upon you personally, but he is at present quite incapacitated by gout.'

Brougham held out his hand and the papers were handed over. In the silence that followed, Blair caught the sound of voices in the hall, but could not make out whether they included Susannah's.

'Am I required to sign these?' Brougham enquired, and Blair was jerked back to the business in hand.

'Er – no, sir. They are simply for your perusal. And your approval, of course.'

Brougham's thick black eyebrows came together in a frown. 'Is there any reason why I should not approve?'

'None at all, sir,' Blair said, gaining a little confidence.

'But Mr Lethbridge would not wish you to be in the dark concerning the negotiations being conducted on your behalf.'

Brougham fixed his spectacles on his nose, and after several seconds of concentration read aloud: ' ". . . the said bridle path bordering the north-eastern boundary of the property to remain as a public right of way the purchaser undertakes to maintain in good condition . . ." ' He looked up. 'Does that refer to the bridle path or the boundary do you suppose?'

Blair looked disconcerted. He blinked very fast and his cheeks went pink. He had copied the report himself, and he had a nasty feeling he had missed out a line.

'If I may take a closer look, sir,' he said, and peered over the curate's shoulder, blinking in the smoke that rose in a thin spiral from the curate's pipe.

'Er – I would judge that that refers to the boundary, sir, not the bridle path.'

'You may judge that I grant you, but will Lord Clifford?'

'Lord Clifford, sir?'

'Is he not Lord of the Manor?'

'Er . . . I believe that is so, yes, sir.'

Brougham stuck his thumb into his waistcoat and glared up at the young man, who could not help reflecting that it was a sight easier to confess to fornication than admit to a slip of the pen.

'Perhaps I should look into this further,' he said.

'I think you should indeed, Mr Harvey,' said Brougham. 'Otherwise I may find myself being required to maintain half the highways and byways of Teignmouth in good condition. That sentence strikes me as sylleptic. Or possibly zeugmatic. Do you know the difference?'

'I must confess sir, I – er –'

'No of course you don't. That would be too much to expect, would it not, of a graduate of Oriel.'

Blair tried to smile at this, but the resulting expression

made him look more pained than pleased.

'I suggest you find out,' Brougham boomed, and rang for Dobbs, who appeared immediately. 'Along with the difference between a bridle path and a boundary.'

Blair found himself outside in the hall.

Dobbs, having only recently assumed the duties of footman to the curate, had been instructed to brush a visitor's hat before handing it over, and he did so now for Blair with such thoroughness that the young man's departure was delayed; and while he stood waiting for the old retainer to raise the nap he became aware of a movement on the floor above.

He glanced up – and then further up – until he was looking directly up the stairwell. Standing on the first floor landing and looking directly down at him over the bannister was Susannah, her fine golden hair loose so that it fell downwards round her face and her petticoats (he counted at least three) clearly visible. For a second – perhaps two or even three – they stared at each other, before Dobbs coughed meaningfully and handed over Blair's top hat.

That was enough: he took the hat and ran out into the road, across the greensward by the cathedral where the daffodils were in bud and the crocuses out. He ran on, past an astonished Bishop who was emerging from his palace in conversation with his financial adviser; he went out of the city gate and strode over Southernhay, throwing up his stick and catching it, laughing and talking to himself and already composing in his mind the letter he would now send to Susannah – the letter that would declare his feelings honestly and beg her to do the same.

It was delivered at the back door by hand of a messenger boy, and it came with a posy of crocuses and early narcissi. Zilla brought them up to Susannah's room where she was about to change out of her walking dress, having recently been visiting at the library.

She slit it open with an ivory paper knife and read its contents in mounting amazement. She was informed that since his brief meeting with her three weeks before, Blair had been able to think only of herself, that he was enraptured, captivated and entirely struck by her, that so great was the effect she was having upon him that his work was suffering and that he could not bear to continue without some firm knowledge as to her feelings towards him. In order to save her from any embarrassment, he proposed the use of a simple signal to indicate her feelings.

She turned the page. By comparison with her own educated hand, his writing looked as though it had been executed at high speed and with a pen given to making little spurtings of ink, so that the page was here and there decorated by little blossoms of black dots. He asked her, on receipt of these flowers, to put them in her window if she felt any similar warming towards him, so that his mind might be set at rest. He completed the letter at right angles to the body of the text with a few lines of apology for thus intruding upon her privacy and declaring that his intentions were 'of the very highest possible order'. With that, he remained her obedient servant, hers to command, etc, etc, Blair Harvey, B.A.

She went down to the kitchen to put the flowers in water, and was coming out into the hall again when her father opened his study door.

'Susannah,' he said. 'Spare me a few moments. I have something to read to you.'

She left the flowers on the hall stand and followed him into the study. As the door closed behind her the newly lit fire pushed out a cloud of woodsmoke into the room. Her father lifted a sheaf of foolscap from his desk and fitted spectacles to his nose.

'Well sit down, child,' he said. 'I can't read to you if you are standing about like a foolish virgin.'

She sat obediently and he began reading from his

treatise. He paced up and down, rolling the words on his tongue, beating time to the march of his sentences, stopping occasionally to ensure that she appreciated a nuance of meaning here or a subtle allusion there; and when she saw Blair Harvey looking in at her from the other side of the road she almost jumped out of her chair.

'. . . preposterous though it may seem to modern minds,' continued the curate, 'this thesis, first put forward by Johann Agricola nearly three hundred years ago, still holds a dangerous fascination for those spiritual marauders in our midst who seek to make their dissent acceptable in the minds of innocent persons but whose insidious purpose is to do away with the most ancient traditions of the Christian church; indeed, for a man who calls himself a Christian to claim that he has a right, through grace, to transgress the decalogue itself must at first glance seem so obviously heretical as to be of no danger to the church; but whether through apathy or ignorance, the truth of the matter cannot be denied and we must state it simply –'

'Papa –'

Dr Brougham stopped in mid prose. 'What is it? Is that not clear to you?'

'Papa – might I be excused? I have . . . urgent business to attend to –'

'Urgent business? What urgent business?'

She coloured deeply.

'Do you not realise that this is due at the printers on Thursday next?' He looked down at her severely, and the breath whistled in his narrow nostrils before he plunged back into the tide of words.

She sat upright in her chair no longer listening.

'You think it reads well, Susannah?' he asked eventually.

She was anxious to give him all the approval he desired. 'I thought it quite excellent, Papa.'

'Truly?'

'Truly, Papa. The force of your argument is most powerful.'

He was content with that, and took out his hunter, flipping it open with his thumb nail and snapping it shut in the way she had seen him do a thousand times before. Licking a little froth from the corner of his lip, he dismissed her.

'And be so kind as to shut the door carefully, else I shall be asphyxiated,' he added, a second too late to prevent another cloud of smoke entering the room.

She took the jug of flowers from the hall and went quickly up to her room, closing the door behind her. Beneath her window, children were making patterns of oyster shells in the gutter, and she stood watching them for a while; when she looked up, she was surprised to see Blair striding across the cathedral greensward towards her.

He stopped, and looked directly up to her window. She was taken by surprise: she had not yet decided whether she would comply with his request for a signal and she knew now that there was no time left. The sound of her father's voice boomed downstairs as he instructed Dobbs on some household matter, and her mind was finally made up. Hardly knowing what she was doing – and yet in a deeper way knowing very well – she placed the jug of flowers on the sill in full view of Blair and then moved quickly back into the room out of his sight, to clasp her hands tightly against her breasts as if by doing so she might slow the wild beating of her heart.

Passion, like champagne, cannot be produced unless it is contained in a strong bottle and stopped up with a wired cork, nor can it be enjoyed until the cork is removed and the effervescence allowed to flow out. It is made, too, from the finest fruit that is without taint of sourness or acid. Thus young men with loving mothers, and young women – especially clergymen's daughters – with possessive fathers make excellent passion, provided they are suitably restrained.

No, she did not actually rise out of the sea like Aphrodite, nor did she make love to her dear mortal Adonis; but she dreamt it and the dream was so real that she awoke trembling at the strange sensations she had experienced; and when she actually met Blair two days later in the city library, where he had tracked her down, the experience was hardly less moving. That first meeting was a breathless, tongue-tied event, impossible to report in dialogue, for communication was effected by means of earnest glances on Blair's part and a heaving bosom on Susannah's; but he managed to suggest a private meeting and as a result, gradually, they became better acquainted.

They met; they talked; they crossed from dumb admiration to shy conversation, and while Dr Brougham worked away at a new thesis, Blair and Susannah fermented for each other, the bubbles of their passion gaining pressure within the strong bottle of society and restrained by the cork of their upbringing.

She could not have admitted to any living soul what thoughts he caused in her. She had seen him statuesque in her mind's eye some weeks before but now, having walked through frosty meadows with him and watched the water rats and coots by the River Exe and walked in Bonhay Copse with the beeches swaying and creaking in the March wind; now when she dreamt of him (by day or by night) she saw him as a living being, one whom she could invite into her arms at will, one who pressed his lips over hers, and whose arms enfolded her imagined nudity.

Sometimes in the evenings she would stand shivering in her night gown before the mirror, trying to see herself as he might see her on their wedding night – wondering if she were good enough for him, praying that he would soon agree to call upon her father and bring their acquaintance into the open.

As for Blair, he found himself in a quandary: he knew

that his feelings for Susannah were so strong that they must be true love, and yet he was terrified of allowing the fact to be known to her father. As the weeks passed, they spoke of the matter increasingly, Susannah voicing her fears that her father would be furious to discover she had been meeting a young gentleman in secret and unchaperoned, and Blair making vague excuses to delay the moment of truth. The longer they delayed – and they were both aware of this – the more difficult it became. Blair eventually felt obliged to explain to Susannah the reasons for his apprehension (though he watered it down a lot and made no mention of Molly) and Susannah admitted to him that her father had been most antagonistic at the mention of his name.

Then one midday towards the end of March they were caught. They had met outside the city in Northernhay, and were walking out towards St David's church when Dr Brougham's trap came along at a brisk pace from the opposite direction. Well wrapped in a kerseymere, the reverend doctor was singing a *Te Deum* for his own edification. He came over the brow of a hill, his voice mingling with the rapid clopping of hooves, a scattering of crows and seagulls following the plough in a neighbouring field.

Blair and Susannah stopped dead, and awaited the inevitable. But strangely, Dr Brougham did not appear to notice them. He went straight past, his eyes on the road ahead, his powerful tenor voice crying out, like the Cherubim and Seraphim, without ceasing.

They watched him drive on towards the city in stunned silence, then Blair turned to Susannah.

'There! He did not even notice our presence!'

But Susannah knew her father too well. 'He did, Blair. I know it! He pretended not to see us in order to heap coals of fire upon me! You must call upon him this afternoon. There is no alternative – no alternative at all.'

He stared back at her; then, bowing his head, muttered

that he would do so, and they hurried back to Broad Gate House to face a different sort of music.

'Say what you have to say,' Brougham growled, standing at the window of his study, his back to the door. 'I have little time to spare.'

'I must confess, sir –' Blair started.

'Confess! I have had enough of your confessing, Mr Harvey!'

Blair put out one foot, trying to appear like a stallion pawing the turf, but more closely resembling a schoolboy at a class of backward ballet dancers. 'Sir – I firmly believe that your daughter and I have discovered a deep and mutual affection.'

Brougham turned and gave Blair the benefit of his most baleful glare. 'And what opportunity have you had to gain such a belief, may I ask?'

Outside, a surgeon's bell clanged by the window. Blair drew himself up and remembered that his mother had once told him that he resembled Lord Byron.

'Sir,' he said. 'I love your daughter, and wish to ask you for her hand in marriage.'

'Oh do you indeed?' replied Brougham with uncharacteristic sarcasm, and proceeded to give the young man his views on the matter, which were not at all favourable.

Susannah was summoned to the study ten minutes later when the front door had closed behind Blair and he was walking away with Brougham's vigorous refusal echoing in his ears. She entered the room confidently – perhaps a little defiantly – and stood before him with her chin up and her hands joined.

Brougham could not help feeling a surge of affection for her. She was his only daughter after all: he wanted the best for her, and Blair Harvey was simply not good enough.

'You sent for me, Papa.'

'Indeed,' he said, pacing his study, his fingers interlaced behind his back. 'Indeed.'

He paused to take a book from one of the shelves that lined the study, and having checked some line from Quintilian that had been bothering him, he closed the volume with a snap and fitted it back into its place.

'Yes,' he said, as if reminding himself, 'I sent for you.' He looked her up and down. 'I sent for you to say that you will have no more trouble from young Mr Harvey, Susannah.' He shot a glance at her from under thick, dark eyebrows. Susannah met it with what he divined as the gentle confidence of one with a clear conscience.

'I have had no trouble at all from him, Father.'

'But you have, Susannah, believe me, you have. That young man is trouble himself, trouble with a capital T. He is a rascal from his egg to his apples, take my word on it.'

She remained motionless, just inside the door. She had prepared herself for opposition from her father, but was determined to overcome it. She had even convinced herself that Blair would have won him over, and expecting that afternoon to mark the announcement of her betrothal had changed out of her walking dress into grey and white silk and had tied a ribbon of dark blue velvet in her hair.

'Mr Harvey has never been anything but gentle with me,' she said quietly.

He noted the flush in her cheek and the sudden rise of her bosom.

'That may be so, Susannah. But has he not led you into deceit? Has he not met you behind my back in the knowledge that I would not approve? Is that the mark of a gentleman?'

She looked down at her hands. 'Father I did ask you if we might invite him to dine with the Groves, but you refused me permission. We met by chance in the city, and our conduct has at no time been anything but respectable. Indeed, his call upon you this afternoon was made with the express intention of repairing any small deception of which we may have been guilty.'

But Brougham was not prepared to let her gentle answers turn away his wrath. 'He has taken advantage of your innocence, Susannah – and of my good will. He has led you down a slippery path, and I have told him as much. I have also informed him that if he troubles you further I shall speak with Mr Lethbridge and have him removed from chambers for abusing the privileges of his profession. Indeed, I have a mind to take that step in any case, for I am beginning to see that it will be better for you, for Lethbridge & Wright and for Exeter in general if Mr Harvey were invited to pursue his doubtful ends elsewhere. The fellow is an adventurer, my dear – a treasure hunter – and you are well rid of him.'

She was becoming very agitated. 'Father – I must ask you not to take that step. It would be most unfair on the gentleman – especially when he is at the very threshold of his career. He has done no wrong, and if he were to lose his position and reputation in this way I would feel personally responsible.'

He smiled quickly. 'That was a brave little speech, Susannah, and I give you credit for it.'

'I wish no credit, Father.'

'My dear,' he said, relaxing. 'Let us forget all about this. It is not surprising that you have been pestered in this way, and I do not expect it will be the last time either. But you must understand that I am your loving father, and I cannot allow the very first fortune hunter to win you so easily. Mr Harvey is an opportunist without means, and from what I have seen of him without many principles either. He is scarcely qualified to be articled to a solicitor, let alone husband to my daughter. So let us put all this behind us once and for all. Besides,' he added, 'I have excellent news for you. The purchase of West Lawn Villa is finally concluded. It is ours. I propose we take the carriage down to Teignmouth on Monday and spend a few days at Cockram's Hotel in order to look over our new acquisition, what do you say? It will take your mind off all this unpleasantness. And think – I hear they have twelve new bathing machines at Teignmouth now, so in the summer you will be able to take a plunge in the sea. I might even venture in myself!'

He crossed the room and held out his hands to take hers, but she shook her head abruptly.

'Susannah! Do you think I have refused him out of spite or selfishness? If so, you are misjudging me. What I do, I do solely for your own benefit. I have the advantage of years, my dear, and there is no doubt at all in my mind that Mr Harvey is a bad lot and that you will be better off without him.'

'Whether that is so or not,' she said in a low voice, 'I cannot escape the fact that I am in love with him.'

He shook his head, chuckling benevolently. 'Come come, Susannah! Love? Infatuation, more like. *Aut amat aut odit mulier*, my dear. Do you know the tag?'

'Yes, Father, I know it very well, but it is not at all true and was probably invented by a man.'

'No doubt, no doubt,' he replied amiably, 'but there *is* a modicum of truth in it nevertheless. Now I have work to do even if you do not, Susannah, so I shall be obliged if you will accept my blessing and continue with your daily round. *Dominus tecum*, my dear, and please remember to close the door gently.'

He moved to open the door, but Susannah's forebearance suddenly ran out.

'No, Father. I cannot let this matter pass so easily. I cannot accept your decision, however much it may pain me to do otherwise. I will admit that I did practice a small deception in not informing you immediately of Mr Harvey's attentions, but I cannot agree that you have a right to decide for me whether or not I shall see him in the future. I have my majority – I am nearly twenty-two. It is difficult enough for me to meet anyone of my own age

54

here in Exeter, and well nigh impossible to meet a gentleman. Nor is my attachment to Mr Harvey a mere infatuation as you claim. I have been conscious of the very deepest possible feeling towards him, and – and – I cannot allow you to shrug him off in this way, Father. I cannot –'

He turned away, paced about, stopped, paced again. It was all damnably awkward. Knowing what he did about Harvey – all that appalling behaviour the young man had confessed to – it was quite out of the question to give his blessing to such a union. He would never be able to forgive himself. But on the other hand he could not possibly explain to Susannah exactly why, for that would break the secrecy of the confessional.

How right Rome was to insist upon the celibacy of the priesthood! Here, yet again, was evidence of the sad mistakes that had been made at the Reformation, and even in this moment of domestic crisis he made a mental note to cite this sort of situation in a treatise on the authority of the Roman Catholic Church.

Meanwhile Susannah stood before him in tears – an unusual sight, for she had always been a brave child, with good control over her outward emotions. The sight of it caused Percy a certain pain, for since Jane's death he had felt remorse for his treatment of her, and had promised himself not to make the same mistake over Susannah, the purchase of West Lawn Villa being a part of his attempt to make up to her for the love he had been unable to show her mother.

But while Percy wished to comfort his daughter and was well practised in offering spiritual comfort to the lady members of his parish, he suffered from that failing not uncommon in priests, doctors and public benefactors of having difficulty in showing love for the members of his own family. He was now quite at a loss.

While he reflected, Susannah went onto the attack. 'What is it you expect of me?' she challenged. 'Total, mute obedience? Will that satisfy you? You have trapped me in this house as surely as you trapped Mama. I have no friends. I am scarcely permitted to leave this house without drawing you a map of my intended route and stating my expected time of return. I have no freedom, Father, no freedom whatsoever. And now, when I meet someone who – who – who –'

She gave way to unstifled sobs, and Brougham made a move to comfort her. He reached out and patted her shoulder, the effect of which was similar to that of pouring cold water on red hot iron.

'What am I supposed to do?' she exploded, rearing away from him like a frightened mare, her nostrils widely dilated, her slightly large teeth bared. 'Am I to be driven underground into further deceit? Is that what you wish? Or am I – am I expected to wait patiently until you are *dead* before I am allowed to lead a life of my own?'

This last shot upset her even more. She turned abruptly and left the room, and he heard her run upstairs and close her bedroom door with a bang.

A minute or two later he heard her door open again. She was coming downstairs. He listened at his own door, wondering if he might attempt a reconciliation. Then he heard the front door close firmly, and he saw from his window that she was walking rapidly away from the house.

Now what? Was she off to see Harvey? A surge of anger went through him: he would not have her disobey him in that way, no by heaven he would not.

Perhaps she had merely gone to weep on the shoulder of her friend Mary Groves. He wasn't so sure he approved of that young lady either, for she had been influenced by her elder brother, who had some very strange ideas indeed.

He took out his hunter, flipping it open and closing it with a snap, and as he slipped it back into his waistcoat pocket was aware of a fierce little attack of gripe that caused him to put his hand to his side in order to ease the pain.

Blair Harvey was emerging from Mr Lethbridge's inner office when Susannah was shown in.

'Miss Brougham!' he said quietly, conscious that her arrival had been noted by the senior partner.

'Forgive me for calling without appointment, Mr Harvey, but I think we have unfinished business to discuss.'

He nodded to dismiss Clannaborough, who was wheezing in the background, having shown Susannah in. 'You should not have come here,' he said quietly.

She made no attempt to hide their conversation. 'Should I not? And why is that, Mr Harvey?'

He looked uncomfortably at the door to Mr Lethbridge's office, then turned to her again. 'Your father has put me on my honour not to see you again. It is not what I wished, you know that –' He broke off, shaking his head. 'I cannot explain, Miss Brougham – indeed, your father assured me that he would explain it all very clearly to you.'

She was still out of breath from her brisk walk along the High Street, and the wind had blown a lock of hair so that it fell across her face. She seemed more lovely to him at that moment than she had ever seemed before. He felt quite off balance: he had been sure that she would accept her father's order not to see him, and her presence here seemed highly dangerous for him. At any minute, her father himself might arrive, and no doubt blame him for speaking to her and have him dismissed.

'I must not see you, Susannah,' he whispered. 'You must understand my position. Your father has already threatened to have me dismissed for unprofessional conduct, and I could be ruined for life if he were to carry out this threat. It is not that my feelings have changed at all, believe me. Simply that – that –'

'Simply that you are not made of the stuff I thought, Mr Harvey,' Susannah retorted, and swept out, slamming the front door so hard that the building shook, and Blair was obliged by Mr Lethbridge to give an explanation. Mr Lethbridge, amused by the storm in a teacup, observed that in his experience women were indeed queer cattle and that they were on occasion given to having such inexplicable tantrums, and that it was all due to the fact that Eve was created inferior to Adam, being made from one of his ribs, and that it was therefore natural for her descendants to feel incomplete, and that this in turn gave rise to strange uncontrolled humours which were linked to the phases of the moon.

Having received this lecture on the mysteries of womanhood, Blair Harvey went off to his favourite inn, where he sat in the front kitchen with a mug of mulled ale while one of the regulars told a long and humorous story about a well loved sow in litter who fell down a well, and the farmer who lowered his ill-tempered wife down on the end of a rope to get her out, who in turn, having attached the rope to the sow, was drowned in the well while the sow was hoisted to safety.

This story ended with the moral that fair exchange was no robbery, repeated several times by several of the listeners, to the accompaniment of much rosy-cheeked Devon laughter, in which Blair Harvey joined as heartily as the rest.

Susannah needed to cool her temper after her brush with Blair Harvey, so she walked up to Mrs Hake's school near Rougemont Castle, where she hoped to meet Miss Groves; but on finding that the latter was engaged in a Bible class, she continued on round the city, pausing on her way to watch a steam tug bringing barges up the river.

Most of her anger was directed at her father, but some was still reserved for Blair, for although she still loved him he had behaved like a ninny and she was disappointed. 'But I have not yet given up,' she told herself as she went up Racks Lane and into Palace Gardens. 'This is only the beginning.'

She started across the cathedral grounds which were now thick in daffodils. As she approached Broad Gate House, she saw that her father's groom was holding a horse by the front door and that a knot of people had gathered. This miniature crowd looked at her with curious faces as she approached, and the whisperings among them convinced her that some crisis had arisen.

She was not kept long in suspense: Dobbs, Mrs Roughsedge, and Zilla were lined up with long faces in the hall, and strange, bestial noises were issuing from the study. On entering, she found Doctor Runciman kneeling on the carpet beside her father, whose face was covered in froth and whose body was racked by the last throes of apoplexy. He seemed to recognise her, for he made an effort to sit up and reach out to her; then, his face twitching grotesquely, he fell back with a thump, and lay still.

CHAPTER 3

However hard she tried, Susannah could never quite escape the memory of those words she had used to her father scarcely an hour before his death: 'Am I to wait until you are *dead* . . .' That single, bitter challenge began to haunt her: she saw herself as having struck him dead. She shut herself in her room for hours at a time, receiving no one, spurning all attempts at consolation on the part of her domestics, speaking only to Zilla, who since Mrs Brougham's death had become Susannah's personal maid and confidant.

A few days after the funeral (which was attended by several disappointed ladies, along with a large proportion of the city gentry) Mr Lethbridge called at Broad Gate House to inform Miss Brougham of her father's will, and through the mists of her grief and self-accusation she became aware that her situation in life had been radically altered.

Life went on; she began to emerge from her slough of despond; she began to think again of Mr Harvey.

She presumed that he would renew his attentions after a suitable period but was not sure how long that suitable period might be. Nor was she sure whether she wanted to see him again, and at times she wondered if her father had been right and that Blair Harvey was too much of a lightweight (in an intellectual rather than physical sense of course) and that she should discourage his attentions in order to leave herself free to find a man of greater maturity and means.

One night at the end of May, Exeter was hit by a freak thunderstorm. Vivid, electric flashes split the sky, and were followed by that awesome sound as of calico tearing which precedes the worst thunderclaps. Unable to sleep through the racket, Susannah drew her curtains back and lay in her fourposter watching the display.

Softly at first, rain began to fall. It pattered upon the dry roofs like the swiftly running feet of thieves; then the deluge started in earnest: it rattled on the tiles and thudded on the gables; it made torrents in the gutters that rushed and gurgled down drainpipes; it sent a cascade of soot down the flue and into the grate, and played a bass drumbeat on her window.

In the middle of all this, the door opened, and in came Zilla.

She was whimpering with fear because one of the lightning flashes had convinced her that she had seen Dr Brougham's ghost. She knelt at Susannah's bedside and begged for comfort, swearing that she could not return to her room in the attic. It was a mere act of human kindness to take her into her bed, and Zilla was quickly calmed; what Susannah could not have known however was that Zilla's need for comfort extended to something more than she was prepared to give. It was not a question of morals so much as of different standards: Zilla had been brought up in a large family and certain caresses between next of kin were regarded as a pleasant relief from the woes of working folk; so when she buried herself in Susannah's arms and lovingly kissed her breasts, her new mistress was understandably shocked.

In the morning, she decided that on no account must she allow such intimacy to take place again, however innocent it may have seemed in Zilla's mind. She took pen and paper therefore and composed a letter to Mr Lethbridge, intimating to him that he might make it known to

61

Mr Harvey that should the young gentleman care to call upon her in order to present his condolences, she would be happy to receive him.

She sent Zilla round with the letter. When she had gone, Susannah was suddenly seized with an impulse to call her back. It was as if she were in the grip of some fateful inevitability which she could not discern – rather as one who, having missed the right turning on a dark night, plunges onward along a strange road in the hope of finding her way home.

He called a week later when she was feeling more cheerful. She heard him downstairs, and laughed at her own nervousness.

Dobbs, troubled by rheumatism that morning, came up the stairs on all fours. He tapped on Susannah's door, entering at her command. She was sitting at her bureau, dressed totally in black, composing one of several letters she felt obliged to write to her late father's relations as a result of the recent finalisation of his probate. A shaft of brilliant sunlight stabbed into the room.

'Yes, Dobbs, who is it?'

'Ma'am,' he said, having changed to that title at her request a few weeks earlier. 'Mr Blair Harvey awaits you in the front parlour.'

She sat very straight backed, considering how she would respond. Her father's death had turned her into a woman of means: she was his sole beneficiary and owned this house, the villa in Teignmouth, all her father's considerable collection of books, together with the rights to whatever royalties his writings might yet earn. She was also the possessor of a large holding of two percents, together with a quantity of gold sovereigns presently held in the vaults of the South Devon Bank.

'Indeed?' she said quietly, and in the pause that followed the noise of Dobbs's breathing could have been mistaken for a patent steam engine in need of olive oil.

'Will I say you are not at home, Ma'am? Or will you go down to receive him?'

She looked at Dobbs, and the hint of a smile came to her eyes – a smile that would have been recognised as a sign of mischief by the lady who had once taken her for Scripture lessons ten years before.

'No, Dobbs,' she said. 'I shall not descend to receive Mr Harvey. Let Mr Harvey rather ascend to wait upon me.'

She listened to him going painfully downstairs, and then heard the brisker step of Mr Harvey, coming up two at a time. When he reached the landing he halted a moment, and she could just make out the sound of his breathing.

'You may enter, Mr Harvey.'

He came to the door, looking dashing in his black frock coat, his face shining as if it had been scrubbed and polished and his side whiskers neatly fluffed. Having him standing there at the threshold of her room, and the knowledge that he was not at ease gave her a pleasing sense of power: the thought occurred to her that she was now in a position to have anything she wanted of him.

He coughed. 'Miss Brougham. I hope you will forgive me for calling upon you –' and he coughed again, his voice having risen to a squeak.

She needed to prevent herself laughing, so she rose from her desk and crossed the room, passing behind him to close the door. She took the opportunity to examine the back of his head, and to admire the thick waves of hair which descended to his collar. Then she faced him, and looked at him so intently that he backed away.

'Are you afraid of me, Mr Harvey?'

'Miss Brougham! What a question!'

'And are you, then?'

'Not at all!' he said, and puffed his cheeks.

'I'm glad of that,' she said softly, and went to her window, turning her back on him to look out over the cathedral grounds.

Blair had prepared a speech offering his condolences,

63

but her extraordinary manner had rendered it quite inappropriate. Really he had no idea what to say, and her air of suppressed amusement did little to put him at ease.

Without turning, she said, 'If you have come to ask me to marry you, Mr Harvey, then I beg you to get on and do it, for I have never enjoyed delay.' She turned. 'And please – no, do not bend the knee to me. I would rather have it from you direct.'

She came back towards him and fixed him with gentle, mischievous eyes.

He made a croaking noise. 'Will you, then?'

'Will I what, Mr Harvey?'

'Be my wife?'

Later, she saw that she had not been nearly so firmly in control of events as she thought at the time.

'Will you be my husband?'

He breathed out. 'Of course. Yes – with all my heart.'

'In that case, I agree.'

His mouth fell open. She could not help thinking that he would have reacted in exactly the same way if she had tipped him a florin.

'You may kiss me, Mr Harvey,' she said.

He took her hand and fell upon it greedily, pressing soft, boyish lips to the backs of her fingers. She looked down upon his head, inwardly amazed at the ease of the conquest, and perhaps a little perturbed by it.

'Now on my lips, if you please,' she whispered, and found herself trembling all over. 'But gently –'

CHAPTER 4

'It is better to marry than to burn,' Susannah said with that bright lavender twinkle in her eye, 'and I fear that if I wait too long for you my dear, I shall burst into flames.'

They were walking along the path between the river and Berry Meadow. The hedgerows were full of dog roses and fledglings, and here and there, like patches on a green quilt, cowslips and primroses grew in profusion.

Blair strolled with her arm linked in his. 'Don't you feel that we shall be considered improper marrying so soon after your father's death?'

They had already touched on this subject: Susannah had never believed in lengthy mournings and was anxious to leave the past behind.

'What of it? If you are seen calling at Broad Gate House every day of the week for the next two months, tongues will wag with just as much ferocity.'

On the opposite bank, a shire horse plodded by, towing a barge loaded with clay.

'So we shall have to call upon the Bishop,' Blair said.

'Why is that?'

'Won't he require to call the banns?'

When she smiled she sometimes showed her upper teeth and gums in a way that he found almost irresistible. 'My dear,' she said, 'let's not have a society wedding. I have no need of a big organ or a choir. Let's be married quietly at St David's.'

She looked back at the barge to make sure that the

coast was clear, then went on tiptoe in order to press her lips against his. He was amazed how devoted she was to him, how delighted she seemed at the prospect of matrimony, and how cleverly she managed to hint at the intimate delights which lay ahead. She reminded him of a painting by Botticelli: her skin was so pale and fine, her hair such a delicate red-gold. The very act of kissing her lightly upon the lips was enough to stir up the most intense feeling, and he felt obliged to disengage himself from her and draw away so that she could not see the exact extent of his arousal.

There was another, equally pleasurable aspect to their union, one that he hardly liked to mention at first, for his visits to Broad Gate House had made him aware that Susannah had inherited a valuable property together with an unusually fine collection of books, furniture and paintings. It dawned on him, slowly, that he was betrothed to an heiress. Curious to find out the exact size of her fortune, he spent an afternoon in the office when Mr Lethbridge was out going through Dr Brougham's probate papers and examining the list of securities and chattels. Seated in his shirtsleeves at the high desk, he totted up a column of figures and arrived at the astonishing figure of twenty-one thousand pounds.

He was left almost breathless at the discovery. He stood in the office and shook his fists to heaven in triumph, so that when Lethbridge entered unexpectedly he had to go quickly to his desk and explain that he had been merely stretching his limbs.

When he waited on Susannah the following day, she came down to him looking more captivating than ever in a dress of green and white.

'I have discarded my weeds,' she announced. 'See – I am in new leaf.' She took both his hands in hers, closing her eyes and trembling in excitement at being with him again. 'Now,' she said, becoming businesslike. 'Let us stop having wicked thoughts about each other for two minutes and have a serious talk, my dear. Sit over there where I can't reach you and tell me what you are going to do after we are married.'

'Do?' he queried. 'I don't understand.'

'Well I do not see how you can continue at Lethbridge & Wright as an articled solicitor if Mr Lethbridge is going to be dealing with you at the same time as a favoured client. I do not wish to interrupt your career in any way, but our circumstances are a little peculiar.'

He stroked his lips and whiskers with the back of his forefinger. 'Perhaps I should tender my notice,' he suggested, hardly daring to hope that a life of ease now lay before him.

'Perhaps you should indeed,' Susannah replied. 'And then we must consider where we are going to live. I shall not wish to stay here for ever, and have always had an idea that I would like to live in the country. We might sell this house, and buy land with the proceeds. A farm perhaps. Think of it – acres and acres of pasture, hundreds of sheep –'

'And pigs?' he suggested.

'Yes, and pigs if *you* will look after them. And hens and geese. And a donkey for the children and a spring cart and a few head of cattle for butter and cream. I shall have you in a smock frock yet, just wait.'

He looked solemn. 'I think it would be unwise to rush too pre-precip –'

'Precipitately?'

'Exactly – into such a purchase.'

She could resist him no longer: she laughed and crossed the room to him, lifting his hand and pressing it to her cheek. 'Would you like to own a farm or two?' she asked. 'I think I would be very happy with you in the country.'

He looked pleased with himself, glancing from side to side in embarrassment and blinking rather fast.

'Now what you should say is that you would be happy with me anywhere,' she laughed.

'I would Susannah,' he said. 'I would indeed.'

She breathed out. 'I so love you when you put on that serious expression, my dear. You look so grand, so wise!'

He smiled and patted her hand, uncertain exactly how serious she was being.

'Mr Groves was saying only the other day that he considered agriculture to be one of the few occupations open to a Christian,' Susannah said. 'Not that we have to follow his precepts to the letter of course, but there may be something in what he says. Agriculture, medicine and missionary work, those were the three callings I think, and I can hardly imagine yourself as a surgeon or a missionary, can you?'

The following Sunday, they went to lunch with the Groves family, walking back with them through the fields to Northernhay House after hearing Mr Abbot preach at St David's. The wheat was almost full grown now but still green, and waist high on either side of the track. The three ladies walked in front with the children, and Blair walked behind with Anthony Groves and the family tutor, a Scot named Craik. Groves had already started at Dublin University, but was not required to take residence there. He was a quiet, sincere man with a gaze that Blair found uncomfortably penetrating. The previous year he had published a tract entitled *Christian Devotedness* in which he taught that it was the duty of the committed Christian to reject the pursuit of wealth and the acquisition of worldly possesions and instead to live on the minimum, hand to mouth, giving away all excess earnings to the poor. Susannah, on telling Blair about this, had added that her own comfortable circumstances always caused her a certain unease in Mr Groves' presence.

It was another perfect summer's day: larks twittered incessantly overhead, and brimstones flapped between the green stalks of wheat, visiting the new poppies and ox-eye daisies that grew along the edge of the path.

68

Inevitably, the conversation turned to spiritual matters – Mr Groves rarely speaking of anything else – and Blair was asked if he considered himself a high churchman.

'I have never darkened the doors of a dissenters' meeting house, if that is your meaning,' he replied lightly. 'No, I regard myself as a middle of the road man. I have little time for the Methodists, and no time for Rome.'

'And do you have time for Christ?' Mr Craik asked.

Blair felt put out by this question. He regarded such matters as strictly private. 'Why of course,' he said easily, 'but I do not believe greatly in trumpeting about it.'

'You are not afraid of being lukewarm, then, like a Laodicean?' Mr Groves returned.

'I beg your pardon?'

Craik and Groves exchanged a glance. They were walking on either side of Blair, who felt that this inter-rogation had something to do with the fact that he was to marry Susannah.

'Mr Groves refers to the Book of Revelation, chapter three, verse sixteen,' Craik said, rolling his r's and shut-tling his glance quickly back and forth between Groves and Blair Harvey.

They had reached a stile and the ladies were waiting to be helped over. When that had been done and the children were about to scamper on ahead, Anthony Groves opened his Bible and said, 'Let us minister the Word.' The ladies reached out hands to the children, who came to heel immediately, looking up at the grownups in silence, while Blair, who was the only gentleman wearing a hat, removed it hastily as a result of a timely nudge from Susannah.

Mr Groves had found the passage he wanted and the little group stood there between the fields of wheat and barley while he read: 'So then, because thou art luke-warm, and neither cold nor hot, I will spue thee out of my mouth. Because thou sayest, I am rich, and increased with goods, and have need of nothing; and knowest not that thou art wretched and miserable and poor and blind and naked . . .'

Blair glanced sidelong at Susannah, and when she glanced covertly back, he was pleased to feel that she was on his side and that she disliked being preached at in a public place every bit as much as did he.

'As many as I love,' Mr Groves was continuing, 'I rebuke and chasten: be zealous therefore, and repent. Behold, I stand at the door and knock: if any man hear my voice and open the door, I will come in to him, and will sup with him, and he with me.'

'Amen,' said Mr Craik, whereupon Mr Groves invited him to lead them in prayer – which he did at some length, asking the Lord's blessing upon Susannah and Blair, that they might grow in grace to serve the Lord.

Blair was not at all sure what to make of all this. Susannah had introduced him to a number of her acquaintances in the city, but these Groves people were in a class of their own. At lunch, the conversation continued on spiritual matters to the exclusion of all else, ranging from the meaning of the Last Supper to the extent of the atonement and theories about ministry and worship in the early church, and though much of this went straight over Blair's head, he gathered from his afternoon at Northernhay House that Groves and Craik were among a growing number of educated men in Exeter, Plymouth and Dublin who sought to make a return to a form of Christianity that was neither Protestant nor Catholic: one whose aim was to approach as near as possible to the original beliefs and form of worship of the first apostles and the churches that sprang up in the century after the crucifixion.

'I cannot help being impressed by their integrity of purpose and transparent sincerity of belief,' Susannah declared as they walked arm in arm back through the city, 'but they make me feel uncomfortable, all the same. All my life I have had to keep my head lowered for fear of the criss-cross of religious musket fire that has gone on around me, and I had hoped that today we might have had at least some secular conversation.'

Blair felt considerably relieved at this: he had been afraid that Susannah had introduced him to her friends in order to have him 'perverted'.

'But wasn't your own mother quite strongly allied to their way of thinking?'

'Yes – but then Father was practically in the arms of Rome, so I have seen both sides.'

'And which is more to your liking?'

She laughed and clung to his arm. 'I prefer neither. I propose that we do not take too much notice of Mr Craik's apocalyptic warnings, and that we concentrate upon loving God and each other and leave the doubtful art of splitting hairs to others.'

He felt very proud of her commonsense and reflected that it was odd how, having been betrothed to her for nearly four weeks already, it was only now that he was beginning to discover her hidden depths.

Susannah had the fourposter taken to pieces and reassembled on the second floor before the wedding, and the other bedroom on the same floor converted into a dressing room for Blair. She ordered new feathers and linen for the bed, replacing the old drab grey stuff she had known all her life with pale green, and hanging rose-patterned curtains instead of the faded velvet. The wedding itself was as simple as she could have wished: she drove with Blair to St David's, made her promises to love, honour and obey before eighteen witnesses, and was quickly out again in the sunshine, a plain ring on her finger and her arm in Blair's. They were young, they were intelligent, they were, above all, modern. They had taken a bold step together, and faced the future with confidence. Riding back together to Broad Gate House, he held her hand tightly all the way, while total strangers waved their blessing to the good looking couple, and an urchin ran along beside the wheels playing tunes in the spokes with a stick.

The house filled with guests: people Blair had never met for the most part, but whom Susannah felt obliged to invite in honour of her parents' memory. The servants dashed to and fro with trays of French wine; Dobbs excelled himself in the taking of coats and the brushing of hats, and Mrs Roughsedge, the cook, was allowed to stand in the doorway of the parlour to listen to the speech made by Mr Lethbridge in honour of the bride and groom.

And then – quite suddenly, it seemed – the guests were gone and the servants sent away and Susannah was alone in her own house with her own husband.

'Are you hungry?' he stammered. 'Would you like to take some supper before we retire?'

She went to him deliberately so that he must take her in his arms. 'I am hungry for you,' she whispered unashamedly, and pulled his head down to kiss him on the lips.

He seemed quite at a loss: the vein in his forehead had enlarged and he blinked rapidly in the way he always did when emotionally stirred.

'Say something,' she commanded. 'Tell me what you are thinking.'

This only served to embarrass him more. She slipped her hands down his arms and linked her fingers with his.

'Do you feel, inside yourself, that you are still a child?' she asked. 'That's how I feel. As if I were twelve years old again and starting on a great adventure.' She looked searchingly into his face, loving his shy youthfulness, his scarcely bristly cheeks, the fluff of whiskers he was cultivating upon them. 'Let us be for each other all and everything, my dear. Let us be so close, so intimate that nothing in the world can separate us.'

He glanced from side to side nervously, and the thought

occurred to her that he was perhaps even more of a child than she, inside himself, and that it would not do to lay too great an emphasis on the fact. He must be helped to prove himself as a man, she thought, and immediately was flooded with a delicious sensation of longing for him.

She released his hands. 'I am supposed to go up first, isn't that the way of it? And when you have taken something to fortify you, you are permitted to – to join me.'

She laughed suddenly and heard her own voice to be a little high pitched. She rather wished that he was better able to take the lead: it would have been exciting, for instance, if he had picked her up in his arms and carried her upstairs. But Blair was quite speechless, frowning now to make himself look masculine. She wondered what on earth could be going on in his mind.

'We shall go up together,' she decided for him. 'Here, take my hand so I shan't be afraid.'

She knew instinctively, like the daughter-in-law of Pythagoras, that a woman who goes to bed with a man must lay aside her modesty with her skirt and put it on with her petticoat. She had daydreamed of this moment so often before that she wanted no further delay; with both parents dead, it seemed to her that whatever she did was of herself and not subject any more to their approval or disapproval. So having felt childlike only minutes before, she now felt quite mature: she had a sudden insight into the importance of what was to take place, knowing in her heart that their consummation must be joyful, innocent and free from all feelings of anxiety or guilt; so she was careful, on entering the bedchamber, to behave as if she were alone and to prepare for bed as she did on any other night of the year. She set about undressing in a matter-of-fact way therefore, her skirts rustling to the floor, her long, fine tresses falling away down her back as she released them from their ribbons. No, it was impossible to behave

73

entirely normally, she knew that, but it was important that Blair should not be made more nervous by any display of apprehension on her part. They had been made one flesh that day: she believed it firmly. He would be feeling every bit of what she was feeling now, and his confidence could only be improved by her own. But there was also, she discovered, a need to show herself to him as she had shown herself to herself in the mirror so often before. She revelled in his little gasp of approval at her hair loose about her shoulders, her neck, her breasts, and the line of her back as she bent to take up her nightgown and slip it over her head. What if it was a display? She wanted to give herself to him completely, she wanted him to possess her entirely, so the sight of him standing there entranced, a boot horn in one hand and his cravat in the other was praise enough.

She climbed into the bed and pulled up the sheet under her chin.

'I am a little afraid, Mr Harvey,' she said, mock-formal.

'There is no need,' he replied, unbuttoning his under-shirt.

'I am glad of that.'

He was careful to pull on his nightshirt before lowering his drawers.

'Your hands are trembling,' she observed.

'In anticipation,' he replied.

'Are you not at all frightened?'

'Perhaps a little, then.'

'It is because you are innocent,' she said. 'If you were a great and practised lover, you would not turn a hair.'

He made a gargling sound that was a laugh. She held back the covers for him. 'Come,' she whispered, and he obeyed.

She knew that the tiny creature depicted in Greek sculpture was supposed to grow to a massive limb that was reputed to be able to give a woman great joy, and in her teenage she had wasted much time drawing profiles of her ideal man. As Blair's profile approximated to her ideal she had expected – perhaps a little illogically – something far more triumphant from him. She had presumed that with the taking off of his clothes he would become for her what she was trying so hard to become for him: the sublime lover, the soul mate, the partner in ecstasy. Susannah, become Leda, expected Blair to become Zeus, and the discovery that she was instead bedded down with a gauche young man whose fumbling hands lost their way and whose final tears, she suspected, were more for his own departed innocence than for the fact that he had made an unsatisfactory penetration and arrived too early was a disappointment to say the least. What an extraordinary, degrading fiasco it turned out to be! A few minutes of desperate clutchings in the dark; a small organ, and no choir.

Well!

When Dobbs brought in *Trewman's Flying Post* at breakfast the following morning, Blair made a move to hide behind it.

'My dear,' Susannah said. 'We have many breakfasts before us. Can't the newspaper wait just a few days?'

He put it down beside his place. She had directed Zilla to lay the table so that they sat side by side rather than at either end, but Blair noted that it was she who sat at the end of the table and he beside her.

She had laid her hand over his. The sun was throwing brilliant rectangles of light upon the pannelling and an erand boy was whistling in the street. He was aware of the thought: she is my wife.

'We shall improve,' she was saying. 'We shall practice assiduously, and become most proficient.'

He found it shocking that she should speak of the act of love even obliquely, just as he had been shocked at her self-confessed desire for him the night before, and the way she had undressed with so little modesty. He had expected something quite different of it all: she should indeed have preceded him to bed and he should have come upon her suddenly. There should have been a struggle and an overpowering, a scream, blood, tears and final adoration. It should have been he who called the tune, he who cracked the whip, but instead she had somehow managed to take over from him the role he was supposed to play just as Molly had done, so that in the middle of it all the memory of that afternoon came forcibly back to him and he had been unable to perform.

Yes, he had wept. He had wept for reasons that he could not understand himself. There had been a feeling of longing inside him when she had turned away from him in exasperation – of longing for the approval and gentleness of his mother and the love and adoration of his elder sisters. What was he doing with this woman in this bed? How could any person change so completely within a matter of hours?

It had been a turbulent night for him, with little sleep. Susannah's way of turning from him had forbidden him to reach out to her and he had been careful to allow no bodily contact between them. He had lain on his back and listened to the mournful tolling of city bells, and in the hour before dawn, when the first sparrows were chirruping outside he had fallen into a fitful doze, waking to find that Susannah was already up and the sun bringing to life the colours in the rose patterned curtains. He had lain and listened to the hiss of water being pumped up to the cistern and the clatter of hooves in the yard; he had closed his eyes and recalled those awful minutes of intimacy the night before. How could it be that Molly had been able to arouse him so skilfully and effect his entry so easily, while Susannah had been so grossly incompetent? She had not helped him at all. She had lain like a log, that was what had been wrong. Molly had somehow managed to open herself to him, while this new wife of his had expected him to enter by a door that was hardly within his reach.

He dreaded the evening already. They would have to go through the whole thing all over again!

He must have sighed, for he felt her hand tighten on his. 'It's not as serious as *that*,' she murmured. She considered a moment then added: 'Besides, we shall not be able to give a repeat performance for a few days, as I've started the blessing.'

'Blessing? What blessing?'

But just then Zilla came in with fresh coffee, and as Susannah seemed to forget to answer his question, Blair decided it was better not to ask again.

What a lifetime those first five weeks of marriage seemed! She tried – yes she *did* try to contain her impatience with him, to overlook his lack of imagination, his self-centred behaviour, his closed mind. She tried to forgive him for being piqued when she discovered he had never read Montaigne and for his extraordinary outburst of anger when she laughed at him for thinking that a vignette was a green vegetable; she bent over backwards (in more ways than one) to accommodate him, to ease his lot, to be the submissive and obedient wife – only to be rewarded, night after night, with a grunt and a peck on the cheek as soon as Blair had completed the little task he seemed to regard as his husbandly duty.

As time passed, Blair came to believe that Susannah deliberately sought supremacy over him, using her know-ledge of languages and literature to score off him, but this was not at all the case as far as Susannah was concerned. She had been quick to see that, for all his Oxford degree and training in law, Blair's education was sadly inferior to her own and that a passing reference to the Phaedo led him to believe she was speaking of a pet dog, and a quotation from Aristophanes left him blankfaced. This caused her inner amusement at first, but quickly became tiresome, for she had to avoid hurting him or allowing him to reveal his ignorance, and resign herself to the fact that she was unlikely ever to enjoy the sort of stimulating conversation she had expected with him. She reflected sadly that she had exchanged a kindly, learned father for a callow, under-educated youth.

To make up for his lack of conversational prowess she returned to the task of educating him in bed, unwilling to accept that they could not attain the delights of love her reading of certain Roman poets had led her to expect. And there was reason for optimism, too: from time to time she began to feel the beginnings of it, and she was sure that if only Blair could be persuaded to persevere longer than two and a half minutes she might win the goal which he was quite unaware she had set herself.

'Let us play a game,' she said one night. 'Let us make believe we are animals! You are a lion and I your lioness. Let us maul and scratch each other, my darling. Let us bite and lick, thus and thus . . .'

But it was no use. His best was never quite good enough for her. She had an ascendancy over him that she had never wanted or campaigned for, and the better she got to know him the more often his remarks seemed to her puerile or ridiculous.

He entered a mood of depression. He took to spending his days out of the house, lunching with merchants and gentry in the city or going for solitary drives in the phaeton. He came home late in the evenings when Susannah had given up waiting for him and had dined alone. He treated her with great civility, but declined to touch her in bed. Then one evening when she was preparing for bed he came to her door in tears.

She turned to him immediately and held out her hands to him. He ran to her and knelt by her dressing table, sobbing.

'I should never have married you,' he wailed. 'I didn't even have the courage to ask you, did I? I'm not good enough for you, Susannah. You are my superior in everything, everything!'

She took him in her arms and ran her fingers through his hair. 'You are the only person I can ever love,' she told him, and felt a little desperate in the saying of it because there seemed in her words a double-layered meaning. 'You are my handsome, strong, wonderful husband.'

This seemed to cheer him a little, and she realised that his sudden outburst may have been caused by a slight excess of port-wine. She soothed him like a mother soothing a schoolboy, and when he eventually smiled she held his face in her hands and kissed him on the forehead.

'You should hear Zilla speak of you!' she said lightly. 'Do you know that the poor girl is besotted by you? She worships the ground you tread! Now doesn't that make you feel better?'

Zilla knew she was a lucky girl, because Mrs Roughsedge was for ever reminding her. She was one of a large family – poor folk – that had been evicted from a tithe cottage near Drewsteignton, and had been saved from the work-house by the charity of Mrs Brougham. It was five years now since she had been brought trembling and pathetically thin to the kitchen door, to be bathed and scrubbed and de-loused by Mrs Roughsedge and set to work as a kitchen maid. In those five years she had learnt all the rules of the household and the skills of service: how to scrub flags, clean pewter, tend a spitroast, use a goffer iron, starch a shirt, wait at table. But she had also become devoted to Susannah who, on her mother's death, had decided to train Zilla as a lady's maid – a position so exalted in Zilla's mind that when she was first told she had gone into a dead faint and had to be revived with salts.

Becoming a lady's maid meant that you became part of your lady's life, that was what Miss Susannah had said to her on her first day. You had to learn exactly what your lady liked to wear and how she liked it folded or laid out for her to put on. You had to learn how to hold her silver-backed brush and brush her long, fine hair without pulling too hard at the tangles; you had to help her with her shoes and be present when she dressed for important occasions. You even saw her undressed in the tub and were required to scrub her white back and pour warm water over her to rinse off the suds, and she confided things to you, little secrets about her likes and dislikes and her happinesses and sadnesses that brought you close together in a wonderful sisterhood. You came to know her so well that you could almost tell sometimes what she was thinking, and in a strange, mystical way, your body sought its own particular harmony with hers, so that when you woke with that dull feeling of physical disappointment, you knew that Miss Susannah would have done the same and you would be able to share with her the unspoken sorrow, the womanly secret that was written so plainly in the pallor of the skin, the colour of the eye, the dull disobedience of the hair.

This was the real reason why Zilla was so lucky: in becoming Susannah's maid she was able to share in Susannah's life, so that what Susannah enjoyed, Zilla enjoyed at second hand, and what Susannah loved, Zilla adored from afar.

So it was true that she adored Mr Harvey, for she had shared Susannah's excitement over him from the first day when he had delivered flowers with a letter to the kitchen door, and within the space of six months, it seemed to Zilla that Mr Harvey had been responsible for the extraordinary change that had taken place in the household. The old order of an elderly couple living in fusty grandeur had given way to the new, of frequent dinner parties and musical evenings, of laughter in the dining room and poetry with the port.

Was it inevitable that Mr Harvey should one day require a bottle of Malaga from the cellar that Zilla could not locate? And was it inevitable that Dobbs should be laid up with rheumatism and Zilla required to play butler as well as tablemaid?

She came back into the dining room where Susannah and Mr Harvey were entertaining the Withinshaws, the Pagets and Lieutenant Agassiz and seeing that Susannah was closely engaged in conversation whispered her apologies in Mr Harvey's ear.

He wiped his lips on the damask napkin Zilla had ironed that morning and excused himself from the table, ordering her to lead the way down to the cellar.

The candlelight flickered among the arched shelves; she bent to examine the rows of dusty bottles again, and Mr Harvey's shadow extended up over the curve of bricks behind her.

'I've looked and looked, sir, honest I have, and I be blowed if I can find 'im,' she explained, then froze as she felt his hands on her waist.

'Put the candle down, Zilla,' he whispered, and when she had done so turned her round to face him. He looked down at her, and the tip of his tongue went round the perimeter of his mouth; then, saying something about this being the vintage he wanted to taste, he almost lifted her from her feet and put his open mouth over hers, forcing his tongue between her lips.

The act lasted only a matter of seconds. He let go of her, grinning in a way she had never seen him do before, his mouth wet and a vein making a zigzag down his forehead. 'Now be a good girl and don't say anything, and maybe there'll be another one for you one of these days,' he said, and she fled up the stone steps and into the scullery.

'Mrs R is in a flutter over Zilla, dear,' Susannah said to her husband. 'The poor girl seems to have got it into her head that you have designs on her!'

He felt a thud in the pit of his stomach.

'I said there could not possibly be any foundation in the

suggestion,' she added. 'There is not, is there?'

He snorted. 'None whatsoever.'

She was brushing her hair before the mirror. He saw her glance at him and smile.

'And what was that for?' he asked, tugging his neck-cloth between his hands. Outside, the cathedral clock boomed the hour. Eleven o'clock. They were retiring later and later these days.

'What was what for?' she countered, dealing with a tangle.

'The little smile.'

'Did I smile? I was not aware of it.'

'You smiled as though you did not believe me,' he said.

'And how does one do that?' she asked. 'How does one smile as if one does not believe someone.' She turned away from the mirror. 'I believe you entirely,' she said. 'I merely told you because I thought you would be amused. I was not at all serious.' She laughed suddenly.

'And there – you laugh like that.'

'I can't help it! You are as red as a turkey, my dear! You look as though you have been found out in the romance of the century!'

The colour went quickly from his face.

'So,' he said. 'What you mean is that you do *not* believe me at all and that you *were* being quite serious. You are accusing me of abusing one of the servants and by implication you are also accusing me of being a liar.'

She felt her heart-beat quickening. There was something strangely enjoyable about arguing when you knew that you had a watertight case. She put down her hair-brush.

'My dear – please let's not make a mountain from a molehill. I have not accused you of anything at all, and am not doing so. You have given me your assurance that Mrs Roughsedge is mistaken, and I have accepted it.'

'Very well, if you will not be honest with me, I shall have to be honest with you. I do not believe you,

Susannah. I do not believe that you believe me.'

'This is becoming ridiculous,' she said. 'I believe that you believe that I believe. If we are to play that game, let us hold a mirror up to a mirror.'

He said nothing.

'Perhaps we should start again,' she said. 'Mrs Roughsedge has come to me with a suggestion that you may have behaved a little cavalierly to Zilla. I am not in the least put out by the news, and I suggest that you tell me what has happened so that we may have it in the open and laugh about it.'

He swallowed. 'So. You are demanding a confession of me, is that it? Well I'm damned if I'll confess to anyone, least of all you.'

'Confess?' she whispered. 'I said nothing of any confession, though seeing you now leads me to think that one may be due. I am not deaf and blind, Blair. I have known Zilla since she was a scrap of eleven. A girl does not suddenly start blushing and running about the house for no reason. I told you – oh – two weeks ago – that she was struck by you, and only a few days later you come up from being with her in the cellar looking as red as a mullet. Then, when I make it easy for you and give you the gentlest of hints, you become unusually defensive.'

'So you did *not* believe me!' he shouted. 'You had me tried and found guilty before telling me the charge.'

She bowed her head, struggling for control. 'All that concerns me is that you and I, as husband and wife, should have no secrets from each other. That is all that concerns me.' She appealed to him: 'What does it matter if you stole a kiss from her? I think I would admire you for it! And I would admire you even more if you could admit it to me instead of adopting this extraordinary holier-than-thou –'

She saw his hand go back as if in slow motion, and there was an explosion of pain across her mouth. In the morning, she told Mrs Roughsedge that her swollen lip had been caused by a midnight collision with her bedpost.

He decided, after that, that he would in future make it a strict policy never to apologise. Her behaviour had been a complete eye-opener to him. He saw her for what she was now. A shrew. She had ensnared him into marriage, demanded too much of him, belittled him and finally provoked him to violence. Was he to blame for that?

He ignored her pointedly for several days in a row. He hid himself behind the *Spectator* at breakfast. He returned to his bachelor haunts in the city, and one night returned to Broad Gate House so full of drink that he fell asleep fully clothed in his dressing room.

It did the trick. It brought her to heel.

She came to him in the study where he sat surrounded by her father's books. She closed the door gently behind her and stood there looking serene in her green and white dress, her hair tied back in a velvet ribbon.

'Yes?' he asked. 'What is it?'

'I have come to ask if you will cease being angry with me and love me a little,' she said.

They were both still very young. Both wanted to love and be loved. Quite without warning, they were in each other's arms.

'Can we be friends?' she whispered when they were calmer. 'Can we put all this behind us and start filling our lives with happiness?'

He nodded his agreement, stroking her brow with the tips of his fingers.

'And will you please never hit me again?'

'I did not hit you, Susannah. It was merely a little slap to teach you a lesson.'

'Indeed?' she replied. 'I think you are much stronger than you realise. A little slap to you is a prize fighter's punch to me.'

'Well,' he said. 'If I say it is the moon, it is the moon, understand? The wife must be subject to her husband, otherwise we shall have anarchy.'

She looked at him very steadily, but said nothing. In the evening, over dinner, she told him that she wanted to move away.

'We cannot go on here in Exeter,' she said. 'This house has never been a happy one, and I'm afraid of its effect on us. I dread another winter here of rain and fog and that bell outside our window every night. I think we should move as soon as possible – to West Lawn. We can put this house up for sale and – if you would like it – you can go into business with the capital. I have already enquired about carriers, too. Kerslakes can move us at a fortnight's notice. We can go at the end of the month, before the worst of the winter.'

He sipped his Marsala. 'Wouldn't it be better to wait until the spring?'

She smiled in a wistful way, looking into his eyes as if searching for what lay behind. 'No, I think not, Blair. I shall not feel inclined to take a long bumpy ride by next April.'

For once she did not have to spell it out. His face lit up with surprise and wonder. He knelt by her chair and kissed her hands reverently, and the following evening, as a reward for being such a clever girl, he took her to a concert in the Royal Subscription Rooms, to listen to the premiere performance in Exeter of some new sonatas by a German composer with an unpronounceable name.

CHAPTER 5

They set out in the Royal Clarence Post on a blustery day in late October, having spent their last two nights in Exeter at Northernhay House, with the Groves. The removal wagons had lined up in Cathedral Close, and the furniture had been loaded in the pouring rain. When the last waggoner had shouted his 'Walk on!' Susannah had gone up to the room that had been hers as a child and stood listening to the echoes of past memories. She had lived in this house since the age of eight and now, on leaving it, she experienced a strange sense of foreboding, as if she were committing herself to some extraordinary future. Looking out of that window, the one which commands a view across to the cathedral and beyond the city walls, she felt that if she stood very still and emptied her mind of every thought and sensation, she might be able to catch a glimpse of what lay ahead.

Blair's boots echoed on the bare boards behind her and she came out of her reverie. He stood beside her, the breath whistling slightly in his nose.

'Glad to be going?' he asked.

She turned her head to look at him and thought, not for the first time, how little she knew of him and how extraordinary it was that she should have committed her life to him so readily. And was she glad to be going? No, she was not; but then she would not have been glad to stay, either.

She slipped her arm into his. 'Yes,' she replied. 'Very glad.'

The journey to Teignmouth was about fourteen miles, and they should have arrived in the afternoon, but soon after leaving Dawlish they encountered a landslip, and the coachman decided it would be necessary to retrace their track and take an alternative route right the way round Little Haldon. They left the coast road and began to climb, and as dusk fell the journey became something of a nightmare. The wind increased in strength and rain squalls thundered on the coach roof. There were frequent delays and long periods of total darkness. Looking forward out of her side window (which rattled abominably) all Susannah could see was a few yards of rough track and the slanting lines of rain. Zilla, who was the only servant they had taken with them from Broad Gate House, was sick because of the motion, and the other passengers sat facing each other, clamping their teeth tightly shut against the smell of her vomit. They went up and down impossibly steep hills, the coachman calling to his team to coax and cajole them on the way up and crooning, 'Easy, easy, easy!' to steady them on the way down, and the dimmed lights of a hill village crept by like a scene in a diorama.

Susannah dozed, and woke with a start to find that her head was resting against Zilla's shoulder.

'We'm nearly there, Ma'am,' the girl said.

'How are you feeling now, Zilla?'

'I'm right as rain, Ma'am,' Zilla said cheerfully. 'I'm lovely.'

Susannah looked out of her window. The coach had descended to the main road bordering the River Teign, and the going was much smoother. As they topped a rise, the new bridge across to Shaldon came into view, and at the same time the coach was buffeted by the wind, which was howling straight in through the harbour entrance.

They came to the first houses and went down a narrow, cobbled street, where the lights of a tavern were reflected in the rain. As they went by, a man was ejected from the front door with such force that he all but went under the wheel of the coach, and Susannah heard a shout of laughter from the revellers inside.

The town seemed to close in upon them: narrow fronted houses leant in on either side, and there was a sudden, strong smell of drains and rotting garbage. When they emerged from this street, the full force of the storm hit them, and Susannah saw that they were close to the shore, where a blanket of whipped spume and foam-streaked waves stretched out into the night.

The coach drew to a halt, and a man looked in through the window. He held a bull's eye lantern aloft and shouted, 'Cockram's Royal!'

They had arrived.

Mr Inman, an obsequious man with lips as thick as a negro's and eyes that shifted rapidly up and down and from side to side while he spoke, took their cloaks. Blair removed his hat, and with a swift downward swing of the arm threw off the water droplets from it before handing it over.

'It ith the low theathon,' lisped Inman, 'and what with the thtorm and the landthlip on the Dawlish road, we prethumed you had turned back to Ectheter.' He looked from Blair to Susannah, and when she caught his eye blushed deeply. 'The thervantth have been thent up already and I fear the kitchen fire ith already banked up –'

Blair tapped him on the shoulder with his silver-headed stick. 'Are you saying there is no supper for us?' he demanded. 'For if you are, you are mistaken. My agent has booked a room for myself and my wife, and a hot dinner into the bargain, so I suggest you rouse the servants and stoke up the fires, or I shall want to know the reason why. And so, for that matter, will Mr Cockram when I inform him of it.'

This last shot frightened Inman so much that his thick lips pouted as if he were about to burst into tears; then, having deposited the new arrivals' cloaks, he led the way into the small dining room, stoked up the log fire, fanned the embers with a pair of leather bellows and hastened out to organise some supper.

'And we shall have two brandies, if you please,' Blair called after him. 'One hot with sugar and one cold without. And – wait a minute, man! I haven't finished with you! Make sure the bed is *properly* warmed on *both* sides.'

Blair warmed his back at the blaze, and Susannah sat down gratefully by the fender. Taking the hem of her dress in the tips of her fingers, she turned it back a few inches in order to dry her feet and stockings, then leant back and closed her eyes.

'I would be quite happy to go without supper,' she said. 'All I want now is fresh linen and a warmed bed.'

Blair bounced on his heels and said they would have a hot dinner that evening or his name wasn't Blair Harvey.

At the same time, they heard voices in the lobby, and a moment later a short, red-faced fellow, who looked as though he had been raised on lean beef and Devonshire cream from an early age, entered. This, it turned out, was Harvey's agent.

'Mr and Mrs Harvey, I presume!' he beamed, and the lights from the chandelier glowed in his polished cheeks. 'John Cobbe, merchant of this parish, as they say. And this,' he added, turning to a tall, narrowly built gentleman whose honest face and kind eyes took Susannah's attention – 'this is Captain Endacott, my sleeping partner and farming friend.' Cobbe bowed to Susannah (who had managed by now to return the hem of her dress to its proper position) and gave his hand to Blair, who explained that he and his wife were to move into West Lawn Villa.

'Of course you are – of course you are,' Cobbe chortled fruitily. 'The whole of Teignmouth and Shaldon know that, for we have seen the caravan of wagons arriving with your furniture yesterday.' He turned and looked down at

Susannah. The fire had blazed up by now, and her face and neck were lit by the flames. Her hair was a little disarrayed, and one end of the bow tied in her hair ribbon had come loose and hung down to her shoulder. She was conscious of Cobbe's appreciative stare, but much more conscious of the quick, shy glance of the captain of dragoons who stood behind him.

Cobbe had recovered from the effect Susannah had on most males at first acquaintance and had turned back to Harvey. 'So what sort of a journey have you had? Pretty damnable, I'll be bound. We've had a smack from Brixham ashore, lost with all hands on Spratts Sands this afternoon, and they say a clipper's in difficulties off Hope's Nose. Not as bad as the storms we had in '23, mind you, and the new bridge has stood up to it excellently, excellently. Mind you, that bridge'll last for ever, Mr Harvey. I was on the committee, you know. Done wonders for the town. Opened up the coast, linked east with west. Bringing in some pretty toll revenue, too. Have you heard that we plan to dredge the entrance? We'll have ships in here of ten and twelve foot draught before long. We'll be competing with Bristol and Falmouth on level terms.'

'Yes, John,' Endacott put in quietly, 'but I think you will have to win your independence first.'

'If your humble servant has anything to do with it we shall, and in double quick time, too,' Cobbe said.

'Independence?' Blair asked.

'From Exeter,' Endacott explained. 'As a trading port.'

For a second time he glanced at Susannah and their eyes met in a delicious shock of mutual awareness.

'We're being bled white,' Cobbe was saying. 'Harbour dues – all going to Exeter. Customs formalities and revenue – all going to Exeter. It's a disgrace. Grossly inequitable. But we'll win our case. What we need is a few sharp brains and a little capital. We'll get up a petition. You're the sort of gentleman we need, Mr Harvey. People who wish to see Teignmouth prosper. People of intelligence and influence. With a modicum of careful planning and sensible investment, this harbour could become one of the principal trading ports in the country, do you know that? Has it ever occurred to you?'

The brandies arrived, and a little while later two helpings of lukewarm beef stew and dumplings, which Susannah was unable to eat. Cobbe and Endacott sat down at the table with them, and Blair was treated to a continuation of the eulogy of Teignmouth and the business prospects on offer to the enterprising young man with capital, until Susannah, unable to keep her eyes open much longer, excused herself and retired for the night.

She was shown to her room by Inman's mother, who had put on her apron and cap for the occasion. She led the way up the wide stairs and into a south facing bedroom on the first floor, lighting an oil lamp, removing the two long-handled bed warmers and reassuring Susannah that her maid had eaten some supper and been provided with a bed.

Nearly an hour later, when Susannah was on the very point of falling asleep, Blair entered the room, having taken several more brandies with Cobbe and Endacott. She had left the lamp burning for him, but he made a noise while using the close stool, and her eyes opened automatically.

'Ah, so you're awake,' he said, standing at the foot of the bed and removing his neckcloth. 'Well that was very interesting, Susannah, very interesting indeed.' He stepped out of his trousers and put them over a chair. 'I don't think we'll regret coming to Teignmouth – or *Tin*mouth as they pronounce it here. No, not at all. Why, the business opportunities make one positively gasp. New roads to be laid, new buildings to erect, the shipping industry just beginning to advance by leaps and bounds.' He stood in his shirt and flexed his shoulders like a weight-lifter. 'I believe that we find ourselves in one of the more exciting eras of history since the discovery of the Americas, Susannah. Everywhere is development, and the more development, the more business, the more business, the more development. Do you know that half the granite being used for the new buildings in London is shipped from Teignmouth? It comes down by rail and barge from some quarry –'

'Haytor,' Susannah said sleepily.

'Exactly! How did you know that? It comes down the Stover and loads right here at New Quay. Then there's the exportation of pottery clay, the resurgence of trade with Newfoundland – we're even importing hides from Argentina! And you know what this fellow Cobbe's up to, don't you? Banking and investment. Export – import. Loans on interest. Even shipping.'

He climbed into the bed beside her and having snuffed the taper, drew the canopy and planted a brandy-smelling kiss upon her cheek.

Just as she was falling asleep, he announced in the darkness: 'Yes, I have a strong feeling that we shall find life very much to our liking here, Susannah. Very much to our liking.' Then he turned on his side away from her, and she was left lying awake, listening to the gale howling in the flues and battering at the sash like some wild animal that was determined to come in.

On going to the window the following morning, Susannah was greeted by a desolate scene: the fishing smack that had foundered the previous day lay upside down on the sands, and a group of women stood huddled together in shawls, mourning their dead.

'The widows and the orphans,' Blair said at her side. 'Poor dears, poor dears!'

'Were many drowned?'

'Cobbe was saying about a dozen.'

She shivered, and Blair, mistaking her feelings, put his arm round her shoulder to comfort her. He admired the profile of her nose against the grey light from the window. 'There is no need to be afraid, Susannah,' he said softly. '*I* shall not be going to sea, though I may invest in shipping. No, I'll let others get their feet wet on my behalf, thank you very much.' He gave her a little squeeze and kissed her on the chin. 'There's a lot of money to be made here, I'm convinced of it. A *lot* of money.'

He took her arm and they went down to breakfast; and in the afternoon, when the gale had abated and the rain given way to intervals of bright sunshine and high, marching clouds, they took a carriage through the narrow streets and up the hill to their new home.

'It is far too big for us!' Susannah said. 'I never imagined it so large from father's description. He called it a "little villa". We don't even have enough furniture for all the rooms!'

They were standing in the wide sitting room, whose south-facing windows overlooked terraced lawns, the upper slopes of the town and the sea beyond. In an adjoining room carpenters were fitting corner cupboards and shelves, and the house echoed with sawings and bangings.

'We shall have to close up two of the bedrooms.'

'Not for long, Susannah. Within a few brief years these walls will resound with the noise and laughter of baby Blairs and small Susannahs.'

She laughed delightedly: there were occasions when Blair managed to hit upon a nice turn of phrase, and here was one of them. Perhaps he is not quite such a barbarian after all, she thought.

'And what are we to do with all Father's books?' she asked. 'We have plenty of parlours and bedchambers, but no library. I hardly like to give them away, and I doubt if a lending library would take them off our hands.'

'In that case we must build a new wing,' he said airily. 'I shall engage an architect at the earliest opportunity.'

She clapped her hands together, delighted at his forthright self-confidence, his willingness to make things happen.

'We shall have a studio and a music room as well,' he mused, patting her hand and feeling very pleased with himself. 'We shall become patrons of the arts, dear, will you like that?'

She turned to him, her face alight with excitement, and her smile revealing her upper gums in a way that never failed to entrance him. He was just about to bend and kiss her forehead when they were interrupted.

' 'Scuse me, M'm,' Zilla said. She had knocked before entering, but had not been heard because of the sawings and bangings in the next room.

'What is it Zilla?'

'Please, M'm, Cook's arrived, and the new kitchen maid and the gardener. They'm waiting on you in the back kitchen being as how you said you be wanting to meet with 'em, like.'

Susannah turned to her husband. 'I must be about my domestic duties, dear,' she said, and pressed his hand affectionately before leading Zilla from the room.

They settled quickly into a new and prosperous way of life. A few weeks after their arrival, Broad Gate House was sold, the proceeds of which were made over to Blair to invest as he saw fit. Encouraged by Susannah, he went into partnership with Mr Cobbe and Captain Endacott, the three men becoming the principle shareholders in a shipping firm set up under the name of Harvey & Co. He replaced Dr Brougham's carriage with a lighter, more elegant vehicle in which he promised to take Susannah for country drives once the baby was born. He fitted himself out in twill trousers and good broadcloth. He engaged a young man called Robson to be his valet, and trained him in the art of laying out his clothes and polishing his boots. By the early summer following their arrival, the Harveys were already establishing themselves as people of property and influence in the town, and the new studio and library wing they had built onto West Lawn Villa gave them a reputation for being both well educated and – in the strictest meaning of the word – genteel.

He considered himself particularly fortunate in the choice of his partner, for Cobbe turned out to be both a shrewd businessman and an excellent companion. Together they invested in what Cobbe saw as the certainty of Teignmouth's development as a major trading port on the south coast; a brigantine was laid down to take advantage of trade opening up with the continent, and the two men were frequently to be seen dining together at the Royal Hotel.

Of Captain Endacott, Blair was not so sure. Having a farm to oversee near Bishopsteignton as well as his interest in the shipping firm, Endacott was not such a regular table companion. He seemed to Blair something of a loner, and for that reason a little too quiet and withdrawn for his liking. No, Blair preferred Cobbe's rosy-cheeked humour any day, and was intrigued to learn from him that the captain was a ladies' man, with a mistress in Exeter.

No wonder he was always so willing to travel to that city in order to negotiate payments of revenue and city dues! He began to see Endacott in a completely new light. He was a dark horse, no doubt of it!

But one afternoon he received quite a nasty shock. He had been visiting in Exeter to arrange a transfer of securities to his Teignmouth bank and was walking along Fore Street thinking of nothing very much in particular, when he saw Endacott emerge from one of those terraced buildings whose gables leant out over the road. Not seeing him, Endacott walked quickly away, pausing to turn and raise a hand to an upper window; and Blair, following the direction of his gaze saw a face there that he recognised – that of Molly Burke.

So that was it, he mused, driving back to Teignmouth.

He had set the girl up and made her into his kept woman. How despicable! He shall not dine at my table again, no by heavens he shall not!

As the carriage went along by the river, the hooves of his two greys thudding rhythmically on the dry surface, he could not help thinking again about his encounter with Molly and the extraordinary abandon with which she had behaved. That was what Endacott was enjoying twice a week! The thought of it appalled and yet fascinated him: it seemed to him quite amazing that a man who appeared to the world as an officer and a gentleman should be cavorting with a little whore. And oddly, he couldn't help feeling wronged, as if Molly had been his personal property and was guilty of disloyalty to him in giving herself to another.

But all this was ridiculous! How can I think such a thing? I have put Molly behind me – and all thoughts of the likes of her. I am a gentleman of means, a husband, a man of honour. What is past is past, and if the captain feels inclined to degrade himself, that is his business.

He deliberately turned his thoughts to another subject, and began to think about his mother. One of his greatest regrets was that she had not lived to see the success he was making of his life. He imagined how proud she would have been, how she would have written to him every single week, endured all the hardships of travel to visit him, first in Exeter and now here in Teignmouth. What times they would have had together, and how full of useful suggestions she would have been for the decoration of the new house and the running of the household!

If only Mama could see me *now* he thought. If only she could see this fine bridge, these ships, that sparkling path of sunlight on the sea!

Even now he could hardly believe his luck in being married to Susannah. He laughed aloud. Twenty-three years old, and all this! It seemed that fortune had positively doted upon him.

The mares plodded slowly up past St James's Church, and Blair turned them into the sycamore avenue that led to West Lawn, outside whose front entrance a small roundabout was planted with brilliant hydrangeas.

Just as he was about to park the carriage and call for Dallmyer to see to the horses, he heard a wail from somewhere inside the house. Jamming on the handbrake, so that the carriage wheels skidded in the gravel, he leapt down and ran into the house, crossing the hall in three strides and going up the polished wooden staircase several steps at a time.

The commotion seemed to be coming from the main bedroom, and within the space of a few seconds Blair had imagined scenes of murder, rape, discovered suicide, robbery at gun point, torture, catastrophic accident – and even a practical joke. He marched down the landing and threw open the door.

'What in heaven's name is going on?' he demanded.

But then he stopped dead. Zilla and the midwife, a plump body with dimples at her elbows, were assisting Susannah who lay on the bed, her face drenched in sweat and her legs splayed; and while Blair stood transfixed in both surprise and some revulsion, she gave one last howl of pain and his son and heir, Benjamin Harvey, came forth into the world.

CHAPTER 6

He had dark red hair the colour of Devon earth, limpid brown eyes and black eyelashes. There was a dimple on each knuckle of his perfect little hands, and he held tightly onto your thumb.

For Zilla, his birth marked the beginning of three idyllic years. That morning, sitting on the lawn at her easel, it had been Zilla Susannah had called to her side to take the message to Mrs Unders that the baby had started. She had flown down the sycamore avenue like a messenger from the gods, her straight black hair flying up behind her and her normally solemn expression alight with the excitement of the moment. It had been Zilla who had rushed up and down the stairs with towels and kettles and smelling salts, and it had been Zilla's hand that Susannah had sought out and held tight during those last miraculous minutes of labour when the baby was delivered.

No wonder she came to regard the baby as partly her own, and no wonder the father sensed her devotion and reacted against it. But what did that matter? Mr Harvey had never liked her since that evening in the wine cellar at Broad Gate House, and had always been on the lookout for a way to get rid of her. She had become used to keeping out of his way, and was confident of her position because Miss Susannah (she still couldn't call her Mrs Harvey) had once told her that provided she did her job properly as a lady's maid Miss Susannah would see to it that she would be well cared for.

In a blurred way that Zilla did not fully understand, there was an unspoken agreement between herself and Miss Susannah, one that dated from that night thunderstorm when Zilla had been so lonely and afraid that she had sought comfort in Miss Susannah's bed. Sometimes when their eyes met by accident, Zilla was sure that Susannah was remembering what had happened, how they had embraced and how Susannah had later told her that it must never happen again and they must not even speak of it. Miss Susannah had made her promise never to talk about it and never again to run into her bedchamber in the middle of the night, not even if there was the most terrible thunderstorm, not even if Mr Harvey was away in Plymouth or Exeter on business. That was the condition she had made for retaining Zilla as her maid after they moved to Teignmouth, and Zilla was prepared to agree to anything at all in order to remain as Miss Susannah's hand maid, and now, Benjamin's dry-nurse.

Mr Harvey wanted Susannah to engage a wet-nurse for the baby, but Susannah refused saying that as she was the one who bore him she was the one to decide who would suckle him, and Zilla was glad of it, for she was required to be in attendance when the baby was put to his mother's white breast, an occasion which, the first time she witnessed it, made love-tears go rolling down her cheeks; and sometimes when the baby was fretful and Susannah absent, Zilla put him to her own breast, gaining more comfort from feeling him suck than did Benjamin from doing so, and she even learned to sing the tune of the German lullaby that Miss Susannah sang, the one that began *Guten Abend, gute Nacht*.

So she sang to the baby, changed him, rocked him, carried him in her arms, walking up and down the lawn in the summer sunshine with him, and later encouraged him to crawl and toddle and know his Mama and Papa. She woke him in the mornings and put him down at night; she went to him when he cried – at whatever hour – and once had a very unusual dream in which she gave birth to a child that turned out to be Mr Harvey's top hat with the silver head of his ebony stick poking up through the crown.

Mr Harvey seemed to think that he and Miss Susannah had an exclusive right to love the baby, and Zilla had to be very careful not to show her affection for Benjamin in his presence. Mr Harvey never actually touched Benjamin when he was tiny; instead, when there were callers in the afternoon, Zilla would be despatched to bring Little Ben down and she would enter the drawing room with him wrapped in his lamb's wool shawl, and Mr Harvey and Miss Susannah and their guests would be sitting in their elegant chairs, and the ladies cooed over him and wondered at the lights in his hair and admired his clear skin and his eyes, and whispered behind their hands to Susannah how progressive it was of her to nurse him herself.

On summer days, they sometimes went down to the Den in the carriage, which Mr Harvey drove himself, to watch the horse racing or the people using the bathing machines or to meet with their acquaintances and walk up and down on the grass in front of the Assembly Rooms. Once, Miss Susannah made fun of Mr Harvey so much that he eventually gave in and went for a bathe. Zilla held Benjamin's hand and stood on the promenade with Miss Susannah to watch as the bathing machine trundled down to the water's edge. Then there was a yell and a roar from Mr Harvey because the water was so cold, and only a minute later the bathing machine was being hauled up the beach again and ten minutes later Mr Harvey emerged from it looking even redder faced than usual with his hair all wet and slicked and his eyelashes stuck together saying that was the first and last time he tried that ridiculous caper, thank you very much.

Another time Zilla overheard Mr Harvey saying that he had made a clear profit of six hundred pounds. She had been standing in the hall wondering whether she should clean Miss Susannah's bedroom silver or go into the kitchen to make sure that Cook was rendering the marrow bones for calf's foot jelly, when he came thundering in with Mr Cobbe speaking of it quite openly, and caught her unawares. Later, when Mr Cobbe had gone, he blew her up good and proper, saying that he wasn't having her creeping about like a spy in his house and she didn't even dare explain that it had been an accident; and even Miss Susannah had been cool to her for several days, so that she went back to crying herself asleep at nights again, the way she used to do long ago, when she was first separated from her brothers and sisters, and her mother and father were in the poorhouse.

Soon after that (just under a year ago now, when Little Ben was two) the post boy delivered a letter for Miss Susannah from her friend Miss Groves, whose brother was out in Baghdad converting the natives.

'Well!' Susannah exclaimed when she had read it. 'That is good news! Do you remember Miss Groves, Zilla? She is to be married and will be coming to live here in Teignmouth this October!'

The person she was marrying was Mr Müller, a German gentleman who preached in a meeting room in Bitton Street. He was tall and aristocratic looking and wore a straight black coat with a small collar and a white neck-cloth wound round and round like a bandage, and no pin. He had thick sidewhiskers that met under his chin and kind, blue eyes that seemed to drill little holes right into your soul. He had a funny German accent, mournful in a way but also warm and sometimes humorous too, and once when Zilla was coming back from the town he had helped her when the kerchief on her breadbasket had blown off, and asked if she knew the Lord Jesus.

Mr Harvey did not think it was good news at all, and he had an argument with Miss Susannah. When they had arguments Miss Susannah spoke very quietly and Mr Harvey usually ended up by shouting. The trouble was,

Miss Susannah was much better at arguing than Mr Harvey, but because he was the master of the house he always had to have the last word and Miss Susannah had to let him. This particular argument lasted and lasted. It rumbled on through August and September, because Susannah wanted to go to the wedding in Exeter and Mr Harvey refused to go with her and refused to let her go on her own. Then, after the Müllers had arrived by stage coach it took a different turn, because Miss Susannah wanted to call on the newly wedded Mrs Müller and Mr Harvey was furious about that, too. 'Very well, God damn it,' he shouted up the front stairs to her one morning, 'go and call on them if you must, but don't expect me to get involved in their meetings and preachings, for I won't, and that's final.' Miss Susannah had been very upset over it all and had been red-eyed in the mornings for a week, until one day Mr Müller and his wife came up the drive to call on them, Mr Müller in his black coat and Mary in the simplest looking grey dress and bonnet; and Susannah had run out to meet them and embraced her friend and led them into the drawing room; and when Zilla brought Benjamin in, Mr Müller had taken him on his knee in the most gentle and loving way so that Zilla loved him from that moment.

What was so different about Mr Müller was that he treated you as if you were his equal, and no one, not even Susannah, had done that. When they were leaving, and Zilla was holding the door open for them, he paused and spoke to her, hoping he would see her lovely face at the meeting one Sunday evening.

'That's not my place, sir,' she mumbled nervously.

'Zilla,' he said, 'the Lord Jesus said, "Come unto me all ye that labour and are heavy laden, and I will give you rest." ' He lifted her chin with his finger and looked down at her as if he were her father. 'I am a servant too, Zilla. I am a servant of the Lord Jesus, and in His sight we are brother and sister.'

Hearing his words thrilled and disturbed her, and Susannah, sensing it, later asked her if she would like to go to one of Mr Müller's Sunday evening meetings.

'I don't rightly know, Ma'am,' she said, and caught herself biting her fingernail, something she hadn't done for months.

'Well if you want to go, I don't mind, Zilla. But you must ask my permission beforehand, understand?'

She understood, yes, she understood. Miss Susannah didn't *mind* if she went, but she didn't want her to go, either. And if Mr Harvey got to hear of it – well, there would be fireworks, that was certain.

So she did not go to Mr Müller's meetings, at least not until after she got into trouble for dropping one of Mr Harvey's precious brandy glasses and he ordered Miss Susannah to take the cost of it out of her wages, sixpence a week for three weeks. Miss Susannah said she really couldn't do anything about that because Zilla had been careless recently and it was time she learnt her lesson, and suddenly she felt that Miss Susannah no longer cared for her and that she was completely alone in the world; she remembered what Mr Müller had said to her, and one Sunday evening listened outside the house where he held his meeting. She heard voices singing without accompaniment: the sound of them flooded out into the summer air and filled her heart to overflowing, so that she walked slowly up the hill under the sycamores in tears, and in the morning plucked up courage to ask Miss Susannah if she might go the following week to hear the gospel.

When Mr Müller read from the Bible or preached, he spoke slowly and clearly so that you could understand every word, in spite of his German accent. Zilla had heard the gospel story before from Mrs Brougham, but that had been when she was only twelve. Now she was twenty, and better able to understand that all had sinned and came short of the glory of God. She was old enough to know that she was as bad a sinner as any, and she loved the thought of having a heavenly Father who could give her the peace that passeth all understanding. Mr Müller said that being saved and coming to Christ was like having a cool drink of spring water when you were dying of thirst. He said that God so loved the world that He gave His only begotten Son, that whosoever believeth in Him should not perish, but have everlasting life. He told the people sitting in the rows of upright chairs (Zilla was right at the back, having slipped in at the last moment before the meeting started) that not even a sparrow could fall without the Heavenly Father knowing it, and that even the hairs on your head were numbered. Then he explained how only a few years before he had been living the life of a wastrel, reading novels, drinking in taverns, neglecting his studies at school and getting into debt. He had even spent three weeks in a prison cell at the age of sixteen for failing to pay an innkeeper's bill, and had been bailed out by his father, who gave him a thrashing.

Zilla listened entranced as the story of Mr Müller's own conversion unfolded, how he had tried repeatedly to mend his ways, and repeatedly failed. Finally he had seen that it was no use relying on himself to live a better life, but that it was necessary to repent his sins and put his trust in the Lord Jesus.

He said this discovery had been the turning point in his life, and that it could be a similar turning point for every person listening to him in that hall there in Teignmouth on that June evening in 1831. All you had to do, he said, was ask the Lord to come into your heart. That was all you had to do.

The meeting lasted a little longer than she had expected, and when she arrived back at West Lawn, Cook was in a flurry because Mr Harvey was waiting for his dinner and Zilla was late, and when she carried in the soup Mr Harvey made a remark about her as if she wasn't there, wondering who the hell was supposed to be waiting on whom. After that he and Miss Susannah had had another of their arguments, and a few days later Miss Susannah told Zilla, when Zilla was helping her wash her hair, that she might go to the Sunday evening meetings in Bitton Street provided she arrived back in time to serve dinner.

So she started going regularly, and had now been to five meetings in a row in spite of the remarks Mr Harvey made in her hearing about going to listen to nonsense preached by a foreigner who couldn't even speak the King's English. She had continued to attend because Susannah had called her into the studio where she kept all her beautiful water colour paintings and told her that it was every individual's right to worship where she wished, and that she must not let what Mr Harvey said upset her, because that was just his way. She had held Zilla's hands, and had swallowed, her nostrils dilating as they did when she was upset and her gentle eyes roaming sorrowfully as she spoke. 'You are free to worship how you like, Zilla, and free to believe what you wish to believe and reject what you wish to reject. Hold onto that freedom, whatever you do, for it is the most precious gift.'

Now, today, Zilla had obtained special permission to attend a meeting held in the Baptist chapel in Shaldon where Mr Müller's friend Mr Craik was preaching. Shaldon was the little village that nestled under the cliffy headland they called the Ness. You got to it by walking across the wooden toll bridge, which was the pride of Teignmouth because it was the longest in the country. The chapel was just up the hill from the main street and it had a proper pulpit because Mr Craik was a minister and had been to a Scottish university. It was such a warm evening and the chapel was so full that Mr Craik directed that the front door be left open to let in the fresh air and to allow the sound of the people making a joyful noise unto the Lord (which he pronounced Lorrrd, rolling the r) go right out over the water to Teignmouth on the other side.

'What shall it profit a man if he gain the whole world

and lose his own soul?' Mr Craik read from the Bible, and Zilla couldn't help thinking of Mr Harvey's polished brown boots and golden watch chain and the profits he was always making from his partnership. Mr Craik leant out over his pulpit and enlarged upon his text for the evening, and towards the end he posed the question, 'What think ye of Christ?'

'O my dear brothers and sisters, please ask yourselves that question now, in the quietness of this evening. Do not delay, for the Lord cometh like a thief in the night. Make this evening the evening that you put your trust in the one who has said, "Suffer the little children to come unto me." Do not delay, for if you do you can be sure that one day you will have to answer that question, whether it be on your deathbed, or on that awful day of Judgement.'

He blew over the pages in his Bible and read solemnly, 'He that believeth in Him is not condemned: but he that believeth not is condemned already.' He paused, and there was a hush, broken only by the barking of a dog; then, quietly, he entreated any person sitting in that hall who had not already accepted the Lord Jesus into his or her heart and confessed Him with their lips, to do so now.

The dog stopped barking. The silence lengthened, and gradually the people sitting in the hall became aware of the sound of sobbing.

It was Zilla: suddenly she saw that she was weighed down by a great burden of sin, a burden which could be taken away by a simple act of repentance and trust. Suddenly, she saw that Christ had died for her and that though her sins were as scarlet, they could be white as snow.

She felt hands at her elbows, encouraging her to stand up, leading her forward, guiding her; she felt the hands of Mr Craik on her shoulders and heard him giving thanks for this little one, who had been lost and was found.

When the meeting was over, Mr Müller and Mr Craik sat down with Zilla and counselled her about the meaning of salvation. They said that now she had accepted the Lord she must grow in grace: that she had been born again, and as a newborn baby learns to sit up, and crawl, and walk and talk, so she must learn to grow in knowledge and faith. They said that if at all possible she should come to the Lord's Table at Ebenezer on Sunday mornings, and that when she was ready to confess Christ Jesus, she would be baptised.

While they spoke, Mrs Müller came and sat with them, and held Zilla's hand between her own. 'When you arrive back in the house, Zilla, go to your master and mistress and tell them what has happened. Tell them that you have accepted the Lord Jesus, and are born again.'

Now, she was walking back over the bridge. The sun was down behind the Ness and the shadows of the ships' masts were lengthening across the water; and as she went along in her cap and shawl, her heart full to overflowing, her head buzzing with what had happened to her that evening, she was repeating to herself in a whisper, 'I be saved! I be saved!'

Having a westerly aspect and an altitude of one hundred feet above sea level, West Lawn Villa enjoyed the evening sun longer than the village of Shaldon, and the last of it was now slanting almost horizontally through the drawing room windows, where the Harveys were entertaining a few acquaintances to an evening of music and poetry.

Susannah had had the Broadwood moved in from the music room and Miss Cox had been persuaded to play. She sat on the revolving piano stool in a white dress of generous cut, her plump fingers appearing to move independently of the rest of her body, in accordance with a method of pianoforte playing known as the Peaceful Wrist.

It was pleasant enough, Susannah reflected, to sit in this room among gentlefolk of similar tastes in the arts and to listen to Mozart – even if Miss Cox's interpretation left much to be desired; and in a way Mozart was well suited to being played in this mechanical fashion, for there was a certain mathematical precision about his compositions which, while admiring them, Susannah found a little too perfect.

She glanced at the faces of some of her guests. They were seated in three semicircular rows with the decorous Miss Cox at the focus. Old Mr Codner was tapping out the time with his forefinger on his knee, and his wife sat beside him, her hands joined in her lap and a look of aesthetic serenity on her face that Susannah knew very well was adopted for the occasion. Commander Tobin seemed to be having difficulty in deciding whether to breathe through his nose or through his mouth, and was having another difficulty of a masculine nature over whether to cross his legs; Mrs Tobin looked extremely bored, but then she always did. Susannah glanced in the other direction at Mr Luny, who had also been in the Navy but had now turned artist, and was often to be seen with palette and easel capturing a view of the harbour or a perspective of the Den. His eyes seemed to be closing of their own accord, and when he jerked them open again, he glanced about to ensure that he had not been detected in the act of catnapping.

Blair was wide awake and his attention fixed upon the fair Miss Cox. He had that half surprised look that made him look younger than his twenty-six years. Susannah was still inclined to regard him as an overgrown undergraduate. He is such a *good boy* she thought, trying to see his slightly protruding eyes, and 'sensitive' bowed upper lip as if he were a stranger.

But he was not a stranger. Having been once shocked at how little she knew of him, it now unnerved her to know him so well and to be able to predict mentally how he would react to a situation and what little unconscious gesture would betray his self-esteem.

What would he be thinking now?

She laughed inwardly, and must have smiled as well, for Blair caught her eye and smiled back.

Yes, she thought, apart from unmentionable stirrings concerning Miss Cox, he is feeling mighty pleased. He is at the centre of culture and society here in Teignmouth, and that is buttering his opinion of himself very pleasantly. To me, of course, he will be quite condescending – especially if the opportunity to make fun of me in front of his friends arises. But nevertheless he benefits more from these little evenings than I, for he makes capital out of the aura of culture we have brought to West Lawn, and though he's never read more than two sentences in a row out of any of Father's books, he always makes a point of entertaining his business friends in the library so that they can see what a literary fellow he is.

Miss Cox had finished her piece, and Blair clapped heartily. She rose from her stool and dropped a plump curtsy; and when Blair insisted she play again her cheeks pinked and she put her fingers to her neck.

'As we have two naval gentlemen in our number,' she breathed, 'perhaps we should have a hornpipe to remind us of the slanting decks and the foaming main,' and with that she immediately sat down again and launched into the tiddle-im-pom-pom.

Blair was delighted, as of course he would be, and Susannah could see from the vein that throbbed down his forehead exactly what was going on in his mind. He was already in brass buttons and buckled shoes, and his jolly tars were scrubbing down the decks and singing at the capstan and walking the plank (or whatever it was that jolly tars did) and overhead the to'gallants were bellying out – as taut, as white and as well filled as the upper regions of Miss Cox's gown.

She felt suddenly angry. She had asked Miss Cox to play Mozart, not a matelote, and she had certainly not invited her to flutter her eyelashes at Blair as she was now doing in an amazingly obvious way. Even her own annoyance irked her, for she knew she should be above such feelings and untouched by the sight of Blair becoming bowled over by yet another pair of – of –

No, she decided. I shall not even think it.

She thought about herself instead. It was all very well making fun of Blair, or these good people who came to her evenings, but should she not first cast one or two beams from her own eye? Wasn't this silly performance on the piano, this wrecking of an evening which she had hoped would heighten the appreciation of the arts rather than degrade them, wasn't that a sketch in miniature of her own situation? For had she not, in marrying Blair, given up something precious, something that could never be regained? Wasn't this the mess of potage she had willingly accepted in exchange?

And what a mess it was, if you looked behind the elegant French furniture, the Persian rugs, the tall, Chinese vases full of tall, English flowers. How detestable were all those nose-pulling acquaintances of Blair's, whose finger ends seemed permanently grubby from the counting of sovereigns and the shuffling of bank and promissory notes.

I am riding to an unknown destination, she thought. I am no longer in control.

Miss Cox had, on Blair's insistence, allowed herself to be cajoled into one more reprise, and now, Susannah noted, her wrists became a little less Peaceful: they jumped up and down like white mice on hot stones; while Blair, captivated by the simplicity and urgency of the rhythm, had taken to banging his feet on the floor to accentuate the 'pom-pom'. Beaming all over his face, practically dribbling in appreciation of Miss Cox's white skin and scrambling fingers, he was encouraging his guests by nods and glances to join in the fun; and while the awful performance clattered on and on, Susannah became aware of a loneliness, a bleak sadness; for although she had organised this evening, and although she had become regarded in Teignmouth as a young woman of talent and culture, she knew that such activities were merely an excuse, a veneer. In her heart she knew that she was simply one of thousands of earnest young women up and down the country who clutched in vain at the coat-tails of genius. She knew that she did not have that mystical energy to take her up, over the ridge of mediocrity, nor the courage to face that ice-cold blast of public opinion which every serious artist must confront.

The knowledge of it angered and humiliated her. What point was there in continuing with her little sketches of Teignmouth life, whether in pastels or prose? And why should she surround herself with people of similarly mediocre minds, why discuss their little imitations of genius and indulge them – as they indulged her – by speaking of their spark of talent, their gleam of promise?

It was all so false! So engineered! She felt an insane need to escape, but knew there was none. If only she could be quite alone! If only she could live simply, if only she did not have to perform the continual smoothings and oilings of polite society!

She knew, now, that she should not have married. She should have had the courage, after her father died, to carve her own course through life, unburdened by the awful obligations of being a wife or a mother.

She imagined an alternative situation with powerful, almost visual, reality. She saw herself alone in Broad Gate House declining the hands of a succession of suitors (however handsome, however intelligent!) and, in her own time, purchasing a cottage high on some moor or mountain where she could be quite alone, quite at peace to discover her genius and give it full rein. Yes, but I would have to have some help, she thought, and immediately saw herself writing in a bare boarded room, the flames of a wood fire leaping at her back and Zilla slipping quietly in with a meal for her on a tray.

The scene was so clear in her mind that she saw herself

look up after Zilla had left the room. What was that person, who was herself, thinking? Or, what would she be thinking? How strange to be imagining a person who was herself but yet the person she could never be! She could see the impossible Miss Brougham sitting there in that little room, the old thatch dangling over a leaded window: she could see her own handwriting on the page – and yet she could not quite fathom what that non-person might be thinking. Why had she looked up so quickly when Zilla had left the room?

Susannah Harvey closed her eyes. Perhaps, after all, it was better to have married, better to have borne Blair's child, better to be surrounded by these safe, respectable people and better to plod steadily on into old age, known and admired in this Lilliputian town as a person of intellect and education.

The hornpipe was over and Miss Cox curtsying for the last time.

'That was lovely!' Susannah exclaimed. 'Quite, quite delightful!'

Zilla heard the hornpipe end as she walked up the drive under the sycamores. Entering by the pantry door, she found Cook asleep in her armchair by the hob, and as Cook did not often enjoy such a privilege, she left her in peace and went through to the hall.

She paused, listening. The drawing room door was open, and she could see Commander Tobin and his wife in profile, listening as Susannah read a piece of poetry.

It had been easy, in the presence of Mr and Mrs Müller and Pastor Craik, to promise to go straight back and witness for Christ, but now that she was about to do so she felt suddenly timid. Perhaps, after all, she should wait until the guests had gone.

She shivered. No, that was what she must *not* do. Mr Müller had said that the sincere witness of one who had recently accepted the Lord Jesus was the most powerful way of bringing others to repentance, and that when the moment came, God would give her the courage she needed and help her to say what she had to say.

She went nearer therefore, and stood in the doorway, waiting while Susannah completed her reading.

It was the poem entitled *To Sleep*, by John Keats:

'. . . Then save me, or the passèd day will shine
Upon my pillow, breeding many woes;
   Save me from curious conscience, that still lords
Its strength for darkness, burrowing like a mole;
   Turn the key deftly in the oilèd wards,
And seal the hushèd casket of my soul.'

Zilla did not understand these words, but they seemed to parallel the emotions she had experienced that evening and made her feel that Miss Susannah would readily understand what had happened to her; so in the silence that followed, she walked boldly into the room and announced what she had been rehearsing all the way from Shaldon.

'Oh Ma'am!' she sobbed. 'I been to the gospel, and I be saved! I be born again!'

She was aware then of astonished faces staring at her. Susannah, with considerable presence of mind, said, 'Never mind, Zilla, I think you're feeling rather tired, aren't you?' and as she was led from the room she heard Mr Harvey say, 'Behold the handmaid of the Lord,' and give a shout of laughter.

But at first it didn't matter about Mr Harvey. It didn't matter that he had laughed or that he started calling you Little I-be-saved. Nor did it matter when some local children ran after you on the way back from the fish market or when Peg the kitchen maid teased you because you blushed at the postboy. All that mattered was that you were saved. Your hand was in His, and underneath

113

were the everlasting arms. You had a Father at last, a Heavenly Father, and you could cast all your care upon Him, for He cared for you.

It was in the mornings especially that it felt different to be born again. You got quietly out of bed so as not to wake Peg and knelt down with your hands joined and gave thanks for another day and asked the Lord Jesus to direct your path and keep you from sin. You asked His blessing upon Miss Susannah, Little Ben, Cook, Peg, Dallmyer, Robson and even Mr Harvey; and when you had finished you went to the window and marvelled at the early dew on the lawns, and wisps of smoke coming from the town, and beyond, the silver ribbon of the Teign and the forests of masts beneath Shaldon and Ringmore.

When you had washed and dressed you went to the nursery and looked down at the sleepy head on the pillow, the dark Devon hair, the black eyelashes, the pink and white skin; you lifted him in your arms and he was warm and sleepy with his thumb in his mouth and his special kerchief scrumped up against his cheek. He stretched in your arms and you kissed him goodmorning and whispered a little prayer with him. You sat him on the washstand and did his face and hands, hushing him for getting impatient, holding his hands in yours and whispering to him secretly about Jesus; and when his hair was brushed and his boots tied you took him down for his bread and milk and half an egg with butter and allowed him to hold the spoon himself, not getting at all cross when he lost his temper over not wanting to drink his milk and went deep red in the face, pouting angrily at you and reminding you of his father.

Yes, you *did* feel a new person in those first few days, and you expected the feeling to last for ever. You wanted everyone to share the feelings of love and happiness you had found in your Saviour. You sang in your heart; you prayed without ceasing; you gave thanks continually for His tender mercies and loving kindness.

114

Sadly, imperceptibly, the feeling of being born again went away. In its place, there developed a new feeling, first of being laughed at and tolerated, later of being disliked, later still of being hated. It was a feeling that seemed to be generated by Mr Harvey, but it spread to other members of the household, so that Peg stopped speaking to her and Cook was abrupt and Robson, Mr Harvey's valet, took pleasure in embarrassing her by pinching her person and making lewd remarks to her when no one else was listening.

Worse, she began to sense a deterioration in relations between Miss Susannah and Mr Harvey. Although they had had arguments from the earliest days of their marriage, there had always been sunny intervals between them, times when the household relaxed and enjoyed their happiness at second hand. Now, whenever Zilla was in their presence, it seemed that they were either preserving one of those hateful silences (which were probably what she feared most of all) or conducting monosyllabic arguments whose cryptic interchanges she found so difficult to understand.

As the weeks went by, it became necessary to avoid contact with Mr Harvey as much as possible. If she met him in the hall, she would flatten herself against the panelling as he went by, and if she saw him approaching she would either slip away into another room or pretend to be so deeply engrossed in her work that she did not hear, or appear to hear, his biting little remarks about the handmaid of the Lord.

Even Ben sensed the unhappiness in the house. Mornings with him turned into a struggle of wills that too often ended in his bellows of rage, which brought Susannah hurrying in to see what had caused the trouble. Susannah was behaving differently, too. It was as if she were afraid to take Zilla's side. Sometimes Zilla saw in her eyes a sadness which she believed to be a longing Susannah felt to reach back in time to the days of innocence when they had been like sisters; when Susannah had whispered secret hopes and imaginings to Zilla, and Zilla had loved her in a very special way.

All that was past now. She was nearly twenty-one years old, and she was one of the saints at Bitton Street. She went to The Lord's table and the gospel and the Bible reading; she struggled to read a few verses of Scripture each day, and she learnt to apply the teaching of the beatitudes and believe herself blessed when reviled and to look forward to the reward that awaited her in heaven.

But in spite of that, after kneeling at her bedside in the evenings and asking His blessing on 'Mr and Mrs Harvey and all the household, and Little Ben, and all those dear to me, and Mr Müller and Mr Craik and Mrs Müller, and Mary Hunt who is with child by Lord Carnavon's coachman' Zilla would slide down into her bed and curl herself in a ball, covering her face with her hands and sobbing silently until she fell asleep.

'I have something I wish to discuss with you,' Blair said one morning, on entering the breakfast room.

Susannah looked up. Blair had taken to having his breakfast brought to him in the library by Robson, and she took hers on her own, with a book for company.

He had brought his cup of coffee in with him and took it to the window, which overlooked the harbour entrance. Four years of good food and not much exercise had thickened him considerably.

'I have had an idea,' he said suddenly, turning back from the window.

She waited for him to continue. He bounced up and down and made a succession of little grunting noises – a sign of impatience.

'Would it be too much to ask you to close up your book for thirty seconds, Susannah? Thank you. As I was saying. I have had an idea. You know the *Eustacia* sails on her maiden voyage at the end of August?'

'No, I had not heard.'

'Yes you have. August the thirtieth is the date. It occurred to me that we might organise a celebration. As I am to have the controlling interest.'

She waited again. It was usually safer not to speak to Blair unless asked a direct question.

'Well? Have you nothing to say at all, Susannah?'

'I was not aware that you wished to involve me in your shipping business.'

'But I do, my dear, I do. My profit is your profit. My capital is your capital. With my body I thee worship, and with all my worldly goods I thee endow.'

She stared steadily back at him, and he turned away.

'I know very little of your plans, Blair. I find it difficult to take an interest in matters of which I am quite ignorant.'

He passed a hand over his face and sighed. 'Very well, Susannah, I shall tell you. Again. The *Eustacia* is a brigantine of 118 tons burthen. I have twenty-six shares, Langmead & Jordan have eight and Messrs Cobbe, Endacott, Mudge and Hennet have four each. Which means, if you have not entirely forgotten your addition –'

'*Will* you not speak to me in that way!'

He smiled, pleased to see that he had successfully ignited her temper.

'Do you wish me to continue then? Or do you prefer to remain in ignorance?'

'Go on, then,' she said. 'But please remember that I am more than eight years old.'

He crossed to the table and helped himself to more coffee from a fluted silver pot. 'What I intend is to experiment with the importation of port-wine, almonds and olive oil. I lunched with Cobbe the other day – and the agent of a fellow by the name of Delaforce who's setting himself up as a shipper of port-wine. We have persuaded him that with the market opening up so rapidly

117

in the south of England, he should consider shipping direct to Teignmouth, which is a full day's run shorter than London and charges lower harbour dues into the bargain. What he needs is someone like myself, with commercial initiative and a controlling interest in shipping, and all *I* need is the opportunity to share his profits.'

Blair nodded to himself and drank his coffee off at a gulp, setting the cup and saucer down on the wide windowsill. 'The opportunities are amazing, Susannah, if you pause to consider them. Dawlish, Teignmouth, Torquay, Salcombe, Plymouth, Falmouth – they're all expanding. Hotels going up every day. We might even supply Bristol and Bath! We could set up a bottling factory and stick our own label on it! Harvey's Port! Think of that!'

He turned to face her, placing the palms of his hands on the small of his back, the thumbs forward round his waist, his coat tails bunched up behind him.

'Well? What do you think, dearest heart?'

'It sounds a good idea, Blair.'

'It *is* a good idea!'

He paced up and down, then stopped abruptly. Zilla had entered to clear the breakfast table. While she did so, he lifted his heels and lowered them slowly, watching the maid's every move.

She loaded a tray with crockery, the milk jug, coffee pot and marmalade dish and had reached the door with it when Blair barked 'Wait!' so imperiously that she stopped dead and a teaspoon jangled to the floor.

'Sir?'

He made no reply, but pointed to his coffee cup and saucer, which she could not see.

'What've I done, sir?'

He pointed again. Zilla's lower lip trembled.

'There's another cup and saucer on the sill, Zilla,' Susannah said gently.

She put down the tray, picked up the teaspoon, collected the cup and saucer – which rattled in her hand as she returned them to the tray – and departed.

'Arrr, arrr,' Blair said. 'I be zorry, zirr, I be zaved, zirr, I be born again, zirr.'

Susannah stood up and faced him. 'Why do you have to torment her like this, Blair? Why? Is there anything you hope to gain by it?'

'She is well paid, well fed, well clothed,' he said. 'And if she cannot take a little ribbing for being born again as she calls it, then perhaps she should be reminded that had she lived seventeen hundred years ago she might have ended up serving breakfast to the lions.'

'I am not amused, Blair. I know you dislike her, and I know *why* you dislike her too, but she has never done anything to deserve this mental cruelty to which you are subjecting her.'

He snorted. 'Ah. I see, I am to have my knuckles rapped again, is that it? Would you like me to hold out my hand?' He did so, and pretended she had used the cane on it, wincing for three imaginary blows and shaking his hand in imaginary pain. 'There, I've taken my punishment like a man. Are you happier now?' He turned abruptly away from her and stared out of the window.

She was silent for a while; then, quietly, she said: 'I do not take her side against you, and I have no wish to reprove you. My only wish is to be able to love and honour and obey you as my husband. To respect you and look up to you. And when I see you making fun of a servant in this way I am saddened, because I can see that you are doing yourself a disservice, and because I know Zilla to be a good soul who would never seek to displease you or me and who even now looks up to you as someone whose actions she should see as an example.'

Blair was not listening. He was watching a scow crossing the harbour bar, heading seaward on the ebb, with men crawling out along the yards to set the course and topsail; he was thinking about his own ship, due to sail on her maiden voyage to Oporto in four weeks' time. He was seeing all the huge possibilities that lay ahead of him: growing wealth, influence, social position. A knighthood, maybe, or a seat in the Commons. In his mind's eye he saw himself addressing parliament, introducing legislation, manipulating vast forces of industry.

'If I have ever done anything,' Susannah was saying, 'that has offended you and which you have withheld from me – or if Zilla has – will you please tell me of it now, Blair, for I cannot see how we are to continue with this friction between us. It is not a case of my being struck by the dissenters at all, you know that. It is simply that I believe Zilla has a right, as a human being, to believe and worship as she wishes, without any persecution from you or me.'

He spoke without turning, still watching the scow, which was now clear of the bar and heading out on the starboard tack. 'She is a dissenter, Susannah, and like every other dissenter she lives up to her name. Not only does she dissent but she *causes* dissent, which she is doing here, now, in my house. That girl is not an influence for good under my roof, I have known it for months. I see her watching me, tiptoeing about, disapproving even when I dare to pour myself a glass of Madeira after dinner. Were we at each other's throats in this way before she burst in on us and told us she was saved? No, we were not. We were living normal, peaceable lives like civilised human beings, and I, simply because I refuse to put on a long face and live like a puritan, or dare to extract a little humour from her black evangelism – I'm blamed. I'm castigated for persecuting her, using mental cruelty. I will not have it, Susannah. I am the master in this house, and I will not have her – or you – acting as the keeper of my conscience and looking at me as if I were the devil incarnate –'

He stopped and turned, for both had heard a sob at the door, and both were in time to see Zilla standing there, the tears streaming down her face, before she turned and ran away down the corridor, through the kitchen, out through the stable yard and down the drive; and having seen her go, Blair stamped out of the breakfast room, saying that if anyone called he would be out driving until nightfall, and would dine with Cobbe at the Royal.

She ran down the hill to Bitton Street and along to the Müllers' front door, where she was admitted by Mary. The house was small, terraced and sparsely furnished: eight months before, George Müller had given up his pew rents in order to start living by faith, never asking for money except in private prayer, and often being reduced to his last few pence before receiving what seemed to him miraculous gifts of food, clothing or money from the most unexpected sources.

He was a tall, heavily built Prussian. Born four weeks before the battle of Trafalgar, he had experienced conversion at the age of twenty and had come to England to study theology. Later, for the sake of his health, he had stayed in Devon, come into contact with the Groves family and through them Pastor Craik, who now lived across the river at Shaldon and who shared Müller's views on matters of faith and worship. The congregation at Ebenezer Chapel, struck by Müller's speaking, had unanimously asked him to become their pastor, and he had accepted, later teaching that, at certain meetings, brethren in the Ebenezer assembly should be given the opportunity to exhort or teach the rest, if they felt led by the Spirit to do so.

When Zilla knocked at his door, he was on his knees in the tiny front parlour begging the Lord to provide, having been living off his last thirteen shillings since the middle of the previous month. He heard the sound of weeping in the hall, and rose to his feet as Mary brought the girl in.

Slowly, they got the story out of her.

'My m-aster says I – I be a – a evil influence! O Sir! He says I be causing dissent!' She hid her face in her hands and sobbed bitterly. 'An' I run out without permission! I can't never go back! I'll lose me position and end up in the poorhouse!'

Mary held her hands and soothed her, and George said that they must lay it before the Lord. They knelt on the bare wooden floorboards and asked for God's guidance; and half an hour later, when Zilla departed to return to West Lawn, the Müllers found a parcel on their front doorstep. It was an anonymous gift of a shoulder of mutton and a loaf of bread.

Reluctantly, Susannah decided that it would be better for Zilla to go to a new household, and after making enquiries she discovered a place for her on a farm near Chudleigh, where the farmer's wife had died in childbirth leaving a fine baby girl for Zilla to love and cherish as if she were her own.

'I be sorry for everything, Ma'am,' she whispered that last morning after making her farewells to Cook, Peg and Benjamin. 'And I won't never forget all your kindness.'

They stood in the stableyard. All Zilla's belongings had been tied up in a coloured kerchief which she carried by the knot.

'Perhaps, if I'm passing, I'll call and see how you are one day,' Susannah said, her mouth going a little out of shape.

Zilla was to walk down to the town and catch the morning stage coach. 'Oh Ma'am!' she wailed suddenly, 'I don't want to go, I don't want to leave 'ee, an' Little Ben!' She hid her face in her hands, sobbing. 'I'll always pray for 'ee and the master. I won't never be as happy as I have been with you as my lady, Ma'am, not ever!'

She was too tearful herself to see the tears glistening in Susannah's eyes, and too overcome to perceive that when Susannah suddenly and unexpectedly embraced her, her mistress's heart was just as close to breaking; but those few moments when they held each other and kissed made a deep impression upon Zilla, and as she went away down the hill to the Den, she reflected that she had seldom been held in anyone's arms, and probably wouldn't be very often in the future.

CHAPTER 7

That summer was unusually fine and warm. The harvest was in early and crops were heavy; moths, bees and June bugs flourished, and there was an atmosphere of sleepy content among the rustics of the West Country. But while cattle moved slowly in the green meadows and apples reddened in the orchards, other, less welcome organisms also prospered. There were outbreaks of typhus, summer diarrhoea and scarlatina; plagues of horseflies, green toads, sheep rot. Taken individually, each outbreak was unremarkable, but taken together, they were reaching alarming proportions.

Unfortunately, the proportions were not alarming enough. Members of parliament were used to quitting those rooms whose windows gave onto the River Thames on hot days when the receding tide left lines of rotting garbage and excrement on the slimy banks; landlords were too crippled by the window tax to think of improving living conditions for their tenants, and in cities like Plymouth and Exeter there was nothing new about the heaps of filth or pools of stagnant water that lay in the central gutters which ran the length of those dark, narrow passages between back-to-back tenements where hollow-eyed mothers and children huddled ten and twelve to a room.

'Another glorious day!' Blair would say each morning on joining his wife for breakfast.

He sat himself down and squared his shoulders. He

gave the bottom of his waistcoat a little tug and took a table napkin from a monogrammed silver ring.

'Another glorious day!' he repeated, and sat back as Peg came in with the choice piece of haddock in butter or the slice of gammon steak or the fried bacon and mushrooms. 'The sun shineth on the righteous man, isn't that how it goes, Susannah?'

'I'm not sure about that,' she laughed, 'but I know that "He makes His sun to rise upon the evil and on the good" so we should not be too self-satisfied.'

He chuckled and grunted to himself and helped himself to quantities of scrambled egg and fried tomatoes from the heated silver dish Peg held at his left elbow.

'Nevertheless,' he said when Peg had withdrawn, 'we are on better terms, and we should be thankful for that, should we not?'

'Yes, we are, and I am thankful,' she said, and Blair looked down at his plate a little embarrassed by his own display of husbandly affection.

They ate in silence a while, and Susannah reflected that it was strange how Blair needed to be reassured and supported by her. Yes, he was right, they were on better terms. He was breakfasting with her again and now seemed permanently in a good mood. His business was doing well and his first ship due to sail on her maiden voyage in a few days. Being his wife for four years had taught her a lot about him: she had discovered that there were two particular qualities which he required in her: the quality of a mother, to give him approval, reassurance and the comfort of her body; and the quality of a daughter, to give him adoration and fearful obedience. The only quality he did not require of her was the quality of intelligence – or at least any sign from her that she might be in any way his intellectual equal. In order for their marriage to be happy, she had discovered that her Blair must have the ascendancy all the time, come what may. She also had to be extremely careful at dinner parties, for

Blair was inclined to be jealous if she talked too long with any one person, male or female. This had caused a number of arguments between them over the years, and she had learnt that Blair regarded her as one of his private possessions, like the leather boots Robson polished so assiduously each morning or the silver-backed hair-brushes he kept, bristles interlocked, on his dressing room table.

Yes, they were on better terms, but Susannah could not help thinking that it was more thanks to herself than to him. For the sake of peace and happiness, she had made the household revolve round him, had instructed the servants to ensure that his likes and dislikes were noted, that his routine was never upset and that his laundry and his meals were presented to him in the right way and at the right time.

It paid dividends. There had been occasions, in the last few weeks since Zilla's departure, when he had come to her and held her hand and talked very sweetly with her, tears appearing in his eyes when he told her how much he valued her and how precious she was to him; and because of the hot nights they had once slept entirely naked together – something which the French did and which she enjoyed considerably; but the next morning Blair had said that it was 'vice' and not to be repeated.

The matter of lovemaking was the most delicate subject of all, and quite impossible to discuss with him. She was sure that it could be made considerably more enjoyable if only Blair could be made to understand that it was an act of love, not merely a perfunctory coupling to be performed with downturned lips and mild disgust. It was disappointing, too, that he had not managed to give her another child.

She suspected she knew the reason: Blair seemed to obtain all the pleasure he required from her by an incomplete and tantalising coupling that left her in an agony of frustration; but when she dared to plead him to

126

make a deeper entry, she had earned a rebuke for using such a coarse turn of phrase.

But I cannot grumble, she told herself. I have everything a woman can ask for. A handsome husband and a thousand a year; a fine son, a good table, a contented household; friends . . .

No, not friends. Acquaintances yes – dozens of them, all proud to be guests of the talented Mrs Harvey and the ebullient Blair. But not friends.

She thought of Mary Müller. They had been close once, in their late teens. They had met on Saturday mornings in the Exeter city library and had borrowed books which they studied together in Northernhay House or at Broadgate. They had tackled Greek together, had discussed syntax and tested each other on vocabulary. But the rift between Susannah's parents had split her loyalties and damaged the friendship, and Blair's strong disapproval of George Müller and all that he stood for had virtually ended it. Zilla's departure had finalised the estrangement. Now, when Susannah and Mary met in the town they would exchange a brief, formal greeting, and go quickly on their separate ways.

There were times when Susannah felt guilty about what had happened over Zilla. Perhaps she should have fought harder to retain the servant. But there was a double reason for allowing her to go: first, that lingering memory on her conscience of a night long ago when the girl had crept into her bed, and second a fear that she might repeat her own mother's mistake and make a rod for her own back by refusing to be subject to her husband. So she did not regret the decision, and instead, to ease her conscience, sent the occasional anonymous gift of money to the Müllers, who – as everyone in Teignmouth knew – were now entirely dependent upon charity, having abandoned the legalised custom of pew rents and a fixed living.

She admired the Müllers for their courage, but she did not altogether approve of it. Mary had given birth to a stillborn child in July, and Susannah could not help agreeing with Blair that if she had been better rested and nourished the child might have survived. Mary's brother Anthony was acting in a similarly irresponsible way: he had subjected his wife and family to the most terrible privations by going out to Baghdad and Susannah could not really believe that he was likely to have much success in his efforts to convert the Mohammedans.

Blair had been quite outspoken about Müller's activities, and never lost an opportunity to attack them. 'All this sentimental religiosity he's stirring up causes discontent and disobedience among the servant classes,' he said one morning, 'and what's more, it's a threat to law and order to abandon the role of pastor as they're doing.'

'But don't you think it was at least courageous of him to abandon his pew rents?'

'Not at all! This "living by faith" is a sham, Susannah. Herr Müller knows damn well that by relying on the goodwill of innocent people he stands to receive a lot higher income than he would from a fixed living – especially as it would have been halved.'

'Halved?' she had asked. 'Why halved?'

'Hasn't he submitted himself to a believer's baptism? It's the law, Susannah, and a very good one too. We had enough trouble from the Anabaptists three hundred years ago to encourage them again. And besides – what would happen if we all followed Herr Müller's example? Where would all the unsolicited sovereigns come from then?'

He was finishing his breakfast. He put his knife and fork together on the plate and pressed his table napkin to his lips.

'Well, well,' he said. 'Men must work and women must weep, Susannah. I shall be in Exeter today to see old Lethbridge, so I shan't be back before seven.'

She followed him into the hall, where Robson was ready with his hat and stick, and Benjamin waiting with Peg to say goodmorning to his Papa before he departed.

128

Blair lifted his son and held him on one arm, turning his head stiffly like a puppet in a Punch and Judy show. 'Well cheeky-chops,' he said in his puppet voice. 'Are we going to be good boys today? No running away from Mama or Peg? Eating up our milksop and minding our p's and q's?'

Benjamin opened his mouth very wide, something he had been taught to do some weeks before when he had a sore throat and which he now apparently saw as a gesture of respect.

'Pees and coos?' he asked. 'What's pees and coos?'

His father set him down on the Persian rug and crouched to speak to him face to face. 'Pleasantries and quips! Pears and quinces! Pens and quills! P-leases and than-kyous.' He patted Benjamin's cheek and stood up, and having put his hat on and taken his stick, went out to his carriage, where the horses were tossing their heads in the sun.

Susannah stood at the breakfast room window as the carriage went down the drive, and watched Blair's top hat disappear beneath the stone wall at the foot of the property. She looked out upon the soft shadow of the walnut tree which fell away down the lawns, reflecting that the atmosphere had improved almost tangibly since Zilla's removal. The day after tomorrow was the celebration lunch and the farewell ceremony for the *Eustacia*, which was to sail on her maiden voyage to Oporto. The invitations had been sent out and her new gown delivered from Exeter. Blair had said that it would be the day he would put the name of Harvey on the map.

Yes, they were already happier. It was better to be Blair's devoted and obedient wife than to allow old ties, old arguments to linger; better to enjoy the sunshine and the good life, the August races, the boat picnics, the walks along this beautiful red-rocked coast; better to pay for front pews in the fashionable (if a little high) church of St Michael's, better to preserve the outward and visible signs of good breeding and respectability.

She shivered, and goose pimples appeared on her arms below the balloon sleeves of her blue taffeta. She told herself that it must be a draught from the hall, but at the same time she could not help feeling that she had caught a fleeting glimpse of something that lay in wait for her round the corner of time.

It was an excellent lunch. Blair had reserved the main dining room of the Assembly Rooms for the occasion and had spared no expense. The principal guests included the roué millionaire William Crockford, the lord of the manor Lord Clifford, Viscount Haldon and the mayor; while seated at the two lower tables, each with his lady, was practically every merchant, squire, banker, shipowner and gentleman in Teignmouth. They sat down to oysters, game soup, roast beef and Yorkshire pudding, gooseberry pie with Devonshire cream, Stilton cheese and vintage port-wine. By the end, when Blair had made a speech encouraging one and all to invest in Teignmouth, and the mayor had replied by affirming that Mr Harvey's enthusiasm and business acumen was bettered only by the charm and beauty of his lovely wife, everyone was feeling in an excellent mood, and ready to take a constitutional stroll through the town to the New Quay, where the *Eustacia* was ready for departure.

As Blair came out of the Assembly Rooms with Susannah on his arm, they were met by Dallmyer, who had brought the carriage down with Peg and Benjamin. This was in accordance with Blair's wishes, because he had insisted that Benjamin was old enough to take part in the occasion.

He lifted the boy down (he had been dressed in a new suit of brown tweed that made him look like a miniature sportsman) and took him by the hand.

'There we are, Master Benjamin. We shall walk with Papa like a little man.'

Benjamin opened his mouth wide for inspection.

130

As the collection of worthies proceeded through the town, the locals came to their windows and doors to watch, and by the time they arrived at the New Quay Inn, a small crowd had already gathered in order to sample the free beer that Mr Harvey had laid on for the occasion.

On board the *Eustacia*, which lay alongside the western end of the granite quay, the brass had been polished and the decks holystoned, and a string of flags rigged from the bowsprit to the truck of the foremast and from there to the main and mizzen masts and down to the stern.

'Stand aside now, stand aside!' Cobbe ordered, making a corridor for the owner and his wife, who now made their way to the dais; and as Blair stuck his thumbs into his waistcoat and prepared to speak, silence was called for and a considerable amount of shushing and hushing went on, accompanied by one or two giggles from some of the girls who had found new friends among the celebrating artisans and journeymen.

Blair said all the right and proper things for a shipowner to say before a maiden voyage, and when he had wished the *Eustacia bon voyage* and pointed out with a tremor that she was named after his own sweet mother, the ship's master proposed three cheers for Mr Harvey. After that Blair, who had for some while needed to relieve himself, told Benjamin to be a good boy and stay with his mother and slipped away to make use of the privy at the back of the New Quay Inn.

When he returned, the preparations for slipping the *Eustacia* were complete. The new steam tug, *Grasper*, had appeared on the scene, belching a column of black smoke from her tall funnel, and the crew of the *Eustacia* were heaving in on the bower anchor, which had been laid to windward in order to assist in unberthing. The stops had been cast off the fore and mizzen sails and the halyards were in hand, ready for hoisting. Wives and sweethearts were weeping and waving and the ship's mate, standing on the cabin roof was bawling out, 'Let go for'd, let go aft!

Hoist the mizzen! Hoist jib topsail! Brace the yards to port!'

Susannah looked back at Blair. He was standing on the dais again, his chest stuck out and his fists clenched. Really how typical this was of him, she thought, laughing inwardly at the pleased-little-boy look on his face. That is what he *is*, she thought: a little boy. That is what all these earnest gentlemen in waistcoats and watchchains are! They are all the same – little boys playing at being men! And we women have to join in their games and make believe that they are gods to be worshipped and adored!

She sighed and looked round for Benjamin, and a sudden, stark chill went through her. He was no longer at Blair's side.

'Blair!' she shouted over the cheering as the ship drew away from the quay side. 'Who is looking after Benjamin?'

'Looking after him?' he returned impatiently. 'What do you mean? You are, of course.'

'But he was with you!'

'Not at all –'

'But you said he was to stay with you!'

'I said nothing of the kind!'

'Then where is he? Where is he, Blair?'

She gave up questioning him and pushed through the crowd to find Peg, who was flirting with one of the journeymen.

'I don't know, Ma'am,' she said, blushing scarlet. 'I thought he were with you, like.'

Susannah hurried back through the crowd, and on the way bumped into Cobbe.

'Little Benjamin?' he said. 'Yes, indeed I have seen him Mrs Harvey. He was playing under those palings not five minutes ago.'

She began praying silently: 'O Lord, let him be safe; O Lord, turn not Thine hand against him.'

Blair was standing on the dais still, waving his hat to the

Eustacia, which was now well out into the river, with the headsails and mizzen set and making good progress in the northwesterly breeze.

'We have lost Benjamin!' she shrieked at him. 'Do you hear me, Blair? We have lost him!'

It took some seconds for the meaning of it to sink in. Then, at last, he took action. He put his hat on and held up his hands for silence. 'Ladies and gentlemen! Silence if you please! Has any one of you seen my son Benjamin?'

The noise and laughter turned quickly to murmurings and shaking of heads. Blair stepped down from the dais and marched off the quay towards the main street. People came up and volunteered their services. Blair took charge. 'Everyone search the town!' he ordered. 'He cannot have gone far! Susannah – come with me. Mr Cobbe – be so kind as to search the waterfront in this direction. Captain Endacott – yes, that way. He may have found his way into some back kitchen.' He turned to Susannah and patted her hand. 'Don't worry, my dear, we are sure to find him very soon.'

At the same moment, a shout came from behind them, and then a woman's scream. They turned back and hurried out along the quay to join the little crowd that was staring down at a patch of calm water where driftwood, scum and garbage had collected against the granite blocks; and it was in this foul corner that Benjamin's body could just be made out, face down and largely submerged, the little arms spread out in cruciform.

By the time a barge pole had been fetched and his body was being lifted dripping from the water, everyone knew he must be dead, and the valley of the River Teign was echoing with the anguish and despair of a mother who had lost her son.

September, October, November, December . . . the months had no meaning, time had no meaning, life – no meaning. She stood at windows, she looked out over the

Channel at the rain driving in from the sea; she sat at her bureau and stared at a blank sheet of paper; she lay in bed all day, the curtains drawn to exclude the grey winter light. One night she ran out onto the lawn in her night clothes and screamed at the racing clouds to bring back her son, and had to be led sobbing back into the house by Blair.

Her grief was punctuated and prolonged by unsought scenes that flashed before her mind's eye with demonic clarity: she saw the body of her son being raised up at the end of a pole; she saw the filth and sludge on his precious face, witnessed again the stream of vile water that issued from his lips when Cobbe tried to resuscitate him by pressing down on his chest. She saw him washed and prepared for his last resting place, that unnecessarily deep pit: she saw him lying in his silken shroud, his infant's coffin decked out with wild flowers which local children had picked when the news of the tragedy had been reported in the *Teignmouth Gazette*. She saw the brass plate which announced his name, his age and the words, 'For of such is the kingdom of heaven.'

Her grief turned slowly to rage. Sometimes she would start up with a pathetic, yelping scream of anger – anger at Fate, at Chance, at Providence – even at God. 'Why?' she demanded over and over again. 'Why? Why?'

One answer to that question presented itself repeatedly: from the very moment of the accident, she had known that it would not have happened if Zilla had remained in her service. Zilla had been so devoted to Benjamin that she would never have allowed him out of her sight. She would have chased after him the moment he ran off by himself; she would have gathered him in her arms, scolding him and cuddling him as she had done so many times before. And Zilla would not have left if only Susannah had stood up for her instead of taking the easy way out. The knowledge of this forced upon her a host of other self-accusations: she had misused Zilla from the start, had led

134

her into vice, had desired her with her body, had made a pretence of being a good mistress to her and yet, when the test came, had failed her.

Thoughts of Zilla led her to dwell upon her own childhood, and she saw that she had been the cause of unhappiness from as far back as she could remember. Her parents had argued over her; she had been a disruptive influence in school; had made faces behind the teacher's back and led an underground movement which sought to undermine the authority of grown-ups and divert her neighbours from their studies.

Wherever she looked she saw signs of her own failings, her own weakness and malevolence. She found cause for shame even in the nursing of her own mother, for had she not become secretly impatient by the daily necessity of waiting upon her, emptying her pans, helping with her pillows, attending her during her attacks? Had she not been covertly relieved at her death?

If she had behaved badly towards her mother, how much worse had she treated her father! How sulky and petulant she had been in his presence after her mother's death! How ungrateful! And at the end, how flagrantly disobedient!

Self, self, self, she thought one December afternoon as she walked along the foreshore. She turned her head against a thin drizzle that stung her cheek. The headland known as the Parson and Clerk looked like a giant elephant at the water's edge. Her boots crunched over pebbles and red sand, and without warning she experienced a vivid insight into what lay at the root of her present misery, what – ultimately – had caused Benjamin to fall off the New Quay and into that filthy slurry of scum and driftwood and excreta.

She closed her eyes and stood swaying and shivering at the shock of it. She was reliving that last argument with her father. 'Am I to wait until you are dead before I can live a life of my own?' she had demanded. She saw herself

135

entering Lethbridge's office and meeting Blair for the first time. She saw the downy hairs on his cheeks, the moist, bowed lips, the glittering eyes, that looked blatantly through her dress; then she was back in her own room, pacing about, pausing before the mirror, longing for him, lusting for him, wanting him not out of pure love but as a base animal, simply and solely for his masculine body, his sex . . .

She ran up the beach shrieking and fell headlong among the boulders.

'I am a murderess!' she sobbed. 'I have murdered my father in my heart in order to gratify the lust of my flesh! I am a murderess and this is my punishment! This is my punishment!'

An hour later, when the light was all but gone, she walked slowly up the drive beneath the bare sycamores to West Lawn, and went straight into the library without removing her cloak. She sat down at her bureau, dipped a pen into the well and wrote in black copperplate:

> I wished my father dead
> I married in haste
> I married for physical reasons
> I misused Zilla
> I failed to honour my father and my mother
> I have belittled my husband in my thoughts
> I have been an ungrateful and disobedient wife
> I have been a neglectful mother
> I have not given to charity
> I am a murderess

When she had done this she laid the pen upon the rack and read over the lines; then, leaving the sheet of paper on the desk top, she went upstairs and stood silent and motionless in the darkness of her room.

Some time later – she didn't know how long – Susannah

became aware of candlelight coming along the landing. The shadows slanted forward along the walls and over the ceiling and she heard the distinctive sound of Blair's breath whistling in his nose. He paused behind her, then came closer.

'Susannah,' he said gently. 'My dear!'

She closed her eyes and clenched her fists. She did not want him here with her; she did not want herself here with him.

'What is this I have found on your bureau?'

It was as if a wooden plug had been inserted into her gullet. She was physically incapable of reply.

The wind moaned softly in the chimney flue, and ivy leaves tapped on the pane. He said: 'You must stop this self-torture, Susannah. It is time to end your mourning and start living again.'

He moved round to face her, and the candlelight threw his features into cadaverous relief, accentuating the nostrils and the line of his brow. He spoke in a slow, serious way she had never heard from him before. 'I am fearful for your sanity, Susannah, do you know that? I have tried to help you, but nothing I say has had an effect. I think that the only person who can help you is yourself. You must make an effort, now, to emerge from this self-imposed purgatory. And as for these lines I have discovered in the library – I have destroyed them, and you must destroy them in your mind. You must shut up your mind against such thoughts, just as we shut out germs and disease.'

She whispered: 'I am no longer worthy to be your wife.'

He stared at her, blinking in the candlelight. After Benjamin's death he had made it clear that he took no blame at all for the accident, for it was not for fathers to play nursemaid; but on the other hand he had not actually laid blame upon Susannah, for he felt that in her nervous state she would be unable to bear it. Now, he saw that she did take the blame and he felt that she would benefit from the generosity of his forgiveness.

'You must not blame yourself, Susannah. It was a moment of inattention, of forgetfulness, that is all, and we are all capable of making such mistakes. But you must not accuse yourself in this harsh way. I do not blame you – indeed, you are completely forgiven.'

There was a certain illogicality in what he said of which he was half aware, but he enjoyed being in a position to act in this magnanimous way, to absolve her of her guilt. And now that he was over the shock and sorrow of his loss, he could not help feeling a little pleased that the event had ended in Susannah that air of superiority which he had found so exasperating in the past. He had the ascendancy now, he was certain of it: provided she could be cured of her black depression, he was confident that in the future she would be a new and better person and a more fitting wife: a wife who listened more and spoke less, who acknowledged her dependence upon her husband and who no longer exercised her intellect and wit at his expense.

He lifted her chin on his finger and smiled. 'No more black thoughts, mmm? Let us put what has happened behind us, Susannah. We must take up where we left off. And who knows – perhaps we shall be blessed with another child.' He set the candlestick down on her dressing table. 'I thought that in the spring we might make a tour of the continent. I have often wished to visit Switzerland, and I am sure the air would be most beneficial to us both. Is that not a good idea?'

There were deep rings under her eyes and her hair was loose and ill-kempt. She looked back at him as if not quite understanding, then bowed her head. 'Yes, I would like that. Thank you.'

'Excellent!' he boomed. 'Now what about dinner this evening? Will you make an effort and come down?'

'If that is your wish,' she murmured.

He took her face in his hands and kissed her lightly on

the forehead. 'I do wish it,' he said, 'for it will be a sign to me that you are on the mend, Susannah, and that is my first wish.'

He went downstairs and put his head into the kitchen to tell the servants that Mrs Harvey would dine with him that evening. Later, when she entered the room in black, he could not help being reminded of his first meeting with her when she had been similarly dressed. But then she had been a blushing girl of twenty-one, her eyes bright with mischief and invitation, while now, though she had applied a little rouge to heighten the colour in her cheek, she was pallid and drawn.

He patted her hand. 'It wasn't so difficult to come down, was it?' he said. 'And you are looking a little better, Susannah. I expect this evening to mark the beginning of a steady improvement.'

There was an improvement, but not the one Blair had expected. Instead of a gradual return to her cheerful, waspish self, Susannah began to adopt an increasingly submissive role. At first, he enjoyed this new meek obedience of hers, for it reminded him of those halcyon days of his youth when his mother and sisters had adored and glorified him. Later, he found Susannah's quiet humility irritating – to such an extent that he sometimes tried to provoke her in order to see again the fire in her eyes.

January and February passed: the snowdrops and aconites flowered beneath the walnut tree, and the crocuses made a yellow and violet display along the grassy borders of the drive. Blair became busier than ever: he was now setting up as a banker in partnership with Cobbe, and a second ship – to be named the *Benjamin Harvey* – was already on the stocks.

But another interest was also taking up much of his time: some months before, he had met a Mrs Pendlebury, a widow of thirty who lived by herself in a cliff-top cottage in a hamlet on the coast road to Torquay. They were placed next to each other at a mayoral dinner given for local merchants to which Susannah had also been invited, but had declined to attend. Mrs Pendlebury had eloquent eyes and languid, white shoulders. She spoke in a low voice and led Blair into intimate revelations about his childhood over the turbot in cockle sauce. At the end of the evening, she remarked that if ever he should be passing Oddicombe and had the time to call upon her, she would be delighted to receive him.

He called, and she was delighted. She sent her maid into the village and entertained him to China tea and fruit cake. She led him into a wide, carpeted sitting room full of chinoiserie, whose windows gave onto the cliff edge and the white-flecked sea beyond. She stood beside a floor vase of tall bamboos and confided that since her husband's death from cholera in the East Indies, she had been the loneliest person in the world. The way she said it convinced Blair that it was his duty as a gentleman to help her combat such awful loneliness, and as he had more than half an idea how that would be achieved, he drove home with his mind in a turmoil.

He had not enjoyed much in the way of husbandly privileges since Benjamin's death, and Mrs Pendlebury's smouldering eyes had contained a very clear invitation. When she had pressed his hand in farewell, he had been almost overcome by the musky odour that rose from that mysterious valley between her smooth white mountains and she, seeing the vein rise in his forehead, had commanded him to come again soon.

The following week he obeyed, and this time Mrs Pendlebury did not bother with the weak tea or the fruit cake. As soon as Titty was out of the latchgate, she fell into his arms and declared – in the intervals between a succession of passionate, open-mouthed kisses – that her whole being cried out for him and that she was his, totally his.

Blair felt, during the amorous wrestling match which ensued in Mrs Pendlebury's satin draped bedroom, that it was more a case of himself becoming hers, totally hers, for Mrs Pendlebury knew exactly what she wanted and exactly how to get it.

Under an hour after arriving at her door, he departed again, having promised to call within a week, and on the way over the Teign bridge he laughed aloud, suddenly realising that he had found himself a mistress.

It was a most satisfactory arrangement. Mrs Pendlebury was a lady of advanced ideas, and expert in practices recommended by Bentham and Place. There was absolutely no danger, no danger at all! Really, he could hardly believe his luck. Oddicombe was just far enough distant from Teignmouth for there to be little risk of gossip, and Mrs Pendlebury's villa was delightfully secluded, lying at the end of a single track. He found, too, that it was quite easy to separate his affair from his domestic life with Susannah – rather in the same way one can separate the contents of a gilt-framed nude in oils from the respectable surroundings of the sitting room where it hangs. There was also the comfortable reassurance to be gained from the thought that not only was he helping Mrs Pendlebury overcome that awful loneliness, but he was also so much boosted in himself by what was going on that he felt quite able to show Susannah much more consideration than he had in the past.

Besides – what he was doing was quite normal among gentlemen of his age and standing in society. Every healthy man needed an outlet of this nature. And look at the alternative – a weekly tumble with a whore, booked in advance for a Thursday afternoon, and the certain knowledge that when you walked into her frilly boudoir someone like Captain Endacott would have walked out only fifteen minutes before.

No, this was the best possible arrangement, and if playing silly games with Mrs Pendlebury (she was Lavinia between the sheets) helped to assuage the flames of her nymphomania, then he was quite prepared to indulge her.

The wound of Susannah's bereavement was beginning to heal now, and in order to occupy her mind, she had set herself the task of putting her father's papers in order. For a month, she had spent every available minute of her time in the library, and as a result was beginning to gain a real insight into Dr Brougham's way of thinking. Having rejected his Romish tendencies while he was alive – perhaps out of duty to her mother – she now felt that she owed her father a debt of loyalty which might be repaid in part by reading his works and divining, from the quantity of correspondence he had received from academics and clerics, a clearer understanding of his beliefs.

She found the process pleasantly soothing: sometimes, while reading a treatise or pamphlet written by her father, she would stop in mid-paragraph and put her head back, remembering the boom of his voice in the study at Broad Gate, or her poor mother's expression as she came out after listening to him reading. How sad it was that they had been so divided, and in retrospect, how unnecessary!

She was thinking along these lines one February afternoon when Blair drove up in his carriage and pair. She watched him through the library window as he stepped down to the gravel and flexed his shoulders before handing over the pair to Dallmyer. What a handsome man he was! And how distant they had become, once again, over the past months! Benjamin's death should have brought them together, but it seemed to have forced them further apart She wished she could understand him better.

He seemed to have changed in recent months: he was more confident, rosier-cheeked, readier to laugh. And I, have I changed? she wondered. Outwardly, yes, for she had set herself the task of being completely obedient – both to her husband and to the memory of her father. Although a small voice within her still made mild protest, she had decided that it was easier and safer to accept that her husband must rule over her and that her will must be subject to his. It was not so much a change as a resignation, an acceptance of the inevitable; and having taken the decision, she felt greatly relieved. The struggle was over: it was no longer necessary to do battle with Blair, to prove her- self to him, find fault in his logic or correct his solecisms. He was a man and she was a woman, and she was coming to believe that the secret of real love – for a woman at least – lay in total submission, a negation of self.

She heard his boots in the hall and rose to greet him. She would have liked to welcome him with an embrace, but that did not appear to be his wish.

'Aha!' he said, looking at the piles of books and the papers strewn about her desk. 'Hard at work are we, Susannah?'

She inclined her head. 'I am putting Father's letters in order. I had no idea he was such a prolific correspondent.'

He nodded in approval and casually picked up the top letter off a pile.

'Those are from Bishop Jebb,' Susannah said. 'He and Father seem to have been very much in agreement on a number of matters. He kept up with many of his students at Oxford as well. I expect there are a few names that you will recognise yourself.'

'Doubtless,' said Blair, and went to the window.

'I had the idea to compile a memorial to him,' Susannah said behind him. 'An anthology of his essays and sermons, and perhaps some personal reminiscences of my own. He once said that I could do worse than become his amanuensis.'

Blair grunted. 'I was under the impression that your recollections of him were not altogether favourable.'

'That is true, but there were happy times, and it would do no harm to recall them.'

He stood with his arms akimbo and lifted his weight gently off his heels.

She went to him. 'He was a good man, I am convinced of it from what I have read these past weeks. I used to detest his theories so, did you know that? But now, having read them over, I find that they are not so far removed from what we hear in St Michael's every week.'

Blair gave a little snort, unable to come up with a more lucid reply because his mind was still full of his afternoon romp with Mrs P.

Susannah had returned to her bureau. 'I found something that might be of interest to you,' she said, and brought him a few sheets of an unfinished letter that was addressed to J.H. Newman. 'Look at the last paragraph. I am sure Father is referring to yourself.'

He scanned the page. The letter appeared to be arguing a case for celibacy of the priesthood, and came to an abrupt ending, as if the writer had been interrupted in the middle of it:

'. . . as recently as last summer, when a young gentleman of most punctilious and upstanding manner approached me after matins one Sunday to ask for guidance on a spiritual matter. I later had the pleasure of hearing his private confession'

'Is that all there is?' he asked.

'Yes. I think those words must have been the very last he wrote, poor lamb, for see – the date of the letter is the very date he passed away.' Susannah took back the letter and placed it on her bureau. 'It made me wonder if I should not follow your example, Blair, and ask the vicar at St Michael's to hear my own confession. I still feel a great load of guilt over Father as you know – and a number of other things. Would you disapprove if I were to?'

My God! he thought. She's going religious! Aloud, he said, 'Not at all,' and shrugged a little huffily.

Seeing him put out, she changed the subject and asked if he had been again to Torquay. He turned quickly.

'Torquay? Why should I go to Torquay?'

She was surprised at his defensive manner. 'I don't know, but you went last week, didn't you? And when you arrived a moment ago I thought the horses looked a little frothy, so it was clear that you had been out of town, and I presumed –' She stopped, seeing she was straying into danger. 'I'm sorry, Blair. It's no business of mine, is it? I should not have asked you.'

He wondered how much she knew, or what she had guessed. The previous week he had been seen coming back from Oddicombe by Captain Tobin's coachman, and the word had come back, via the kitchens, to Susannah. He had explained it by saying that he had been to visit an old legal colleague, and she had appeared to believe him completely; but this sudden question out of the blue was unnerving.

'I hadn't realised you took such an active interest in my comings and goings,' he said dryly.

She longed for him to show her some little sign of affection. She went to him and gave him her hands. 'My husband,' she whispered. 'My dear husband. I was not meaning to be at all inquisitive. But I sit indoors all day and I cannot help being a little interested in your activities. I would not be a proper wife to you if I were not.'

He relaxed a little and misquoted: 'For I could love you twice as much loved I not honour more.'

She gave a quick laugh, then bit her lip.

'What do you find amusing?'

'It's nothing, Blair.'

'It must be something, Susannah, otherwise you would not be pink as a carnation.'

'Very well, but please don't be offended. It is simply that you have misquoted Lovelace. The lines are not at all as you said them.

'And how do they run, precisely?'

' "I could not love thee (Dear) so much, Lov'd I not honour more." '

'Isn't that exactly what I said?'

'No! You said "For I could love you *twice as much*."
That means that your love would be greater if your love of
honour were less! I am quite sure that your lady love
would not be at all pleased about that!'

He went suddenly white in the face, and two pink
patches appeared on his temples. 'What exactly are you
hinting at, Susannah? Are you accusing me of something?
May I be allowed to know?'

'Accusing you? Not at all!'

'I thought,' he said, his breath coming in little puffs and
gasps, 'I thought – since you allowed my son to be
drowned by your own negligence – that you had put away
this sly, insinuative way of yours, but I see now that I was
wrong. Did you think me so obtuse that I would not see
through your devious way of interrogating me? Am I to be
put on the rack and questioned every time I walk into this
house? Is my wife to use a spy glass on the horses' flanks
in order to judge what distance I have travelled?'

Her eyes widened in fear. 'Please – my dear. I was not
accusing you. Indeed I have no idea how we came into this
extraordinary argument –'

He shook his arm free of her hand, and on the way out
of the library met Peg, who had come in with the post and
wanted to know if he and the mistress would take tea in
the library together.

'I shall take nothing at all with your mistress – in the
library or anywhere else,' he said, and took his letter up to
his dressing room.

It was from his eldest sister, who wrote every year on
the anniversary of his mother's death. He stared at the
neat lines of roundhand, hardly able to take them in; then,
leaning against the chimney piece and bowing his head, he
wept – not simply at being reminded of his mother's
passing, but more particularly at the knowledge that he
had entirely forgotten her anniversary and had, on that
very day, cavorted adulterously with Lavinia Pendlebury.

146

CHAPTER 8

On a blustery afternoon the following April, Blair drove back – or rather, set out to drive back – to Teignmouth in his gig. He had been to Plymouth on business and had broken his return journey at Brixham, where he had spent the night after dining with a client.

His conscience had been severely pricked by his sister's letter and Susannah's chance remarks. It had seemed to him that his dear mother was still keeping an eye on him, and that events had conspired together to produce a deliberate condemnation of his behaviour with Mrs Pendlebury. It was almost as if Lavinia and his mother were competing for his affection: though he had been frightened by Susannah's suspicions, he had been far more disconcerted by the thought of his mother's disapproval from beyond the grave.

He knew now that the memory of her had been his sheet anchor ever since leaving Oxford. Everything he had done or set out to achieve had been prompted by her memory. It had been she who had given him confidence to make his way in the world, and without the steadying influence and the continual awareness of 'what Mama would have thought' he knew that he might well have gone down the drain. Why – he might even have taken up with whores, like Captain Endacott!

The road out of Brixham climbed steeply to a height of some two hundred feet above sea level, and from here Blair could see, over to his right, the rocky headland of

Hope's Nose which stood out black against an angry sea. Fishing smacks were running back to Brixham to seek shelter from the freshening gale, and a formation of naval frigates was pressing westward under reefed topsails. The wind buffetted the carriage and blew out the pony's mane, and Blair – who had extended his mourning for Benjamin, and was still in black – turned up the collar of his coat.

While he drove, he wrestled with a new temptation. The fact was, he had avoided Lavinia in the past eight weeks mainly by having had no cause to travel past her lane. Now he could not escape the uncomfortable knowledge that his route took him past her turning, or that it might be pleasant indeed to call on his *femme fatale* for a little light intercourse.

It seemed, with every clop of his horse's hooves, that the time of decision approached. Within the hour, he would actually go along past the signpost to Oddicombe; within an hour, he might be wrapped once more in her glorious, soft embrace.

Can I do without her? he wondered. Yes, provided a substitute could be found for the bodily delights she afforded him. But what possible substitute could there be apart from another mistress? That was the terrifying part about it: now that he had progressed so far in the art of love (and he humorously regarded himself as a bachelor of that art rather than a master) he had become prey to an insatiable hunger for it. Nor was it any use expecting satisfaction from Susannah, for though they preserved the outward appearance of being happily married, they had little true affection for each other. That, he decided, was normal in a marriage: one did not *love* one's wife. One could only love one's mistress. (Or one's mother, of course.)

He was losing his patience with Susannah. Really she had a great deal to answer for: all those occasions on which she had belittled him or made herself out to be his superior! From that point of view, there was a certain rough justice in his liaison with Lavinia, for it evened up the scales and rendered Susannah's distant humility easier to bear. Let her make her sly innuendoes! Let her act as a self-appointed conscience to her husband! Let her see how far along the road to happiness that might take her!

He came to the junction where the Brixham and Kingswear roads joined to descend to the coast, and having negotiated the turning, he was just encouraging the pony into a trot when he saw ahead of him a familiar figure.

George Müller was the last person Blair wanted to meet that day, but the road was empty and it would have been worse than boorish to ignore the fellow; so as he came up with him, he slowed and gave him a good-day.

'Are we travelling in the same direction?' he asked a little foolishly, for it was quite obvious that they were. 'Would you care for a lift?'

To his horror, Müller accepted, and a moment later they were side by side, a little cramped for space, two large men in black with totally opposite aims in mind; for while George Müller's thoughts dwelt almost constantly on spiritual things, Blair's were seldom far from matters of the flesh.

Damn, damn, damn, he thought, realising that he had indeed intended to call upon Lavinia. But with 'German George' beside him he saw that it might be tempting providence to claim that he had a pressing engagement in Oddicombe.

He was thinking along these lines, and reflecting that perhaps Müller had been sent by fate to keep him on the straight and narrow, when his passenger broke the silence.

'Allow me,' he said in his gutteral English, 'to enquire after your good wife, Mr Harvey? Is she keeping in good health? Since your sad loss last summer, she has been much in our prayers.'

'Thank you kindly, she is well,' said Blair, and shook the reins to speed the animal.

They started down the hill. 'If it is of any comfort to you sir,' Müller ventured again, 'I am fully persuaded that every child snatched away from this world in the innocence and beauty of infancy finds rest with Him in glory.'

Blair was inclined to tell Müller to mind his own damned business, but thought better of it. 'He was a good little boy and a baptised Anglican,' he said. 'That is enough for me, Herr Müller, and I suspect that it is enough for Almighty God.'

'So,' said Müller, and fell silent.

Blair was annoyed at being led into a discussion of spiritual matters so easily, and decided to seize the initiative. 'And yourself, Herr Müller? How goes your little band of brethren? Do I understand you are considering removal from Teignmouth?'

Müller recognised the veiled hostility in this question. Over the past year, there had been an increasing antipathy towards him among the non-believers in the town, and he had for some time felt that he would have to make a change. Craik had already moved to Bristol, and only a few days before Müller had accepted an invitation to spend a fortnight with him in order to test the water and find out whither the Lord would have him go.

'It is a possibility,' he replied. 'I shall make no decision which I do not see to be the Lord's will for me, however.'

They had descended to that stretch of the road that runs along the flat by Goodrington Sands. To their right, waves crashed and thundered on the beach, and seabirds wheeled and cried, swooping down over the foam and soaring upward in the air currents.

'And how will you go about discovering the Lord's will?' shouted Blair, who had by now decided that if Müller was to ride with him, he might as well have some entertainment out of him.

'The Lord speaks to them that wait upon Him, Mr Harvey.'

'Oh yes? And how does He speak?'

Müller prayed silently for help. He was aware that much of the antagonism he had experienced in Teignmouth was the result of the influence of worldly people like Blair, who could not bear to see others finding joy and hope in the gospel of Christ.

'I shall not presume to give you the answer to that, sir, but we read in the scriptures that "all things work together for good to them that love God." Of that I am convinced afresh every day.'

'You mean by the gifts of money and food you receive? Is that the work of the Lord then?'

'I believe it to be.'

Blair might have left it at that, but an inexplicable stirring of anger spurred him on.

'It would not, do you suppose, have anything to do with people feeling sorry for you, or perhaps thinking that they can salve their consciences by making anonymous donations to a man of God?'

'I do not look into the motives of others,' replied Müller gravely. 'I have difficulty enough with my own.'

'Oh yes? I was under the impression that you were very strong in the faith. Indeed, I heard that you had claimed a miracle for yourself only recently. A matter of a burst blood vessel, wasn't it?'

This was a story that had been going about since February, when Müller had suffered a mild internal haemorrhage, and in the face of all advice from his doctor had insisted upon continuing to preach, making such a rapid recovery that he regarded it as plain proof of the hand of God in the matter. The story had gone about Teignmouth, and on the strength of it, Müller had started praying with sick believers to restore them to health.

'I have never claimed a miracle for myself, and I pray that I shall never have the presumption to do so,' he replied. 'It is true that the Lord has seen fit to answer my prayers in remarkable ways, but it is to Him that all glory for it is due.'

'Hmmph!' went Blair, who was thinking that Müller was getting a bit big for his spiritual boots. 'So – all you have to do is have faith, and you get what you want, is that it?'

They were passing through Paignton to Hollicombe.

'Not what *I* want, Mr Harvey. What the Lord wills.'

Blair sensed an easy victory here. 'So what you have to do, I suppose, is first find out what the Lord wills, and then ask for it? Is that it?'

But Müller was not to be drawn into the paradox of predestination. 'Sir,' he said gravely, 'if you are sincerely interested in discussing matters of the spirit, then gladly will I answer your questions, but if you are only intent upon making a mockery of things I hold precious, then I must beg you to excuse me.'

Blair looked more surprised than he was. 'I am entirely serious,' he said. 'I have never been more serious in my life!'

Müller glanced quickly at Blair, and was not deceived by his air of false sincerity; but having accepted a lift, he believed it was his Christian duty to witness to this man, whom he regarded as an agent of the powers of darkness.

'Then I shall try to explain,' he said. 'Two years ago, in London, I was restored through prayer from a bodily infirmity under which I had been labouring for a long time, and which has never returned since. This answer to prayer, along with several others, has led me to the conclusion that it has pleased the Lord – in some cases – to give me something like the gift, rather than the grace of prayer.'

'The gift rather than the grace? And what does that mean, Herr Müller? Is there a difference?'

Having asked this question, Blair felt a little pang of annoyance at showing so much interest.

'Indeed there is,' Müller was saying, 'for according to the gift of faith, I am able to do or believe something the not doing, or the not believing of which would not be sin;

while according to the grace of faith, I am able to do or believe something, respecting which I have the word of God as the ground to rest upon and, therefore, the not doing or not believing of it would be sin.'

'A very fine point!' shouted Blair over the roar of wind and waves. 'But a bit too fine for the likes of yours truly!'

'Let me give you an example then, so you may grasp it more fully: the gift of faith is needed to believe that a sick person may be restored to health, for there is no scriptural promise to that effect; while the grace of faith is needed to believe that the Lord will give me the necessaries of life, if first I seek the kingdom of God and His righteousness, for there is a promise to that effect in the sixth chapter of Matthew's gospel.'

'So what it amounts to,' said Blair, confident that he could now crush the whole silly theory once and for all, 'is that if I have the gift of faith, all I have to do is ask the Lord, and I can make this pony and trap fly over Torquay and set me down five minutes later in Teignmouth. Is that not the case? Don't I recall something about mountains and mustard seeds?'

'Mr Harvey, *you* could not make this trap rise in the air, or any other heavy object. We know that to be an impossibility and against the immutable, God-given law of gravity. But if the Lord willed it, He could raise us up – indeed, He has promised that the saints *will* one day be caught up in the air to be with Him in glory. So I am thinking that it will be of greater benefit to your soul if you would ask first for the free gift of salvation through our Saviour's death on the cross. I know that you are a businessman, Mr Harvey, so let me put it this way: "What shall it profit a man if he shall gain the whole world and lose his own soul?" Those are the words of our Lord, sir, and I think you will do well to consider them. And now,' he continued, 'if you will very kindly put me down at the corner here, I shall be grateful, for I am to preach in Torquay this evening, God willing.'

With that, George Müller slung his knapsack over his shoulder, shook Blair warmly by the hand, and having murmured a last blessing upon him, stepped down to the road.

Blair drove on, feeling quite bewildered. He had presumed that the fellow was going to Teignmouth. He had presumed that he might yet score a few points off the solemn German – but here he was with his thoughts in a turmoil and a gnawing resentment at the way George Müller had managed to penetrate his defences.

Scowling, he drove the pony hard up the hill out of Torquay and along the coast road past Babbacombe.

The signpost to Oddicombe came into sight. It was like a direct challenge to his manhood. He swung the gig off the main road at the last moment.

'And George Müller can go to hell,' he muttered.

The gig went down the narrow lane between high banks; his hands were busy with the reins and the brake to steady Minnie, whose hooves were inclined to slip on so steep a gradient; and his mind was already full of thoughts about a roaring log fire in front of which he and Mrs P would toast muffins after variations on a diverting theme in a feather bed.

These imaginings were rudely interrupted as he reached the entrance to Mrs Pendlebury's drive, for emerging from the tunnel of hazel saplings was a smart carriage and pair driven by a gentleman of somewhat stylish appearance. As there was not enough room for the gig and the carriage to pass in the lane, Blair was obliged to carry on a few yards in order to let the other man out.

'Thank you, Pastor!' said the gentleman; and the confidence of his manner, the jaunty wave of his hand and – so it seemed to Blair – even the knowing glint in the eye of the nearside gelding, all shouted one particularly unwelcome message.

Blair proceeded down the hill feeling doubly insulted:

154

first, at having his place in Lavinia's favour so abruptly usurped, and second at being mistaken for a man of the cloth.

It was impossible to turn in the lane, so he went on down to the hamlet of Oddicombe, which consisted of a few thatched cottages perched on the slope; and deciding that he might yet heap a few coals of fire on Mrs Pendlebury's head, he parked the gig by some railings, tethered the pony and set out on foot along the cliff path that led beneath his mistress's window.

Having reached a strategically useful position where he was sure he would be seen from her sitting room, he turned his back on it and stood gazing out to sea.

She will see that it is I, he told himself, and she will know that I have been misused.

For a while he allowed himself the luxury of imagining her hurrying out to ask his forgiveness. He saw her on her knees in the sea clover, her arms round his legs, begging him to return to the bosom of her affection.

But it was cold there on the cliff edge, and he felt suddenly tired of all this foolishness. A jumble of thoughts, memories and hopes jostled for front place in his mind. He thought of his childhood days and Oxford; he recalled his ambitions to cut a figure in the world, to lead a public life, a life that would leave its mark upon the history of old England. It seemed to him that by taking up with Lavinia he had severed the link between himself and his mother – had broken a mystic umbilical, so that he could no longer turn to her in his thoughts for guidance or congratulation. If only she were still alive! If only she could come and stay with them at West Lawn! If only he could turn to her and say, 'See, Mama, how well I am doing in the world! See what a clever, successful son you have!'

But I am neither clever nor particularly successful, he mused, watching a brigantine a mile off shore which seemed to be having difficulty putting about. I am like that ship out there, coming up to the wind but falling back onto the same tack again, never holding a steady course through life, never able to grasp hold of my destiny.

Women, they were to blame. Petted by them in childhood, intrigued by them in youth, misused, belittled and degraded by them in manhood.

He hunched his shoulders against the wind and watched the brigantine make yet another attempt to come about. He saw the headsails flap, the crew man the lee braces, and a long feather of spray go up as another wave crashed against her bows. There – she had failed again, and was now in stays, making sternway for some seconds before the helm was reversed and she payed off on the port tack once more.

Gradually, his interest in this ship replaced that in his own affairs, and he found himself wondering why she was unable to put about. 'Or why does she not wear?' he muttered aloud, before replying to himself that she could not do that because she was already too close inshore. He was so absorbed in the ship's predicament and so full of theories about jammed rudders and incompetent seamanship that he was unaware of Mrs Pendlebury looking down on him from her window, and of the curtains being drawn to exclude him.

He had an idea what had happened. The master must have been hugging the shore in order to avoid the effects of the east-going flood tide; the wind had then veered a point and headed him, but the force of the waves upon his port bow was repeatedly preventing him from standing out on the starboard tack to safety.

There is going to be a ship wrecked here this afternoon, he thought grimly, but could not help feeling a little excited at the prospect. Beneath him, spray was leaping thirty and forty feet in the air as the rolling waters smashed down upon the rocks and fallen boulders, and he shivered at the thought of being thrown into such a maelstrom.

156

'And up she comes again,' he said to himself, watching intently as men moved about her decks and the wheel was put over. He saw the bows lift out of a wave and plunge down into the next, and this time the headsails were not let go but held fast – presumably in the hope that they would be backed and would thus bring the head round. For a moment, this seemed to be successful, but just when he was sure she must now pay off on the new tack she was hit by a gust of wind that sent her backwards, the big sails thundering and cracking, and one of the headsails blowing out and going quickly into shreds.

The wind whistled sharply in the sea grasses, and a lash of spray found its way over the cliff, stinging his cheek. 'I shall watch her put about,' he promised himself, 'and then I shall continue home – and the lovely Lavinia can go cool her porridge.'

But the brigantine had failed again. 'I'm damned!' Blair whispered. 'Now she really is in a fix!'

He was able to look down on her now and could hear the shouts and curses of the master and crew. They scurried about the decks like insects: some handing the foresail, others preparing an anchor for letting go. But they are too late, too late, Blair thought. They are embayed, can't they see that they are already doomed?

From somewhere to his right and below him he heard a shriek. Women and children were going down through the trees to the shore. Suddenly he wanted to do likewise – to share with them the witnessing of disaster.

He hurried back along the cliff path, through the hamlet, over a stile; and slipping and sliding in the red mud, he followed the villagers down a goat path that plunged almost vertically through a wilderness of brambles, ash saplings and wild clematis to the sea some two hundred feet below.

On reaching the dark stones of the beach (he had fallen twice on the way down, and his coat was covered in red clay) he was surprised to see how many people had already gathered. They were poor folk – women and children, in shawls and tatters – and he was the only person among them of any breeding.

A cable or so off shore, the ship was making one last desperate attempt to come through the wind; but the seas were breaking all round her now, and it was clearly a vain hope. Within minutes she would be carried down upon those rocks, and those of her crew who were not immediately drowned as the hull broke up would be pounded to their deaths.

You could hear the wind shrieking in the masts and stays now, and the great sails came thundering down as the halyards were cut. An anchor had been dropped, and as the head came round to face the seas, a bigger wave swept over the vessel and its foaming crest took a man with it: for a few moments he was visible to the spectators on the shore, and then he was lost in the chaos of broken water and surf.

It was then that an old woman, quite toothless, approached Blair Harvey and clutched at his sleeve with knobbled fingers. When she spoke, her mouth became a dark round hole surrounded by black wrinkles.

'We can zee 'ee be a man of God, zirr,' she howled in his ear, 'so will 'ee not lead us in prayer like, for that the good Lord may deliver they poor souls?'

In a sudden flash of insight, he saw it all: the vocation to be a benefactor, the punishments he had received for past sin; the chance meeting with Müller and their spiritual conversation about faith; the extraordinary coincidences not only of meeting Mrs Pendlebury's lover face to face but also of having this ship founder on this part of the coast, and to be mistaken twice within the hour for a man of God. It was as if the Lord had spoken to him directly through the cracked lips of this old peasant woman in her black shawl: he was filled with a sudden, invincible certainty that a new path had opened up before him, a path that would change his life radically and irrevocably, a path that would be stony and difficult to follow, but one that would give him direction where there had been doubt, and confidence where there had been a lingering sense of inadequacy.

They had turned to him and were waiting for him to give a lead. He experienced a deep, spiritual ecstacy: sinking to his knees on the wet pebbles, he threw back his head, and clasped his hands, and called upon the name of the Lord.

Long after midnight, Susannah awoke to the sound of wheels on gravel beneath her window. She had expected Blair back that afternoon, but when he had not arrived had presumed he would come the following day. She lay in bed listening to the wind and rain, and a little while later saw the line of yellow candlelight creep under the door as Blair came upstairs.

She sat up in bed.

'My dear!' she said. 'You are soaked! What on earth has happened?'

He fell to his knees and took her hands, and in a trembling voice, a quite different voice, began to tell her about the shipwreck and how, after he had prayed, the anchor rope had carried away and the ship had been driven miraculously down onto a narrow strip of sand; how he and the village women had laboured in the raging surf to help the crew to safety, and how only one man had been lost.

'And afterwards, when they were safe ashore, the good people of Oddicombe asked me to go with them to the village and give thanks, Susannah.' He stopped, and wept for several moments. 'They asked me to lead them in a simple form of worship. And – I led them in prayer, my dear. Without difficulty, without shame. I knew then – with a wonderful, miraculous certainty that here was the way which the Lord wished me to follow. Oh my dearest Susannah! I have been so touched and humbled this night!'

159

Her heart went out to him: they wept in each other's arms.

'They brought a Bible to me and asked me to minister the Word to them. I turned to St Matthew and read them the Sermon on the Mount, and then continued reading straight on for nearly an hour. Oh Susannah, I have been such a great sinner! And yet I know that though my sins be as scarlet, they can be white as snow – indeed *are* as white as snow, for I have this very evening prostrated myself before the Lord and repented of my sins! Kneel with me, I beg you dearest! Kneel with me now and let us be one with each other and with the Lord!'

She felt that her heart was breaking: it seemed to her that she had found a new husband, a husband whom she could now love, respect and gladly obey; so she knelt at the bedside with him and they joined hands as Blair brought his dear Susannah to the feet of the Lord.

'But why did you go to Oddicombe, Blair?' Susannah asked the next morning at breakfast.

He blinked rapidly and glanced out of the window. 'That was the extraordinary part about it, dear,' he said. 'Do you know – I had no reason at all to do so, but simply felt drawn to go down to the cliff and watch the storm.'

They walked down the hill, and broke the news to the Müllers. George and Mary fell on their knees immediately to give thanks, and the Harveys joined them. Afterwards, Mary told Susannah that her ears were ringing with the sound of heavenly rejoicing.

CHAPTER 9

Brother Müller was to depart on a fortnight's visit to Bristol that morning, and while he and Mary were still on their knees with the Harveys, three other brethren from the Bitton Street assembly called. These were Starling, a large butcher with three chins, Tozer, a gentleman's outfitter, and Synge, a quiet, well spoken man whose natural sincerity immediately struck Susannah.

These three stared in amazement at the sight of Mr and Mrs Harvey on their knees, and quickly joined in the thanksgiving for their miraculous conversion; Mary's father (old Mr Groves) also joined the saintly celebration, and it was unanimously agreed that they should go along together to Ebenezer Hall to pray together before brother Müller departed.

The chapel faced down the hill from Bitton Street: it had no organ, no pulpit, no altar, no nave, no aisle, no kneelers. All was simplicity, nothing adorned in any way. By the time the Harveys arrived with George and Mary, a number of other brethren and sisters had already arrived, so that the prayer meeting that followed was attended by more than thirty of the saints.

'We give thee thanks O Lord for these dear lambs who were lost and are found,' Müller prayed, and several of the brethren added emphatic amens.

Afterwards, the conversion of Blair and Susannah was somewhat eclipsed by Müller's departure, whose Bristol visit was seen by many as a sure sign that he might be leaving Teignmouth for good.

They clustered round him outside the chapel and shook him by the hand, some of the women weeping and one brother embracing him and begging him not to stay away too long, and before he set out to catch the post chaise from the town centre, he turned back to the Harveys and exhorted them to read the Scriptures, to give themselves up entirely to the Lord, to pray without ceasing and to witness for Christ at the earliest opportunity.

'Come back with us,' Mary Müller said when her husband had gone. 'Spend this first day with us in prayer and praise.'

Lunch was potato broth and yesterday's bread. Mary urged her guests to have second helpings, telling them that there was plenty, so Blair accepted, earning a quick look from Susannah, who was sure he was eating Mary's supper.

'You will not find these first weeks at all easy,' Mary said when Mr Groves had led them in prayer. 'Indeed, it is our experience that the newly converted are more likely to backslide in the first month than at any other time. It is necessary to throw yourselves entirely upon the Lord, to witness for Him and to live for Him.' She smiled lovingly to Susannah, for whose conversion she had been praying regularly for the past six years. 'Do try to attend all our meetings at Ebenezer, too. And read, read the Scriptures. My dear husband says that like sponges dipped in water, we should be dipped in the Word. We should be thoroughly soaked and saturated in it so that we are entirely occupied and taken over by the Holy Spirit.'

During the afternoon they were introduced to several other of the Ebenezer saints who, having heard the extraordinary news, came in to share in the rejoicing and bring gifts of food and money. Blair beamed so much that his face muscles ached, and as there was not much for supper both he and Susannah returned to West Lawn that evening feeling hungry and emotionally exhausted.

They were met by Peg, who had been keeping a look out for them. 'Cook's been ever so worried!' she said. 'We didn't none of us know where you were at, like! We kept your dinners hot, but Cook's all in a froth and says it's spoiled and being as how she knows you be partial to silverside, sir, she be in a right state!'

Blair felt his digestive juices becoming enthusiastic, and saw in his mind's eye a plate of boiled beef with carrots and dumplings; but he ordered Satan behind him and told Peg that he and Mrs Harvey had had their fill of better food that day than even Cook could prepare.

Peg looked dismayed.

'Child!' Blair said. 'I speak of heavenly food. Do you understand?'

'No, sir, I can't say as 'ow I do, sir.'

'Very well. Run and tell Cook that we shall not require dinner tonight, but that I wish to speak to all the servants together at six-thirty tomorrow morning in the breakfast room.'

'All of us, sir?'

'All, Peg. And that includes Dallmyer and Robson and old Litton.' He placed his hands on the girl's shoulders and looked down into a pair of bewildered eyes. 'I have something of the very highest importance to impart, something that will affect you to all eternity.'

With that, he took Susannah's arm and they went upstairs, leaving Peg to rush back into the kitchen and tell Cook that she thought the master had finally gone off his rocker.

It was the first time they had been alone together that day, and to Susannah it was like the first night of a spiritual honeymoon. When Blair came into the bedroom in his night shirt she was already in bed; but he asked her to kneel with him once more while he prayed and read a passage recommended to them by brother Synge from Romans vi. While he did so, she became aware that their relationship as man and wife had altered in some indefinable way: she felt much closer to him and more at one with him – a feeling that was immediately confirmed as soon as they were between the sheets.

The following morning, Dallmyer and Robson brought six upright chairs in from below stairs and put them along the wall in the breakfast room, and at six-thirty the other servants came in, old Litton the gardener rolling the catarrh about in the back of his throat, and Mrs Stapleton whispering to Sal, the new kitchen maid, to keep an eye on the bacon.

Blair waited for them to sit down and stop fidgeting before getting to his feet to address them.

'The day before yesterday, your master and mistress underwent a change so radical and all-embracing, that we feel it necessary to inform you all of it,' he began, and the line of servants glanced about in embarrassment, occupying their fingers and lips in all those little pickings and scratchings so common among the lower classes. 'That night, through the grace of our Lord, we repented of our sins, and accepted the free gift of salvation.' Blair's voice trembled and his eyes glistened. His domestics gazed at him in mute amazement. 'And in order that you, the members of my household, may share with me the joy of salvation, I have decided that from henceforth we shall assemble ourselves together each morning for prayer and the reading of the Scriptures. Further, I am confident that each one of you will wish to share with me and Mrs Harvey the glorious knowledge of salvation through faith, and to this end I earnestly desire you to attend at the preaching of the gospel at Ebenezer Hall. And now,' he concluded, taking up a large Bible that had once belonged to Dr Brougham, 'I shall read to you what I read to the humble folk of Oddicombe on the night before last when, through the miraculous power of Almighty God, twenty-three souls were snatched from certain death by shipwreck.'

While he proceeded to read the Sermon on the Mount,

there came an increasingly strong smell from the kitchen, and Cook whispered to Sal to take the pans off the hob, but this idea was quashed by a fierce look from Mr Harvey; so when Peg brought in the breakfast ten minutes later the porridge was scorched, the fried eggs hard and the bacon done to a dark frazzle.

Blair walked down the hill to his offices in New Quay Street. He had put on black as usual, being still in mourning for his son, but today he was conscious of having done so for a new reason, seeing himself in the mirror as a great evangelist in the making – just as he had previously imagined himself as a Lord Chief Justice, benefactor, member of parliament, captain of industry and banker.

This new vision of his future self was more tangible than those previous, however: when that old woman had implored him to lead them in prayer it was as if his own mother had been speaking to him through her, and he had a vague feeling that she must be watching him even now as he took a narrow back alley through the town.

A man of God: that was how he had appeared to them, so that was what he must be. And there was no doubt that the safe beaching of that vessel had been a miraculous answer to his prayer: the ship had been clearly doomed and the likelihood of her being driven up between those rocks and onto that small stretch of sand impossibly small. It was a miracle, there could be no doubt of it, and he, Blair Harvey had been instrumental in bringing it about. Could there be any clearer sign to him of the way in which he must go? He had appeared to that loathsome fellow in a carriage as a man of God and then to the women on the beach. His prayer had been heard. This was his true vocation. The knowledge of it sent a shiver of happiness and pride through him. 'I am the Lord's and He is mine,' he said aloud, and strode in through the modest front door of Harvey & Co.

The offices were on the first floor and his own was panelled in oak and decorated with half-models on the walls and a polished brass binnacle cover on his desk. He gave his usual brisk goodmorning to Northway, the clerk, and went to his window to look out over the Teign where a sea breeze was sending catspaws pattering over the water.

Northway cleared his throat behind him. 'Mr Cobbe will be late in this morning, sir, owing to the necessity of carrying out the progress inspection aboard the *Benjamin*.'

'Very well,' replied Blair, and seeing Northway about to leave, called him back. 'Spare me a moment of your valuable time,' he said, and the young clerk whose narrow body looked the thinner for his outsize cast-offs, obeyed.

Blair looked him up and down and felt his own heartbeat quicken. He had resolved to witness for Christ at the very first opportunity, but doing so even to a junior employee was something of a hurdle. He pressed his lips tight together and blew out his cheeks, blinking rather fast and looking not unlike that species of frog which blows itself up before emitting a powerful, horn-like boom.

'Do you know Jesus?' he enquired.

'I beg your pardon, sir?'

'I said – do you know – do you know Jesus?'

Northway smiled nervously and put inky fingers through his blond hair. Mr Harvey occasionally asked trick questions that turned out to be jokes at the expense of his employees, and he was anxious not to be caught out.

'Do I know Jesus, sir? Well now – no, I can't say as how I do, sir. Not personally that is.'

Blair felt his pulse quicken in anger. 'In that case, Northway, you do not know Him at all, for last Thursday night when the *Fair Intention* foundered at Oddicombe, I came to know Him as my Friend and Saviour.'

Northway, being the youngest of eight and used to keeping his end up, was not long at a loss for words. 'In which case I offer you my hearty congratulations, sir, if congratulations are in order,' he said, and bowed out.

Blair returned to his desk and opened the *Teignmouth Gazette*, upon whose front page was a report of the wreck and a short history of the master who, the report ran, 'by his skilled use of a bower anchor contrived to manoeuvre his ship in such a way that it was driven up upon a safe beach, thereby saving all but one of his gallant crew.'

He threw the paper down in disgust. How typical this was of the world, to warp truth and give man the glory! He was still pacing about the office thinking about it when Cobbe entered ten minutes later.

'Morning Mr H,' he said cheerfully, and shot an inquisitive glance first at the newspaper on Blair's desk and second at the solemn look on his face.

Blair nodded briefly in reply, and wondered if it would be wiser not to say anything about his conversion on this occasion.

But Cobbe, his cheeks pink with cheery optimism and his eyes glinting with make-money humour was not to let him off the hook. 'So what's all this we've been hearing about your goodself then?' he enquired, bending to look out of the window at the dray of beer barrels arriving at the New Quay Inn.

'I don't know, Mr Cobbe, what have you been hearing?'

'Well,' said Cobbe, and stuck his thumbs into the armholes of his plaid waistcoat, 'A little bird told me that he saw a certain young shipowner in a black coat coming out of Ebenezer chapel last evening with our friends the brethren. What is it, got a guilty conscience over our lady friend in Torquay have we? Cold feet? Or a whiff of the hell fire?'

Harvey's face went white, and anger spots appeared at his temples.

'I'll lay you a magnum of best port-wine to a pint of scrumpy that you'll be over it in a fortnight, you old toper,' laughed Cobbe and dug Blair in the ribs with his thumb. 'Are you on?'

'No sir, I am not "on", as you call it,' Blair managed,

having shouted inwardly to the Lord for help. 'Nor will I be "on" for any wager in the future, for I am turned away from all such behaviour. I am a child of God's now, a servant of the Lord Jesus, and I will be obliged to you to respect the fact.'

Cobbe was inclined to shout with laughter at this, but the tears in Blair's eyes warned him against it, so instead he contented himself with an 'oh dear, oh dear, oh dear!' and left the office shaking his head in despair.

The implications of his conversion took a few days to reach Blair, who in his naïve way had scarcely bothered to think about them until they glared him in the face. But one by one they dawned: he began to see that if he were indeed to cast in his lot with the brethren at Ebenezer, he would no longer be able to lunch with business acquaintances in the Assembly Rooms or take a drink with Cobbe in the Royal; nor could he take any more of those short-cuts in his shipping deals or buy favours of his auditors with a well timed crate of French wines or a side of prime beef obtained for next to nothing from Captain Endacott. All that worldly behaviour had to be put behind him for good: it would have to be bread and cheese in his office for lunch and straight home in the evenings to take Susannah down to Ebenezer for the prayer meeting, the ministry of the Word or the gospel.

There was another problem, which his intensive study of Scriptures quickly presented, and this was the embarrassment of financial wealth. Every evening, on returning to West Lawn, he could not help looking at the Persian carpets, the Italian oils, the French furniture and all the other *objets d'art* and sigh inwardly, knowing that these heirlooms of Susannah's were a spiritual encumbrance.

'We should sell all we have and give alms, Susannah,' he said one evening. 'The Scriptures are quite clear on the matter, and we shall have to be guided by them, sooner or later.'

'I should be sorry to see all these things go,' she said, 'and though I know I should not feel attached to them in any way, nearly all are reminders of my parents. Really I don't feel that they belong to me, but that rather I am their custodian.'

He paced about the library, pausing at one end to lift himself gently off his heels. 'That is a specious argument. It matters not a jot what we feel in the matter, only what is the will of the Lord. If we feel led by the Holy Spirit to sell our possessions and give to the poor, that is what we must surely do. It is easier for a camel to pass through the eye of a needle than for a rich man to enter the kingdom of heaven, is it not, and we should do well to dwell upon that a little more and less upon our sentimental feelings for inanimate objects.'

They were taking tea from a Wedgwood service. Susannah sat by the bar fender, her grey dress spread out round her feet, her auburn hair tied simply in a black ribbon. 'Then let us not rush into anything my dear,' she said. 'Let us wait upon the Lord and be confident that He will guide us in His own time.'

The matter was temporarily dropped in favour of others which appeared more pressing. One was the question of whether Blair should ride in his carriage down to the office each morning as previously, for some of the town urchins had taken to following him and shouting blasphemies at his back; Susannah felt that if he used the carriage he would prevent the occasion for sin among the children, but Blair (who had by now even rubbed his topcoat against a wall to make it look shabby) held that it was his privilege as a Christian to accept the buffeting and sneers of the world, quoting Christ's teaching as his authority.

'In that case you have more courage than I,' Susannah said.

'It is not my courage, dear, but the courage of Christ Jesus in me. As long as my hand is in His, I am safe against all words of abuse.'

He was surprised and gratified at his own rapid progress in spiritual matters and the speed at which he passed from darkness into light. Having neglected his studies at school and university, he now found that his mind was eager to absorb as much from Holy Scripture as he had time to read. He plunged eagerly through the gospels and the epistles and made fond comparisons between the simple life of the new brethren and that of the earliest Christians. He rejoiced in the certainty of his salvation and was thrilled by the knowledge that all he needed was the Bible and the guidance of the Holy Spirit in order to be brought to a fullness of truth and understanding. All other learning, all other science, philosophy, metaphysics and literature was wasted breath now: he could laugh with relief at never again having to feel inferior because of an inability to quote Catullus or turn an epigram: such intellectual tricks were of the world and could be scorned and set aside. All that mattered was that he should, as a newborn babe, desire the sincere milk of the Word.

'Listen to this, listen to this!' he exclaimed one evening when they were reading together in the drawing room, and read out 1 Peter ii 5. 'Ye also, as lively stones, are built up a spiritual house, an holy priesthood, to offer up spiritual sacrifices, acceptable to God by Jesus Christ.'

Susannah turned her head to one side, puzzled at what he should find so exciting.

'Don't you see? It means that we are *all* priests! All members of a holy priesthood, built up like living stones, to make the church of God. It refutes the whole structure of clericalism. We have but one high priest, namely Christ Jesus, and every man who elevates himself as vicar or curate or pastor or bishop is merely echoing the great Romish evil. "Call no man father upon earth" . . . our Lord told us that Himself. And yet the Church of England is part of the state! It willingly accepts the model of Rome, while at the same time claiming to be in opposition to it! What a generation of vipers and hypocrites, Susannah!

And how blessed are we to have been brought out of such darkness!'

They attended every prayer meeting, Bible reading and gospel service that was held at Ebenezer during brother Müller's absence, and by the time he returned were already anxious to be admitted to full fellowship in the breaking of bread. But there was one hindrance which had to be overcome first, in that they had not yet applied for believer's baptism. Although opinion was divided on this question, the majority felt, with Müller, that the presence of an unbaptised believer at the Lord's Table would prove a stumbling block to the saints, and Blair's mind was considerably exercised on the matter. Both he and Susannah had been baptised and confirmed in the Church of England, and presumed at first that further baptism was unnecessary.

Brother Müller urged them to think otherwise. 'Two years ago when I went to preach at Sidmouth,' he told them one evening when they had returned with him to his lodgings for further ministry and prayer, 'I was present while three sisters of the Lord had a conversation on this subject, and my opinion was asked. I said, like you, brother Harvey, that I did not think that I need be baptised again, whereupon one of the sisters asked me if I had read the Scriptures and prayed with reference to the subject, and I had to admit that I had not. "Then I entreat you never more to speak of it until you have done so," she said, and I saw the force of the remark, for while I had been preaching for some time that we should receive nothing that cannot be proved by the Word of God, I was at the same time advocating the error of pedobaptism.'

Blair laid it before the Lord and searched the Scriptures, and within a week became convinced that he was being led by the Spirit to request baptism. 'Only by going down into the water and dying with Christ can we say that we are truly born again,' he told Susannah.

'But my godparents made promises for me at my

171

baptism, and I later endorsed them at my confirmation,' she returned. 'Were those promises and that confirmation therefore worthless?'

'Yes, that is the easy way out, isn't it? Are you quite sure you do not say that because you are afraid of the shame and indignity of public baptism? Can you be sure of your salvation if yet you are not willing to share with Christ this tiny part of His shame and indignity? That is the great difference, the gulf, between pedobaptism, which has become nothing more than a fashionable event for parents to coo over an infant, and believer's baptism when the old sinful person goes down into the water as Christ went down to Hell, and the new man rises with Him, to immortality.'

It was late May: over a month since their conversion. They walked down the lawn arm in arm, pausing to view the neat ranks of peonies, wallflowers and violas in the herbaceous border. Two days before, amid much sighing and weeping, brother Müller, his wife and father-in-law had left finally for Bristol where he was to take over the eldership of Gideon and Bethesda with brother Craik. Teignmouth was therefore left with brothers Tozer, Starling and Synge to oversee its activities, and Blair already had the idea that before long his own influence and education would earn him a place in that oversight.

'You see,' he went on, feeling increasingly confident that he was led by the Holy Spirit, 'the question is closely allied to that of our worldly possessions. It is a question of becoming dead to the world. We must die with Christ, and we must be seen, by the world, to die with Christ.'

Susannah bent to examine her polyanthus. 'Are you to give up your business then?' she asked.

He considered. This was a particularly difficult question. He had read Anthony Groves's famous tract *Christian Devotedness* by now, but had not yet rationalised the matter of his business interests to his own satisfaction. 'As yet,' he said, taking Susannah's arm again as they con-

172

tinued their walk, 'I am not privy to the mind of my Lord on the question, and I must content myself by waiting patiently for Him to reveal His will. Perhaps we shall feel led by the Spirit to take our Lord's words literally as have brothers Groves and Müller, I do not know; but we should bear in mind that passage – I think it is in First Corinthians – in which Paul says that there are diversities of gifts, but the same spirit. It may be that Our Lord wishes us to remain within our present stratum of society in order to be a better witness to gentlefolk like ourselves.'

'It would certainly be a blow to the servants if they were to lose their positions as a result of our conversion,' Susannah remarked, and they stopped at the foot of the lower lawn, where a weeping beech was in new leaf.

'Heaven forbid!' Blair said. 'No, I confidently expect that their position will be improved beyond all measure, for I shall insist upon their being baptised at the same time as ourselves, in the way that so many households were baptised in the first days of the church.'

'But what if they refuse?'

He puffed his cheeks a little, looking as if he were about to sound a trumpet. 'I do not see, in all conscience, how they could remain in our service if they are still in darkness, Susannah. After all, a house divided against itself shall not stand, and it would be impossible to have some servants believers and some not.'

She felt a little pang of fear, as if, once again, some dark inevitability lay ahead which she could not quite discern.

'Do you mean that you would dismiss a servant for refusing baptism then?'

'No, I do not say that at all, for I have faith that my Lord will bring each one of them to a knowledge of His grace. The question will not arise therefore, and it need not concern us.'

He beamed, pink cheeked and boyish, and they started up the slope again to the house.

*

The question of baptism became increasingly pressing with the passing of each Lord's Day. 'My heart will not be at peace until I can follow my Lord's command and remember Him in the breaking of bread,' Blair said one day a few weeks after their conversation on the lawn. 'I know that you are reluctant to apply for it to the brethren, but I am firmly persuaded that it is the Lord's will for us so to do, and to take full fellowship with the believers.'

He was about to depart for his day at the office. Since their conversion, the atmosphere at West Lawn had changed: Peg no longer sang in the kitchen after breakfast and Robson no longer pinched her bottom; while Cook was continually in a grey temper and for ever persecuting Sal for her clumsiness and stupidity.

'Let us lay it earnestly before the Lord in prayer today, Susannah,' Blair suggested, taking her hands in his. 'Let us entreat Him to lead us into all truth, so that we may be at one upon the subject this evening and feel confident to approach brother Synge about it after the meeting.'

She stood at the window and watched him go down the drive in his old black coat and unpolished boots, and felt an inward desperation at the thought of having to go through with it. She didn't want to walk into the sea in front of a crowd of laughing townspeople. She had no wish to be pressed down under the waves by brother Synge or even, for that matter, brother Newton from Plymouth who was coming to be regarded as a leader of the brethren in Devon.

She left the breakfast room and went along the passage to the library, where she stood surrounded by the loaded shelves of her father's books.

It was not simply a matter of disliking the physical experience of baptism at all: it went much deeper than that. Her loyalties were being split all over again. She had already made a start on the memorial to her father and had read most of his works since Benjamin's death. She did not accept all his ideas, but she understood them and was attracted by the logic of some of them. Dr Brougham had argued that the time was ripe for the Anglican Church to return to its apostolic origins, to repair the rift with Rome and return into the original unity of the early church. How extraordinary it was that the aims and beliefs of the brethren at Ebenezer tended in exactly the same direction and yet in exactly the *opposite* direction! Both her father and these new brethren advocated a return to Christian orthodoxy, and yet each pointed to the other as the epitome of error, the latterday Babylon.

She sat at her bureau for a long time, staring vacantly into space, examining her fingernails, sighing with closed eyes. Could it be that it was the Lord's will for her to embrace a belief that was so directly opposed to that of her father? On the other hand, how could she possibly defy her own husband and refuse to be one with him in baptism? If she believed in nothing else she believed in the sanctity of her marriage vows: yes, she had perhaps entered into them lightly, but that rendered them no less binding. And having been guilty of disloyalty to her father, having murdered him in her heart, was she now to make the same mistake with Blair?

She opened her Bible and continued her reading of St Luke's gospel, praying for guidance while she read.

Woe unto thee Bethsaida! . . . and thou, Capernaum, which art exalted to heaven, shalt be thrust down to hell . . .

She continued on through the parable of the Good Samaritan and the story of Mary and Martha; she read again the account of Jesus teaching his disciples to pray, and of the good and bad gifts; she saw those words, *blessed is the womb that bare thee and the paps which thou hast sucked* and remembered her own mother using Christ's rejoinder to refute the Maryan doctrines of the Church of Rome.

Then, a little while later a passage leapt at her from the page:

But I have a baptism to be baptised with; Suppose ye
that I am come to give peace on earth? I tell you, Nay,
but rather division: For from henceforth there shall be
five in one house divided three against two, and two
against three. The father shall be divided against the
son, and the son against the father; the mother against
the daughter, and the daughter against the mother; the
mother in law against her daughter in law, and the
daughter in law against her mother in law . . .

She shut up the Bible and put it aside, unable to read
further, and paced about the library in agitation. It
seemed that for every instruction or assertion she could
find in Scripture she could also find an opposite, and the
more she read and prayed, far from growing in certainty
and assurance as did Blair, the more she became tortured
and confused.

She stared down at the Persian rug by the bay window
where a bright triangle of sunlight crept imperceptibly
across the room. Really it would be easier to turn her back
on both doctrines – to abandon Christianity altogether,
whether Protestant, Catholic, Anglican or dissenting –
and live in the world and for the world, boldly accepting
whatever eternal punishment the Almighty chose to mete
out to her.

And if I were not married I could do that, she mused,
and for a moment imagined herself again in that impossible country cottage, alone with her books and her writings
and a small, close circle of true friends.

Blair found Susannah still in the library when he arrived
home that afternoon. He rang for Peg to bring in the tea
and settled himself in his favourite chair by the window,
and Susannah saw that he had something to tell her by the
pleased look on his face and his impatience with Peg to set
the tray down and leave them alone.

'Now then,' he said when Peg had gone. 'I have taken a

176

decision and arranged an auction. Mr Hartwell informs me that the earliest he could hold one is in the first week of July, so if we are baptised at the end of this month, the two events will be conveniently linked.'

'An auction?' she asked. 'Did you say an auction?'

'I did indeed, Susannah, and I feel very much at peace in my heart over it too. As soon as I walked into Mr Hartwell's offices I knew that the Lord was guiding my footsteps, and when I came out again, why, I could have shouted for joy.'

'But what do you wish to sell?'

He made a broad sweep of his hand. 'Everything but the necessities. All our effects. It came to me with great force this morning, dear. The Lord spoke to me direct. I saw that in His wisdom He wishes me to remain in business, but that I am led to abandon all worldly possessions.' He beamed. 'We shall lay up treasures in heaven, Susannah, where the moth and rust cannot corrupt.'

She was quite at a loss for words, and he took her silence for acquiescence. 'I thought we might go down this evening for the ministry of the Word, and afterwards inform brother Synge of our intention. It will convince him of our sincere desire for baptism and will ensure our earliest acceptance into fellowship –'

She turned quickly, a spot of colour in each cheek and a hint of the old fire in her forget-me-not eyes. 'These things are not yours to auction, Blair. I inherited them from my parents.'

He said nothing for some moments, as if seeing that a battle was about to start and deciding on his tactics.

'Susannah! You say you inherited them from your parents? Don't you accept that every good gift comes from God? Don't you believe that we are nothing without Him?'

'Yes, I do believe that. But I believe also that I should honour my father and my mother –'

'Honour them, yes, but not their riches! We have gone

over this a dozen times, and you have never once raised an objection. I have laid it before the Lord, Susannah, and He has guided me upon the matter.'

'All the same, I know that my father would not have wished me to disperse them. I do not feel they are mine to sell, Blair, but rather a collection of which I am the custodian –'

He laughed in a way that she could see he intended to be kindly, but its effect struck her as the reverse. 'You *know*? You say you *know* what your father would have wished? How can you say that? How can you be so sure?'

'Because I am his daughter!' she replied heatedly, and tossed her head so that a lock of fine hair fell over her brow.

He relaxed, confident of victory. 'Exactly, exactly,' he chortled. 'And I, being by adoption one of the sons of God am led to believe that I know the mind of my Heavenly Father with far greater accuracy. It is His will that we sell our goods and give alms; the Scriptural direction is perfectly clear. What is more, it is also clear that He made the woman to be subject to the man and has directed wives to be obedient to their husbands. We are one flesh, Susannah, and you are bound to obey me till death us do part. We must not be unequally yoked, nor riven with all manner of disputations.'

She was sickened by this new way he had of larding his conversation with biblical reference, and turned away from him, her shoulders shaking in powerless rage; while Blair, seeing that he had achieved the victory, paused a moment to savour it before telling her, 'When your heart has been softened on the matter please inform me, Susannah, so that we can go forward together to brother Synge and take up our cross in baptism,' and with that he left her to weep alone in the library while he mounted the staircase to his dressing room in the total conviction that it was his privilege to know the Lord's will, and his duty to see that his wife obeyed it.

Downstairs, Susannah went from room to room, admiring her earthly treasures. She ran her fingers along the polished grain of the Broadwood; she picked up the fine porcelain figures from the piecrust, recalling her very earliest memories of her parents; she stared at the wonderful portrait of her mother done by Sir Joshua Reynolds. How dare he arrange to sell these beautiful things without reference to her! And how dare he place her yet again in this dichotomy of loyalties!

She felt herself buffeted back and forth between two high walls of conscience. It is my duty to obey my husband, it is my duty to honour my father and my mother, it is my duty to seek out and follow God's will. I must be meek because I am a woman, I must be obedient because I am a wife. Why? Why? Because you murdered your father, because you slept with Zilla, because you caused your son to drown. Watch and pray that ye enter not into temptation, Susannah; die to the world: go down into the water even as your son Benjamin went down into that foul corner of scum and filth and garbage . . . .

Her shriek brought Cook to the kitchen door in time to see the mistress run away upstairs to her room. She flung herself down on her bed and gave way to hysterical weeping, which took the form of a succession of little muffled yelps like those made by a rabbit when given alive to an adder; and only when Blair had come to her, and put his arms about her, did she become calm.

He sat with her on the bed, bringing her head close, under his chin. He talked quietly and persuasively of the love and infinite wisdom of the Lord. He fondled her, smoothing his hand up and down her arm and gently brushing the undersides of her breasts.

'This is the last struggle of Beelzebub to win over your soul, dearest. But it is over now and he is beaten. You are safe in the everlasting arms.'

'I keep seeing Benjamin!' she whispered. 'In the water.

179

I see him, Blair – as he was, when they lifted him up . . .'
She turned to face him. 'What has happened to him? Is he
in glory?'

Blair was conscious of a new responsibility as a husband. From now on, Susannah would be dependent upon
him for guidance and spiritual leadership.

'We cannot know the answer to that until the last day,'
he said gently, 'when the books are opened. But if, as is
possible, Benjamin died in disobedience, then let that be
the most powerful lesson to us both: for if he died in
disobedience, how much more important is it that we
should live in obedience.'

He released her, and took his Bible from the bedside
table, opening it at Genesis iii 16. 'You have heard these
words before, Susannah, but I want you to listen to them
now with new ears: "Unto the woman he said, I will
greatly multiply thy sorrow and thy conception; in sorrow
thou shalt bring forth children; and thy desire shall be to
thy husband, and he shall rule over thee." ' He lifted her
chin and looked into her sad eyes. 'Is your heart still
hardened, dear? Surely not! Make the decision joyfully,
now that you have started on the upward path toward it.
Go on with confidence and without faltering.'

She gazed back at him and he could not help thinking
how lovely and fragile she was now that the Lord had
subdued the fleshly rebellion in her.

'Will you agree to baptism then?' he asked. 'And to
selling what we have and giving alms in accordance with
Christ's teaching?'

She felt utterly broken. Dimly, she saw the possibility of
running away and abandoning her house, her husband and
her home; but how could she live? She had no money of
her own, it was all made over to Blair. She was his chattel
as surely as all those fine things he intended to put under
the hammer. There was no point in resisting further: she
could not win, however hard she tried. Perhaps, too, this
feeling of being in ruins was good and preordained and in

accord with God's will: perhaps it was necessary to be brought down into this depth of humility before being able to live for Christ. So she bowed her head and whispered her consent, and Blair let out a great gust of relief and offered his thanks to the Lord.

'As you are feeling out of sorts I shall go alone to the ministry,' he said, 'and will apply for baptism on your behalf as well as my own.'

She remained sitting on the bed, and listened to the sound of his steps going down the stairs; and while the evening sun sent level rays across her room, the thought went round and round in her mind that there were only a few weeks remaining before she would go down into the water and die to the world.

'. . . for we ask it in the name and for the sake of our Lord Jesus, amen,' said Blair, and opened his eyes.

Morning prayers were over. Mrs Stapleton got painfully up from her knees, and the other servants did likewise, old Litton indulging in a short but useful piece of coughing which held the promise of a satisfactory spit in the privy as soon as his old legs could get him there.

But while Mrs Stapleton headed for the door and Peg and Sal brushed their aprons with their hands, Blair took the head of the table and ordered them to remain a few minutes longer.

He placed his slender fingers on the mahogany and turned the corners of his mouth down, as if there were a nasty smell under his nose. The servants resumed their seats along the wall, each clasping the Bible that had been provided for their individual use. He invited them to turn to the sixteenth chapter of the Acts of the Apostles, and this caused a flurry of whisperings and rustling pages among all except old Litton and Sal, neither of whom could read more than their own names, and who were therefore excused the labour of following.

When they were ready, he began to read. In the past ten

weeks, having read from the Scriptures every morning, he had begun to develop a style of his own, pausing after texts of particular importance, or tapping lightly with his fingers on the table to emphasise certain words or phrases. Now, he read to them the account first of Lydia who was baptised with her household, then of a certain damsel from whom Paul cast out a spirit, and then of the imprisonment of Paul and Silas and the miraculous earthquake which brought about their release.

'And they spake unto him the word of the Lord, and to all that were in his house. And he took them the same hour of the night, and washed their stripes; and was baptised, he and all his, straightway.' Blair closed up the Bible and placed it reverently on the table before him, allowing the silence to lengthen before addressing his household.

'Last night, at Ebenezer, I solemnly applied for baptism to brothers Synge and Starling on behalf of myself, my wife and all my household, and I speak to you now to inform you of the fact and to express my earnest wish that we shall all be baptised together, as was the custom of the earliest Christians, so that it shall be a witness for the Lord in this dark town of Teignmouth.' He paused, looking up and down at the row of faces before him, and glancing briefly at Susannah, who sat by the window sill where a bowl of early sweet peas brought a delicate colour that contrasted with the darker panelling.

'And further, having been greatly exercised on the matter all night and for several days past, I am led to the conviction that should any one of yourselves harden his heart and choose to remain in darkness, then I shall be obliged, with sadness in my heart, to release that person from my employ.'

He picked up the Bible again and turned to Matthew xii. 'For every city or house divided against itself shall not stand,' he read solemnly, and gazed again at the servants in order to let the meaning sink in.

Later, when Mr Harvey had departed to his offices, Cook called a meeting in the kitchen. She was approaching fifty now, a woman with arms made muscular from the pounding of dough, and a fierce independence caused by early widowhood. She waited for Litton to scrape his boots and requested Robson to move his chair away from Sal's, then called for silence.

'So what are we going to do about it?' she challenged, her back to the rows of kitchen plates on the bracket.

'Do about what, Mrs Stapleton?' Peg said, supporting her bosom upon folded arms.

'Don't 'ee never listen?' Cook scolded. 'He's giving us an ultimatum, that's what. He's saying that either we get ourselves baptised or we find another position.'

'Get under or get out like, innit?' Dallmyer added, and nodded wisely.

'Don't 'ee want to get baptised, then?' Sal enquired.

'Want to? A woman of my age? Not likely! I'll not make a fool of meself! I'd rather go into the poorhouse!'

'I wouldn't say that, I wouldn't say that,' Litton rumbled.

'No one's baptising me, that's certain,' Dallmyer said.

'What about you, Robby?'

The valet pressed his white hands together, his large eyes sliding back and forth from Sal to Peg. He blushed, and mumbled he'd seen the light and felt bound to follow his master's example, though it wasn't clear from this whether he meant Blair or his Master with a capital M.

Mrs Stapleton turned to old Litton. 'Well, Addy? You'll never be going into the sea with that chest of yours?'

Mr Litton hacked obligingly and said he wasn't at all sure.

'I don't see what else me and Sal can do,' Peg said, ' 'cos there's few enough positions in Teignmouth as it is, and there don't seem nothing wrong with it, do there? I seen 'em at it last summer: you get a bit laughed at, but what's that? Bit o' laughter never 'urt nobody.'

'*I* want to be baptised,' Sal blurted, and flushed immediately.

'In that case you're a silly girl and don't know what's good for you,' Mrs Stapleton said crossly. 'If we all stuck together Mr Harvey'd have to think again. As it is, well I just don't know, but I'll say this clear out: I'll not be dipped in the sea for a king's ransom, and if it means I lose my position, so be it.'

She repeated this message in gentler terms to Susannah, who had taken a chair onto the lawn to enjoy the sun. 'No disrespect, Madam, but I can't find it in me to go along wi' it. I'd like to remain as cook but if Mr Harvey can't have me in the house like 'e said, then I'll have to go, and Addy Litton's asked me to speak likewise for him on the matter. I'm sorry, Madam, but there it is like, but what has to be has to be, and all I can do is wish it otherwise.'

Susannah, aware that the matter was already out of her hands, accepted this resignation without opposition, along with Dallmyer's a few minutes later when he came to tell her that as there was a position for a coachman vacant with Lord Clifford he thought it for the best to leave as soon as possible.

'So we shall have no cook, no gardener and no coachman,' she told Blair on his return that evening. 'Unless you are prepared to reconsider what you told them this morning.'

He snorted at the suggestion. 'I shall certainly not reconsider. I would not dream of it. They will not hold a gun to my head in this way. No, I shall let them go and have their trade union under someone else's roof.' He crossed to the sitting room mantel and rang a brass bell. 'Peg,' he said when she entered a few moments later. 'Run along and ask Cook to come and speak with me.'

Peg's face fell. 'Sir – she's in the middle of straining the broth for the calf's foot jelly!'

'That can wait, Peg. I wish to see her immediately. And Dallmyer, if you please.'

Peg hurried out. Susannah folded her hands in her lap and gave a barely audible sigh. Blair ignored it. He sat upright on a velvet upholstered chair, the tail of his coat like a black tongue on the Axminster.

Cook arrived, and a minute later, Dallmyer.

'Mrs Harvey has told me of your decision,' Blair started, 'and I understand that Litton is of like mind.'

'That is so, sir, yes,' answered Mrs Stapleton, and closed up her mouth so abruptly there was almost a snap.

A clock of gold and porcelain chimed melodiously on the mantel. It was half-past six. In an hour, Blair and Susannah would walk down the hill to Ebenezer for the prayer meeting.

'I wonder if you understand the exact nature of that decision, Mrs Stapleton, and you, Dallmyer. I wonder if you are aware, for instance, that it is not merely this temporal household that you are choosing to turn your backs on, but also the eternal household of God?' Blair puffed his cheeks out and stared first at one, then the other. 'Do you understand that those who have heard the gospel and yet turn away from it are doubly guilty, for they re-crucify Christ and are inevitably destined for the lake of fire, and endless torment down the halls of time? Had you given thought to that?'

Mrs Stapleton looked from side to side. Dallmyer, a stocky man in knee breeches with bowed legs and a fiery complexion sucked his teeth audibly. 'I believe in God, sir, always have, an' I reckon that's good enough for any man. "Love God and honour the King," sir, that's my motto.'

Blair reached for his Bible and began to search for a suitable text, and there was silence in the room while he blew pages apart in Timothy and Philemon. 'Ah well, I cannot find the passage at the minute,' he said eventually. 'But I am quite sure that I have the authority of Scripture in this.' His manner softened: 'Come – let us kneel together and beg our Lord's pardon for contemplating such a course. Let us ask Him to show us the way.'

But Mrs Stapleton was not to be persuaded, and before Blair could get to his knees she came out with a firm, 'No. I don't believe it, sir, and I won't believe it, neither. I was baptised when I was a babe in arms and brung up as a good Christian, and I've no reason to think I'll go into any lake of fire, nor am I going to get meself baptised to save me job. I'm sorry sir, but that's the beginning and the end of it.'

'That goes for me, sir, as well.' Dallmyer said, looking at his boots.

'And Addy Litton an' all,' Mrs Stapleton said, and turned to Susannah to add: 'I'm sorry about this, Ma'am.'

Blair stood up, and towered over the recalcitrants. He was wearing his hair longer these days: it was brushed straight off his high forehead and was thick and wavy, like a mane at the back of his head. 'In that case I shall say to you now what the Lord will surely say to you at the last day: "I never knew you: depart from me, ye that work iniquity." '

'Is that it then, sir?' Mrs Stapleton enquired, sticking her chin defiantly in his direction and slanting her head a little to one side. 'You giving us the sack?'

'I am not giving you the sack, Mrs Stapleton, nor am I pushing you out. No, it is you who are turning away into darkness, let us be quite clear about that.'

'In that case, if I'm going into darkness, you won't be wanting my fingers in your pastry this evening,' she replied, and turned on her heel.

Dallmyer opened his mouth to speak, thought better of it, and followed her out.

Blair stood in the bay window looking out over his garden. 'I was not too harsh with them, was I Susannah?'

She said nothing, so he looked back at her. 'What are you thinking? That I have done wrong?'

'No, no,' she replied absently. 'I was not thinking that.'

'Then you approve of my action?'

'Is that for me to say? Provided you have acted in accordance with your conscience, you have no need to be concerned.'

He turned back, and looked out at the neatly tended lawns and flower beds, and after another long silence gave a little snort and said, 'I never did like that woman's gravy.'

The baptism was announced to the public ten days in advance by means of a notice that was put up outside Ebenezer chapel. The people of Teignmouth were informed that, God willing, Mr Benjamin Wills Newton of Plymouth would visit Teignmouth for the purpose of preaching in the open air on the Den at six-thirty in the evening of Sunday 24 June, after which the public baptism of five brothers and sisters in Christ would be performed in the sea.

The buzz went quickly round the town that the five to be baptised were Mr Harvey and his household, and the subject became a humorous talking point in the local taverns. People knew that Harvey's cook and coachman had left him, and old Litton had been found dead of pneumonia in the porch of St Michael's soon after being dismissed from West Lawn; they also knew that all the priceless treasures of West Lawn were being put up for auction, and there was speculation about whether the Harveys would keep their promise and give away the proceeds to the poor. As for the fun-loving Peg and the poor simpleton Sal, people said they were more to be pitied than blamed.

The day approached; the day arrived. It started sunny, but by mid-afternoon a bank of cloud had moved in from the west and the sea was looking uninvitingly metallic, with short waves tumbling in rapid succession on the shore.

In West Lawn, where Peg's culinary hopelessness had obliged Susannah to take over command in the kitchen, and Litton's departure had caused Blair to wield a hoe for the first time in his life, there was an atmosphere of nervous anticipation. Susannah had had white cotton dresses run up for Sal and Peg, and had herself decided to wear her everyday dress, telling herself that the occasion of her baptism would be the last on which she would wear it. Blair had discovered his old cricket outfit in a trunk and looked oddly sporting for the ceremony, while Robson had borrowed a seaman's outfit and looked extraordinary in smock and serge.

They set out in a group a little after six, Blair and Susannah arm in arm and the servants following behind. They went down the sycamore avenue and past St James's, where the evening bells were summoning more conventional worshippers to evensong.

A crowd was already gathering by the time they reached the Den. Faces were peering out of windows along Powderham Terrace and urchins were playing and tumbling in the sand. At the water's edge, beside two bathing machines hired for the evening, forty or so brethren and sisters from Ebenezer chapel had gathered, and there was a noticeable increase in the numbers of gentry taking an evening constitutional on the promenade.

Brother Starling had been elected to lead the singing before the meeting opened, and as soon as the Harvey household arrived announced the first hymn, which he pitched a fraction high so that some of the ladies had to sing an octave below for the high notes and some were inclined to shriek:

> Come to the living water come!
> Sinners obey your Maker's voice!
> Return, ye weary wanderers home,
> And in redeeming love rejoice.

The wind strengthened perceptibly. White horses appeared out at sea, and Susannah saw Blair look at the water and shiver.

Brother Newton, the elder from the Plymouth assembly, led the meeting in prayer. 'Pour down O Lord thy plenteous blessings upon these thy humble servants who now take up their cross,' he prayed, a neat, dark figure, his hands gripped tightly together at his waist. 'May they find new life in Thee, and may other wanderers be raised up to the Lord through their witness.'

They sang another hymn. During it, the crowd of spectators increased considerably. How many were there now, Susannah wondered, glancing quickly back. Three hundred? Four? She felt suddenly sick and found herself to be trembling all over.

Brother Newton was speaking of the last days. He was warning of the antichrist and the tribulation. He was appealing to those who had ears to hear, to turn to the Lord Jesus before it was too late. He enlarged upon the meaning of baptism by immersion and explained the symbolic representation of Christ's descent into hell and resurrection. The wind carried his voice up and away toward the curved facade of regency buildings along the sea front, and as he spoke some of the spectators edged closer to listen.

While they sang one more hymn, brother Newton went into one of the bathing machines and appeared a minute later having removed his topcoat and donned a huge pair of waterproof waders. He beckoned to Blair, and together they walked down into the surf.

'Blair Octavius Harvey!' shouted brother Newton over the sound of the waves. 'Dost thou confess that Jesus Christ is the Son of God? Dost thou believe in thy heart and confess Him with thy mouth?'

'I do!' bellowed Harvey, upon which Newton placed one hand in the small of Blair's back and the other on his chest, pushing him backward into the waves; but because of Blair's weight and size was unable to bring him up again immediately, so that Blair spent all of five seconds under the water and came up spluttering and coughing and gasping for breath.

The urchins on the beach whistled and cheered and ran round in circles, while brother Starling led the believers in the first verse of a baptismal hymn:

> Beneath the mystic waves of death
> Obediently we go;
> And thus, O Lord! our part with thee
> In death and burial show.

Susannah was next. Some people said she was weeping when she went down into the sea, but no one could be certain. She submitted herself entirely to the arms of brother Newton, and after it was over walked back to the bathing machine with her hands joined and her eyes fixed upon the darkening sky.

Then it was Robson, then it was Peg and finally Sal, who let out a great shriek as she was pushed into the sea, and who came running up the beach in nervous giggles afterwards.

'O Ma'am!' she said loudly and clearly inside the bathing machine, so that those standing outside could hear every word. 'I think they seen my titties through my dress, like!'

Walking back after the prayer meeting following the baptism, Susannah experienced an unexpected feeling of release and happiness. It was done now. There was no going back: she could never be unbaptised, she was committed.

She clung to Blair's arm. Brother Synge had prayed most lovingly at the meeting, and she had wept in spite of a valiant effort not to. She looked up at Blair and was thankful to have him as her husband, to be able to lean

190

against him and obey him.

He patted her hand and stopped. They stood facing each other, alone together in the tunnel of foliage of the drive. 'We shall be happy now, dear,' he whispered.

'Yes, I believe it,' she replied.

He kissed her lightly on the forehead; she wanted him to hold her – wanted him to crush her in his arms. She wanted to be in him, and wanted him to be in her. But instead he looked gravely down at her for a moment before taking her arm again and going on up the drive to the house.

They were met by Peg, who had gone on ahead with Robby and Sal. She stood in the porch, white faced.

'What in the world is the matter?' Susannah asked.

Peg stood wringing her hands and shaking her head and saying, 'Oh Ma'am! Sir!'

At the same time a voice called from the drive, 'Good evening!'

They turned. It was Miss Cox in a layered taffeta.

'Is everything all right?' she enquired. 'I saw a wagon outside your door when I came back from evensong but I didn't like to intrude as I knew it was – it was your – ah –'

She looked from one to the other, a neat parasol in her small white hands, a reticule hanging by a silver chain over her arm.

'We've been visited, Ma'am,' Peg said. 'Thieves. All the silver and plate! All gone!'

They left Miss Cox in the drive and went inside. All the smaller oil paintings had gone from the drawing and dining rooms, together with every figurine, miniature and portable clock.

They went into the library and looked about them at the rifled drawers and strewn papers.

Blair went down on his knees. 'We thank thee O Lord, for giving us this sign, for teaching us so clearly to scorn the love of our possessions and to count for nothing the value of household gods.'

Susannah turned away from him and found on the carpet a musical box which had been given her by her mother for her tenth birthday. She held it sadly in her hands and opened the lid. The delicate notes sprang forth in the silence, and she recalled, in spite of herself, the words of the song she had learnt at her mother's knee:

> The price I offer, my sweet pretty maid,
>> Singing, singing, buttercups and daisies,
> A ring of gold on your finger displayed,
>> Folde dee!
> So come, make over to me your ware,
>> In church to-day at Strawberry Fair.
>
> Rifol, Rifol, Tol-de-riddle-i-do,
> Rifol, Rifol, Tol-de-riddle-dee.

CHAPTER 10

'At fifteen shillings, ladies and gentlemen,' announced Mr Hatwell, looking over his spectacles at the gathering of bargain hunters in the library at West Lawn. 'For the first time. For the second time –' The gavel came smartly down and the last item in the auction – a dumb waiter – became the property of a pleased and blushing Miss Cox, whose earlier purchase of the Broadwood had been the surprise of the day.

'Ladies and gentlemen, that concludes the auction,' Mr Hartwell called, raising his voice to be heard over the buzz of conversation. 'May I thank you for your attendance and custom, and at the same time remind you that Mr Harvey has made a special request that all lots be removed from the premises by tomorrow afternoon at the latest, thank you.'

The auctioneer stepped down from the raised platform, and the buyers, spectators and busybodies prepared to leave. In the hall, Susannah and Blair stood together and nodded their goodbyes. The Tobins, the Cliffords, and other erstwhile friends shook them by the hand and murmured pleasantries, each avoiding what was uppermost in everybody's mind, namely that having sold their possessions the Harveys had effectively locked themselves out of polite society for good.

Peg brought tea into the drawing room when the last of them were gone. Her pattens echoed on the bare boards as she came in. Every carpet and rug in the house had been taken up: every ornament, every last piece of Wedgwood and crystal had been sold. The very building seemed numbed by the shock of it.

'So now,' Blair said, slowly stirring his tea, 'all that remains to be sold is the books.' He looked across at Susannah, who sat in a cheap wicker chair. 'Will that sadden you, dear?'

'Perhaps,' she said. 'But I am resigned to it.'

Outside, a pigeon cooed sleepily in the walnut.

Blair leant back in his chair and opened his knees in a way Susannah had always found slightly offensive. 'On reflection, I'm glad we decided to take them out of the auction,' he said. 'And not simply because they might fetch a better price in Exeter, either.'

'Are you thinking of keeping them after all, Blair?'

His eyes swivelled. Now that the auction was over, the house seemed oddly quiet. It was one of those sultry summer days when trees and plants droop, waiting for the cool of the evening.

'Would you like that?'

She looked down at her hands. 'I thought we had agreed to sell them.'

He made a series of little grunting noises. 'We did not agree to sell them, Susannah – only that we should be rid of them. We agreed that they represent a symbol of worldliness that we can well do without. We agreed, did we not, that the highest Christian must necessarily decline the pursuit of science, knowledge, art, history – except so far as any of these things might be made useful tools, for immediate spiritual results.'

She was tempted to reply that when the books were gone, he would still have his Oxford degree while she would be left with nothing – but resisted the temptation, confident that Blair would enlarge upon his theme and come to his decision without any further assistance from herself.

He had gone to the window and was now standing with

his back to her, flexing his shoulders and bouncing gently on his heels. It was a sure sign to her that he was about to make a special announcement.

'I think we should burn them,' he said. 'Yes, I think we should burn the whole lot. Books, papers, manuscripts – even your memorial, Susannah. Are they for edification? No they are not, and therefore, I say, to sell them would be to accept money from the devil. We should have a holy bonfire, have done with the lot. All that pagan mythology, all that tendentious, papist – yes, Sal, what is it?'

'Gentleman's gentleman just brought this, sir,' said the maid and crossed the room to bring him a sealed letter.

He nodded to dismiss her and broke the seal. It was from a firm of solicitors in Plymouth, and was written in elegant copperplate with swooping tails on the g's and y's, and a quaint use of the old fashioned s.

Sir,

The sale by auction of your household effects has recently been brought to our attention, and in view of other circumstances to which we are privy, we beg to advise you not to dispose of the proceeds from the said sale before first consulting with ourselves.

While we are aware of your generous and admirable intention to donate the monies raised to charity, we feel it incumbent upon ourselves to inform you that it will be greatly to your advantage, and to the advantage of the religious body of which you and your wife have recently become members, to grant us a short consultation before putting into effect your charitable intent.

To this end, we propose a private meeting between yourself and our Mr Digby in the Royal Hotel, Teignmouth, on Wednesday 4 July 1832, where the pleasure of your company is requested at lunch in the private dining room at twelve o'clock, noon.

We shall be obliged, sir, if you will advise us at

your earliest convenience of your acceptance, so that if you are unable to attend, alternative arrangements can be made.

Assuring you of our respect and duty,
We remain,

Ignatius Pulvertaft
for Messrs Digby, Hawkins & Digby.

Blair frowned over this for some time before handing it to Susannah.

'Will you accept?' she asked when she had read it.

'If I judge it to be the Lord's will, yes,' he said. 'But my first reaction is to reject it out of hand. To me, that letter smells of mammon; I should be very surprised if Messrs Hawkins and Digby are inviting me to lunch out of any altruistic motive. No, I suspect "our Mr Digby" will turn out to be a young fortune hunter who thinks he can make a fast sovereign by taking advantage of my Christian charity.'

'But you will never know what they wish to suggest unless you accept,' Susannah observed gently.

'I shall wait upon the Lord to guide me upon the matter,' he said, and left it at that.

Whether the Lord guided him, or the prospect of a free lunch at the Royal appeared too tempting an offer to refuse, not even Blair himself could have told: his decision to accept being – like most of his decisions – the result of an amalgam of intuitive desire, pious intention and inward rationalisation. The result was that he presented himself as requested at Cockram's hotel and was led along carpeted corridors by Inman, who gushed about how pleathant it wath to thee Mr Harvey again after all thethe weekth.

The private dining room was an elegant place with brocade curtains and striped wallpaper. The pillar-and-claw dining table was by Adam Smith, and a gilt and

196

painted sofa occupied the wall under the sash windows. Having lunched here with private clients before, Blair could not help feeling pleased to be back in such prestigious surroundings.

A gentleman in a brown coat and pale beige trousers was looking at himself in the gilded mirror over the mantelpiece when Blair was shown in, and when he turned, Blair received a little shock that caused him to go redder and blink faster than usual.

'Mr Harvey,' said the gentleman as Inman withdrew. 'Charles Digby. Delighted to make your acquaintance.' His eyes twinkled mischievously: he was an aristocratic looking man, a good five years older than Harvey, with humorous, hooded eyes and neatly trimmed whiskers. 'Though – I believe we have met before, haven't we? On a windy afternoon in Oddicombe, if I remember rightly.'

Blair looked puzzled and claimed he didn't recall the occasion.

'But you must, you must!' said Mr Digby cheerfully. 'You were coming down the hill in your gig, and I mistook you for a pastor! But then you were in mourning, weren't you? For a close relative, was it?'

'My son.'

'Ah, your son, yes indeed, how tragic that was.' Digby unstopped a cut glass decanter with a very wide base – the sort that is found on board ship. 'A glass of sherry, Mr Harvey? Or is that against your religion?'

Blair felt himself getting hot. 'I will take a glass, thank you,' he said crisply.

Digby indicated the sofa to Blair and took one of the Trafalgar dining chairs himself. 'Of course you are something of a celebrity in Oddicombe, aren't you, Mr Harvey? Since that very afternoon when the *Fair Intention* foundered. They tell me that there was an article in the *Christian Witness* on the subject which described the affair as a miraculous answer to prayer.'

Blair tapped his knee self-consciously, unsure whether

197

Mr Digby were making fun of him or not. He knew that here was a ready-made situation in which to witness for the Lord, but there was something in Digby's urbane manner which utterly forbade it.

'I believe something was written about it, yes –' he ventured.

Digby told him he must not hide his light under a bushel so, and put his tongue rather obviously in his cheek. Blair began to feel distinctly uncomfortable.

Mr Digby then changed tack, and began to take pains to put his guest at ease. He drew Blair out about his mother, his sisters and his home background, and discovered that he had originally been destined for a career in law; and before they sat down to the soup he insisted upon another bumper of sherry.

The meal was excellent. A fine Dover sole was served with a most delicate Muscadet wine, and while they ate, Mr Digby regaled Blair with such charming conversation that it was quite impossible for him to raise the question of exactly why he had been invited; and by the time Inman came in with the Hine and the balloon glasses, Blair was becoming happily impatient to hear from his host what it was that might be so much to his advantage.

Mr Digby pushed his chair back from the table and gently swilled the golden liquid about in his glass, unconsciously proving, by the way he held it, that he was something of a connoisseur.

'You will forgive my asking,' he remarked casually, 'but would I be correct in believing that you were at one time acquainted with a Mrs Pendlebury?'

Blair Harvey looked into his brandy glass, which was already emptier than Mr Digby's. He felt suddenly old, and pale – but not very superior.

'I think you were, weren't you?' coaxed Digby. 'At least, many of the folk in that part of the world believe you to have been.' He smiled, and winked knowingly.

Blair felt a positive thud in his chest. When he spoke,

his own voice sounded to him as if he were being strangled. 'We were – er – passing acquaintances, yes.'

'Only passing acquaintances? We were under the impression that you were rather firm friends, Mr Harvey.'

'Firm friends . . .' echoed Blair.

'What does it matter what you were!' said Digby generously. 'All that matters is whether or not you will contest the lady's sworn affidavit that you are the father of her child.'

Blair disgraced himself at this point, behaving entirely predictably by closing his eyes, groaning and saying 'Oh God, oh God, you can't do this to me, please, no.'

Mr Digby had experience of such situations and waited for the waves of remorse and shock to pass – but did so a little apprehensively, for it seemed by Mr Harvey's sudden change of colour that he might at any moment return his soup, his sole and his saddle of lamb upon the pristine white damask tablecloth.

'We are not doing anything to you, Mr Harvey. We are simply acting on the behalf and at the behest of our client.'

Blair had put his head in his hands and was swaying the weight of it back and forth upon his elbows. His mind was racing with brief, unsavoury recollections: of Lavinia writhing naked in his embrace, her sweat-damp body heaving and arching in ecstasy; of her eyes rolling upward in their sockets at the moment of her wild delirium, her voice mannish in the gusty appreciation of his voluntary service.

He gave a strangled cry.

'Come, Mr Harvey, it's not the end of the world! Worse things happen at sea, you know. Besides, our client is making a most generous offer. She is aware of your peculiar situation and of the necessity of avoiding any scandal that might disgrace your name or . . . what are they called, the people you are identified with in Teignmouth? "Brethren" is it?'

The silence lengthened, and Digby waited. When Blair

eventually took his hands from his face he looked as if he had aged ten years. 'What is she . . . offering?'

The lawyer joined his hands and leant on the table. 'Excellent,' he said. 'I knew you were a man to see the sense of civilised negotiation, Mr Harvey. What she is offering is to accept from you a once-only settlement to cover the cost of her removal to Italy – which she felt obliged to make for the sake of appearances – and the upbringing and education of your son. Really she is acting in an unusually charitable way towards you. She has even requested that we convey to you her warmest good wishes and her assurance that your secret will never be divulged by her.' Mr Digby beamed and sat back in his chair, taking a pocket watch from his waistcoat and flipping it open in a way that was horrifyingly reminiscent of the late Dr Brougham. 'Always provided you agree to her terms, that is,' he added, closing the hunter with a snap.

'How much does she want?' Blair croaked.

Digby rose from the table, and every last trace of humour vanished from his expression. 'Five thousand pounds sterling is the absolute minimum we have advised her to accept, in return for which we shall be pleased to draw up an agreement – at no cost to yourself, I may add – that will make it clear that you are absolved of all financial, physical and moral responsibility for your child.' He moved to the door. 'I think there is little more for me to say at this stage, and no doubt you will wish to think it over. Perhaps you would let me know your reaction by Friday? Forty-eight hours should be long enough for you to make up your mind. And as we are dealing in round figures, I know that the cost of our luncheon today can also be comfortably borne by your goodself. For which I thank you. Good day, Mr Harvey, and please be sure to let me have your answer by this time on Friday.'

After he had gone, Blair sat dazed and motionless, hardly able to believe what had happened. There was a timid knock on the door: Inman entered.

'I trutht everything wath to your thatithfacthon, Mithter Harvey?' he enquired, fluttering a white hand over the table and licking some small bubbles of froth from the corner of his lip.

Blair could not permit himself to speak. He rose from the table, threw down a sovereign and stalked out: out of the hotel, out of the Den, out of Teignmouth; and somewhere along the rocky coast towards the Parson and Clerk, he faced out to sea and bawled: 'Damn her! Damn her and all her sex!'

Unfortunately, damning Lavinia provided only a short-lived catharsis, and when he had shed a few tears of pity for himself and rage at the flawed teachings of Messrs Bentham and Place, he sat down on a piece of red stone, placed his chin on his fist and – looking like a clothed anticipation of Rodin's Thinker – set about reasoning his way out of the predicament.

He considered the possibility of contesting Lavinia's claim. What would that involve? He would have to retain the services of a lawyer for a start, for he could not venture alone into the maze of litigation such cases inevitably dragged behind them. And even if he employed the best lawyer in the country, he could not see any real hope of proving that the child was not his. He knew instinctively that it must be: during his liaison with Mrs P, she had often assured him that he could call upon her whenever he liked – at any time of day or night, on any day of the week. She had declared herself his, utterly his, and he could not believe that another lover could have enjoyed similar favours at the same time.

He shuddered, and threw a stone into the sharp grey waves.

There were other considerations. He had been seen by the maid on more than one occasion, and Digby's assertion that he was famous in Oddicombe was a fairly accurate one. The very fact that he had not returned after that night the *Fair Intention* foundered had probably added to the mystery surrounding his name, and if all this came out (he closed his eyes at the horror of it) all the adulation would be immediately reversed: he would be reviled and hated, and the infamy of his adulterous conduct would be muttered and whispered right across the county.

And what about Susannah? he wondered. It would break her completely – just when she was beginning to regain her confidence.

He proceeded with a few mental calculations. The sale of effects had raised nearly two thousand pounds, which left three to be raised from capital. He would have to cancel his order for a third vessel right away, that was certain; and he would also have to cash in nearly all of his remaining two percents. He would be left with only a slender margin for emergencies and repairs.

He stood up and picked his way down to the water's edge. 'We shall be poor,' he informed a gull which sat on the waves a few yards out, eyeing him suspiciously. 'We shall be down on our uppers.'

The gull flew away.

He went back over his internal arguments, trying to find an escape route. Then he wondered if his new-found faith might be of assistance, and tried to lay it before the Lord. But in a strange way this matter seemed to lie outside the Lord's jurisdiction, for whatever course of action he followed involved either further sin in deceiving Susannah as to his loyalty or a scandal so horrendous it would turn the brethren at Ebenezer into a laughing stock. The situation seemed to present a clash of principles, a contradiction of moral values: either he must be prepared to perpetuate a deceit for the rest of his life, or he must plunge himself and the woman he loved (yes, on reflection, he *did* love Susannah) into abject misery from which they might never recover.

Then, stealthily, another avenue of action presented

itself to him, and this was suddenly attractive. What if he went back to Susannah and told her that he had made a terrible mistake – that his conversion had not been a conversion at all? What if he told her, bit by bit, the truth of why he had gone down to Oddicombe beach that afternoon, and why his conscience had been so easily pricked by a cackling old woman? What if he admitted the whole ghastly story and at the same time suggested to her that they uproot from Teignmouth, sell up the shipping and banking businesses and go right away together, to start afresh – to leave all this mess behind them, brethren and all?

The idea of it made him shake and sweat: he felt as if he were looking God in the eye – he had never been quite so honest with himself before. And where did such a thought come from? Was it of God or of the devil? He spoke aloud, experimentally: 'Get thee behind me, Satan . . .' and put his head in his hands, trying to pray. Am I saved? he wondered. Or has it all been an act, a part I have been playing? He shook his head from side to side, as if to rid himself of the torment. What guarantee was there, if he slid back into the world, that he would be able to retain Susannah's love? Would he not be lowered in her sight? How could he ever hold up his head again? She might even find cause to separate from him, to draw away from him on account of his despicable behaviour – wasn't there a verse somewhere about that?

He tried to pray direct to God. Although in the months since his conversion he had adopted the practice of referring to the 'Lord Jesus', his childhood habits still remained in his private prayer and he still pictured the Almighty as a Herculean figure whose head blotted out the sun and whose all-seeing eyes looked down upon him from a white-bearded, craggy face. This was God: the God of Abraham and of Isaac, the God who had led the Jews out of the wilderness, the great I Am who would one day sit upon the throne of Judgement.

Perhaps He has placed me in this situation deliberately, he thought, not thinking to ask himself whether God might ever allow anything to happen un-deliberately. Perhaps I am being confronted with the enormity of my sin so that I may be tried in the fire and hardened in God's forge, to be a mighty tool, a weapon for the Lord. Perhaps there is blessing in this, after all: perhaps this is my chance to make amends – to pay the price of past misdeeds in order to be able to put them behind me and walk in the paths of righteousness.

Here at least was some consolation, for he could see that God might be singling him out and giving him a special cross, a secret burden – a thorn in the flesh that would serve as a continual goad to urge him on.

He began to make his way back along the shoreline towards the Den, and as he went he developed this new, encouraging way of viewing what had happened. He began to see that the Lord, having saved him from eternal punishment and raised him up to be one of the elect, was choosing to submit him to special trials, in the manner of Job. Here was something in which he could take holy pride, for was not he, Blair Harvey, a far mightier sinner than most? He had attended enough gospel services to know that every good testimony was prefaced by references to an early life of profligate sinfulness, and he could see already that when the time came for him to preach the gospel he would be able to tell a powerful story indeed. Had not his need of salvation been far greater than that of the average man? And was it not evident that his Lord was now tempering him like steel in order to fit him for the great ministry that lay ahead?

With these thoughts tumbling about in his mind, he made his way up the hill to West Lawn, and as he came up the drive and saw Susannah dead-heading the tea roses by the sundial, he experienced a sudden return of confidence, a certainty that the Lord was directing his path and that he was being tested and would not be found wanting.

204

She joined him on the gravelled forecourt, taking his arm and asking him if he had had a good lunch.

'A good lunch?' he repeated a little distantly. 'Yes, a good lunch.'

'And what of your host? Was he the fortune hunter you expected him to be?'

They strolled arm in arm into the orchard, where greengages and damsons ripened on the boughs.

'No, he was a most respectable lawyer.'

'Then what did he have to say, Blair?'

He paused a moment before replying, although he had already prepared in his mind the answer to this question.

'He has made a suggestion regarding the disposal of our funds to which I feel obliged to give serious consideration.'

'You mean – a business proposition?'

He glanced at her, frowning and puffing his cheeks. 'No, Susannah, there is no worldly profit for us in it. Rather, it is a scheme to benefit the needy in a way that is close to my heart.'

'Then what is it, Blair?' she laughed, pressing his hand and leaning against him.

They had stopped beneath a cherry tree. Blair looked very solemn, and sounded solemn too: 'There is a verse – in St Matthew isn't it? "Let not thy left hand know what thy right hand doeth." I propose to abide by that.'

'You mean – keep it a secret from the world?'

'Yes.'

She looked up at him as if seeing him in a new light.

'That is a wonderful, brave idea, Blair.'

'It is not of myself, dear, but of the Lord. He has told us that when we give alms it should be in secret and has promised that our Father which seeth in secret shall reward us openly.'

They proceeded into the vegetable garden where, since Litton's departure, the groundsel and dandelions had started to overgrow the rows of beetroot, leek and endive.

'How much shall we donate?' Susannah asked.

'Quite a large sum,' he replied, and glanced upward at the sky.

'And may *I* know who will benefit?'

'I think it better not, Susannah.'

She knew already that she was on dangerous ground: she had seen a change in Blair from the moment she had taken his arm in the drive; and while she admired his reason for keeping his alms-giving a secret, she could not help wondering if there might be some motive for him to do so that was not entirely based upon the directive in the gospel according to St Matthew.

'Then – if I am not to know who will benefit, may we send a proportion – say three hundred pounds – to Anthony Groves in Baghdad? You know how much in need they are, Blair, and I believe we should do all we can to support those in the mission field.'

Blair appeared to take particular interest in a pair of bullfinches that flew, one after the other, up to a birch tree on the edge of the property.

'I would like to know the destination of the money,' Susannah went on, feeling a little carried away. 'After all nearly everything we sold came originally from my parents, and you may trust me entirely with the secret. Can't we act as one on the matter dear? May I not know who will benefit from our gift?'

'It is not *our* money, Susannah. It is the Lord's.'

She released herself from his arm and turned away, filled suddenly with unwelcome suspicion. What if he were deceiving her? What if he were planning to invest it secretly in some tea plantation or tin mine? But even the thought of it filled her with a sort of dread, for she had forced herself to believe very strongly that she must be subject to him, that she must obey him in all things. I must not even suspect him, she told herself. He is my husband, we are one flesh. If I do not trust and obey him, we are lost. There is no other way.

She turned back to him and took his thick red palm in her hands. What did it matter what he did with the money? Had she not been thinking only a matter of an hour before how happy she was to have been released from the captivity of her worldly possessions? Had she not rejoiced in this new freedom?

'Provided it goes to a good cause, dear, and I am sure that it will, then I do not wish to know how much is donated or who is to benefit.'

When she looked up into his eyes she saw tears there, and was suddenly moved with love for him; and he, in a rare gesture of affection, took her gently in his arms and held her, staring over the top of her head in bleak resignation to the loneliness of the decision he had taken.

'By the way,' Susannah said as they were about to go back into the house. 'I have some news also. We are to be blessed, God willing, with another child. In January, I expect.'

She had been thinking about this little speech most of the afternoon and had waited for the right moment to deliver it; but Blair, having learnt in one afternoon that he was fathering two offspring by different women could only reward her with a look of stunned surprise.

It was not a happy season for Blair, after that. He spent two sleepless nights wrestling with his conscience, and on Friday afternoon met Mr Digby again and gave his assent to the contract between himself and his former mistress.

That was bad enough, but the actual business of raising the capital sum and making it over to Lavinia was far more painful, for even his most expert rationalisations could not quite hide the fact that he was perpetrating a deceit that would have to burden him for the rest of his life. In the space of a week, he felt himself age ten years: he was assailed by swirling phantasies and nightmares in which he found himself occupied in filthy copulation with Lavinia; he was pursued by fleeting glimpses of everything that was most evil – of fornications, of murders and of the vilest bestiality. All this he had to bear alone, with the result that just when he should have been rejoicing in his salvation, he appeared to the brethren and sisters of Ebenezer as a brother of gloomy countenance indeed.

Each Sunday morning, the Harvey household sat like a family at the breaking of bread, with Peg, Robson and Sal sitting between Blair and Susannah. Now that they had been received into fellowship, each was allowed to break off a piece from the cottage loaf that was passed round on a plate, and to sip from the goblet of wine.

With brother Müller gone, there were few brethren available to minister at Ebenezer, and for the time being Mr Synge, a man of education and position, had assumed the eldership.

A quiet, earnest man, Synge lived comfortably just outside Teignmouth, and had recently been in correspondence with Captain Hall of Plymouth, a naval officer who had resigned his commission in order to follow the Lord. The subject of their correspondence had been the mode of worship to be followed among the brethren, Synge being an ardent anti-clericalist. He was particularly keen to groom newly converted brethren for the task of ministering the Word, and had been quick to see that in Blair Harvey he had a man with a natural gift for leadership among the saints.

One of his principle beliefs was that brethren of like mind should join together in pairs and go out to preach the gospel 'by two and two' in accordance with Mark vi 7, and he prevailed upon Blair to accompany him. They went out every Saturday and Lord's Day, riding on horseback as far as Ashburton, Bovey Tracey, Chudleigh and even Moretonhampstead. Synge conducted prayer meetings and Bible readings in the cottages and preached the gospel outside church gates in the summer evenings; and Blair acted as his listener, the 'plant' round whom larger audiences gathered.

In spite of all Synge's encouragement, Blair found himself quite unable to speak in public. Before his baptism, he had confidently expected to play an active part among the brethren, secretly regarding himself as Müller's natural successor. Now, however hard he tried, he found himself forcibly prevented from opening his mouth.

He knew the cause of it only too well: it was a sense of being unworthy. He felt as if he had signed away his spiritual birthright and had been struck dumb as a punishment. He began to worry more and more about his salvation, and became most fastidious about his personal cleanliness, washing his hands frequently and insisting on a clean shirt every day of the week.

Susannah was aware of his difficulty (though not of its cause) but kept silence about it for some time before broaching it tactfully.

'I wish you would minister one of these days, Blair,' she said one day when they were lunching together after the breaking of bread. 'I am sure you have the gift of it, and I know the brethren are expecting it of you.'

'I have not felt led to do so as yet,' he said, 'nor can I promise that I ever shall be.'

'But is it because you are apprehensive of speaking in public?'

He carefully removed a piece of gristle from his mouth. 'Perhaps.'

'If it would be of any help to discuss any subject upon which you are exercised, I would be happy to listen,' she said. 'It might help you if you voiced them to me, at least.'

'I am not sure that any person can be of help, Susannah,' he said, 'but only the Lord. I must trust Him to lead me to speak in His own good time.'

'But couldn't you prepare a ministry as every clergyman and pastor up and down the country does? And just as some of the brethren here do, too, I suspect. Brother Tozer's ministry last week on the tabernacle struck me as very carefully rehearsed.'

He explained why he could not do that, enlarging upon the necessity of allowing the Holy Ghost to direct the course of worship among the brethren. 'It would not be of the Spirit,' he concluded.

'Then why not prepare something and wait until it *is* of the Spirit?' Susannah suggested, and for a moment that forget-me-not twinkle returned to her eye and she added, 'or would that be cheating?'

He rewarded her with his loftiest disapproval. 'I shall never speak or minister unless I feel positively led by the Holy Ghost, Susannah. To do otherwise would be to deny the whole basis upon which we meet as brethren in the Lord.'

So he continued to attend the meetings at Ebenezer in silence, bowing his head during the prayers and joining in the hymns, but otherwise taking no active part in the impromptu form of worship that was being developed and refined not only in Teignmouth but in Dublin, Plymouth, Exeter, Bristol and an increasing number of towns and villages in the south west.

Then at the beginning of September, brother Synge drew Blair aside one evening after the prayer meeting and suggested that he might like to travel with him to Ireland to attend a conference. It was to be held later that month in Powerscourt House, the seat of Lord Powerscourt, whose daughter Lady Theodosia was associated with the brethren of the Aungier Street meeting in Dublin.

'I truly believe that you will find it to be of nourishment to the spirit,' he said. 'I attended the conference last year, and found blessing in listening to brethren who are specially gifted in the ministry, and I think that you will find similar benefit from it.'

Blair put the idea to Susannah later that evening. 'Brother Synge is planning to go to Dublin a week before the conference and stay on for a week after, and has asked me to go with him,' he said, and looked more cheerful than he had at any time since his meeting with Mr Digby.

210

Susannah thought it was an excellent idea, but knew Blair too well to say so.

'Do you think we should afford it?' she asked.

'Let us ask the Lord, Susannah, and act as He directs us.'

Two days later, he informed her that he was sure it was in the Lord's mind for him to go. He did not deceive her in this either, for he had indeed heard the voice of the Lord, urging him to get away from Susannah and West Lawn for a few weeks in order to seek spiritual renewal.

So it was decided, and when he set out for Plymouth to take the steamer to Dublin with brother Synge a week later, he did so with a feeling of considerable relief – quite unaware that Susannah watched him go in exactly the same mood of inward rejoicing.

When he was gone, she came back into the house and stood in the hall, actually laughing to herself in relief. Until that moment, she had not fully appreciated how heavily Blair's solemnity and depression had weighed on her, and the knowledge that she had the house to herself for a full three weeks caused an almost hysterical gaiety.

'Anything the matter, Ma'am?' Peg asked, from the kitchen door.

'No, nothing at all, nothing at all. But wait – don't go away, I have an idea.'

Peg looked at her curiously, wondering if her mistress was going to have one of her nervous attacks.

'There is still a little summer left,' Susannah said, 'and I think we should make the most of it and take a picnic to the Ness. So I would like you to prepare a hamper and ask Robby to get the spring cart ready and Jehu harnessed. We shall picnic on the cliff top and have our lunch *al fresco*.'

' "We", Ma'am? Who's "we"?'

'All of us! Yourself, Sal, Robby and I. It will do us all good to get out into the open air for a change.'

An hour or so later they set out, jammed together in the spring cart. They rattled across the Teign bridge and crawled up the steep, zig-zag hill, the servants having to get out and push for the last hundred yards before reaching the crest.

They walked the pony down over green turf, and when Robby had taken Jehu out of the shafts and put a straw hat on over his ears to keep away the flies, the rather unconventional party of lady and domestics spread a cloth on the grass and sat down to cold roast beef with lettuce and cucumber and a delicious apple and gooseberry pie with thick yellow cream. This was accompanied by quite a lot of inconsequential chatter from Sal, who always talked a lot when she was nervous, and was nervous because of Robby's increasingly warm attentions.

After the meal (following some whispering and giggling between Sal and Peg) Peg asked Susannah if they might be allowed to play hide and seek, and Susannah astonished them by announcing that she would join in.

'But what about –' Peg started.

'What about what?'

Peg blushed furiously. She had fattened in the last year or so and was now like a large suet dumpling, with rosy cheeks and blond hair parted down the middle.

'What about your condition, Ma'am?' she whispered, to which Susannah replied that provided they didn't mind counting to a hundred instead of fifty she would not have to hurry unduly while finding a hiding place.

When Sal heard she was going to have to count to a hundred she said, 'Oh Lor'! I don't know as if I can count that far, Ma'am. I'm lovely up to twenty or thirty, but I gets all mixed up with they seventies and forties.'

Robby explained that she would have to count five times to twenty, and indulged himself in the pleasure of taking her hand while he showed her how to use her fingers for the purpose.

'Well I'll do me best, Ma'am,' she promised dubiously.

212

'I can't say fairer 'n that, can I?'

After hide and seek they played tag, in which Susannah did not take part, and then Robby suggested they play leapfrog. Peg said it wasn't seemly, however, so they returned and sat with Susannah, who told them about the times she had had when she was a little girl. Robby made a daisy chain for Sal, who went very coy when he put it round her neck, and Peg told her not to be so daft. Listening to Susannah talk, it seemed as if there were far more than only six or seven years difference in her age and Peg's, because she could actually remember hearing the news about the Russian victory over Napoleon at Borodino, and it seemed to Peg, Sal and Robby that she had been brought up in a quite different world – a world of dandies and heroes and phenomenal wealth.

So they sat on the cliff top and talked and giggled, and Robby pretended he needed to prop himself up by placing his hand on the turf behind Sal's back; and later in the afternoon, when they stopped at a farm for a special treat of hot scones, raspberry jam and Devonshire cream, Peg told Susannah that she hadn't enjoyed herself so much in one day ever before.

'Nor me, Ma'am, neither,' Sal said earnestly. 'Can we do this every day while he's away?'

'Hush, you, what a thing to say!' Peg scolded, and glanced at Susannah whose eyes danced in controlled amusement.

'No, Sal, we can't,' she said, 'and I don't think you'd enjoy picnics nearly so much if you had to have them every day.'

'I *would* Ma'am!' Sal protested stoutly. 'Honest to God, I would! I really would!'

She knew exactly how Sal felt, for she had often felt the same herself. Why indeed could not life be a picnic every day? Why did one have to grow up and lose all the enthusiasm and spontaneity of childhood?

Travelling back in the spring cart, she felt saddened by the glimpse of carefree happiness the four of them had shared that day and the uncomfortable knowledge that it could only be a glimpse. Perhaps the servants sensed her mood, for they fell silent after the planks of the Teign bridge had ceased rumbling beneath the wheels, and when they drew up in the drive outside West Lawn, Peg quietly told Sal to go straight into the kitchen and get the kettles on, while Robby jumped down to hand Susannah down to the gravel as if he were a flunky and she a marchioness.

She went echoing down the bare hall and into the library, the one room which remained more or less as it had been before the auction. Yes, she thought, the picnic is indeed over. She took an old – almost ancient – volume from one of the lower shelves by the door. It was the second volume of Quintilian's *Institutione Oratoria*, whose treatise on the nature and end of oratory had been given her as an area for study in her teens. She had already lost most of her Latin: though the lines were familiar, their meaning was gone. All they contained now was the memory of her father hearing her construe in his study on a Saturday morning – his learned benevolence, his unceasing encouragement.

She put the book carefully back among the other eleven volumes of the work and wondered again what she should do about Blair's idea of a 'holy bonfire'. How could she allow him to destroy these beautiful volumes? She had grown up among books, had been taught from her very earliest years how to treat them, how to hold them, how to turn the pages in order not to crease or tear them. The printed page had become sacred to her in a way she had presumed it was sacred to every other thinking person – Blair included. Although he had let the matter drop since his mysterious lunch with Mr Digby, she felt she knew him well enough to see that having announced his intention to burn her father's books, he would do so sooner or later.

But what am I to do? she wondered. Am I to take issue

with him all over again? And even if I do, will he not quickly overrule me?

Peg had come to the library door.

' 'Scuse me, Ma'am, but where will you be taking your supper tonight?'

She turned. 'I shall only require a little soup and some bread,' she said, then added on an impulse – 'and I shall take it with you in the kitchen. There is no need to set a table for me.'

'But Ma'am –' Peg started, horrified that her mistress should stoop so low.

'If we can take our lunch together in the open air, Peg, we can sup together in the kitchen,' Susannah told her. 'I shall be in directly.'

She forced a little of her previous cheerfulness at the meal and had them laughing about the practical jokes she used to play on her governess, but it was not the genuine gaiety they had shared that afternoon, and the servants were well aware of it.

'I shall take the stage coach to Exeter tomorrow morning,' she told them before retiring for the night. 'I have business there, and will not be back until late. Now let us kneel and thank the Lord for the day he has given us and the happiness we have shared.'

It was the first time she had prayed aloud in this way, and she felt that, as a woman, she could not address the Lord in the formal style used by the elders at Ebenezer; so instead she used the form she had been taught by her mother, the way those earlier dissenters had used. She spoke simply, directly and briefly, and when she ended by saying 'in Jesu's name, amen' and rose from her knees, Sal was sniffing and her eyes brimming with tears.

'Whatever is the matter?' Susannah asked her.

Poor Sal: she had had a long day and an exciting one. Robby had kissed her for the first time, and she had enjoyed herself more than she could explain. She was soon to be seventeen: she hadn't seen her mother or her brothers and sisters for over five years, and Susannah's gentle prayer had touched some tender chord in her. Suddenly she let out a wail, and Susannah found the girl in her arms.

'What is it? What's happened?'

'Oh Ma'am, oh Ma'am!' Sal sobbed, 'It's 'cos I love 'ee so, that's what, an' I don't never want to lose 'ee!'

The result of this outburst was that Susannah felt her own eyes beginning to overflow too, and she had to make a quick escape from the kitchen; and when she was safe in her own bedchamber with the door closed she went and stood at the window for a long time, letting the tears run silently down her cheeks and splash on the sill, her heart filled with that ache that comes from thinking how life might have been if only . . . .

Exeter presented a dismal scene the next day when she arrived there a little before eleven: the cholera epidemic was only just past its height, and evidence of it lay at every turn. Smoke billowed about the huddled tenements from tar barrels placed by the City Health Board to combat the disease; a funeral bell tolled, and the lime-whitened streets were deserted except for dogs scavenging in the gutters and a one-horse hearse taking one more victim to the burial ground outside the city wall.

She alighted from the coach in the High Street and walked quickly along to the offices of Lethbridge & Wright, holding a kerchief to her nose as a precaution.

It was a long time after the jangling of the doorbell had ceased before the front door opened a crack.

'Yes?' snapped a disembodied voice.

'I have come to call on Mr Lethbridge.'

'Stand back!' said the voice, and when she did not immediately obey repeated, 'Stand back!'

She stepped away from the door, which opened further to reveal a much changed Clannaborough, who was now very bent and pinched and whose entire loss of teeth had turned his nose and chin into nutcrackers. He inspected her in silence for several moments, and it dawned on Susannah that he was assessing whether or not she was likely to be infected.

It was clear that he did not recognise her.

'Name?' he demanded.

'Miss Brougham,' she said without thinking, then shook her head and corrected herself. 'Mrs Harvey.'

He regarded her suspiciously. 'What business have you with Mr Lethbridge?'

'I am a client,' she said, drawing herself up a little. 'He is my lawyer.'

'Step inside quickly then, we don't want any more foul air in here than's necessary,' Clannaborough said, and led the way into the familiar hall.

In the outer office, an absurdly young looking articled clerk sat in shirtsleeves at the same high desk Blair had once occupied. Susannah could not help looking at him with interest – as if time might suddenly jump back and she might find herself once more waited upon by that handsome young man whose frank, penetrating stare had once disarmed her.

When she was announced, Mr Lethbridge came to the door of his office to welcome her. Like everyone she had seen in Exeter that morning, he looked old, worried and tired.

'Hard times, hard times indeed,' he said, indicating a chair to her and taking his seat behind the big teak desk that was piled with briefs and testaments. 'Had I known you intended to visit Exeter I would have advised against it at this time, you may be sure.'

She asked after his health and that of his family. He told her, grimly, that he had lost his cook three days before and his beloved wife a month before that. 'If I were in your shoes, Miss Susannah, I would not spend one minute longer in this accursed city than I had to. But – now that you are here – I am at your service.'

She was nervous of telling him the reason for this personal visit. Although she had given much thought to it since Blair's calm announcement to destroy her father's books, the decision she had taken was not going to be easy to put into effect.

'I think you may have heard of our sale of effects,' she started.

'I have indeed,' Lethbridge returned, with a hint of disapproval in his tone. 'There was a full column in the *Flying Post* on it. Indeed, I would be dishonest to hide from you that I was shocked and disturbed by your husband's decision to sell such a collection of treasures.'

'It was a joint decision, Mr Lethbridge,' she said quietly.

'Was it indeed,' he said gruffly, and left it at that.

She looked at her hands, which lay clasped in her lap. 'The reason I have called on you today is to ask your advice as to the disposal of my father's books.'

'Don't,' he said abruptly.

'I beg your pardon?'

'I said don't. Don't dispose of them, Susannah. I regarded your father as one of my closest friends. I had great admiration for him. If you sell his books – that fine collection – he will turn in his grave.'

'That is what I wish to ask you about,' she said. 'It is not that I wish to sell his books. All I wish . . . is to have them removed from West Lawn. The collection is too large to be taken on by Croydon's Library, and it occurred to me that you might know of some suitable home for them, where they would be cared for and appreciated.'

Mr Lethbridge looked across his desk at her, his eyes intense beneath thick, white eyebrows. He could not be sure exactly why Susannah should wish to have her father's books removed from West Lawn, but he had heard gossip about the conversion of the Harveys that had put one or two shrewd ideas into his head.

'So you are proposing, if I understand you correctly,

218

that your books be taken into – ah – safe keeping, but that they should remain your sole property. Yes?'

She glanced quickly up at him. 'Would that be possible, Mr Lethbridge?'

He noted her heightened colour and wondered exactly what lay behind this strange request; but as a liberal he saw himself as the champion of womanhood, and had the delicacy not to enquire further.

'I am sure it would not be too difficult to find a library or college whose patrons would be only too glad to take on such a fine collection,' he mused, 'but you will have to give me a few days to make enquiries.'

There was a silence.

'All I wish is that the books be removed from Teignmouth and given a good home,' Susannah said.

He nodded. 'We can do better than that. I can draw up a document now that will place the books in your sole name, Susannah, so that you or your offspring may take the benefit of them whenever you desire.'

She let out an involuntary sigh: he guessed that he had relieved her of a great burden. 'And if you will grant me power to act for you in the matter, I think I can guarantee to find a suitable home for them and to make all the necessary arrangements for their removal.'

'I am greatly obliged to you,' she whispered. 'And if – if you could make those arrangements without delay –'

'I shall put it in hand this very day,' he said, and each was secretly aware that they were joining together in a small conspiracy against her husband.

As she emerged from the front door of Lethbridges, she nearly collided with Captain Endacott.

He had come from visiting Molly only minutes before, and the sudden meeting with Susannah put him in high colour.

'Mrs Harvey,' he said, raising his hat. 'I do apologise.' He clicked his heels and bowed from the neck.

She inclined her head, pleased to see him. 'Captain!

219

What brings you to Exeter?'

'I visit regularly. On business, you understand.'

'Business,' she echoed, a gleam of mischief in her eye. 'Of course.'

He fell into step beside her. 'And yourself? Are you returning to Teignmouth today?'

'Yes, on the stage coach. It leaves at two, isn't that right?'

'I have no idea – I have not travelled on a stage coach in five years.' He turned to her as if sharing a confidence. 'They're so uncomfortable, don't you find? And the people with whom one is obliged to travel . . .!' A thought occurred to him. 'If you could bear to travel with me, Mrs Harvey, I am returning immediately in my gig.'

They had stopped by the pillared entrance of the guildhall, where a miserable wretch sat glumly in the stocks.

Susannah hesitated. She had heard about Endacott's reputation with women but found him extremely attractive, nevertheless. She was conscious of his admiring glance and the quickening beat of her heart.

'I should be most honoured by your company,' he said gently.

Their eyes met for an infinitesimally small flash of time, but in that moment she knew that they shared the same longing, the same desire.

'It is very kind of you,' she managed huskily.

'Then you accept?'

She heard herself answer in the affirmative, and accepted his arm as they crossed the High Street. She wondered if she were dallying with Lucifer, but could not really believe she was. Nor could she believe her luck: for a few brief minutes, all she knew was that fortune had smiled upon her, and that in this man's company she was indescribably happy.

He drove fast out of the city, the grey gelding's hooves pounding rhythmically on the road with such enthusiasm that it seemed to Susannah that the animal must have guessed her secret.

'I think your new way of life must suit your constitution, Mrs Harvey,' Endacott remarked as they went through the village of Alphington. 'I have never seen you looking so well.'

'I caught the sun yesterday,' she explained. 'We took a picnic to the Ness, and I forgot my parasol.'

'And your husband – I understand he is touring Ireland?'

She told him about the Powerscourt conference, being careful to play down its purpose in order to avoid embarrassing him.

'And this new way of life you have embraced. Do you find it congenial?'

She had not wished to speak to him of spiritual things, and hoped that they would soon get off the subject. 'It is no harder than the life we led before,' she said lightly. 'Indeed, I sometimes think that to be relieved of so many social obligations is a considerable blessing.'

Endacott did not wish to dwell on such matters either, but as so often happens when people of like minds are together, their conversation assumed a will of its own and led them where they had had no intention of going.

Wishing to pay her a gentle compliment, he said, 'It must be pleasant indeed to have a firm faith, a sure belief. I think people like yourself may be more envied than you imagine, Mrs Harvey.'

'I am not at all sure of that, Captain!'

'Well I *am* sure,' he insisted. 'You . . . you are an excellent example, to my mind, of what a Christian should be.'

She felt a strange sensation of panic. She did not wish him to regard her as a good Christian at all.

'You should not presume that outward appearances necessarily reflect the inner state, Captain,' she said.

'Not in most cases, I agree. But your case is special.' He

touched the rump of the gelding with the whip end, and they sped along beside the Exe estuary. 'You have found an inner peace which gives you a marvellous serenity.'

'If that is so, then it is not of myself,' she managed, and hearing herself was conscious of her own ineptitude and cowardice. Why could she not speak to him of spiritual things as she should? Why could she not witness for Christ as she was supposed to? She understood now why Blair had had so much difficulty over speaking in public, and felt a little pang of guilt for having teased him about it.

In the event, it was not at all necessary to force the conversation or steer it in any particular direction, for Captain Endacott was clearly intent upon drawing her out. So as they went along at a spanking pace he questioned her about her views on life after death, original sin, repentance and salvation; and she, feeling drawn to this serious, shy and gentlemanly dragoon, disguised her feelings for him by speaking as sincerely as she might of her own conversion and of the sense of release it had brought, so that by the time he dropped her at the rear entrance to West Lawn and she was making her way along to the house through the orchard, Captain James Endacott of the King's Own was well on the road to salvation.

It happened so quickly and naturally that Sal later didn't really understand how it could have happened at all. Robby started it. He came straight into the kitchen after taking the mistress down to the stage coach in the morning and put his hands up under her bosom from behind. She was up to her elbows scouring the pots and she didn't know how to stop him. Besides, he made her go all throbby inside when he pressed himself against her bottom and all she could do was whisper he didn't ought to. Then Peg came clumping in and he had to stop, and when he said he had to go and polish the brasses Peg said that was a likely story. 'Just you be sure and keep him in his place,' she said. 'I seen him looking at you, I know what 'e be after, I do.'

In the afternoon, Peg went down to the town. The *Eustacia* had arrived that morning on the tide: she had come flying in over the bar under headsails and mizzen and berthed out in the river off New Quay. She was back from Oporto, and Peg's man friend, the one she wasn't really supposed to see any more now she was in fellowship, might be coming ashore. The mistress wouldn't have let her go down to see him, Sal knew that, but that didn't worry Peg, and the excitement was shining in her face.

It was funny being all alone in the house, with Robby working in the garden. She didn't have much work to do once she'd scrubbed out the larder and made sure the copper was full so that her mistress would have hot water for a bath when she returned; so she went upstairs and tiptoed into her master's dressing room, a place where she wasn't allowed really, and when she was standing by his chest of drawers Robby came in behind her and practically made her jump out of her skin.

This time, when he asked her if she liked him doing that she said yes, it was lovely. He kissed her neck and put his arms round her waist. He held her hands and led her to the narrow flight of stairs and up to the servants' rooms on the second floor. He pulled her gently up behind him and took her into her own room: he lay down with her on the narrow bed, and there they were, face to face and hands to hands and lips to lips, lovely it was, and what he did was something wonderful, because it set something buzzing inside her and made her feel all kind and motherly and it didn't feel at all wrong, neither, because she'd always been a good girl and they were both saved: it didn't feel wrong, but after a bit Robby went all quiet and sort of jerky, and he said they would have to stop, and when she asked him what's the matter he said, 'I nearly gone and been and done it, an't I?'

So they stopped, and she went back down to the kitchen and started peeling carrots and potatoes and slicing onions for the soup, and Robby went back out to the garden; but some time later, when she was blowing up the kitchen fire with the bellows, he came to her again.

'Sal,' he kept saying. 'Sal.'

'We mustn't Robby. Least – not in the house.'

'Outside then?'

'It's sin, Robby.'

'I got to, Sal. It'll be worse sin if I don't.'

'Not here though! Not in the house!'

'In the stable then.'

But she couldn't do it in the stable either, not with the horses watching, she couldn't do it, and told him so; so they went along by the kitchen garden wall to the potting shed. There wasn't anywhere to lie down, so she felt safe, but they got carried away all the same and he said they didn't have to lie down. He said he could be obliged if she bent right over and put her face down among the pots of geraniums and cyclamen, and when the door unlatched and started banging in the wind he was already there and it was so good she said it didn't matter. And the door banged in threes, BANG-bang-bang, BANG-bang-bang and she didn't care because it was the most important thing in the world that he came right on all the way in and when he did he slid in like a sheet of flame and the geraniums smelt funny and the door was banging and she felt an O go out of her, an O and another O; she heard Robby whimpering and crying out; there was one more, much smaller o and then it was over, but definitely good, definitely worth it even if it was sin and the only part wrong with it was it didn't go on long enough.

They went back into the house. 'Well,' she said. 'That's me, Robby. I'm a fallen woman, an't I? Do anything with me now, you can. Play tunes on me if you want.'

But he didn't want to talk about it. He left her alone and went off by himself, down to the cellar, and she was so frightened and lonely about what she'd done that she went to him, hoping they could do it again. But he said no they couldn't, he wasn't interested in her, and there was a sort of ache deep inside her, because she felt empty without him. She couldn't understand why he had been so keen before and was so take-it-or-leave-it now. She wanted him to touch her, kiss her, love her; she followed him round the house and hung onto his hand, and they ended up down in the library with him sitting in the big wicker chair with his legs wide apart like how the master sat in the evenings. She wanted him so much she couldn't leave him alone. She sat down on top of him, trying to make a game of it. She tickled and stroked him; she blushed and giggled; she said, 'Want to play with my titties, Robby?' and he did, he took them out, both, and squeezed them together and made the ends tingle with his fingers, and that's what they were doing when a shadow moved.

It was the mistress. She was standing outside the window looking in, only she wasn't looking exactly because although her mouth was wide open, her eyes were tight shut.

She was very gentle and understanding. She spoke to Sal on her own and said we were all frail sinners, all made the same way, all given to temptation and weakness of the flesh. Her lips quavered and a single tear went slowly down her cheek. She read from the Bible a piece that said that every man should have his own wife and every woman her own husband. She said that they had been weak and had given way to fornication, but that it wasn't the first time Christians had yielded to such temptation and it wouldn't be the last. But they couldn't go on living under the same roof unmarried, not after this. Either one must go or they must be joined. She said she didn't have the power to send Robby away because he was the master's, and although she didn't want to send Sal away, that was what she would have to do if they didn't marry.

The trouble was, she said, that now they had started this it was like lighting a fire that you couldn't put out. She said that the only way to quench it was to be given in marriage, otherwise they would burn for each other and the same would happen, or worse. 'Tell me honestly,' she said. 'Have you given yourself to him?' and she didn't have to explain what she meant because Sal knew that she had, and bowed her head, nodding to admit her guilt. The mistress said nothing at all for some time after that, but instead did a wonderful thing: she put her arm round Sal and comforted her, and whispered that she, the mistress, was no better herself and was every bit as much of a sinner; that life was full of such temptations and that the only way was to cling to the Saviour.

After that, she sent Sal away to wait in the kitchen while she spoke to Robby. He spent a very long time in the library with her and when he eventually came out he was pale as a white cabbage.

'What's going to happen?' she asked. 'What she say we got to do?'

He stood in the kitchen doorway and looked round the room as if he thought it was haunted.

'Isn't no choice, is there?' he said. 'We got to be married, Sal. That's the beginning and the end of it.'

CHAPTER 11

Powerscourt House stood in one of the most romantic and picturesque regions of County Wicklow, to the south of Dublin. Some fifty years before, the previous Lord Powerscourt had landscaped the grounds and had been so pleased with the result that he had commissioned a jobbing poet to write a eulogy of the 'finished Seat'. Choosing to remain anonymous, the versifier preserved for later generations the 'gilt Profil' and the 'pictured Colonnade', the 'fretwork Ceilings' and 'historic Walls' – along with a liberal sprinkling of towering woods, soft carpet walks, enamel'd vales, mossy banks, crystal springs and that *sine qua non* of the eighteenth-century hack, the ideal grove.

It was here, where arched Hesperian windows drank the Noon, and fluted Dorics reared the rich Saloon, that the second Powerscourt Conference took place in the fourth week of September, 1832.

The theme for the conference was that of 'prophecy and the truths connected with it' – a subject of pressing importance to contemporary minds, who regarded the wars, revolutions and pestilences of the previous fifty years as sure signs that the world was entering the last days.

At the first session on Monday evening, the bedrock of Christianity was examined in biblical references to Emmanuel, God with us. On Tuesday, the prophetical character of each book in the Bible was discussed, with special reference to the three great feasts of the Jews, the blessings pronounced on Jacob's sons, the parables in the gospels and the letters to the seven churches in the Book of Revelation.

Wednesday's deliberations pursued the questions raised by Tuesday's discussions. Should we expect a personal antichrist? If so, to whom would he be revealed? Were there to be one or two evil powers in the world at that time? And by what covenant did the Jews, and would the Jews, hold the land?

Between sessions, earnest men in black broadcloth paced together upon the rain-damp lawns. They discussed the decadence of the established church, the doctrine of open ministry, the expected fate of the Israelitic Remnant, and the vexatious question of the ante-millenial Parousia.

But that year, there was a conference within a conference, an élite of young men who met privately for prayer after the day's meetings were over. It was these young men who were beginning to believe that they had been called out by God to leaven His church and bring about a return to an apostolic fervour unknown since the first and second centuries AD.

Although they would have abhorred even the suggestion, this élite group at Powerscourt was laying the foundations for a new religious movement – one that did not recognise itself as anything other than the true church of God, a sect that regarded all sects as abhorrent. Many of them, like Müller, Craik, Newton and Bulteel had had theological training and had practised as curates or pastors; some, like Sir Edward Denny, Captain Hall and Lady Theodosia Powerscourt were people of rank or title; nearly all, like Francis Newman (the brother of John Henry Newman), Robert Chapman and John Bellet were educated men whose contemporaries at university had included some of the most brilliant minds of the century. Born mostly between 1795 and 1810, they had grown up during the struggle against Napoleon and its aftermath and now felt themselves possessed of a special purpose, an ideal planted in them from their earliest years; and having achieved their academic victories, they now sought a higher excellence.

Among these urgent, unctuous and largely unsmiling brethren, one man stood out, head and shoulders, from the rest. His name was John Nelson Darby.

Born in 1800, the godson of Horatio Nelson, he was a few weeks older than Macaulay and a few months younger than J.H. Newman. After a brilliant start upon a legal career at Dublin University, he had thrown worldly ambition to the winds and taken holy orders in the Church of Ireland, starting work as a country curate in the Wicklow Mountains. There, he had gained a reputation as something of a saint among the peasant Romanists. Travelling everywhere on horseback and subjecting himself to a murderous daily routine of reading, preaching, praying and writing, his identification with poverty had driven him ever further from respectable clericalism, and ever deeper into primitive absolutism.

By the autumn of 1832 his leadership, charisma and grasp of the Scriptures had already won him considerable influence among the new brethren, and he was beginning to adopt an increasingly dominant role in this movement which, while regarding itself as the only true church of God, was to develop into one of the narrowest and most exclusive sects ever associated with Christianity.

It was Darby's voice that was most often heard on Friday, the last day of the conference. Having delved the previous day into the apocalyptic prophecy of the Book of Daniel, the assembly now sought to take their conclusions and apply them literally to their own lives.

What light, they asked, did the Scriptures throw upon present events and their moral character? What was the next event to be looked for and expected? Was there a prospect of a revival of the apostolic churches before the coming of Christ? And what were the duties arising out of present events?

Darby was in no doubt as to the answers, for he believed that the Holy Ghost was leading him into all truth. Bible in hand, he asserted that there was indeed a revival of the apostolic churches under way, and hinted that some of the new apostles might be found present in that very banqueting hall where the conference was being held. He pointed to what he saw as clear indications in the Scriptures of a 'secret rapture' before the millenium, when the elect of God would be caught up in the air to be with Christ before the tribulation. Confidently, he predicted that the next event to be looked for was the coming of antichrist, and with equal confidence he spoke of every true Christian's duty to withdraw from the denominated churches and to meet together in all simplicity after the manner of the new Brethren, whom he now saw as the only true successors to the first Christians.

Swarthy, haggard and resolute, there was no stopping him. In a fast, compelling delivery, he averred that not only should Christians admit no pastors or hierarchy in the church but that the very notion of a clergyman was tantamount to a sin against the Holy Ghost.

'The Scripture is clear,' he declared, sticking his chin out between sentences as if challenging any person present to contradict him. 'I am not talking of individuals willingly committing such a sin, but of the thing itself – pure, dreadful, and destructive evil – the very cause of destruction to the church. The word *clergyman* lies at the very root of that denial of the Holy Ghost, and I am perfectly satisfied – however this dispensation may be prolonged to effect the gathering of souls out of the world of God's elect – that it has sealed its destruction in the rejection and resistance of the Spirit of God.'

The words poured out so fast that his hearers were not always able to follow his peculiar grammatical constructions and obscure biblical references, but what matter?

This was heady stuff, and many were carried away by the sheer torrent of his argument.

'Now, God is not the author of confusion or disorder, nor of schism, but the enemy of souls is. But if a clergyman have the exclusive privilege of preaching, teaching et cetera – which they claim – then *must* it all be evil. Therefore I say that the notion of a clergyman involves the dispensation, where insisted upon, in the sin against the Holy Ghost.

'Let any layman ask a clergyman who has been converted to God whether he believes the mass of the bishops are appointed by God? He must say No!

'If we go to India, the persons to be soothed over and won so that the gospel should not be hindered, are the clergy; go to Armenia; go to Egypt amongst the Copts. Go to the churches in Palestine and wherever the Armenian church is spread, the facts are the same. Go to the Greek church: the same. Their Papas or priests, the ministers and sustainers of all the corruption and evil of the church, are the great hindrance to all missionary and spiritual exertion. Their churches are fallen; *therefore* they proportionately estimate the *clergy* and they do not the gospel. Why, the very term "my flock" that we hear from the lips of so-called vicars and parsons up and down the country is a shocking blasphemy, for such as use it place themselves in the place of Christ . . .'.

There was one last prayer meeting held among the Brethren members of the conference, when other members were already departing. Darby attended it, and prayed at some length that they might be kept from error and led into the truth, and afterwards, when he was on his way across the wide, viscountial hall, he was accosted by a tall, heavily built man a few years younger than himself, with a high forehead, thick wavy hair and a lordly manner.

'Brother Darby?' he began, blinking rather fast. 'Might I trouble you for a few minutes of your valuable time?'

They stood beneath the portraits of past Powerscourts

which marched, frame by gilded frame, up the wide staircase.

'But of course,' Darby replied, his manner surprisingly gentle and charming now that he was addressing neither the conference nor Almighty God.

They strolled side by side in the magnificent entrance hall, beneath a Georgian shellwork ceiling of unparalleled splendour.

'It concerns the sure knowledge of salvation,' Blair started a little uncertainly, for at close quarters Darby was a most imposing figure, with short cropped hair, sharply pointed sideboards, a predatorial nose and thin, compressed lips that seemed ready at any moment to seek out and refute error wherever it might be found. 'I – I came to the Lord some five or six months ago, and was baptised by brother Newton.'

Darby's expression changed fractionally at the mention of this name. A year before he had met Newton at Oxford, at the time of Bulteel's famous attack on the established church, and there had been an uneasy relationship between the two men from the start.

'But . . . I must confess that since my baptism, certain of my past sins have been brought most forcibly to my mind, and I have suffered grave doubts as to my salvation,' Blair concluded, and had Sal or Peg witnessed his timidity, his rapid blinking and the pumping vein in his forehead they would have been quite amazed. 'I would cherish your advice upon the matter, brother Darby,' he added, 'for I have been singularly impressed by the force of your speaking this week, and am quite convinced that you are indeed led by the Holy Ghost.'

Darby put his Bible under his arm and his chin in his hand, and when he gave his answer did so with that assurance and authority that had already inspired so many followers. ' "By grace are ye *saved*, through faith," ' he quoted, and taking Blair by the upper arm led him out into the night so that they stood in the damp September wind. 'See these blocks of stone,' Darby said, indicating the granite construction of the main entrance to Powerscourt House. 'Once they were part of a hillside or mountain. They were *in the world*. They had to be quarried, hewn out of the rock in order to be shaped and used in the building of this house.' He gripped Blair's arm. 'Here is what God has done for you, my brother in Christ. You are like unto one of these stones: you have been hewed out and set apart, you are destined to be cut and fashioned so that you may be placed in God's appointed building. And this cutting and fashioning – do you know what it is?'

Blair shook his head.

'It is the process of *sanctification*, which means separation, setting apart. Just as this stone here was once a rough-hewn piece of rock and had to be shaped and fashioned, so you, though you may feel yourself unfit, are nevertheless hewn out and separated from the quarry wall, that you may be made one with Christ's heavenly mansion. "For by one offering, he hath perfected *for ever* them that are sanctified." '

They went back inside. Darby put his hand on Blair's shoulder. 'Rejoice evermore,' he said, his intense blue eyes piercing deep into Harvey's soul. 'Pray without ceasing. Hold fast to that which is good. And the very God of peace will *sanctify* you wholly and make you *fit* for his heavenly mansion, so that you shall be preserved *blameless* unto the coming of the Lord.'

That said, he lifted his hand, and without further word strode off down the corridor, leaving Blair in a daze of inspiration and wonder.

Set apart! Hewn out and separated! Fit! Sanctified! Blameless! The words echoed about in his mind for days after. It was as if a huge, heavy door had finally clanged shut upon all his past sin, so that it could be put behind him, out of mind, forgotten.

He regarded himself as a changed man after that brief encounter with J.N. Darby, and it would hardly be an exaggeration to call him that, for Blair was by nature the sort of person who leaps from fresh start to fresh start, forever turning new leaves and beginning again. Just as he had felt himself to be a new person when he first arrived in Exeter and tore up Dr Watling's letter – or first encountered a whore, or met Susannah, or confessed to Dr Brougham, or arrived in Teignmouth, or fell to his knees upon Oddicombe beach – so he now considered himself to be at the beginning of a new phase in his life, as he trotted along the Devon lanes one afternoon a week or so later, on his way from Barnstaple to Drewsteignton.

The week after leaving Powerscourt had been full of incident. He had accompanied brother Synge on a preaching tour of southern Ireland and had visited Cork and Queenstown, Tralee, Listowel and Limerick. He had witnessed the appalling poverty among the potato-eating peasants and had seen for the first time the superstition and idolatry among the Catholics, who prayed openly to graven images of their saints, or crawled up and down cathedral steps on their knees in order to win indulgences of the temporal punishment they believed due for their sins. What darkness was there present! And what a blessed time it was with brother Synge, to be able to assist in the bringing of free salvation to all those with ears to hear!

He had travelled back to Bristol instead of Plymouth after his Irish tour in order to spend a season with brothers Müller and Craik; and after that he continued down the north coast of Devon to spend a night with brother Chapman.

Chapman was a tall, imposing man of a kindly disposition and mild temperament. He welcomed Blair into his house, and the two men spent several hours of prayer together, along with William Hake and an itinerant preacher by the name of Gribble, who had had much success with the gospel in the scattered villages and hamlets of Devon. But right at the end of their fellowship, Chapman had made a suggestion to Blair which caused the latter a certain inner alarm.

'If, on your journey to Teignmouth, you could find it in yourself to stop by at Drewsteignton and minister the Word,' he said, 'I am sure the few brethren there will count it a great blessing, for they are in much darkness and will benefit considerably from your fellowship.'

Blair had hardly felt able to say no to this, for since his week at Powerscourt he had adopted that grave and godly manner of the brethren so completely that it was becoming second nature to him; and while he had not actually preached the gospel himself while on tour with brother Synge, he had allowed Chapman to presume that he had.

So he assented, murmuring that he felt greatly humbled in his spirit at the thought of it, but that he was confident that the Lord would use him as He saw fit. Accordingly, Chapman wrote a letter of introduction to brother Holman of Drewsteignton, in which he commended his brother in the Lord – a letter which Blair felt that he could not very well tear up.

From Barnstaple, he had taken the road that follows the course of the River Taw, and had passed through the villages of High Bickington and Chulmleigh before heading south to North Tawton and Whiddon Down; and having forked left by Hobhouse Quarry he went up over Shilstone Moor, and on along a narrow lane that led beneath tall beeches, whose leaves were falling in russet blizzards in the October breeze.

He had given a lot of thought to what he might say to the brethren at Drewsteignton that evening and had decided (after laying it earnestly before the Lord) that the fifteenth chapter of the first book of the Corinthians was a most suitable passage upon which to speak, as it not only contained the elements of the gospel for the unconverted but also appropriate words of comfort and exhortation to

235

those brethren and sisters who had already been raised up.

On the face of it, what he had to say seemed simple enough: they would start with a hymn, and he would lead them briefly in prayer. Then he would invite those with Bibles to turn with him to the chapter and he would read it straight through before selecting certain verses for special comment. He would bring out the gospel message in the simplest possible terms for the benefit of the humbler of his listeners, and finally close by re-emphasising the triumphant nature of the last verses of the chapter, which refer to the trumpet sounding and the dead being raised.

The road steepened a little before he reached the crest, and he began the gentle descent towards the village. But as the church and the two neat lines of terraced cottages came into view, and the sound of a hammer on a hot horseshoe came to his ears, he became aware of increasingly nervous butterflies fluttering about in his stomach.

He needed just a little more time, he decided, before going on into Drewsteignton and making himself known to brother Holman; so turning off the road, he dismounted and tethered the animal before taking a solitary walk over the common.

He came to a stone wall, climbed it, and sat down upon it, so that the village was in view about half a mile distant, with the wooded hill plunging steeply down beyond it to the course of the river Teign.

So, he thought. Here we are. You are about to make your *début* at last, Mr Harvey. He saw how it would be: how he would be made welcome in brother Holman's tiny cottage, how he would be given the best country fare the thatcher and his wife could provide; how they would expect him to say a few words of prayer before the meal and how, afterwards, a dozen or so villagers would crowd in to listen to him speak.

He closed his eyes, listening to the gentle hissing of the wind in the granite stones, and the ting-ting-ting of the smithy. Then he heard a thudding and scuffling, a sniff and a snort, and when he opened his eyes beheld a herd of calves approaching to take a closer look at their black-coated visitor. They trotted confidently up to him until the leading brethren and sisters were within a couple of yards, whereupon they stopped abruptly, planting their fore-hooves in the soggy turf, their eyes huge and innocent, their noses moist and shiny.

'Good afternoon!' said Blair, glad to have his mind taken off what lay ahead. 'And how are you all this afternoon, my dear children?' He plucked some grass from the wall and held it out, and the calves, jostling to get a good view, elected one of their number and pushed him forward to accept it. Blair laughed aloud. What a splendid audience they made! What attentive, furry ears they had, and what trusting, speculative eyes!

'I shall be fortunate if my hearers are so attentive this evening,' he said aloud, and reached out to touch the hard forehead of the nearest heifer.

They remained gazing at him, as if waiting for an important announcement.

He glanced about. He was well out of earshot of the village here, and quite alone with them. Why not? he wondered, and addressed his audience.

'Well then, my lovelies. If you are so anxious to listen, I must needs minister to you. So if you will turn with me to the first book of Corinthians chapter fifteen, we shall read together from the Scriptures.'

Thus, with the calves edging nearer and blowing moistly through their noses, Blair Harvey began his dress rehearsal.

The following afternoon, on arriving at West Lawn, he was immediately aware of an indefinable change, but such an awareness may have been caused as much by his own inner change as any alteration in the high gables and leaf-spattered lawns.

Robson appeared from the stables as he rode up. He touched his forelock and welcomed his master back: but there seemed a change in him too, as if he had undergone some significant experience during Blair's five-week absence.

'Is all well?' he enquired of the servant, and Robson looked shiftily away and confirmed that everything was most satisfactory.

He went into the house, and was greeted by Susannah. She came out of the sitting room and took both his hands in hers, giving thanks for his safe return. There was a healthy bloom in her cheeks now and her pregnancy was more apparent. Absence had made the heart fonder, too: he could not help feeling pleasantly drawn to her, and remembered those early days before their marriage when he had practically worshipped at her feet. And the extraordinary thing was, he felt shy of her!

'Have you missed me?' he asked gruffly.

They sat down side by side on the settee and she pressed his hand against her cheek. He had forgotten so much about her! Seeing her now – as if with new eyes – he realised how lucky he was to have such a gentle, loving woman for his wife.

'I have missed you, yes,' she told him, 'but I have also valued our time apart – as I am sure you have, too.'

He blinked for several seconds, recalling the edgy toleration that had prevailed between them before his departure.

But all that was in the past. He launched into a detailed account of his tour: of the voyage from Plymouth to Dublin and the arrival among the brethren at Aungier Street; of his travels among the peasant folk of southern Ireland and the conversions that brother Synge had, through the Lord, achieved; but most of all of Powerscourt, and of Lady Theodosia and brother Bellett and brother Dorman and brother Darby.

Brother Darby came in for particularly effusive praise. 'What a man, Susannah, what a man! Why – he held the whole conference in the palm of his hand! He spoke as – as one having authority! And he dealt with matters that have hardly been approached honestly since the days of the first apostles. There were moments when it was easy to imagine that one was listening to the apostle Paul himself . . . or perhaps Peter, for brother Darby is a most forthright man with a manner that is as direct as it is godly.' He paused, shaking his head in wonder. 'Yes, my dear, I have had my mind opened to wide horizons these past weeks, and God willing, I hope to be able to share something of what I have learnt with yourself and the brethren at Ebenezer.'

'Did you speak at the conference yourself, dear?' she asked.

He glanced down at her slim white hand, which lay in his own, and adopted that humble manner he had found so attractive among certain of the brethren in Ireland.

'Not at the conference, for I was not led by the Spirit to do so. But last night I preached the gospel for the first time, Susannah.'

'Bravo!' she exclaimed, and clapped her hands together in a way he found deeply satisfying.

'It was in Drewsteignton. You cannot imagine the welcome I was given by the good people of the village – it was quite overwhelming. I spoke on first Corinthians fifteen. You know it? – "by the grace of God I am what I am" – and do you know the front room of that little cottage where I spoke was so full they had to open the window so that people could stand outside and listen! And afterwards – afterwards, Susannah, when I was supping with brother Holman and his family, one of the domestics from the vicarage came in and fell on her knees before us to confess the Lord and repent of her sins. What a blessed time it has been, dear! What a truly blessed time!'

'We have not been without our excitements,' Susannah said after a pause, and when Blair did not prompt her to continue added: 'Sal and Robby are married.'

Blair gazed out of the window at the rain which had started to fall since his arrival, still reliving his evangelistic début. When her words sank in, he turned quickly.

'Married, did you say?'

'The day before yesterday. I had expected that you would have returned to us by then, but your letter announcing the later date of your arrival was not delivered until the morning of the wedding, and I felt it better not to postpone it.'

'Married! But they are mere children, Susannah!'

'Yes, but they came to me and declared that they had discovered a deep fondness for one another, dear,' Susannah replied, looking very directly into Blair's eyes. 'As they are living under the same roof, I thought it best that they marry straight away. You understand, Blair. They were . . . burning for each other.'

He took a deep breath and began pacing the room, one hand behind his back.

'Nevertheless, you should have awaited my return. Marriage is not to be entered into lightly, especially by young children in the Lord such as these two domestics.'

She bowed her head. 'I did lay it before the Lord, dear. Really I felt that there was no alternative in the circumstances.'

'Where are they staying?'

'I have given them the large garret bedroom. They seem happy up there.'

'I have no doubt of that,' said Blair, and pursed his lips disapprovingly.

'And some more news. Captain Endacott is raised up to the Lord, dear. He is converted to Christ. He began attending the gospel soon after your departure, and only last Lord's Day he applied to brother Synge for fellowship.'

Blair stopped pacing. 'Endacott? I can hardly credit it! Why the fellow's a – a –'

'He is born again, Blair. He has put off the old man entirely.'

Blair was not sure he found the conversion of his business partner welcome news at all. It seemed to lessen the importance of his own conversion apart from anything else. Endacott of all people! Why – everyone knew he kept a mistress in Exeter! The fellow was the most abominable womaniser!

'I understand there has been some disagreement between him and Mr Cobbe,' Susannah was saying. 'Though the exact nature of it is not known to me.'

Blair grunted. It seemed to him that the equilibrium of his life had been entirely destroyed during his absence.

'There is one other matter to which I must draw your attention, dear,' Susannah was saying. She rose from the settee and offered him her hand. 'Come, I will show you.'

She led him along the corridor to the library and pushed open the door. He could hardly believe his eyes. Every last book had gone from the shelves.

The room had been gutted. Even the furniture was gone. He stood looking from side to side at the bare shelves, still unable to accept the clear evidence of his eyes. 'What is the meaning of it?' he whispered. 'Is this your doing?'

'Yes, it is, Blair. I knew that you wished to be rid of them, and I thought to surprise you on your return. You are not angry, are you?'

He glanced quickly at her. There were times when he could not be quite sure what was going on in Susannah's mind. He had an uncomfortable feeling that she must have known very well that he would be angry and that she was now deliberately using soft answers to turn away his wrath.

His lips quivered. It looked as if he might be about to burst into petulant tears. 'What have you done with them?' he asked, dangerously quiet.

Susannah joined her hands demurely and gave him an approximately truthful account. She said that she had heard, quite by chance, that the Devon and Exeter Institute was seeking to extend its library and one of the patrons – the town clerk of Exeter – was anxious that Dr Brougham's collection be preserved intact. He had made arrangements through Mr Lethbridge for the books' removal without charge, and as far as she was aware they were therefore back in Exeter and gracing the shelves of the Institute library in the Cathedral yard.

'I was very happy to make the arrangement, dear, as I know that my father could not have wished for a more suitable resting place for his precious volumes, and I am sure you will agree that they will be better appreciated there than in our custody where they are simply gathering dust and making extra work for the domestics.'

'You had absolutely no right to act in this way without first consulting myself,' he said. He went to the window, peered out at the rain-damp orchard, then spun back to face her. 'You had absolutely no right.'

She coloured a little, but said nothing.

'I shall have them back,' he said. 'I shall have them returned. Those books are my property, Susannah. They became my property when you were given in marriage. That is the law, do you understand? That is the law. I shall write . . . no, you must write to Lethbridge immediately. You must inform him that you have acted inadvisedly and foolishly – and without the consent of your husband. Do you understand?'

'I understand, yes, but I cannot agree to the writing of such a letter, Blair. I do not wish to cross you in this matter, but I see no reason why we should ask for their return. You yourself told me that you had a mind to destroy them, and I am firmly of the belief that to take such a step would be a mistake.'

'Those books,' he said, and he began pacing again, his

footfalls echoing in the empty room, 'those books were of no spiritual benefit whatsoever. They were papist for the most part. Worldly. Half of them were in Latin, the language of the most evil empire this world has ever known. The language of the latterday Babylon. By attempting to preserve them, you are defending an evil, Susannah. Make no mistake about that.'

'There were Bibles in the collection, Blair. Were those evil?'

'Some of them, yes. The Douai version for one. Much of that is ill-translated and quite misleading to innocent souls.'

'So you would destroy those too?'

'That is not for you to ask, Susannah. I will not have you trying to catch me out in that way. Nor will I tolerate your going behind my back to dispose of property which is not yours to dispose of. I will not have it.'

'In that case I apologise, Blair, but I fear the deed is done, and cannot be undone.'

'We shall see about that.'

She said nothing.

'I shall be obliged if you will write the letter immediately,' he said. 'I will write a covering note.'

'Didn't I make myself clear, Blair? It is not in my power to ask for the books back. They are not my property.'

'They are not your property, no – but mine. Nevertheless –'

'They are not yours either, Blair. They have been made over to the Institute. Mr Lethbridge drew up a document, a deed, which transferred ownership. I do not understand the details of it of course – they were quite beyond me – but I do know that I have no further control over them, and that to write to ask for them back would be quite futile.'

He turned away from her, and she saw his fists clenching and unclenching, the long nails not unlike an eagle's talons. Almost all of what she had told him was the truth,

243

though she had omitted to say that the document she had signed before witnesses contained a clause to the effect that she reserved the right for herself and her offspring to have a proportion of the books on loan from the Institute at any time should she choose to do so. She had expected an explosion from Blair and had prepared herself for it: she had been determined to retain control, and never to give way to anger. Now, looking at his angry back, she knew that she was on the point of victory. She knew that though Blair might huff and puff he did not have the inner resources to put up much more of a fight. In a way, she wished he had: she would have liked to see him drive off to Exeter then and there to confront Lethbridge and make a scene. But when it came to the point, he was a coward in such matters, and she knew it.

He turned suddenly, and she was taken by surprise by his red face and blazing eyes.

'Damn you, woman!' he whispered. 'Damn you!'

It was an argument that could never be finally resolved, a lingering sore that never healed. Books, learning and academic study became subjects that brought a sneer to Blair's lip, and though the disposal of her father's library was seldom mentioned, the knowledge of it lurked between them, so that each knew that the close friendship Susannah had hoped for on their wedding day could never be theirs.

It seemed to Susannah that she was caught in the worst sort of trap: a trap with an open door, a trap that purported to be a haven. Having committed herself to the Lord's service she had also committed herself, in accordance with the teaching of Scripture, to remain subject and obedient to her husband, so that although she may have been technically disobedient in the matter of her father's books, she still felt obliged to defer to him in every other area, for not to do so led inevitably to damnation and eternal punishment.

It was a quite illogical state of affairs, a self-contradictory position. But she could not see any alternative to accepting it. All she could do was try to keep a small compartment in her mind separate and private to herself: a compartment where she could hide away from Blair's pontifical authority, a compartment where she could retain the relics of her true self, the happy, innocent child she had once been – the original, genuine Susannah.

CHAPTER 12

'A slate is a slate,' Cobbe said three days after Blair Harvey's return from Powerscourt, 'whether it be six inches by ten or sixty feet by a hundred.'

'Not so, not so!' Blair replied, becoming heated. 'You know, I know – we all know – that the Exeter city corporation lays down a scale of charges, and that scale, under the heading of "slates" refers to roof slates, not slabs of mountain, if you will forgive the hyperbole.'

'In that case they should say what they mean,' Cobbe retorted. 'And until they do, I see no ill whatsoever in declaring each piece of slate of whatever size as one slate.'

The meeting of partners had been in progress for an hour, and little headway had been made. Sitting at the gate-leg table on the first floor of the New Quay office, Messrs Harvey, Mudge, Hennet, Oxtoby and Cobbe and Captain Endacott had gathered to discuss Cobbe's disagreement with Endacott over the payment of town dues, and what had originally appeared to be a matter of very little consequence was now threatening to split the firm apart.

'What we require,' Harvey was saying, 'is a legal schedule of charges, published at regular intervals –'

'Yes we have heard that at least twice from you, Mr Harvey,' Cobbe retorted. 'You have already given us the benefit of that little gem of originality.'

This burst of sarcasm brought the discussion to a temporary halt, during which the partners glanced surreptitiously at the two main contenders.

'Let us try to preserve a modicum of common courtesy at least,' observed Captain Endacott. 'Cheap jibes will profit us nothing, after all.'

'Here here,' echoed Harvey. 'Thank you, James.'

Oxtoby, the representative of the banking firm of Langmead & Jordan, removed a pipe from his mouth and said, 'Until an agreement as to responsibility for compilation of manifestos is reached, little further progress can be made.'

'I make the returns and I take the responsibility,' Cobbe declared.

'Not so,' Harvey returned. 'As principal shareholder and titular head –'

'Perhaps we should hear the Captain's views?' Mudge suggested. 'After all he is the person who raised the first objection.'

They turned to Endacott, who glanced nervously from side to side before speaking. 'I can't deny that I have been aware of – of certain irregularities,' he admitted quietly, 'and while the collection of town dues is conducted by the Exeter city corporation in a slovenly and even arbitary way, I am now persuaded that we are not thereby absolved – and can never be absolved – from our duty to obey the spirit as well as the letter of the law, and render unto Caesar the things that are Caesar's.'

'Well said, brother,' Harvey murmured. 'Well said indeed.'

'I wish to make it quite plain,' announced Oxtoby, 'that my firm disassociates itself entirely from any hint of sharp practice.'

'My sentiments entirely,' Harvey added.

'And mine, and mine,' snapped Cobbe. 'When have I ever suggested otherwise? All I am saying is that while I can bend over backwards to accommodate the Exeter authorities, I am not prepared to throw backward somersaults for them. So if slates be charged at a ha'penny a dozen, then let us only ship the largest slates, and if those bureaucratic dolts believe a pipe of port to be smaller than a tun, then let us not disabuse them.'

At this point old Mr Hennet, who had fallen asleep, began to snore and had to be roused by the Captain. He raised his head from his arms and blinked vacantly, as if surprised not to find himself in bed with his wife.

'Gentlemen,' began Blair, joining his hands beneath his chin as if about to lead them in prayer, 'Two years ago, I would not have hestitated to support Mr Cobbe upon this matter, for I know as well as any other the injustices suffered by the merchants of this town at the hands of Exeter. Further, my conscience would have remained easy upon the question of making profits by a little winking of the eye at nonsensical regulations. But now, as a servant of Christ Jesus, I am led to believe that my yea must be yea and my nay nay. Yes, we can save a few pence by shipping slates the size of tables instead of ten by sixes; yes, we may profit a shilling or so by winking at the difference between a Winchester chaldron and a Newcastle. But where is the eternal gain? Mr Cobbe may believe that he is achieving an important advantage for the firm, and I grant that he may wish it from the best of motives. But if we look into our hearts, can we deny that such practices constitute a deceit? Can we be confident such deceit will not earn for us a more terrible, eternal loss?'

With the exception of Endacott, who murmured a quiet amen, the partners shifted uneasily. They had heard one or two sermons of this nature from Blair, and were not well disposed to hear more.

Cobbe drummed his short fingers on the woodwork. 'And who do you propose shall carry out this new, sea green incorruptible policy, Mr Harvey?'

Blair cleared his throat. 'I am sure that we can reach an amicable agreement, as partners –'

'Partners?' shot back Cobbe. 'Partners? On paper, perhaps, but hardly otherwise, for since your perversion into dissenting religiosity you have paid more attention to your Bible than your business.'

'I have no reason to be ashamed of that!' Harvey exclaimed, and the vein started pumping down his forehead.

'I am not suggesting that you should, Mr Harvey – not at all. Only that if you wish to spend your time preaching to the yokels, then I consider it only right that I should have a free hand to run the business as I see fit.'

'As you see fit, exactly, exactly,' Blair cried, 'that is precisely where we differ, Mr Cobbe, that is the precise nub of the question, is it not? You are content to trust in your own judgement, while I, I prefer that of my Lord and Saviour. For what will it profit a man if he gain the whole world and lose his own soul? Can you answer me that? Well can you?'

'Mr Harvey, Mr Harvey,' Cobbe returned, tipping his chair back and laughing. 'If I wish to have a sermon from you, I will come along to your little God-box on a Sunday evening, but until that unlikely date I will be grateful to you if you will leave such matters to the right time and the right place.'

'You see?' Blair appealed to the others, as if to obtain their agreement that the ball was out. 'You see? When the devil is confronted, he resorts to cheap sneers. But God is not mocked, gentlemen. He sees our innermost thoughts and hears our feeblest cries, as the good Captain here will, I am sure, testify –'

But Captain Endacott was not to have the opportunity to witness for Christ, for Cobbe rapped on the table and stood up, his chair screaming on the boards as he did so.

'That's enough!' he shouted. 'I wish to hear no more of this holier-than-thou claptrap. I'll make you an offer instead, Mr Harvey – and you, Captain, as you seem to have been taken in by all this. I'll offer you a hundred and eighty pounds sterling for each and every one of your shares in this firm. If you're prepared to sell, I'll buy you out. If not – then I'll offer my own shares at the same price, and if you meant what you said just now I'm sure you'll feel guided or led or moved, or whatever it is that you do feel, to buy me out, for you will not wish to have my devilish influence upon your firm. Well gentlemen. I'll leave you to think that over, and if you see me at this table again, it will be as the senior partner and controlling shareholder.'

Harvey and Endacott remained behind to discuss the offer after the others had gone. Endacott turned his chair away from the table to stretch his legs, while Blair paced about the room or paused to peer out at a sloop beating out on the ebb.

'A hundred and eighty pounds,' he repeated to himself. 'At least we cannot accuse the devil of offering a paltry sum.'

'Are you thinking of accepting?' the Captain asked.

Harvey sighed through his teeth. 'All I am thinking, James, is that we must act in accordance with the Lord's wishes. That is all I am thinking.'

'The question is, how does one discover exactly what is the Lord's will?'

Harvey stopped pacing and glanced back at his brother in Christ. Now that he was used to the idea of Endacott's conversion, he rather enjoyed the prospect of teaching him and helping him to grow in grace.

'We must lay it before the Lord, James. We must take it to the Lord in prayer.'

'I shall certainly do that,' Endacott agreed cheerfully.

'Better that we combine here and now and offer it up in all humility as brethren in the Lord. Do you not agree?'

Endacott felt himself colouring. This total reliance upon the spiritual guidance of the Holy Ghost could be some-what unnerving.

'Very well,' he said. 'Certainly.'

Harvey was already getting down on his knees, but got

up again very quickly when he found he was kneeling on a nail. His second attempt was more successful, however, and when Endacott had followed suit and the two men were kneeling side by side at their chairs, the question of whether to accept Mr Cobbe's offer of a hundred and eighty pounds per share was put to the Lord.

All his instincts told him to sell out. Hadn't Susannah always longed to live in the country? If he sold out now, they would have enough to do so: West Lawn would raise a handsome sum, and they could up sticks and remove from damp, smelly Teignmouth for good. He knew where they would go, too: on his travels through Devon he had discovered a most beautiful district right on the edge of Dartmoor where the River Teign had its source. How fitting it would be to remove from this worldly watering place and go back to origins geographically as well as spiritually! He could buy a few hundred sheep to graze on the moor and start a new little community of Christian brethren – yes, there would be a fine occupation for a man of God! He pictured a thatched farm cottage, some head of cattle, lush fields of arable land, and in one of the outhouses an upper room, furnished, in which he would lead the believers in prayer and the breaking of bread. My name would become known in the county, he reflected. Our little assembly would become a gathering place for weary souls.

How attractive the idea was, and yet how insidiously tempting as well! How could he be sure that he was being guided by the Lord, and not by vanity or financial expedience? He prayed for a sign, and for several days was morose at home and too preoccupied with the matter to take an active part in the meetings at Ebenezer.

One morning he drove over to Shaldon in order to inspect the progress being made on the *Eustacia*, which was in for careening and repainting. Walking round with the yard manager, a whiskery fellow in a peaked cap

251

whose asthma caused him to wheeze with every breath, Blair saw that the name of the vessel was being repainted, and paused to watch the care with which the man steadied his brush, placing his right wrist against his left to do so.

'This is a new man is it not?' he remarked, congratulating himself upon his own powers of observation.

'Ay, sir,' wheezed the manager. 'Old Arthur Prettyjohn passed away three month ago, but Bill here's as fine a signwriter as you'll find anywhere.'

'Signwriter . . .' Blair muttered to himself, and while the manager went on about his business, remained watching the man at work for some time.

Standing there on the foreshore under the sweeping lines of the ship's bow, he saw at last what he must do. Here was an artisan taking infinite pains to repaint the name of his lamented mother. That name would be seen in its decorative copperplate letters up and down the south coast of England, on the continent and even as far away as Newfoundland and North America. How could he allow it to trade under the direction of an evil man such as Cobbe?

'I have been led to see into the mind of my Lord,' he announced to Captain Endacott the following Lord's Day when they lunched at West Lawn after the breaking of bread. 'There is no question but that we must buy out Mr Cobbe.'

Endacott glanced at Susannah. 'I fear it will stretch our resources,' he observed.

'Of course it will, James. Of course it will. But I am led to see that though they be stretched to the very limit, we cannot allow Mr Cobbe to use ships named after my own mother and son to ply a dishonest trade.'

'Could you not sell him your share on the condition that he changes the names of the vessels?' Susannah suggested.

Blair shook his head. 'He would never do it. He is so immersed in superstition that he would esteem it bad luck to change them.' He turned back to Endacott. 'Besides, if we retain control, it can become a blessed work for the

252

Lord. The people of this town will have the benefit of a truly Christian – *truly* Christian – firm in their midst, yes, and one that will provide a living proof of His handiwork in the prosperity He will bring to our efforts in His name.'

So the decision was taken, and with the assistance of most of Endacott's remaining capital, Cobbe was bought out. A new sign went up outside the New Quay office which read 'HARVEY & ENDACOTT, SHIPOWNERS', and Cobbe, having suddenly become richer by over two thousand pounds, used his capital to make several shrewd purchases of land in the locality, the value of which was to treble in a decade when the railway came to South Devon.

Susannah gave birth to a daughter in the new year, and three months later Sal produced a premature son that died within a week. Susannah was having difficulty with her milk, and as Sal was so full of it that it sprang from her breasts in slender white fountains, little Theodosia was handed over to be suckled by the domestic, a move that angered Robby considerably.

Susannah's next baby, another girl, arrived thirteen months after Theodosia and was named Grace. For the few months between the weaning of Theodosia and the birth of Grace, Blair had directed that Sal be loaned to a local orphanage as a wetnurse, so that she would be kept in milk and ready to relieve Susannah of the burden and discomfort of feeding the new baby.

A third daughter arrived in March of the following year and was called Beatrice. After her birth, Susannah hoped for a respite from her labours and tried a few experimental tactics in dissuasion. But by this time Blair was riding a wave of self-esteem born of considerable evangelical successes and was not of a mind to take no for an answer when he sought to exercise his husbandly rights, so within a very short time Susannah was pregnant again.

She was not at all pleased at the discovery.

'I am being turned into a machine,' she said one summer evening when they were preparing for bed. 'All I am required to do is satisfy my husband and bear him baby girls.'

He put his thumbs behind a pair of braces she had embroidered for his thirtieth birthday.

'It is fortunate I know you so well, dear, for if that remark had come from anyone else, I would have felt obliged to denounce it as an outrage to Christian motherhood.'

'Nevertheless, you do not have to endure what I have to endure, Blair. You do not have to suffer the megrims and the sickness, the pains in the limbs and the feeling that you are no longer a thinking person so much as a *thing*, or at best an animal, a she-animal, whose sole function is to satisfy her mate and reproduce his offspring.'

'That is a disgraceful thing to say, Susannah. You are my beloved wife and the mother of my lovely girls.'

'Maybe so, but I do not feel inclined to be the mother of any *more* of your lovely girls.'

'Perhaps you will not be.'

'What does that mean?'

He went to her and placed his hands on her shoulders, looking at her reflection in the dressing table mirror. 'I have been asking the Lord for a son this time,' he admitted, and smiled as if he had been caught stealing an apple.

'I see.'

'So . . . if we have faith, we shall be sent another Benjamin.'

'I could not call a son Benjamin again, Blair. It would be too painful.'

He snorted. 'Nonsense. Benjamin was my father's name. Benjamin Harvey is a name much esteemed in the home counties.'

She put a comb through her hair. 'Well there is little point in discussing it until we know that it *is* a boy. And if our past record is anything to go by, it seems unlikely that it will be.'

'I disagree,' he said, moving away. 'If we ask the Lord for a son and have faith he will surely send us a son.'

She gave a sudden little laugh, then stopped herself. Blair turned quickly: laughing to herself in that way had been one of her early faults which he had corrected when they were first married.

'May I enquire what you find amusing?'

She went behind the screen to put on a nightgown. 'Nothing of importance,' she said.

'I would like to hear it though.'

She wondered if she could quickly manufacture some fictitious thought for him, to deflect his curiosity; but it was not in her nature: she felt driven to speak her mind, however much it might anger him.

'I was thinking that God must already know the sex of our next child, is that not so?'

'God knoweth all things,' Blair declared solemnly from the other side of the screen, and lowered his trousers.

'And further, I was thinking that once a child is conceived in the womb, its sex is already determined. So although I am only two months gone, I am carrying either a male or female embryo. That is so, isn't it?'

She heard him grunt impatiently. 'What are you trying to say, Susannah?'

'Isn't it obvious? If the sex of my baby is already determined, what possible point can there be in praying for a son?'

' "Ask and it shall be given unto you",' he quoted solemnly. 'God makes no provisos or codicils to His divine promises. He does not give a stone when we ask for bread. All that He requires of us is that we should have a little faith.'

She came out from behind the screen and found him in his nightshirt. 'I can see that we might reasonably ask the Lord for a son at some time in the future, Blair, but to

255

pray that this child should be a boy seems to me to be a presumption, for we are asking God to do something which He may already have determined otherwise.'

He drew himself up. 'Are you saying that God is *unable* to alter the sex of our child if He so wishes, Susannah?'

'Not unable, unwilling.'

'But my dear! He has clearly told us to ask Him for our needs. See how brother Müller goes from strength to strength in Bristol! He has never once asked for money from any person, but as a result of prayer is being deluged with gifts for his orphanage! Would that have happened had he not laid his life at the Lord's feet and asked Him for all his needs?'

'We cannot know, can we? And besides – asking for financial donations is a little different from asking for a child of a particular sex.'

'It is not at all different. Why, if you say that you are striking at the very foundations. You are denying our Lord's omnipotence.'

She sighed quickly, becoming upset. 'I was not saying that at all,' she whispered. 'I was simply saying that we should not *presume* . . .'

'Well? Go on.'

She shook her head. 'It is of no matter, Blair. I should not have raised it.'

'Then let us kneel and approach the throne of grace.'

She knelt beside him obediently, but there was still a thread of rebellion in her. She didn't want this baby, and couldn't convince herself that she did; but at the same time knew that such resistance to the Lord's will was sinful, and prayed to be delivered from it.

Blair had preached in Newton Abbot that afternoon and had brought two souls to the Lord. He gave thanks for this at some length before asking blessings upon a home-made litany of people: herself, Theodosia, Grace, Beatrice; the domestics, the saints at Teignmouth; the Müllers, the Craiks, and the Groveses, who were suffering terrible trials in Baghdad.

Having added her amen, she climbed into bed with him, and moments after the candle was out felt his hand at her shoulder to pull her towards him.

His breath smelt of hot milk and sanctity. She lay back and did her wifely duty – remarking to herself that it was odd how nearly all the converts he made were young women, and that after such evangelical successes, he was always more demanding in bed.

Afterwards, when Blair's breathing was becoming deep and regular, she lay awake and allowed herself the luxury of thinking about Captain Endacott. She knew she should not think so much about him, but the harder she tried not to, the more forcibly he invaded her mind. What she feared was that she might let slip some hint of her feelings towards him, whether to Blair or Peg or Sal or any of the brethren or sisters, or even to James himself. Whatever happened, no one must ever know. She must keep so firm a check upon herself that she must not even arouse suspicion by being over-formal or distant with him: she must allow their acquaintanceship to develop as it might have done had they felt nothing at all for each other.

And there – how could she presume that he felt for her as she felt for him? She did not even dare look for signs of it, though she could not help noticing them. She loved his grave good manners, his quiet concern for her wellbeing, his deference to her opinions, her ideas. Could it be possible that he was holding back in exactly the same way and for the same reasons? Sometimes over lunch at West Lawn on a Lord's Day or during those summer outings on his farm organised for the brethren and sisters of Ebenezer and their families – or even sitting in the meeting with him in the row behind her – she would become aware that something said or done had sparked off in him reactions

257

which she shared exactly. She did not even have to look at him to know this, just as a musician does not have to look at two violins to hear that they are in tune. She knew it intuitively. It was a telepathy between them that seemed heaven-sent but which she knew she should regard as evil.

Sometimes she wondered if she was imagining it all, and that these tremblings and yearnings she suffered were merely symptoms of a nervous disorder. Blair had said that there was no such thing as nervous disorder – that all such difficulties came about as a result of sin. She knew, too, that even to think of a man as she sometimes thought of Captain Endacott was as sinful as the physical act of adultery itself. The knowledge of it terrified her. Why was it that she should be tormented by such thoughts, when every other married sister in the assembly should appear so content with her lot as a woman, wife and mother? Why should she be condemned to rage inwardly in this way? And why, above all, did her own body yearn so desperately for a relief that she knew could be hers, a relief which she was occasionally granted in her dreams, one which Blair achieved almost nightly on his own behalf but which she was repeatedly and monotonously denied?

Every Lord's Day after the breaking of bread, Captain Endacott came to lunch at West Lawn. The three walked up the hill together, and the men discussed the morning's worship over the cold pork and bubble-and-squeak.

'I thought brother Synge spoke well,' Harvey might commence after grace had been said and the salt passed. 'Though I could not help noticing that he exercised our patience a little in the multiplicity of Scriptural passages to which he referred.'

Such a remark would set the discussion going. Sometimes it was the Atonement, sometimes the Tabernacle, sometimes the Seven Churches, sometimes the Rapture of the Saints. Although Endacott had immersed himself in the study of Scripture since his baptism nearly two years before, Blair still retained the ascendancy over him, which he exercised with a complacency Susannah found quite staggering.

The trouble with religious virtue was that it was quite unbearably boring; but when it involved the obligation to believe that your tiny circle of doctrine was the only true doctrine and that all other human beings were in error and destined for hell fire; when you were expected to look forward to the end of the world and take joy in the belief that you were living in the last days; when you were expected to take positive delight in the hope that you might be alive upon this earth on that day of days when Christ descended with a shout to catch up the saints and take them into glory – the result (as far as Susannah was concerned) was a sort of living death in which all intelligent questioning was forbidden, all mischievous gaiety frowned upon and all planning for the future qualified by that expression she was beginning to detest: 'if the Lord tarry'.

'Too many babies, not enough domestics,' she would tell herself, looking at her reflection and noting the deepening lines of strain, the first grey hairs, the pallor in cheeks that had once been a delicate pink. But her situation had not been brought about simply by repeated childbirth, and she knew it. No, she was like one who, having committed herself to crossing a marsh, finds herself so bogged down that she knows her only hope is to continue in the hope of reaching firmer ground. There was no going back, but no guarantee that she would reach the other side either.

She *had* to go on. She believed the Bible to its last iota; she clung to the promises of salvation and eternal life in the desperate certainty that if she ceased to do so she would one day have to answer for it at the judgement seat and, doubly damned for receiving the truth and rejecting it, would be cast down into the fires of hell.

Blair woke with a start. Susannah was lying on her back

259

beside him, making little sighs and moans to herself, writhing in a way that seemed to him almost bestial. It was getting light: he could make out her hair upon the pillow, her open mouth, her eyelids fluttering; and suddenly her body arched upward in some sort of devilish ecstasy.

He shook her roughly by the shoulder.

'Susannah! Wake up!'

Her eyes opened, and her head rolled to one side. She was panting like an animal.

'What was it, a dream?' he asked.

She gazed up into his face. Even now she seemed to be in a trance.

'Just a dream,' she whispered. 'Yes, only a dream.'

It was not the first time it had happened. He lay back and tried to sleep. A cock began to crow in the distance. He wondered if she were ill, but he was beginning to suspect something far worse.

She began watching him covertly and discovering new reasons for disliking him. She came to detest the resonant boom of his voice, the thunder of his nose when he blew it in a silk handkerchief, the noises he made in the morning on the close stool and the smell that hung about the landing as a result of his daily motions. She blamed him for making her pregnant with a child she did not want and rebelled inwardly at his lordly pronouncements. She even began to hate the sight of his fingers turning the pages of the Bible at morning prayers, and the downward turn of his mouth as he addressed his Lord after breakfast.

And yet her very hatred terrified her, because she felt that through it she was murdering him in her heart as she had murdered her father. She felt like a secret agent in her own household, a traitor to the very name she bore. She began making excuses to escape his presence, pleading morning sickness, headaches, nerves – anything to keep away from him, anything to avoid further occasions to think evil of him. She spent hours on her knees asking

God to help her find again the love she had once had for him, and for a while she felt these prayers were beginning to be answered; but then she would say or do something to incur his displeasure, and he would tilt his chin sideways and look down his straight nose at her to reprove her or talk down to her ('And how are we this merry morning, Susannah?') and that black and green hatred would rise up again and she would have to turn away in silence, afraid that if he so much as touched her she might lose control and tear lumps of flesh from his face with her fingernails.

At the same time, she knew that she must never allow him to discover her feelings. It must all be bottled up, all prevented from escaping. She must appear to him and to the domestics and the saints as a demure sister in the Lord, she must exercise an iron control. Always at the back of her mind lay the fear that she might lose that control, and of the consequences that would follow. She would lose her reason: he would have her put away. He would be the one who received the murmurs of sympathy, while she would be sent in a closed wagon to the Exeter asylum, to rot her life away in rags and filth, with the cathedral bell tolling out the hours, and old memories coming back to haunt her.

Blair was not as insensitive as Susannah had presumed, in fact if he had spoken his thoughts to her she would have been shocked at how much he had guessed. But like Susannah, he believed that the only solution to such problems was control. They were man and wife, mother and father. They were head of a household and a family. They must fit his conception of normality, they must appear to be as one; so just as Susannah was afraid of being committed to a lunatic asylum, Blair was equally afraid that she might lose her mind or run away or give in to vice. He prayed about it secretly, and looked into his own heart to see if he had committed some sin that might be the cause of this renewed unhappiness at West Lawn.

But he found none: since paying off Lavinia and selling his goods, he could discover no major errings from the Way. His hand was in the hand of the Lord, and he was walking in the paths of righteousness: however uncomfortable the conclusion might be, there was only one, namely that Susannah herself was to blame for her present unhappy state and that it was his duty to lead her out of her slough of despond upward into the light of His abounding love.

But one evening when he returned from a two-day tour of north Devon, he was greeted by Mrs Unders the midwife, her hands and arms pink from hot water and her grey hair escaping from her cap.

Susannah had lost the baby. She was sitting up in bed with a look of bleak triumph in her eyes, and when he went in to comfort her, each found that there was nothing to say.

He left her quickly and went to his dressing room; and there, standing at his bow-fronted chest of drawers, he put his head in his hands and wept – for Susannah, yes, but more especially out of impotent anger at the loss of the baby, and a feeling that God had let him down.

A year passed: the new Queen came to the throne, the country was full of talk about Reform and Socialism and the Rights of the Workers. In Teignmouth, the shipowners and merchants struggled on against the tolls and taxes levied by Exeter, which effectively prevented them from competing on level terms with such ports as Bristol, Falmouth and Liverpool. In the Harvey household, Blair and Susannah practised that self-control and tolerance which was necessary to preserve intact a marriage without love.

Susannah had a good reason now for keeping him from her bed: after her miscarriage Blair had called in Dr Cardew to attend her and he, after a careful examination, had recommended to Blair that they avoid childbirth 'and if possible the assuaging of bodily lusts' for the time being, and when he had let a little blood and questioned both parties upon a number of apparently unrelated topics, departed with his fee of two guineas in his pocket.

Having followed Cardew's advice for six months, Blair called him in again and paid a further two guineas for the privilege of being told that venery with his wife might recommence.

He announced the doctor's decision with what he considered to be great tact. He smoothed Susannah's hand between his own and told her that she was to be allowed to fulfil her function as a wife once more.

She was already in bed: he had come to her from his dressing room, having rubbed a little vaseline into his hair and brushed it back from his forehead.

'So tonight, I shall join you again, dear.' He looked down at their hands. 'Or perhaps I should say, we shall be joined.'

'I fear we shall not, Blair. I'm sorry, but we cannot. I have the blessing.'

He detested the way she referred to her menstruation as the blessing. It seemed to him that the term flew directly in the face of God's directive to Adam and Eve to go forth and multiply.

'Would Eve have called it a blessing?' he asked her, 'No, she would not, for it would mean another opportunity lost to bring a child into this world.'

'In that case I have the *curse* and must be excused,' she replied.

He gave way, and retired to his separate bedroom to contain his desires for another few days.

When he repeated the proposal, Susannah said that she felt she was not yet ready to recommence their relations.

'But the doctor has pronounced you fit, dear. He was quite clear on the matter. He told me straight out that there was now no reason at all why we should not enjoy all the legitimate pleasures of our marital state.'

'Nevertheless it would not be a pleasure for me,' she said quietly.

He stared at her for several seconds, then pouted and stamped out of the room.

She continued to refuse him with diabolical obstinacy for several weeks after, until he lost his patience and called upon Dr Cardew for a private consultation. The doctor took several notes and looked very grave.

'I fear that this may be a matter which is beyond my powers to put right, Mr Harvey,' he said, fingering a small, white beard. 'As you know I have examined your wife and have found her to be in excellent physical health.'

'But how can you say that? You yourself have admitted that she suffers from languors and I do not have to be a physician to know that her nerves, her vapours, are far from normal.'

Doctor Cardew inclined his head. 'Ah yes, Mr Harvey, but such symptoms may be induced by causes other than physical ill-health.'

Blair uncrossed his legs and frowned. 'What do you imply by that, sir?'

The other hesitated a moment, then took pen and paper and began to write. 'I shall recommend a book to you, Mr Harvey, which you may find of interest and of assistance in dealing with your wife's aversion to your attentions. I have a copy of it myself, but I would rather you obtained your own, for I find it an invaluable reference.' He passed the slip of paper across his desk. 'There is the address to which you should apply.'

Blair looked at the doctor's scrawl. ' "Three essays . . ." Three essays about what?'

Dr Cardew stood up to terminate the consultation. 'I think you will find at least one of them of interest, Mr Harvey. I would not like to say more than that at this stage. Perhaps I could tender my account to you within the next few days?'

Two weeks later, the book arrived in the post. It was brought into the breakfast room by Robson, who in the three years of his marriage had become increasingly surly.

Blair put it by his plate without a word.

'What is it? It looks like a book,' Susannah said. 'Aren't you going to open it?'

'In my own good time,' he said, and allowed Peg to help him to a slice of buttered haddock.

After prayers, he went into the library (which had become his study) with the parcel, and when Susannah went visiting and passed the window, she looked in and saw him engrossed in a small, black-covered volume. This was not entirely unusual, for he was beginning to build up a small collection of works by authors among the brethren, so she presumed that this must be some new commentary from the pen of brother Darby. But something about his manner towards her during the days following the arrival of the book began to change her mind. That evening, for instance, he came in abruptly without knocking as if in the hope of catching her at something, and asked her outright if she would not now allow him his rights as her husband, and when she bravely stood her ground and told her that it was her right as a wife to refuse him, he stared intently at her for several seconds before slamming out of the room.

The feeling that he suspected her grew stronger by the day. It was as if he had decided to place her under the closest surveillance. She could not spend five minutes alone in her room without her solitude being suddenly disturbed by an unannounced arrival; when she remarked one evening that she felt tired and would retire early, he looked up sharply, as if her casual remark had given him one more vital clue. The following Lord's Day, at the breaking of bread, he provided her with another cause for alarm: quite out of context, he read out the first chapter of the Epistle to the Romans, laying a subtle emphasis upon the twenty-sixth verse.

The beginnings of a suspicion began to form in her mind, and she saw that if she could look at the book which had occupied so much of Blair's time over the past few weeks, she would be in a better position to understand exactly what was in his mind and causing these strange innuendoes.

But it was not easy. He kept the book locked up in his desk, and was very careful about the personal custody of his keys. She considered ways in which she might get at these keys and have a duplicate cut, but the very thought of that deceitful and underhand action pulled her up short and made her see to what depths she was already sinking.

Then one morning as she emerged from her bedroom, she was presented with a solution so simple that she hardly knew what she was doing until she had done it. Blair was upon the close stool and his dressing room door open. There, on his chest of drawers were his keys. It was over in a minute: she took them, ran downstairs, unlocked the drawer in his bureau where he kept the book, ran back up to his dressing room and replaced the keys as she had found them.

At breakfast, he remarked that she appeared to be trembling, and when she made light of it and said that she was perfectly well he stared intently at her again. 'Are you sure, Susannah?' he asked. 'Will you promise me that you are concealing nothing from me, that you are unassailed by any sort of sickness, whether of mind or body?'

'I am perfectly well,' she declared. 'I have never felt better.'

It seemed that he would never depart, and she was terrified that he might look in his drawer and find it unlocked. But he did not, and as soon as he had left the house and was striding away down the drive, she went quickly into his study, and took the book in her hands for the first time. It was a medical treatise with a very long title:

THREE ESSAYS

First
on the disorders of People of Fashion
Second
On diseases incidental to literary and sedentary Persons (with proper Rules for preventing their fatal Consequences and Instructions for their Cure)
Third
On Onanism: or, A Treatise upon the DISORDERS produced by MASTURBATION: or, the EFFECTS of Secret and Excessive VENERY.

by S.A. Tissot, D.M.

Translated from the French by Francis Bacon Lee, M. Danes, A. Hume, M.D.

She bit her lip and turned to the third essay, which appeared to be well thumbed, and found in it passages that sent the colour flaming to her neck and cheeks. One particular passage was underscored, with 'N.B.' added in Blair's hand:

'A common symptom in both sexes, and which I rank under this article, as it is more frequent among women, is the indifference which this infamous practice leaves for the lawful pleasures of Hymen, even when their inclinations and powers still remain; an indifference which does not only induce many to embrace a life of celibacy, but even accompanies the nuptial bed. In the collection of Dr Bekkers, a female acknowledges that this practice had gained so complete a domination over her senses, that she detested the lawful means of assuaging the lusts of the flesh.'

She found herself breathing rapidly with outrage and embarrassment. Did Blair suspect her of this? It certainly

267

seemed so, if the way he had underlined some words three times was anything to go by. And why had he sent for this book? Who had told him of it? She turned the pages and found other passages with Blair's marginal notes and underlinings:

'The English Onania is replete with confessions, that cannot be read without horror and compassion: the disorder seems to make even greater progress with women than with men . . .' And another: '. . . there is another kind of pollution, which may be called *clitorical*, the known origin of which is to be traced so far back as the second Sappho

Lesbides infamem quae me fecistis amatae:
and which was so much too common amongst the Roman women, at the time when all morality was lost, that it was more than once the subject for the epigrammatists and satirists of that age . . .'

She turned the pages back and forth, finding new horrors of symptoms and consequences. Hysterical fits . . . shocking vapours . . . incurable jaundices . . . cramps in the stomach and back – there seemed no end to the variety of fearful results brought on by the malady, and nearly all led to premature death.

But here was a yet more horrifying passage, drawn to her attention by another marginal note in Blair's hand:

'Women have been known to love girls with as much fondness as ever did the most passionate of men, and conceive the most poignant jealousy, when they were addressed by the male sex upon the force of love.'

Beside this passage Blair had written one word: 'Zilla'.

She put the book back in the drawer. It was all too horrible to contemplate, too vile, too scandalous. She went to the window, pressing her forehead and drumming her fists against the cold glass pane.

'He thinks I am filthy, filthy, filthy!' she sobbed.

There was only one way out, she had no alternative. She must go to Blair this evening, tonight. She must beg his forgiveness for withholding from him what was rightfully his. They must resume relations immediately and continue them, however much she detested it, however many children she might bear.

It was a second repentance: Blair accepted it from her as if he had been confidently expecting it for some time.

Surprisingly, she found that if she forced herself to concentrate upon his finer qualities and rigorously suppressed all filthy thoughts and inclinations, she was able to achieve a sort of semi-contentment that was enlivened from time to time by moments of real happiness in the company of the domestics and her children.

When she became pregnant again in the new year, Blair received the news with joy and tender affection. He sat with her and patted her hands between his own.

'This will be our son,' he said, beaming at her with moist eyes. 'I have been asking my Lord for him for the past two months, and I know in my heart that His answer is now on the way.'

She looked down at her lap and smoothed the pleats of her dress with a pale hand through which blue veins showed.

'Do you believe it Susannah? Will you have faith as I have that the Lord will give us this good gift?'

'I will try, Blair,' she nodded.

He was quite overcome. Tears rolled down his cheeks and he called her his little rabbit, an endearment he had not used since Benjamin had been drowned, and which had once amused and delighted her.

As for the little black volume of essays by Monsieur Tissot, she never saw it again, and no reference was ever made to it.

CHAPTER 13

Blair became one of the elders of Ebenezer in the spring – a member of that select group of brethren known as the 'oversight'. Along with brothers Synge, Starling and Tozer, he became responsible for the spiritual guidance of the assembly and its temporal administration.

He threw himself into his new role with enthusiasm. Every Friday evening the oversight met in one of each other's houses, usually finding it necessary to remain in session until two or three in the morning to discuss tricky doctrinal problems such as whether Mrs Clapp should be reproved for wearing beads at the breaking of bread, or what stand should be taken on the matter of Captain Endacott's private use of tobacco. There was also the question of how open open ministry should be – a problem that recurred every time a young brother with too much self-esteem and not enough learning stood up on a Lord's Day morning to exercise his powers of public speaking. This was a serious dilemma, and one that was never to be completely resolved, for having condemned the clergy and all tendencies towards pastorship, the brethren found that the other side of the coin could be equally dangerous, with newly converted upstarts claiming their share of spiritual guidance and misleading the saints to an alarming degree.

'If I have to listen to brother Longbottom holding forth upon Jonah in the belly of the whale once more, I really do not know if I shall be able to contain my impatience,' Susannah remarked one Sunday.

Blair patted her hand and quoted I Timothy ii 11, saying that women should learn in silence with all subjection.

He was beginning to feel that he was at last making progress. He was head of an increasing family; his wife appeared docile and obedient; his domestics were well disciplined and Christian. Though he knew that his orthodoxy must by definition involve a deliberate abandonment of worldly ambition or a 'career' (for what would it avail a man even to become a second La Place if, after thirty-five years' study, the Lord descended from heaven, snatched up all his saints to meet him and burned to ashes the works of the earth?) he still harboured a need to be at the forefront, to run with the leaders. To this end, he attended every conference on prophecy and gathering of the elders from other assemblies that he could. He never turned down an invitation to speak, and spent much of his working day studying the Scriptures or preparing his next address.

Susannah's latest pregnancy presented him with a new challenge. Since her miscarriage, he had felt led by the Spirit to believe that she had lost her baby through her own lack of faith: the more he thought and prayed about it, the more convinced of it he became. Now, it seemed to him that they were being presented with a second chance.

'Can we in all conscience ignore the fact that we failed the test last time, dear?' he asked one evening. 'No, we cannot. Can we pretend that we are not hopeful of a son this time? No, that neither. Therefore, I say, let us approach the Lord in all humility and ask again for the gift of a son. Let us ask in confidence and in faith.'

She made no attempt to argue with him, and the new item was included in his shopping list of night prayers. A few weeks later, the same request slipped out by mistake during breakfast prayers, and that afternoon Sal announced proudly to the butcher boy that Mrs Harvey was going to have a son because Mr Harvey had asked the Lord for one.

The story went quickly round the town and became a subject for lighthearted gossip in the alehouses. Bets were laid, the odds favouring another girl, for although some held that as red followed black on a roulette table so a run of daughters must eventually end in a son, the majority pointed to the many cases of girls-only families which were common at the time.

Captain Endacott remained a close friend of the family. Never having benefited from a university education, he looked up to Blair for his aura of learning and his ability to turn a phrase; Blair, on the other hand enjoyed Endacott's company, appreciated his capacity for hard work and basked in the reflected glory of his rank and family background.

Since breaking with Cobbe, most of the everyday administration had been shifted onto Endacott's shoulders, and although the dragoon was not well suited to such responsibilities he accepted them with humility. When trade slackened and competition from other ports grew fiercer, he thought nothing of dipping into his capital to subsidise repair costs or pay crew wages, and having partly mortgaged his land to buy out Cobbe, it wasn't long before he was asking the South Devon Bank for further loans; so while Blair travelled about in happy ignorance of the firm's decline, Endacott put on a brave face and saw his worldly assets quietly slipping away.

He was a great favourite with the Harvey household, and became almost an uncle to the children. One reason for his popularity was that from time to time he invited them over to his farm for an event he called 'afternoon tea', a treat invented by his cousin the Duchess of Bedford and staunchly supported by the importers and retailers of the beverage.

He sent his carriage over to West Lawn one Saturday in August, and they rode sedately along beside the Teign in it, the children looking like blonde dumplings in their sun bonnets, and Susannah, who was now in her last month of pregnancy, holding a parasol against the damaging rays of the sun.

Captain Endacott and his housekeeper Mrs Hammet made them all very welcome indeed. A trestle table had been set up in the shade behind the farm house and large quantities of provisions made available. There were cottage loaves fresh from the oven, rich yellow butter the good woman had churned herself at five o'clock that morning, jars and jars of clotted cream, fruitcakes groaning with sultanas, and a quantity of damson tartlets the pastry of which gave sure evidence of Mrs Hammet's lightness of hand. To wash all this down, as an alternative to the special Cavendish tea, there was cool whey for the children and apple juice for the domestics.

It was one of those hot, sultry days that could give way to thunder: a dark hammer-head of cloud hung over the hills to the north, and a heat haze was turning the villages of Ringmoor and Shaldon into shimmering mirages on the other side of the Teign. For once, Blair seemed to have abandoned his grave manner and was behaving with that natural good humour Susannah had found so attractive in him before they were married. The conversation was lively too – with Endacott asking her opinion of the new reforms, the role of women, and the dangers inherent in Rousseau's idea of a social contract between gentry and the labouring classes.

After they had eaten and Blair had given thanks, Endacott suggested that Peg, Sal and Robby take the little ones down the meadow to see the bull in the next field, something Theodosia had been pestering him about since her arrival, and Blair – anxious for the children's safety – decided to go with them.

It was the first time that Susannah had been alone in Endacott's company since the day they had travelled back from Exeter nearly five years before. For a few minutes they were silent, Susannah self-conscious of her condition, and Endacott's finest instincts aroused by it.

273

They watched the others going down through the hay field, Blair an incongruous figure in black, up to his knees in daisies and poppies, and little Grace's sunhat bobbing along beside him like a white boat upon a sea of grasses.

'What fine children they are, Susannah,' Endacott remarked. 'You must be very proud of them.'

She made no reply, but her colour heightened at his use of her first name.

'I cannot help thinking that had my own dear wife lived we might have been blessed with children too,' he went on, and glanced covertly across the table, wondering what thoughts were troubling her, longing to draw her out – and yet afraid of overstepping the limits of propriety.

She sighed deeply, and looking away from him said quietly: 'I do not feel at all proud of them. I hardly feel that they are mine.'

It was as if two prisoners, kept in solitary confinement for years, had been unexpectedly allowed permission to talk together in the prison yard.

'How is that?' he asked gently.

She turned back to look at him, and he saw her eyes scanning his own face. Tell me, he wanted to say, tell me everything that is in your heart.

'I do not deserve them,' she said. 'They are fine children, yes – but that is no thanks to me, no thanks at all, and I have no reason for any sort of pride in them. Indeed,' she went on, and he was aware that she had needed to say these things for a long time, 'since my – since Benjamin died, I have found it difficult to display affection to any person. It is as if something in me died with him, so that I have become only half a person, and no sort of mother at all.'

He saw her struggling for control, and his heart went out to her. 'My dear – you are the finest, gentlest and most loving mother possible, and I will not hear otherwise of you – not even from your own lips.'

She shook her head and regarded him with a wistful

tenderness that made him shout inwardly that he loved her.

'And yet I think you must, Captain Endacott. I do not say it lightly. I may appear to others as a loving mother, but the truth of the matter is that I feel nothing at all for those three little girls. Nothing at all.'

'Then why is there a tear in your eye when you say it?'

She looked away. 'Self pity, probably. We're all good at that, aren't we? But still – I expect this one will be a boy, and that will make a change, won't it?'

He was amazed – and a little embarrassed – by the open way she referred to her unborn child; but at the same time he was gratified by it, believing that in making him her confidant in this way, she was tacitly admitting to deeper feelings towards him than those of a mere acquaintance.

'But – do you *believe* it will be a son?'

She avoided his gaze, and spoke as if quoting a formula. 'Blair says that if we have faith as to a grain of mustard, we should not be afraid to ask for what we sincerely desire.'

'And what do you think, Susannah?'

'Is what I think so important, Captain Endacott?'

The sound of the children's laughter came to them from the other end of the meadow. He said: 'Would it be improper of me to ask that you call me by my first name?'

She looked away again and whispered so softly that he barely caught her words: 'Yes, James, it would.'

He looked down at the scrubbed boards of the trestle table between them, and again they were silent.

'Your opinion does matter to me,' he said at length. 'I would not ask it simply to have an echo of your husband's. I believe you have a fine – an acutely perceptive mind.'

'Whether that is so or not, you must surely agree that in matters of faith, a perceptive mind is a positive hindrance, especially in a member of the weaker sex. I would like to believe as firmly as Blair that I am to bear him a son, but I fear I lack the gift of faith.'

'The gift of faith? Does not every Christian have the gift of faith?'

'Have you not read brother Müller's *Narrative*? He differentiates between the gift and the grace of faith very clearly in it. For instance – the grace of faith is required to believe that the Lord is risen and will come again in glory; but the gift of faith is needed to believe that the sick can be healed by prayer or the naked clothed or – or –'

'Or, that one's wife will bear a son if you ask it?'

'Yes.'

The others had gone on down to the ha-ha. Blair was twirling Grace round and round so that her feet skimmed over the turf.

'If you do not have the gift of faith, *I* think that you are blessed with many other gifts every bit as precious,' Endacott said suddenly.

She relaxed, laughing. 'Oh, yes! A paragon of talent and virtue!'

He regarded her with grave, kind eyes. 'You have the gift of silence, the gift of being able to listen, the peace that passeth all understanding.'

The colour shot to her cheeks and neck. They were suddenly back at the Royal Hotel, she sitting at the fire and hastily turning down the hem of her dress, he transfixed by her loveliness.

'You can have no true idea as to my character,' Susannah told him. 'Outward appearances are often misleading, are they not? And besides – it makes me uneasy to hear myself complimented for qualities which I know I do not possess.'

'I was not attempting to compliment you, Susannah. I was merely voicing my appreciation of certain aspects of your nature. I felt it high time to do so, for I think that you do not often hear the truth about yourself.'

She looked down at the rough grain of the table, her hands, a lady-bird crawling painstakingly up the milk jug. 'I think you may be approaching the limits of propriety,

Captain Endacott,' she said very quietly.

'In that case I apologise. The last thing I wish is to offend you in any way. Believe me –'

But she glanced quickly at him in warning: Blair was approaching up the hill with Grace on his shoulders and Theodosia trotting beside him, holding his hand.

'Please let us never speak in this intimate way again,' she said quickly before they could be overheard. 'I am sure you understand why.'

'I understand,' he replied, and stood up to lift Grace from her father's shoulders and plonk her down on the table, bending to retrieve her sun bonnet which had fallen on the flags.

Blair had caught the sun and was perspiring freely. He mopped his face with a handkerchief.

'Well then, well then!' he boomed cheerfully, 'And what have you been talking so earnestly about to the good Captain may I ask, Susannah?'

The baby started in the early hours of the morning, just a week later. By the time Sal had been sent off to fetch Mrs Unders, and Peg and Robby despatched to fetch towels, stoke fires and boil water, Susannah was well on in labour, with the pains coming every few minutes.

Pandemonium reigned. The children awoke and began bawling their heads off; Theodosia climbed out of her cot and toddled about the landing trailing a long white nappy behind her and getting under everyone's feet, while Blair took himself off to his study to beseech the Lord for the last time over the sex of the baby.

Sal arrived back in a panic. 'Peg! Peg! She's not there! She's out on a call!'

They lifted their skirts and ran upstairs. Robby had been busy lighting candles and lamps, so that the interior of West Lawn was better lit than at any time since the days when the Harveys had thrown society parties. Susannah lay on her back in the fourposter, her belly making a huge

277

mound under a single linen sheet. Her face shone with sweat and she grimaced as a new contraction came.

There was no question of sending for an alternative midwife: there was little enough time left as it was. She gave her instructions for the delivery. Peg was told to tear up one of Blair's shirts to make a bandage, and Sal sent off to fetch a pair of scissors. Theodosia had to be shooed out of the room and Robby invited to play nursemaid to her and the other two while Peg and Sal got on with the business of helping Susannah with the birth.

It was a remarkably quick delivery: Susannah was by now well practised in the proceedings and knew how to assist matters with the maximum efficiency – in fact not having Mrs Unders there to boss her about and tell her that it was as well to feel plenty of pain was a relief, for she felt free to have the child in her own way, pushing when she knew she had to push and resting when it was time to rest.

She pulled the sheet up to her armpits and opened her legs wide. 'Can you see anything yet, Peg?' she asked. 'Can you see the head?'

Peg had attended previous births but was terrified nevertheless. Her podgy hands fluttered nervously about over the centre of operations and she uttered a succession of anxious little noises.

'The head, Ma'am?'

'The baby's head! Can you see the baby's head?'

'I got the scissors like you said, Ma'am,' announced Sal, entering the room and wiping them on her apron.

'I *can* see something,' Peg reported. 'Though I be blowed if I know if it's a head, like.'

'It's not his feet is it?'

'I don't know, Ma'am. Half a mo –'

But Susannah was in no position to wait even half a moment, for the strongest contractions were now upon her. She gritted her teeth and pushed, grunting in a way that at first shocked Sal but later made her feel much closer to her mistress because she realised that at moments like these women were but women, whether high born or not. She pressed a cool flannel to Susannah's brow and whispered words of comfort therefore, and when Susannah asked her to take her hand did so gladly, thinking it an honour.

'Ma'am!' Peg exclaimed a few contractions later. 'I can see 'im! I can see 'im! 'E's coming out a treat!'

Susannah laughed and panted; tears streamed down her face – and then her laughter changed to a sudden gasp that ended in a high pitched scream. She put her head right back and screamed and pushed and pushed and screamed, and –

It was over: every muscle in her body was trembling. She opened her eyes. Peg was holding the child up, the umbilical trailing.

'It's a boy, Ma'am! Look, Sal, it's a boy!'

She slumped back on the pillow.

'Tie the bandage in two places,' she managed. 'Tightly now. Let me see. No, twice round, then a double knot. Tight. Give me the scissors, Sal.'

Peg held the baby for her. She said a prayer – for herself, for the child – and snipped the cord.

'Now give her to me.'

'It's not a her, Ma'am. It's a he.'

'Just give her to me, Peg.'

'Shall I run and tell the master?' Sal asked.

'Yes, go and tell him,' Susannah said, and taking the child in her arms held it naked and whimpering to her breast.

It was dawn: a breathtaking beautiful August dawn, the masts and spars of the ships in the harbour projecting through a shallow layer of mist, and the grass and trees at West Lawn hung with gossamer upon which dew drops glittered like sequins.

Dressed in a black coat and stove-pipe hat, Blair

Harvey walked down under the sycamores to Bitton Street, experiencing for the first time what it meant to sing in his heart.

He overflowed with gratitude: he whispered aloud his blessings upon the Lord. Stopping at a street corner, he opened his Bible and read out the whole of the ninety-sixth psalm, so that Annie Hawke the dairy maid stopped to stare at him before continuing on her way down the hill, the pails of milk swaying from the yoke upon her shoulders.

He called at the houses of brother Synge, brother Starling and brother Tozer. He knocked on their doors and called up to their windows. 'My dear wife has been delivered of a son!' he called up to brother Starling, who stared sleepily down in his nightcap. 'Will you join me for praise and prayer?'

If Ebenezer chapel had had a bell he would have rung it. He waited outside to welcome those who had heard the good news and came to join his thanksgiving, and when a dozen or more were assembled led them in an impromptu act of worship in which he announced that his son would be called John Nelson, after his beloved brother Darby.

Afterwards, he stood at the door of the chapel shaking the saints warmly by the hand, tears of happiness glistening in his eyes. It was only now that he realised how much of a strain he had been under, for although he had insisted to all comers that he firmly believed the Lord would send him a son, he had suffered secret fears that his faith might not be strong enough after all.

As there was some time to go before he could reasonably expect Peg to serve breakfast, and as he didn't wish to become involved in the post-natal chaos which he knew from past experience would ensue, he decided to take a turn round the Den, and took the opportunity to spread the news to every delivery boy and street crier he encountered, so that within half an hour most of Teignmouth knew that Holy Harvey had got his son.

280

It was nearly eight o'clock by the time he arrived back at West Lawn: Mrs Unders had at last arrived, Sal was giving the girls their milksops in the nursery and Peg was stirring the porridge in the kitchen.

'Mr Harvey, sir,' said Mrs Unders, wiping damp hands on a cloth. 'Your wife has been asking repeatedly that you visit her as soon as you return.'

'Nothing wrong I trust, Mrs Unders? All well?'

'All very well indeed, sir, now that I have had an opportunity to put right some of the mistakes made by your domestics.'

She stood aside for him and he went upstairs to Susannah's room. The cradle had been placed by the bed and the baby's head was just visible under the kerseymere blanket. Susannah looked pale and drawn; there were dark rings under her eyes and her hair was drawn tightly back from her face and tied with a ribbon of dark blue velvet.

He fell on his knees beside the bed and gave thanks.

'He is not at all like his sisters, is he?' he observed, peering down at the infant. 'He is dark and they are all fair. And I think he has his grandmother's features. O Susannah! Susannah!'

'Blair,' she said. 'Blair —'

But his effusion of thanksgiving continued. He paced the room, joined his hands under his chin, went to the window, and flinging it open announced to the world, 'I have a son! A son!' He was gripped by a new idea. 'My dear — let us dedicate him, here and now, to the Lord's service. Let us —'

'Blair — it is not a son. It is a daughter.'

He turned slowly, blinking in bewilderment.

'Peg was mistaken, Blair. I discovered it almost immediately, but you had already left the house.'

'Mistaken? How can she have been mistaken?'

Susannah knew the reason, but could not possibly explain. She was physically exhausted and wished simply

281

that Blair would accept what she said without further argument.

But of course he would not.

'She cannot be mistaken,' he muttered. 'It is quite ridiculous. You are lightheaded, Susannah, that's what it is. Nervous imagination. Sal has informed me quite clearly that it is a boy. I have celebrated the fact with the brethren.'

She sighed, closing her eyes. 'Yet it is a daughter, Blair. I have seen with my own eyes. And I am not at all lightheaded nor am I suffering from nerves. I am tired, yes, but I do know that my baby is a girl.'

He turned away. 'I will not believe it.'

'You must believe it, dear. It is the truth.'

He began to look as though he might burst into tears at any moment. 'I have asked my Lord for a son and I have been told we have a son. We have given thanks together as brethren and sisters in the Lord –'

'Am I to blame for that? Could you not have visited your wife to give thanks with her before announcing the birth to the world? Was your public celebration so much more important than our private rejoicing?'

He went quickly to the cot and removed the blanket from the infant, which immediately began to cry. 'I will see for myself,' he muttered. 'I will not believe unless I see it with my own eyes.'

He lifted the baby from the cot. Susannah reached out her hands, begging him to be careful. 'Please – let me do it, Blair. Let me show you.'

He allowed her to take the baby. She removed the blanket in which it was wrapped and lifted a long gown to reveal the pathetic little body, the kicking legs, the tied umbilical.

'There,' he said immediately, 'It is a boy.'

She began to weep. 'It is not a boy, Blair. See. It is not a boy.'

Even now he could not accept it. It was too horrible,

too gross, too terrible . . .

'What is it, then?' he croaked. 'Some sort of monster?'

She wept the more bitterly. 'No! Not at all! This . . . part is a little enlarged beyond the normal, that is all. She is my wonderful, healthy, lovely girl, Blair, and I wish to call her Thamasine.'

'It is *not* normal,' he said, his lips white and quivering. 'It is a monster.'

'She is not! I will not have you call her that! She is quite, quite normal, I am sure of it!'

'How can you be sure? What possible knowledge can you have of such matters? It is perfectly clear that there is something wrong. Why else would Peg and Sal be mistaken?'

'I know because I know!' she hissed. 'I know because I am a woman!'

He snorted. ' "Because you are a woman"! That's meaningless. I shall have Dr Cardew examine it. He is a little more expert on such matters.'

She blazed at him. 'I will not have Dr Cardew examining her! I forbid it! My child is a daughter, and I am more expert than any doctor in this matter. Do I have to spell it out for you Blair? Do you know so little about me after all these years?'

He stared intently back into her eyes, and the beginnings of an awful realisation began to dawn. 'Very well, Susannah. How do you know? How are you expert?'

She put her head in her hands to control herself, then said in a low voice, her head turned away from him: 'I know because I myself am similarly formed. Now do you understand? Now will you accept that she is a girl?'

He went back to the window and looked out over the harbour. After a while Susannah said more calmly, 'I wish to call her Thamasine Jane. I hope you have no objection to that.'

'Call it what the hell you like,' he said, and quickly left the room.

*

All his suspicions about her came flooding back. If she was indeed deformed in this way, didn't that explain the difficulties they had experienced since the very first night of their married life? Didn't it support all the hints and innuendoes that Dr Cardew had let drop?

He went down to his study, unlocked his bureau and took out Tissot's essays. Yes, he thought so. There was a passage which referred to this very monstrosity, a passage which he had passed over, never thinking for one moment that the doctor – who had examined Susannah, and who must have known – had intended him to see its implications:

> 'Nature has been pleased to give some women a semi-resemblance to man; this has, upon slight inquiry, given rise to the chimera which has prevailed for some centuries, of hermaphrodites. The supernatural size of a part which is naturally very small, and whereupon M. Trouchin has given a learned dissertation, produces all the miracle, and the shameful abuse of this part, all the evil. Some women who were thus imperfect, glorying, perhaps, in this kind of resemblance, seized upon the functions of virility. The danger of this kind of pollution is not, however, less than that of the other sorts of masturbation: the effects are equally shocking, all these paths lead to emaciation, languor, pain and death . . . .'

He stared at the words, feeling a strong sensation of evil, an inward panic. He began to see it all quite clearly now: it had been Susannah's physical abnormality that had led to her tendency to excessive passion, and that in turn had caused her perverted affection for Zilla; and if her relationship with Zilla had been on some sapphic level, then all the rest must also be true: she was given over to

Onanism, in the grip of it. Why, her very deformity and that of her child were probably themselves brought on by the hateful practice!

He left the house on foot and walked rapidly up the hill, away from the town. He climbed up over Little Haldon, striding over the heathland, staring down upon the patchwork of fields where the ricks stood yellow and gold, and cattle moved slowly in green pastures.

How could he ever show his face among the brethren again? How could he continue in business, when he would be a laughing stock from Teignmouth to Tavistock and Plymouth to Portland Bill?

Everything he had worked and prayed for was in ruins. Just when he had been making progress – real progress – in gaining his place among the leaders of the brethren, he was suddenly reduced to one who would be sniggered at by every cheap-jack and ostler in the county.

He sat down on a boulder to think things out. Sheep grazed round him, looking naked after recent shearing. Below him, the escarpment dropped rapidly away to Bishopsteignton, the Teign sparkled in the sunshine, and the hills beyond faded to a distant blue. Taking out his Bible, he turned automatically to that passage he had read to the villagers of Oddicombe after the wreck of the *Fair Intention*.

Blessed are ye, when men shall revile you and persecute you and say all manner of evil against you falsely for my sake. Rejoice, and be exceeding glad: for great is your reward in heaven . . .

He looked up at the little clouds that sailed overhead, remembering odd snatches of his past life, his childhood. Had there ever been a moment in which he had not believed himself to be 'special', to have before him some great task in life that would make its mark upon history?

He began comparing himself with the Lord in the wilderness, when He was tempted by the devil. He was being similarly tempted now: he could throw it all up and turn his back on God, he could claim – with some justification – that God had let him down.

But I am not the one who has been let down, nor am I being punished, he mused. It is not through any lack of faith on my part that a son has not been born, no, but on Susannah's alone. She was the one being punished, for God must surely know that he, Blair Harvey, was strong enough to bear this setback and offer it up to His glory.

He knelt among the sheep droppings and began to pray earnestly and sincerely for guidance, and soon felt much calmer in his mind. He knew what he must do: he was quite sure that he had been led once again to see into the mind of the Lord.

Northway, who had abandoned the firm at the same time as Mr Cobbe in order to stay with the latter as his senior clerk, admitted Blair Harvey the following morning when he called at Cobbe's office. He smirked and told Harvey to take a seat, and a moment later Blair heard Cobbe's laughter coming from an inner office.

Northway emerged again.

'Mr Cobbe is engaged in pressing business,' he said, trying not to smile, 'however, he says that if you care to meet him in the New Quay Inn at one o'clock, he will be happy to hear whatever it is you wish to say to him.'

Blair walked out and stood on the sea front, where a schooner had been beached and careened. He knew very well what Cobbe was up to. He is bent upon extracting the last ounce of entertainment out of my unfortunate situation, he said to himself. But I shall have my reward just as he shall have his.

The New Quay Inn was well patronised as usual when he arrived at one. He elbowed his way across to where Cobbe was holding court to a circle of acolytes and business acquaintances.

'Mr Harvey! Talk of the devil!' Cobbe said, and there

was a shout of laughter. 'I understand you are to be congratulated over the birth of your son. Or was it a daughter?'

'I have come on business, Mr Cobbe,' Harvey said shortly. 'I shall be grateful if we could have our discussion in private.'

Cobbe waved a hand airily. 'I have no secrets, Mr Harvey. You may discuss anything you like with me before my friends.'

'Very well. I am offering my business for sale, and am giving you first refusal. A few years ago you offered a hundred and eighty a share. I am now asking only a hundred and fifty. I think it is an opportunity you can hardly afford to miss.'

Cobbe sucked in his cheeks and looked into his glass of brandy. 'You're wasting your time, Harvey,' he said in a totally new tone of voice. 'Those two ships of yours are falling apart. They're a liability, not an asset. I wouldn't take on that firm of yours if you paid me a hundred and eighty a share to do it.' Cobbe drained his glass and held it straight out to the barmaid, who refilled it immediately. 'So if that is all you came to see me about, our business is concluded.'

On his way out through the crush, someone called him back. It was a local fisherman looking very solemn and touching his forelock. 'Beg pardon for bothering you sir, but could I trouble you for some advice?'

The talk in the bar subsided suddenly, and Blair experienced a little heart palpitation at the thought that he was about to be called upon to witness for the Lord.

'Certainly you may,' he said with more confidence than he felt.

The fisherman looked from side to side shamefacedly. 'I don't know as if I like to ask 'ee, sir.'

Some of his friends urged him on, and the ship's boy from the brig *Miriam* was suddenly attacked by uncontrolled giggles.

'Do you wish to speak to me in private?' Blair suggested.

'No, sir, I'll not trouble you. It's just – just –'

'Well?'

The man turned back and grasped one of the local girls who was standing behind him. He dragged her forward, all mirth and bosom and ringlets. 'What I want to know, sir, is – is this 'ere a boy or a girl like, 'cos if it be a boy then I got a problem!'

The laughter rang in his ears all the way to Bishopsteignton.

'I cannot remain in Teignmouth,' he told Captain Endacott, whom he found overseeing the serving of one of his heifers. 'I am firmly convinced that this is no longer my place. I have always found more success among country people, as you know, and my wife is in urgent need of a change of air.'

The bull having achieved a satisfactory union, the two men strolled back up to the farmhouse, and stood on a plat of ground that overlooked the village.

'I have to ask you as my brother in the Lord if you will take over the reins from me, James. And if you can find it in your heart to pay a modest price for the shares remaining in my name, I shall count it the act of a Christian and a gentleman.'

Endacott looked thoughtful: the shipping business had already drained away most of his capital, and he did not relish the thought of taking sole responsibility.

'Would it not be prudent to delay any final decision until next year?' he suggested. 'After all, it seems to me that the Lord would not wish your wife to have the burden of moving house with a babe in arms.'

'I expect it will survive,' Blair said under his breath.

'What of West Lawn? Will that be sold?'

'It will have to be. I shall need the capital to purchase another property.'

'But look here, Harvey – can't you see that this little

setback of yours will quickly be forgotten? Are you sure you are not making it into something far bigger than it really is?'

Blair set his teeth and breathed out impatiently. 'You don't understand a half of this, James, not a half. I have laid the matter before the Lord, there is no doubt in my mind as to His wishes for me.'

Endacott accompanied him to the trap. 'I shall be sorry indeed to lose your fellowship,' he said. 'And that of your dear wife. I would urge you most sincerely to reconsider –'

But Blair was already slapping the bay rump of his gelding with the reins and moving off, and Endacott, watching him going away down the track to the road, found himself wondering what Susannah felt about all this, and whether she longed for a meeting with him as much as he did for a meeting with her.

On arriving at West Lawn, Blair was informed of a new crisis. Peg came bustling out of the kitchen, where Sal was sobbing bitterly.

'It's Robby, sir,' she announced.

'What about Robby?'

'He's gone, sir. Upped and left her. Put a note on her pillow saying he's gone to London and won't be coming back. Says he's had enough of our way of life, seemingly, sir.'

He went into his study, and stared moodily out of the window. 'So be it, so be it,' he muttered aloud, and smacked a fist into the palm of his hand. 'We shall shake the very dust of Teignmouth from our feet, Mr Harvey. We shall seek pastures new.'

He smiled suddenly, realising that he was now the head of a household comprised entirely of women, and unable to prevent himself comparing his situation with that of Endacott's bull, sent in among a herd of cattle.

PART TWO

Babylon

CHAPTER 14

Susannah received the announcement that they were to remove to a small farm on the edge of Dartmoor with outward resignation, though she could not help having doubts as to Blair's ability as a farmer. When she suggested tactfully that taking on ten acres and a hundred sheep might turn out to be more of a burden than he presumed, he squashed her with his usual condescension.

'There is no magic about ploughing a field beyond a strong arm and a steady eye, Susannah, and I have both. Nor do I anticipate great difficulty in putting a ram among ewes and trusting in the Lord to provide the increase. Besides – are we so lacking in faith that we must question His holy will? Are we to fall into the error of putting worldly reasoning before spiritual obedience?'

'I was only thinking of yourself, dear. If you employed a capable manager, you would be freer to pursue your evangelical activities, and you would also be able to learn the business of farming with less risk to crops and livestock.'

He snorted loftily. 'I think you will be better advised to concentrate your attention on the running of the household and the care of my children, Susannah, and leave the important decisions to your husband.'

She was used to such treatment now – almost took it for granted. Since Thamasine's birth, he had been careful to preserve a cool courtesy towards her, while at the same time making it quite clear that he resented and disapproved of the new arrival; and although he claimed to have been moved by the Spirit to minister in the country, Susannah was in no doubt that he was in fact simply running away from the loss of face he had suffered before the brethren of Ebenezer.

In a number of subtle ways, she found herself and Thamasine being separated from the rest of the household. Whether this was intentional on Blair's part she could not be sure, but she could not help noticing, for instance, that when he referred to the three elder daughters it was always 'my little girls' or 'my treasures', while if he found himself obliged to refer to Thamasine it was 'your child' or even 'number four'.

He particularly disliked Susannah nursing Thamasine herself, a practice he looked upon with such obvious revulsion that she felt obliged to avoid all mention of it. Once, when she was sitting in her room with Thamasine at her breast, Blair burst in on her, stopping in the doorway when he saw what was going on.

'Oh,' he said. 'You're feeding it, are you?'

She was inevitably hurt by such treatment, but it had an effect upon her which Blair could not have intended: the more he rejected and resented Thamasine, the more protective and loving Susannah became, so that by his very disapproval, Blair drove mother and daughter into a closeness that was to grow into an inseverable bond.

September passed: West Lawn was put up for sale, and Endacott persuaded to buy Harvey's shares in the firm at eighty pounds each – a purchase that reduced the Captain to a budget that was virtually hand to mouth. Susannah saw little of him now, and though she could not be sure felt that Blair might have had something to do with the fact that Endacott now occupied a seat in the meeting that was well removed from their own.

Blair arrived home one evening looking pleased. 'The purchase is concluded!' he told Susannah, holding her hands between his. 'We move three weeks tomorrow.'

Her heart sank.

'Well, don't look so down in the mouth, dear!'

She shook her head, looking down at his tapering thumbnails. 'We seem to have taken this decision so precipitately, Blair. I wish I could be sure, as you are, that it is a wise course.'

'Have you not always wanted a cottage in the country? I have heard you sighing for one a hundred times!'

'That was before I had four children, dear. And we are not as young as we were, either. I have no idea what the house is like apart from what you have told me; I don't know how we shall educate the children – or even if there are enough beds for us to sleep in!'

He released her hands and went to the door. 'You will just have to have a little faith in me, won't you Susannah? You will have to accept that your husband is not quite the ninny you so obviously believe him to be.' And with that he left her standing at that windowsill where she had stood so often before, looking out over the grey roofs and the grey harbour, where black smoke from a steam packet was spreading out in a flat cloud over the town.

The day of their departure dawned wet and windy, identical weather to that experienced on the journey from Exeter twelve years before. Soon after dawn, four carrier vans and a closed carriage came up the drive, and their effects were loaded. Captain Endacott arrived unexpectedly to wish them farewell: he pressed Susannah's fingers to his lips, asking God's blessing on her before handing her into the carriage. Grace and Bea sat on either side of her, facing forwards, and she carried Thamasine in her arms. Peg, Sal and Theodosia sat facing the rear, all three in a state of high apprehension and excitement.

Blair, who had chosen to make the journey on horseback, had gone to say a few final words to the coachman about the route.

'Mama,' said Theodosia while they waited to depart, 'who will live here when we are gone?'

'I don't know, Theo. The house hasn't been sold yet.'

'Will it be sold?'

'I expect so.'

'Then will we ever come back again?'

Susannah sighed. 'I don't know. I shouldn't think so.'

'Can't see into the future, can we?' Peg remarked. 'No one can do that.'

'Papa can,' Theodosia remarked, with that total confidence in her father's ability sometimes found in five year olds.

'Oh yes? And how does he do that?'

Theodosia tossed her head impatiently. 'Papa says that one day *quite soon* there will be a trumpet in the sky, and we shall be caught up.'

Susannah let out an unintentional snort, which sounded dangerously incredulous.

'Mama!' scolded her daughter. 'Didn't you know *that*?'

Blair looked in, and saved her from further scorn. 'All ready for the off, are we?' he asked cheerfully.

The carriage jerked and swayed: the sloping lawns, the walnut tree and the house slipped away out of sight, and as the convoy turned right to take the road out of town, Susannah settled back against the green leather, holding Thamasine's head to her cheek for their mutual reassurance.

They travelled north along the Teign valley at first, then struck out over Bovey Heath to Bovey Tracey. It rained almost constantly throughout the journey. Susannah would have preferred to stop on the way in order to be able to nurse Thamasine in privacy, but this was not possible because Blair was intent upon reaching their destination well before nightfall. As a result, Theodosia saw her little sister at the breast for the first time, an experience that caused her to ask in amazement, 'Mama! What are you doing now? Are you giving her a drink out of your chest?'

296

After Bovey Tracey, the road climbed steeply up to Moretonhampstead. They passed through densely wooded areas where deer cantered gracefully off at their approach; they were held up by cattle on the road, a village funeral and the Chagford hunt. On arrival at Chagford itself – a small market town with a curious pile of ancient stones at its centre – the coachman consulted with the landlord of the Ring o' Bells on the state of the road up to Brimstonedown.

Overhearing the conversation, Peg threw her hands to her mouth. 'Is that the place we're going, Ma'am? Brimstonedown?'

Susannah reassured her: 'They have strange names in these parts, Peg. Our neighbours are Batworthy and Frenchbeer.'

'Still, I could've done without a name like that,' Peg said, shaking her head so that her chins wobbled all the way down her neck.

After descending the hill out of Chagford, they began the long, slow climb through Waye, Thorn and Teigncombe. Low branches scraped on the carriage roof, and the lane was so narrow and high banked that it was impossible to see anything but occasional glimpses of the surrounding countryside, which appeared to consist solely of small, wet fields.

'Mama,' said Theo. 'What do you think would happen, if the horses slipped and we went sliding helter-skelter down the hill?'

'We would just go on sliding down the hill, Theo, wouldn't we?'

'But what would *happen*?'

'I expect we should all end up in a very untidy heap.'

Theodosia considered this reply for some moments, then asked: 'Would we be backsliders then?'

'No,' said her mother, sighing inwardly. 'Not that sort of backslider.'

'Then *what* sort?'

The carriage came to a halt with a creak; Blair was shouting directions to the waggoners. Looking diagonally ahead, Susannah saw their new home for the first time: a grey stone building perched on the edge of the moor, with a field dropping steeply away before it and a jumble of barns and outhouses on either side. Hooves clattered on wet stones and the carriage wheels crackled and squeaked; they alighted, stretching their cramped limbs and looking round at their new surroundings.

For a few moments, silence descended: an ancient, eery silence composed of mists and moorland, the distant bleating of sheep, and a feeling that invisible eyes were watching from the halls of time.

The shock of their changed circumstances was not long in arriving. Within minutes of the furniture vans departing, Grace had lost her balance and scraped her knee, Bea had lost control of her bladder and was sitting on the kitchen flags in a pool of her own making – and Blair, bitten by the shepherd's wall-eyed dog, had lost his temper.

The house had been prepared for their arrival, but was neither as clean nor as dry as Susannah would have wished. Peg and Sal were set to work immediately: unpacking essentials, scrubbing out the kitchen and making up the beds, while Susannah, having nursed her baby and put her down in the cradle, began organising supper for the children. While all this was going on, Blair conducted a lengthy conversation with old Gus, who had come down from the moor to see the new arrivals in. Gus was the complete shepherd: tall, leathery-skinned, bearded and smocked, and blessed with that gentle voice and mild Devon manner born of many seasons of lambing and shearing, dipping and ramming.

Having finally ended his conversation, Blair came to the kitchen door and watched the women at their work. As there was nothing he could think of to do before dinner, he enquired if he might be of any assistance.

Susannah's patience snapped.

'Yes, there *are* one or two ways in which you might help, Blair,' she replied, her sleeves rolled up and her hands wet. 'You may find the candles so that we do not have to go to bed in the dark. You may take an axe and chop wood. You may light fires, draw water and bring in the potatoes from the barn – and when you have done that there are those boxes to unpack, and you will doubtless want to decide whether we shall sleep with our feet to the north or the south tonight – a decision that may tax you, as I see we are between two rivers here, and I know that you like to sleep with your feet pointing at water. Does that answer your question? Do you require any further instructions?'

He stared at her open mouthed: she had never spoken to him like that before – not even in the earliest days of their marriage, when she had been so quick to belittle him. But he said nothing, and went back out to the yard, returning ten minutes later with an armful of wood. He lit the fires and pumped water up to the tank, and on his way through the kitchen Susannah touched his arm and whispered an apology for what she had said.

So the first day ended: the three little ones were tucked side by side into a feather bed, and when they had eaten mutton stew and boiled potatoes, the remainder of the household retired for the night.

Donning a flannel nightshirt in the tiny room he shared with Susannah and the baby, Blair Harvey was gripped by an uncharacteristic faltering of self-confidence, with the result that he prayed with unusual sincerity that the Lord might guide them and keep them; and much later, when the wind was sighing over the moor and a vixen screaming in the forest of South Park, Susannah awoke, and finding Blair awake at her side, reached out to him and welcomed him into her arms, whispering his name and for once receiving from him some of the love and warmth which she needed so much.

Any illusions about an idyllic country life were quickly banished. It became immediately apparent that if the household and farm were to be properly managed, master and mistress would have to work as hard or even harder than their employees. Without Robson to assist in the house and without money to afford a manservant, Harvey was forced to take on tasks he had never dreamt of performing. He found himself mending walls, splitting logs, clearing drains and digging ditches, and in doing so discovered that an Oxford education was a positive disadvantage. It led one to place too much reliance on the printed word: when the spring cart required repair, he would have gladly exchanged his whole knowledge of Virgil's *Georgics* for an hour's instruction in simple engineering.

To eke out the household budget, Susannah persuaded him to purchase a couple of Devonshire Reds in milk; and having consulted a neighbouring farmer's wife on the care of these animals, she managed to maintain an adequate supply of dairy products for the family. She cleaned out the dairy, whitewashed its walls and taught herself how to milk, churn and make cheese; and though Blair would have been the last to admit it, this aspect of the farm contributed more to the health of the family than any of his Dartmoor sheep, whose fleeces were fetching pitifully low prices at the wool factory.

Winter came, and with it hoar frosts and blizzards. Arriving in from a day on the moor with old Gus, Blair sat before the kitchen fire, his leggings steaming, and ate his supper like a peasant, the plate balanced on his knees. Once a week, the women boiled up quantities of the peat brown water that seeped down off the moor, and he took a hip bath, the suds clinging to the mat of hair on his chest and the beard he was cultivating to act as a muffler.

There were never enough hours in the day: they rose at four-thirty in the morning and worked until seven at night, and still felt themselves slipping by degrees into poverty.

Even Theodosia was forced into employment: given strict instructions on the care of her younger sisters, she bossed them about, played schools with them, insisted upon hearing their prayers at the most unlikely times of day, and rocked Thamasine so determinedly that the wooden cradle made a thundering, quick-march rhythm that echoed through the house.

Unable to afford a governess, and unwilling to send her daughters to the infant school in Chagford, Susannah taught her children herself. In the summer, when eagles soared overhead and the Rhode Islands pecked in the dust, she sat on the kitchen step reading stories aloud and hearing Theodosia answering Mangnall's *Questions* and Grace stumbling through her first reader; and so informal was her method of teaching that the girls hardly realised that they were at school in her class, with the result that all were literate by the age of five. Such rapid progress set them apart from the local children they saw on market days in Chagford, and because they accompanied their parents to the Brethren's Room at Wonson for the breaking of bread each week, they were similarly set apart from the daughters of gentry. As a result, the Harvey children grew up in the certainty that they were special in an exclusive way, for while they shared the poverty of the common people they did not share their lack of learning, and while they shared the good breeding of the gentry, they did not share their worldliness. Such differences caused them to look down upon the world. They were set apart, in a high place. Their Papa was educated and their Mama had once been wealthy, and yet each had put away these mainstays of human esteem in order to follow the Lord.

So they humbled themselves in the satisfying knowledge that by doing so they would be exalted, and the family became ever more close knit – almost like a royal family in which the king and queen jealously guard the princesses to keep them from being sullied by contact either with too

301

little learning or too much luxury.

As the years passed, the memory of their life at West Lawn receded until it assumed the quality of a dreamlike pre-existence, a folk memory that was evoked from time to time by Bea in particular, who, on occasions of special misery would wail, 'I want to go back to Tinmuff!'

'Me, I wouldn't mind neither,' Peg muttered gloomily one black morning while ladling out the porridge.

But there was no going back. They had sold their possessions, they had put their trust in the Lord. However poor they might be, however ill-shod, wet, cold or miserable, they could at least rejoice in the knowledge that with every setback and hardship patiently borne, they laid up for themselves fresh treasures in heaven, where neither moth nor rust can corrupt.

Spring came round again – the fifth since their arrival. Another severe winter had reduced Harvey's flock by almost a third, and with the depression in agriculture being felt right across the country, prices were plummeting and the wool factory at Holy Street was in danger of closure.

Blair was making his way down off the moor. He had been out with his flock all day, and had found a ewe bleating over her lamb which had been drowned in one of the rock pools on Chagford common. He had knotted its forehooves together and was now dragging it down the path from Castor Rock, and its dam was trotting along behind, bleating pitifully.

From this part of the common he commanded a view of his property. He could see the slate roof of the farmhouse nestling beneath the ridge, and the small stone rectangles that enclosed his fields: Park Field, Middle Field, Break Field, Hole Field and the Field-behind-the-house. To the north of these fields, the ground dropped away rapidly to the cleve of the North Teign; to the east, the valley ran away down to Chagford. And there was Susannah, in long grey skirts, lifting leeks with Thamasine, who looked like a clockwork marionette from this distance.

He stopped a moment to watch them, and the ewe stood bleating behind him.

Where am I going? he wondered, leaning on his crook and narrowing his eyes at the horizon. Was this farming life truly what the Lord had desired for him?

He had often been troubled by such misgivings, but had never voiced them to a soul. It was lonely, being the only man among so many females. Sometimes he had been tempted to go away down the hill to one of the villages where he was not known, and enjoy a quiet ale among the yokels, but so far he had managed not to weaken. Nevertheless, the devil was still at his elbow, still ready at any moment to wreck the ship and make him a castaway.

He set off again down the hill, and the ewe continued along behind him. He dragged the carcass into the yard and allowed her to follow; then he picked up the lamb in his arms and went straight into the kitchen with it, where Peg glanced back at him with no indication of surprise. He went on through the kitchen and closed the inner door to leave the house by another, and when he disposed of the dead lamb and returned to the kitchen, he found that the sheep had entered and had been introduced to an orphan lamb he had brought down off the moor the day before. He watched the process of adoption: the lamb had already taken to its surrogate mother and was pushing its nose eagerly up under her teats, its tail shaking in delight. Though he had used this trick several times before, it never failed to surprise him how easily a ewe could be taken in.

While he was standing there, he heard hooves clattering in the yard, and a man's voice he recognised.

'Hulloa! Anyone at home?'

He strode out to make the traveller welcome.

'James! My good, good friend! My brother!' He turned as Susannah and Thamasine came in from the vegetable patch. 'See who's here, Susannah! We are not quite forgotten after all!'

He sat in the front kitchen, the centre of the whole family's interest and curiosity. Though Blair had been back to Teignmouth a couple of times, Susannah had not, so she was anxious to hear from James all the news of the town, the sisters at Ebenezer, the school, the library and whether Miss Cox was married yet to Mr Luny.

'Do you remember Captain Endacott, Theo?' Blair asked, but she shook her fair curls in uncharacteristic shyness.

'*I* remember him!' Beatrice announced, and her mother laughed and said she couldn't possibly, because she had been only three.

Grace climbed onto her father's knee and put her thumb in her mouth, regarding the captain with slow, sidelong eyes that seemed to have already gained some instinctive knowledge of the art of seduction.

'And this is little Thamasine!' the dragoon exclaimed, reaching out to shake a finger with the four year old, who regarded him with intelligent brown eyes from her mother's lap. 'I think you must be prospering, Harvey, or that this bracing Devon air is working some miracle, for I have never seen such good looking children!'

Blair took his cue and began to tell a tale of woe: how the winter had culled his sheep, how farm labourers were hard to come by and expensive to pay, how he was managing practically singlehanded now that old Gus had fallen ill and how the market for wool was being killed off by Australian imports and the boom in the textile industry.

While they talked, Sal made up bread and milk for the children's supper, each of whom was required to be kissed by their 'uncle in Christ' before being taken off to bed. Peg went off to close up the hens and fill the woodbasket, so that for a few minutes Endacott was left alone with Blair and Susannah.

'So what brings you up to Brimstonedown, James?' Blair asked. 'And how fares the world of commerce?'

Endacott stared at the hob, where mutton stew was seething in a blackened pot. 'I've had something of a setback, to tell you the truth,' he said, and looked suddenly dispirited. 'The long and the short of it is, I'm being forced into liquidation. My creditors are foreclosing. It's the end of the road, I'm afraid. I've got to sell up to avoid bankruptcy.'

Harvey blinked in astonishment. 'I can't understand it – I can't understand it,' he muttered. 'Why – the company was nicely afloat only a year or so ago –'

'No,' Endacott said, taking out a roll of tobacco. 'May I?' he asked Susannah, and proceeded to fill his pipe when she gave permission. 'No, I have been struggling for a long time now. I have been half expecting it.'

'But – why didn't you say? Why didn't you come to me?'

Endacott couldn't answer: he simply shook his head, smiling apologetically.

'Have you suffered any major losses?' Harvey asked. 'I mean – the *Benjamin* and the *Eustacia*, are they still in commission?'

He began to explain the reasons for the company's failure. There had been no major catastrophe, simply a decline in Teignmouth's fortunes as a trading port.

'I'm not the only one in this position,' he said. 'There are others going to the wall. All the money's going into this new railway, that's the trouble – money that would be better spent improving the harbour, to my mind. Our friend Mr Cobbe is making money hand over fist, as you may well imagine, and laughing up his sleeve at me when we pass in the street.' He turned to Susannah. 'As for the town, you would hardly recognise it. They have had to rebuild the bridge – which was falling down with wood rot – and are now cutting a great swathe below West Lawn for the new railway. We also have a stink from the gasworks every time the wind's in the northwest –'

'But are you no longer living in Bishopsteignton?' Susannah asked.

He shook his head. 'I sold up last autumn – to pay off my debts, you understand. No, I have lodgings in Bitton Street now, just a step from the meeting hall. But I am in good company. Do you remember brother Parnell from Dublin? He is now Lord Congleton and has taken the humblest of houses quite nearby. I have supped with him on several occasions, and he has not a single carpet in his house and the sparsest sticks of furniture imaginable! – but that is out of choice rather than force of circumstance, of course. No, you would see great changes if you returned. It's progress, progress, progress everywhere, and the devil take the hindmost, if you'll excuse the expression. Langmead & Jordan have failed, and Wise & Co also.' Endacott sighed again. 'So perhaps that answers your question, brother Harvey, as to what has gone wrong.'

Harvey took matches from the mantelpiece and lit a lamp which flared up on the table between them and sent a wisp of smoke to the ceiling. He went to the doorway and looked down over the valley, where lights were twinkling among the trees.

'Are you saying that you wish me to take the firm back from you, James? Is that it?'

'I am saying nothing at all, beyond informing you of the position,' Endacott said. 'I thought you would want to know, before the crash came. If you wish to take back the company and all the debts that go with it, then you are welcome to them. But I cannot continue myself. I have no idea what I shall do, for I shall not have a single penny left to my name by the time the creditors have been satisfied.'

Peg returned to the kitchen to find them in silence. She set down the wood basket and added a log to the fire, then took the lid off the pot and prodded the dumplings.

'Join us here at Brimstonedown,' Blair said suddenly. 'Come and work the farm with me. I need capable hands

306

and could do with some agricultural knowledge too, for most of the lads who work for me here hardly know a rick from a reap hook.'

'My dear –' Susannah put in, 'we cannot possibly – we have no room. Captain Endacott is very welcome to stay the night, but this house is simply too small for him to stay permanently –'

'In that case we shall make it bigger, eh James? With our own two – nay, four – hands. We can push out the west wall, and build rooms in the attic while we're about it for the children. What do you say to that?'

'I didn't intend to suggest this at all,' Endacott started. 'I would not like you to think –'

But Blair was already carried away by his brainwave. 'Never mind what we think! We are inviting you to come and work with us for the Lord, James! Now – what do you say? Will you throw in your lot with us?'

Sal had come down from hearing the children's prayers, and stood at the door. Peg turned back from the hob, her face shiny from the heat, a trail of blonde hair hanging down to her lip.

'Very well, I accept,' Endacott said quietly, and the two men gripped each other warmly by the hand.

Watching them, Susannah knew that she should be as pleased as they at this decision, and although her first reaction was one of happy anticipation, this was quickly overtaken by a fear that James's presence in the house might present new opportunities and temptations that she would find hard to resist.

CHAPTER 15

It is a well-known fact that a man may appear in one way to his family and in quite a different way to the world at large. An extrovert will often appear as a jolly, companionable fellow to his slight acquaintances while being known in the bosom of his family as ill-tempered, moody and tyrannical. Conversely, the introvert, regarded by the world as aloof, will often – once his door is closed and he is relaxed with his dear ones – become warm-hearted, gentle and amusing.

Harvey and Endacott were in some ways representative of these two types, though neither was aware of it. What each was conscious of however was that the renewal of their partnership was a most welcome event, for Harvey had for some time missed the bustle and companionship of Teignmouth, the nightly meetings at Ebenezer, the politics of the oversight and the jaunts into the country to preach the gospel; and Endacott had pined for those occasional times he had spent as a guest at West Lawn when he could enjoy the family atmosphere with Susannah and her children. Suddenly – providentially – Endacott was provided with a friend who had the confidence to put ideas into effect, while Harvey was presented with a man who could act as listener and sounding board.

Such partnerships are common, but the strange part about them is that they can be seldom observed in their entirety, the behaviour of the partners undergoing subtle changes as they move from one circle to another. If an invisible observer had been able to accompany Endacott and Harvey wherever they went together, he would have witnessed an almost magical change in each as they entered the home and left it.

Outside, organising the building of a new extension, prodding the rumps of prospective purchases at market or negotiating prices for root crops and hay, it was Harvey who beamed and talked and laughed and held centre stage; while the moment they arrived home for supper and the children came in from their games among the druidical circles on the moor, it was Endacott whose company was in demand, and who was turned into a much loved, honorary uncle.

When he read to them in the evenings, they clustered round him, arguing over whose turn it was to sit on his knee. They loved the way he never talked down to them but always presumed them to be on his own level of intelligence: they found that if ever they asked him a question, whether it concerned wild flowers, world events or his opinion on the origin of the stone circles, they knew they could be sure of an honest answer, or failing that a promise that he would see if he could find out. And in the middle of such discussions, when the children were clamouring for his attention, his glance would sometimes meet Susannah's and a spark of affection would leap across the gap between them, causing James to forget what he had been saying and incurring his listeners' impatience.

In Harvey's company, he was a different person. Soon after coming to stay, he saw that there were many ways in which the management of the farm might be improved, but being a tactful person he made no attempt to force his views. Instead, he encouraged Harvey to air his theories, and took the opportunity of planting a few seedlings in Blair's mind without his ever knowing it.

One topic in particular came up repeatedly, and this was the falling profitability of sheep farming, which was already a dark cloud on Harvey's financial horizon.

'Give me your honest opinion, James,' he said one day when they were on their way back from Chagford. 'What would you do in my situation?'

It was early summer now. Riding in single file with Harvey in the lead, they passed through woodland carpeted with bluebells and cowslips where the evening sun was sending broad bands of light down between the trees.

Endacott contemplated the broad back of his companion, quite certain what he would do were he in Harvey's situation, but less certain whether Harvey would be willing to accept advice.

They crossed over by Leigh Bridge, where the North and South Teign Rivers join forces, and emerging from the forest began the laboriously steep climb up North Hill to Teigncombe.

'If the wool market is in permanent decline as you say, then you may indeed be right to consider abandoning sheep farming,' he said. It was a carefully worded suggestion: Harvey had not actually announced that he was thinking of giving up his sheep, but Endacott had guessed as much from the drift of their conversation that day.

He saw Harvey nod to himself. 'In other words – change to cattle, eh?'

Endacott could not help smiling. He had been quietly planting this idea in Harvey's mind for the past three weeks.

'I do not specify cattle necessarily,' he said. 'One might consider pigs for instance –'

'Swine, James? Never!'

'Then there is the possibility of concentrating on arable crops. They can yield good returns to the farmer who is not afraid of hard work, and who uses the latest methods.'

They plodded on in silence for a while. On either side, the banks of the lane were radiant with wild flowers, and the hedgerows rang with birdsong.

'No,' Harvey said eventually, 'I am quite persuaded

that the Lord has given me a talent with livestock, and I believe I should not bury it.' They passed through the tiny hamlet of Teigncombe, where five thatched cottages dozed round a ruined chapel, and a labourer's wife in a cap and apron was hoeing a diminutive vegetable patch. When they came to the five-barred gate that led into Brimstonedown, Harvey reined in his mare.

'Stop a minute, James,' he said importantly, and throwing back his head, closed his eyes for a few moments' prayer.

'Do Thou show us the way, O Lord,' he breathed, and Endacott whispered an amen.

They entered the yard and dismounted. Thamasine was singing in French a song her mother had been teaching her. She ran out to meet them. 'Papa! Papa – listen!' – and she began to sing again.

He brushed her aside. 'Susannah!' he said, and went into the kitchen. 'My mind is made up. I have been led to see what the Lord wishes for us. We must sell our flock and change to dairy farming. As soon as possible, right James? We shall go down to Chagford next Saturday and return with the finest herd of milking cows we can lay our hands on.'

Thamasine tugged at his coat. 'Papa, may I sing for you now?'

The change from sheep to cattle took longer than the week Blair had presumed. Tactfully, Endacott convinced him that if the job was to be done at all it must be done properly, and that meant providing fodder, dairy and shelter for the cattle before they arrived. He made a plan of the fields and suggested a rotation of crops to provide roots, cabbage, hay and pasture. He designed a cowshed that was decades ahead of its time in which a drain ran down the centre between the stalls so that the place could be washed out, and suggested a rearrangement of gates and fences to allow the herd to walk the minimum distance when they were brought in for milking.

'But we have always milked in the field!' Harvey objected. 'Why should we not continue to do so?'

'Provided they have only a short distance to walk and are not hurried, it should not strain them,' Endacott told him, 'and milking them under cover has great advantages in time saving and hygiene.'

Blair blinked and nodded to himself. 'Hygiene, yes, that's the thing,' he said, and as they walked down along the edge of South Park to the river, he expounded the origins of the word and the importance it played in the management of dairy cattle, so that by the time they reached the bottom of the ravine, Endacott was almost convinced that it had been Blair who had raised the subject in the first place.

The choice of livestock was another area in which Endacott had to exercise a little tactful control on his partner, for as soon as the sheep had been sold, Harvey was all for buying the first likely looking dozen beasts that came under the auctioneer's hammer; but Endacott, pointing out a sagging back here, a restless eye there or a poorly pronounced milk vein somewhere else, managed to teach Blair to recognise a good cow when he saw one, with the result that they eventually made a purchase of eight fine Devonshires.

The two men drove them up from Meldon Common one Saturday evening in July: they came lumbering and splattering their way up through Teigncombe, and Susannah brought Peg, Sal and the children out to watch as they were herded into Hole Field, in front of the house.

Harvey was as excited as an admiral with a new fleet. He walked about admiring each one in turn, handling their udders, slapping their rumps, passing a hand along their backs and holding their tails to one side to examine their vulvas.

Susannah could not help being infected by his enthusiasm: the animals did indeed look very fine, and she was sure that dairy products would be in greater demand than wool.

'Were they expensive?' she asked. 'Have we any money left at all now, Blair?'

Harvey looked at Endacott and laughed. 'Put it this way, dear –' and he made a grand gesture at the cattle, which were already helping themselves to the long grass, 'you are looking at the remains of my capital. There is my all.' He turned back to her with uncharacteristic, worldly fatalism: 'If we fail with these lovely ladies, we're sunk!'

It was one of those events that mark a turning point in the family history. There was an impromptu party to celebrate it: the children were allowed to stay up late, and they all took supper together at the big deal table in the kitchen, Susannah and Blair sitting at either end, with Peg, Sal and Endacott on one side and the four girls on the other. There was a great deal of chatter and laughter – mostly from the children, all of whom wanted to have a turn at milking and churning and skimming cream.

Bea wanted to give each cow a name, and the choice of suitable ones exercised their imagination for some while. Theo wanted names like Twinkle and Daisy and Buttercup, but Grace, having an eye to finding favour with her father, suggested names from the Bible. Susannah suggested that as there were eight of them, each should choose a name.

'But we add up to nine!' Bea exclaimed, having counted on her fingers.

'I don't count!' Susannah said, to which they all cried that she did.

Then Endacott said that he didn't mind not naming a cow, because he was only a visitor and not family, to which Bea said that he was *her* family anyway. Harvey, being rather silent during all this banter, said that he would settle the argument once and for all by naming his own cattle himself, a decision that caused some dismay.

Then Sal came into her own and displayed a talent for

recitation: brought up on a farm until the age of ten, she could remember a few lines of doggerel with that precision sometimes found among the illiterate, and her performance brought forth gales of laughter on all sides:

'She be broad in 'er rib an' long in 'er rump,
A straight flat back wi'out never a 'ump;
She be wide in 'er 'ips an' calm in 'er eye
An' fine in 'er shoulder and thin in 'er thigh.

She be light in 'er neck an' small in 'er tail
An' wide at the breast and good at the pail;
She be fine in 'er bone and easily fed,
The dairyman's dream – that's the Devonshire Red.'

When the giggles and imitations had died down, Susannah said that it was long past Thamasine's bedtime, but before Sal was allowed to take her up, Blair announced that they would give thanks. The Bibles were fetched down from the chimney piece and one of Harvey's favourite passages from the Song of Solomon read; after that the chairs were pushed back from the tables and faces buried in hands as they knelt in prayer.

Later, in the privacy of their room, Blair confided to Susannah that the change from sheep to cattle opened up a new opportunity for them.

'As soon as the extension is built, I shall start work to convert the hayloft to a room,' he said.

'A room?'

'An upper room, furnished.'

'You mean – start a new assembly?'

'Yes indeed, Susannah, that is exactly what I mean.'

'But we are so few, Blair!'

'Not so very few. We shall be five in fellowship from the start. And consider: how many people already walk from Teigncombe and Yeo and Waye to the meetings in Chagford or Wonson? We are at a crossroads here,

314

Susannah, and I think our numbers will quickly swell.' He saw her smile. 'What do you find amusing in that?'

'Blair – not by any possible stretch of the imagination can we consider ourselves to be at a crossroads. We are perched on the very edge of the back-of-beyond.'

He said nothing, but looked a little sulky.

'Have you discussed it with James?' she asked, and regretted doing so immediately.

He went to the window and looked out between the curtains. An owl screeched. When Blair turned, she recognised in his expression a malevolence which she had not seen there for a long time.

'No, I have not discussed it with Captain Endacott, Susannah. But I am grateful to you for mentioning his name in that way, for I have another small matter to discuss with you.'

In the silence, she felt her heart thud heavily. She had a good idea of what was coming, and knew that it was not entirely undeserved.

'I have noticed that the good Captain is becoming . . . shall we say a little over-popular in certain quarters. With the children. And yourself. Is that a fair judgement?'

She knew that whatever she said would carry little weight with him. It had been impossible to live under the same roof with James and not grow increasingly fond of him, and out of the question to treat him as anything other than one of the family. The very fact that she could not behave to him like her children and throw her arms round his neck when he came in from the fields only made matters harder for them both.

'He is popular, yes,' she said carefully, 'and I am not ashamed to admit that I find him the easiest possible lodger, and a person with whom I am completely at ease. But to say he is "over-popular" seems to me a contradiction in terms. He is liked equally by us all, Blair, and I have never known him say or do anything that could be construed as at all improper.'

'I see,' he said.

'What do you see?'

He grunted moodily, but said nothing more until they were in bed.

'I wish that if you have something to say, you would say it, Blair,' she blurted out eventually. 'I am sure that if you are harbouring some thoughts about James it would be better to tell me plainly about them rather than – than making innuendoes which I cannot readily understand.' She felt a little out of breath, and knew she should not go on, but was by now carried away. 'After all – they only serve to sow unease and distrust between us –'

'Distrust?' he snapped. 'When have I ever said anything about distrust? Who has given whom cause for distrust, Susannah?'

She sat up in bed and put her head in her hands. 'You know what I mean, Blair. You are implying – insinuating – that Captain Endacott is becoming too fond of me –'

He exploded. 'I implied *no* such thing! I said quite clearly that I thought he might be becoming a little *over-popular* in some quarters, which to me indicates that the flow of affection is in exactly the reverse direction from that which you suggest. Now, Susannah. Would you care to start again? Or are we to allow the sun to go down upon our wrath?'

It was the worst argument they had had since leaving Teignmouth, and it left Susannah full of that old hopelessness and despair. For several days, a cloud of despondency settled upon Brimstonedown: meals were held in almost complete silence, the children glancing at their elders in bewilderment.

About a week after the arrival of the cattle, when Susannah was working alone in the dairy, Endacott came to her to talk privately. He stood at the door and watched her rinsing out a box churn.

'Susannah,' he said, 'I have something I must say to you.'

She up-ended the churn to drain and set it down beside the sink. She stood in profile to him, her wet hands on the churn, waiting to hear what he had to say.

'I can't help being aware that – over the past week – there is some difficulty between yourself and your husband.'

She trembled visibly. 'Please let us not speak of it, James. I would rather not discuss it.'

'No,' he said with that grave gentleness which made her ache inside with love for him, 'I must say this. I have to tell you –'

Her knuckles whitened: she leant on the draining board shaking her head.

'It will do no good,' she whispered. 'Please –'

'Susannah – you must hear what I have to say. I have to take action to relieve the present situation. And I have taken a decision – a decision which I wish you to know about in advance so that the news will not come as a shock to you when I announce it publicly.'

She turned to look at him: for a moment it seemed that the dam of their self-control might actually burst, and that they would find themselves wrapped tight in each other's arms; but the moment passed.

'I am going to take a wife,' he said in a sad, flat voice.

She bowed her head resignedly. In the silence that followed, it seemed that they were jointly mourning the passing of an impossible hope.

'You understand my reasons, I know that,' he said quietly, and she nodded.

'And I do not have to put into words the true force of my feelings, Susannah. Do I?'

She shook her head.

He swallowed noisily. 'Nevertheless I would like you to know that – you are my dearest – dearest –'

He was going to say 'friend', but the word refused to

come out, so that when he withdrew in complete confusion, Susannah was left, after all, with the clearest impression of his feelings towards her.

She turned back, raging inwardly at what might have been, and set about cutting the junket.

Endacott left for a short stay in Exeter soon after, and made several more visits at weekly intervals. On his return one summer evening nearly two months after his announcement to Susannah, he invited Harvey to take a stroll with him, saying that he wished to speak privately, and Blair, who liked to think of himself as the Captain's mentor and spiritual guide, readily agreed.

They stood on Chagford common now: Harvey a fraction taller than his companion and heavier in build, his hair like a thick mane at the back of his head. He had shaved his beard recently and now sported a handsome pair of muttonchops, which he was inclined to smooth with his fingers from time to time. By comparison, Endacott looked remarkably trim, having avoided the coarsening of middle age which was already apparent in Harvey's leonine features.

Below them, in a mosaic of greens and golds, the patchwork of this ancient part of old England spread out; and from it rose a mixture of rural sounds that complemented the view. From Yeo cornmill a mile down the hill, the watery thump of the paddle wheels provided a rhythm as steady as a metronome's, while the ringing of a hammer on hot iron from the smithy at Thorn added its own counterpoint. The echoing birdsong provided the melody in this rustic symphony, and all the time, like the steady murmur of an inattentive audience, the two Teign rivers roared down-hill to their confluence at Leigh Bridge.

It had been a successful summer for Harvey. The alterations to the buildings were complete, and the change to dairy farming had gone ahead smoothly. Endacott had taken over much of the day-to-day management of the farm, leaving Blair free to pursue his work for the Lord. Meanwhile the womenfolk milked, skimmed, churned and pressed in a strict routine devised for them by the Captain.

There was another cause for quiet self-congratulation: a fortnight before, the first meeting had taken place in the new Room. Before the event, Harvey had canvassed for support in the surrounding hamlets, with the result that the first Lord's Day breaking of bread was attended by seven brethren and sisters in addition to the members of his household. That first gathering of saints had been a memorable occasion indeed: the humble surroundings of the converted hayloft, the little circle of chairs, the plain table set with bread and wine had created a thrilling atmosphere of simple orthodoxy. If this was not the way the very earliest Christians had worshipped, nothing was, and the impromptu prayers and unaccompanied hymn singing had stimulated a spiritual fervour in the worshippers hardly known among the communicants of any established church. When, at the end, Harvey had led them in prayer, thanking the Lord for thus bringing them together and making reference to the promise 'where two or three are gathered together in my name, there am I in the midst of them', there had been an invincible conviction among all present that the Saviour was indeed in their midst – invisible, but more powerfully present under those old, worm-eaten rafters than under the soaring arches of any Anglican minster or papist cathedral.

He had plans, too: to start prayer meetings and Bible readings during the week, to preach outside the gate of St Michael's in Chagford on Sunday evenings; and in a few weeks' time, when the Anglicans were perpetuating their pagan ceremonies in the festival of harvest thanksgiving, to hold a special gospel mission in the Room at Brimstonedown.

The only blot on this peaceful landscape now was the change he had seen in Susannah since their bedtime tiff two months before, for although he could not bring himself to display any affection for his youngest daughter (however determinedly she pestered him for attention) he had thought that his difficulties with Susannah were at an end. Now, it seemed they had returned to those dark times of West Lawn memory, when hardly a word passed between them from one day to the next.

Still reflecting on these things, he was surprised to have his thoughts interrupted by Endacott's calm announcement that he was considering marriage.

'Marriage?' he repeated, blinking in astonishment. 'Marriage to whom?'

Endacott rolled a pebble nervously back and forth under the sole of his boot. Molly had stipulated, on agreeing to be his wife, that on no account must he reveal the truth about their long relationship or her humble beginnings. 'I – er – have been acquainted with the person concerned for some time,' he explained.

'My dear James! What a dark horse you are!' Harvey pumped his hand up and down. 'May I be the first to congratulate you!'

They continued their walk up the moor, Blair striding along, one arm behind his back, the other swinging energetically. 'Tell me more! Where is the lady from? And what of her family?'

'She is living in Exeter, though she comes originally from Dublin.'

'From Dublin! Then she will know the brethren at Aungier Street? Brother Cronin and brother Stokes – and our beloved brother Darby himself!'

'No – I think not. I think that is unlikely.'

Harvey sniffed a rat. 'Is she not the Lord's, then?'

'Not yet, no.'

'I see,' said Harvey.

'Though I have every expectation that she will be

brought to repentance in the near future,' Endacott added.

Harvey glanced across at the captain. 'Bring her up to Brimstonedown, James. We'll have her converted in no time!'

Endacott looked a little uncomfortable. He had felt morally obliged to ask Molly to be his wife, but was doubtful whether she would be able to settle to the country life.

'Nonsense!' Blair replied when he voiced these fears. 'Any woman can be made to adjust to her surroundings, as you have seen with my Susannah. Give her a roof over her head and firm discipline, and she'll eat out of your hand. No, I think you need have no qualms about her adaptability. She'll soon see what's good for her. Besides, the air here is the healthiest in England. She'll be a new woman within a fortnight! Is she a complete heathen, then?'

'She was brought up a Romanist, though she has not retained any parts of that faith beyond a few childhood prayers and superstitions.'

Harvey snorted. 'The *whole* of their religion is superstition!'

'Then I have your approval, Harvey?'

'Of course you have my approval! I shall look forward to bringing your intended to the feet of the Lord!'

Endacott touched his moustaches with the knuckle of his forefinger. 'I – ah – have to tell you that we have already made arrangements for a quiet wedding in Exeter three weeks from now. On Saturday the twenty-third, to be precise.'

'But that is the day of our gospel mission here at Brimstonedown! You cannot possibly miss that, James!'

'I thought we might travel from Exeter immediately after the marriage in order to be here in time for the first meeting in the afternoon.'

They had arrived at that massive dollop of granite

known as Castor Rock, which marks the high point of Chagford Common. To the west, shot pink by the descending sun, the sheep-dotted moorland rolled away as far as the eye could see, while Cawsand Hill was already a dark mound against the evening sky.

'Nevertheless, it is very short notice,' Blair observed.

'Yes – but I think it best, once the decision has been taken, to marry without delay. I am conscious of certain – certain responsibilities towards her which I cannot, as a Christian, ignore.'

Blair put one and one together and made three. 'She's not with child is she James? Is that it?'

Endacott flushed at the suggestion. 'No, not at all. Molly is a woman of the – the highest moral standing, though perhaps of a lowlier origin than ourselves. No, it is merely a case of her being in straitened circumstances, while I, having been acquainted with her for many years, feel responsible.'

'Molly? Did you say her name was Molly?'

'Yes, Molly Burke. You are bound to like her, Harvey, I am sure of it. She has a most warm and engaging personality, and as I informed you, I have a positive expectation that she will be brought out of darkness. Of course we have discussed the prospect of her joining us at Brimstone, and I think she may be amenable to taking over as housekeeper from your wife, who I am aware is greatly overburdened with work . . .'

Blair was hardly listening. He had turned away from the Captain and was staring unnaturally down at the lichen-covered boulders, his mind full of vivid memories.

'There is no question of allowing him to bring her here,' he told Susannah in the privacy of their bedroom that night. 'And I have told him as much.'

'But you cannot forbid him to marry, Blair!'

' "Be ye not unequally yoked together," ' he quoted. 'The Lord's directive is quite clear.'

322

'But isn't James confident that he will bring her to the Lord? They will not be unequally yoked if that is the case.'

He stood at the window unbuttoning his shirtfront. 'Yes, that was my first reaction, Susannah, but if you look behind the facts of the case you will quickly see that our poor gentle Captain is being hoodwinked. Here is a woman in straitened circumstances who has seen the chance of a husband and the security of a Christian home. Little wonder that she is agreeable to conversion! She can see which side her bread is buttered and is undoubtedly taking advantage of James's charity.'

Susannah sighed impatiently. 'Why is it that you must always impute such doubtful motives upon others, Blair? Surely we know James well enough to trust his judgement? And even if she is still in darkness when she comes here, I doubt if she will remain so long. Your daughters will have her converted within a week even if you or I do not!'

Harvey was vehemently shaking his head. 'Not so, not so. Brother Darby has repeatedly warned of the trials and difficulties attendant upon those who marry unbelievers. More often than not it is the cause of backsliding rather than of conversion, and to claim as James does that one has hopes that she will come to repentance is mere whistling in the dark.'

'Let him bring her to the Lord before he marries her! Then you cannot possibly object to her coming here!'

'But I can – and will. Consider: what guarantee do we have that any act of repentance she may make will be genuine? James has told me of her situation and of her humble origins, and I can only conclude that she is an adventuress who is seizing upon the chance of making a good marriage. Now think – think, Susannah – of the effect the presence of such a person might have upon my household! Captain James, actually living in marital conjugation with one who is in darkness! Think what a stumbling-block she would be to my daughters, my domestics – even to yourself!'

She was silent for some time while she unplaited her hair and brushed out the tangles.

'You accept what I say?' he asked.

'I have little choice, Blair. I am bound to remain obedient to you as my husband. But I cannot help recalling that you had no qualms about remaining in business partnership with James when he was an unbeliever.'

'That was quite a different matter,' he said. 'And besides, if this woman comes she will be living here with us as one of the family. She will be an extra mouth to feed.'

'And another pair of hands to help your wife and domestics – a fact which may seem trivial to yourself but which would make a great deal of difference to me. And should we not think of James a little? Why should the poor man not take a wife? Why must we condemn him to live without the comfort of a life partner?'

'There is nothing amiss with bachelorhood, Susannah. Brother Darby himself forewent marriage to our beloved sister in Christ, Lady Theodosia, in order to commit his life to the Lord.'

'That is brother Darby's affair. I seem to remember that we ourselves married somewhat in haste for fear of the temptations of – of the flesh. Indeed we agreed that it was better to marry than to burn, and it seems to me that Paul's direction applies more aptly to James's case than it did to ourselves.'

During this last little speech, Susannah had flushed very red and had become clearly agitated. Blair saw this and administered the cruellest dart: 'The real reason you wish James to marry, Susannah, is because you cannot trust yourself, is that not so? Will you admit it?'

She turned away from him, but he pursued her.

'Do you think I am quite blind? Do you think I have not seen your exchanged glances, or have failed to notice how frequently you agree with each other in conversation?'

She bowed her head. 'I am fond of James – I will not deny that, Blair. But I have seen equal fondness of others in your eyes before now –'

'Oh yes? And when was that? Please tell me, I'd like to know!'

'I would not lower myself or the persons concerned by mentioning names,' she said very quietly. 'But I will say this. If you prevent James from bringing his wife here, I doubt whether he will remain with us for long. And then we shall be back where we were before his arrival. You will lose not only his company, but also his knowledge of agriculture and his assistance in the building up of an assembly here – and unless we can somehow convince the children and domestics that you have played no part in his departure, you will lose their goodwill also, to say nothing of my own. I think perhaps you should consider these factors, should you not? Before coming to a final decision?'

The trouble was, he felt completely indecisive. If he allowed Endacott to bring Molly to Brimstonedown he would be running risks of recognition that hardly bore thinking about, while if he forebade him he could see that Susannah's forecast would almost certainly prove correct and he would find himself isolated and hated within his own house.

Nor did he feel that he could call upon the Lord for guidance: as in the case of Lavinia Pendlebury's settlement, this seemed to be a question that lay outside the divine aegis; and while he knew that such an attitude was unscriptural and raised all sorts of imponderable questions about divine omniscience and predestination, he could not escape it.

During the weeks that followed, he thought of little else. He took long, solitary walks in his fields and over Dartmoor; he stood with his cattle (which he had named after Greek goddesses); he contemplated the tumbling brown waters of the Teign; and in the evenings as soon as supper was over, he went to the small room at the back of the house which he had made into his study, and where he kept his books and tracts by brother Darby, to brood silently over his dilemma. Staring into the candle flame as he had stared so long ago in Mrs Mudge's lodgings, he tried in vain to reconcile himself to the idea of sharing the same roof with a common harlot.

Would she recognise him? He thought not. Provided she had no idea of his identity, and provided Endacott had never pointed him out to her, the chances were that his muttonchop whiskers and coarsening features were sufficiently far removed from the choirboy appearance of his youth to make an adequate disguise. Besides, it was now seventeen years since that afternoon when he climbed the greasy pole, and the girl – or woman, for she would be over thirty by now – must have bedded down with dozens of men since. But there was no guarantee that she would not know him, that was the terrible part. For all he knew, she might even now be laughing at the prospect of renewing his acquaintance.

He tried to get Endacott to delay the wedding, but failed. He felt unable to press his case too hard for fear that either Susannah or the Captain might turn the tables on him and ask why he was so prejudiced against a woman he had never met. Slowly, he felt his authority being eroded: when the domestics heard that the Captain was taking a wife they were delighted, and their enthusiasm quickly spread to the children.

The more he pondered the problem, the more he became tortured by the memory of that afternoon with Molly. Having suppressed the incident for so long, it now leapt into the forefront of his mind with a vividness he found terrifying. He began to see her face everywhere: the dark eyes, the heavy eyebrows, the wide, sensual mouth; he heard her low, husky voice in his dreams, and once while he was kneeling to lead the household in prayer after breakfast, the vision of her white body and wantonly parted limbs rose up before him so that for a few moments he relived the horror and shame of it all, and the knowledge that she had taken from him an innocence that could never be recovered.

Later, he found himself gripped by an even more insidious obsession, for he discovered growing up inside him a feeling that by taking his innocence she had taken possession of his soul. That was why he had found it necessary to confess to Dr Brougham; that was the tap root of his repentance upon Oddicombe beach – and it was this same instinctive sense of belonging to Molly that now led him into a perverse desire to meet her again, so that in the last days before Endacott's departure for Exeter, he dropped his arguments against her coming and allowed events to take their course.

There was a tap on the door. He had been working on his gospel address for the mission on Saturday. Outside, drizzle was falling in bleak grey curtains over the moor.

'Come in!' he called, and Grace appeared, standing prettily before him, her head tilted coquettishly, her hands joined.

'Papa,' she said importantly. 'Mama says that Uncle James is about to depart, and do you wish to speak with him before he does so?'

He set down his pen and followed Grace along the stone-flagged corridor to the kitchen, and from there into the yard.

Endacott had put the pony between the shafts of the trap, which he was taking to Exeter. He had put on a plain suit of good twill, and had trimmed his whiskers.

'So, James,' Harvey said gruffly. 'You're off, are you?'

'Yes indeed,' he said in the clipped, military way he sometimes used when ill at ease.

'Well – you know my feelings well enough already, so I

shall spare you any further counsel,' said Harvey, though he was unsure in his own mind what his feelings really were.

Endacott put one foot on the mounting step and prepared to climb into the trap. 'I have given it further thought, Harvey, and have been much exercised in my mind by the Lord. I see now that you are indeed right to express doubts about having Molly to stay here while she is yet an unbeliever, so I have decided that if I do not succeed in bringing her over to eternal life, I shall not return here with her on Saturday.'

'You mean – you will not marry her?'

'No, not that, as I'm committed and can't break my word. All I am saying is that I shall respect your judgement and keep her separate if her heart is hardened and she refuses to approach the mercy seat.'

He climbed up and took the reins in his hands. 'So if she is not with me when I return on Saturday, you will know that my next stay will be but a short one, to collect my worldly possessions and to take leave of you again.'

Susannah came out with the children to give the Captain their blessing. They stood in the fine drizzle and gazed up at him as if he were about to travel to the antipodes.

Blair reached up to shake him by the hand. 'May the Lord look with favour upon your endeavours,' he said gruffly.

'Pray for me – and for Molly,' Endacott replied, and Susannah, whose eyes were full of tears, unfolded her arms and waved him goodbye.

The children raced to have the privilege of opening the gate for him, and the trap clattered out into the lane and went away down the hill to Teigncombe.

While they watched him go, Thamasine took the opportunity of waltzing with Ruff, an elderly but very loving sheepdog that had once belonged to old Gus. She put his forepaws on her shoulders and her hands on his black and white coat, and together they moved solemnly about on the wet stones outside the kitchen door, Ruff's ears laid back and a look of tolerant suffering in his soulful brown eyes.

When he saw them, Blair flew immediately into a rage. 'What is that child doing?' he demanded of Susannah.

'Blair – my dear – it is only a game –'

He marched up to the dancing pair, and taking the dog by the scruff of its neck, threw it to one side. 'As for you, you repulsive infant,' he said standing over his five-year-old daughter and shaking his finger in her face, 'you are never to abuse yourself with an animal in such a disgusting way again, do you understand? Symbol of the devil, that is what a dog is, and to embrace one in such a way is to embrace Satan himself!'

Thamasine stared up at her father while this tirade went on, and gradually her face crumpled, her mouth trembled and turned down and she burst into tears. Susannah went to her rescue, taking her by the hand and leading her inside.

'Make sure she is washed, Susannah,' Harvey called after them. 'And she is to go without her supper tonight so that the lesson will be the more forcibly impressed upon her mind!'

Susannah made no verbal reply, but instead spoke volumes to him with a quick, lethal glance.

He needed to be alone. He went out past the new extension at the end of the house, and took the track up past a line of ashes and rowan trees into Park Field. Down in the corner, his cattle stood by the stone wall that separated his property from the forest of South Park. As he approached, they swung their heads round to watch him, their eyes full of bovine stupidity, their hooves sinking in the soggy turf. He went among them, smoothing their backs and slapping their bellies. He whispered nonsense to them, enquiring after Hermione's health and congratulating Antigone upon the damp sheen of her hide.

Talking to his cows could not take his mind off events, however, so he went on down the steep path that led into the wooded ravine of the Teign.

He stood and meditated for a long time by the river, the noise of which drowned all but the determined song of a storm thrush, which was experimenting with its variations nearby. He felt that his life was slipping away out of control. He stared at the tumbling waters, which leapt and rushed over slime-brown boulders.

'I could as soon stop him marrying her now as bid these waters cease their flow,' he muttered, and turned to climb slowly back to the house.

Saturday arrived. It was raining when Peg and Sal called the cows in, but soon after breakfast the overcast gave way to blue sky and tuberous white clouds that sailed overhead like full rigged ships in a following gale.

There was a great deal to be done: Saturday was a churning and baking day, and the Room had to be prepared for the gospel service that evening. Sal and the children were required to sweep the yard, and Peg and Susannah hoisted a banner which announced: I AM THE WAY THE TRUTH AND THE LIFE.

Endacott was late. The children hung about in the lane watching for the trap, and the house filled with an atmosphere of suppressed anticipation. Peg and Sal whispered to each other about having a new housekeeper; Susannah kept glancing out of the kitchen window, and Blair sat in his study trying to concentrate on the preparation of his gospel address.

Eventually, after prolonged badgering from her children, Susannah allowed them to go up to the hut circles on the moor, from where they could keep a look-out for the Captain, and the three girls walked hand in hand over the grass, with Thamasine dawdling along behind.

As always, Theo took charge. She ordered them to sit in a line on a piece of granite and began firing questions at them in the way she presumed was used in village schools.

'Name the colours of the rainbow! Name the Seven Wonders of the World! What are the first five books in the Bible? Spell Constantinople!'

Thamasine became so excited at these questions (to several of which she knew the answers) that she rolled backwards onto her shoulders and kicked her feet in the air. For this, she was deservedly shrieked at by Grace, and made to spell Mesopotamia.

'What does it mean?' Theo asked.

'Between rivers!' they all shouted.

'Which rivers?'

'Tigris and Euphrates!'

'And which are the two ancient kingdoms of Mesopotamia?'

They didn't know the answer to that, so Theo, who had learnt the answer from her mother that morning, told them.

For a while, the questions had run out.

'*We* live in a Mesopotamia,' Bea said, twisting a long, fair curl round her little finger.

This was a favourite topic of conversation among them, and Grace took it up immediately. 'That's the Tigris, and that's the Euphrates,' she announced, pointing first to the North and then the South Teign valleys.

'We are the children of Mesopotamia!' Bea said.

'Mama called us the daughters of Babylon,' Grace interjected, 'and Papa was *very* vexed with her.'

'That's because of the cities of the plain,' Theo said darkly. 'They were in Babylon. At least, I think they were in Babylon.'

'What *are* the cities of the plain?' Bea asked.

'They're like Exeter and Plymouth,' Grace said airily. 'You know – where everyone's in darkness.'

'And you know what they're called?' Thamasine whispered. 'They're called –'

'Ssssh! You mustn't say it!' Theo told her.

But Thamasine had already done a headstand, and from this position, with her face hidden by folds of clothing and her short legs pointing skyward she announced with vigorous delight: 'Sodom and Gomorrah!'

'Thamasine!' they shrieked.

Grace said they ought to tell Papa, but Theo said no, because Mama had said that they were not to say or do anything that day that might upset him.

Grace turned to Thamasine. 'You are a wicked child,' she said, using their father's style to reprimand her, 'and though you go unpunished now, be sure you will have to give account one day, when the books are opened.'

Thamasine stared back and said nothing. She didn't like the way Grace's lower lip turned outwards and the holy voice she affected.

'I wish Uncle James would come,' Bea said, effectively taking their attention off their youngest sister, and they stared moodily down the hill.

But there was no sign of the Captain, and a little while later they were called in by Susannah to have their hair brushed and their hands and faces washed before going up to the Room to hear the gospel.

Thamasine sat with her mother and sisters in the front row. 'Now remember,' her mother had said while brushing her hair for her half an hour before, 'you must try to listen to what Papa is saying, Thamasine, and ask the Lord Jesus to help you be a good girl. And you are not to swing your feet under your chair, nor are you to look round.'

'Like Lot's wife?' Thamasine asked, wincing as the brush pulled at a tangle.

'Well, perhaps a little like Lot's wife, yes.'

'*I* won't be turned into a pillar of salt,' Thamasine said.

'No, I don't expect you will, but I wouldn't risk it if I were you.'

'If you were me, there wouldn't be a you to say that,'

Thamasine had observed precociously, and her mother had smiled and said that the conversation had gone quite far enough.

And there – she was swinging her feet again. She glanced across to see if Mama had noticed, which she had. Really it was very difficult to be good, because being good was so dull.

She looked at her father. He was seated at the head of the Room behind a table upon which lay his spectacles, his hymn book, his Bible and a glass of water. He was praying. Papa was always praying. He said you should pray without ceasing. When he did so, he leant back in his chair and closed his eyes, clasping his hands together on his chest, and Thamasine often wondered exactly what he said to the Lord and whether he could actually hear the Lord talking back. When she prayed, it was like talking to herself inside her mind, and the only way she could get God to say anything was by imagining it, in the same way as she imagined conversations with the farm animals.

There were two chairs behind the table, and the empty one was for Uncle James. Papa was angry that he had not arrived when he said he would, and Thamasine was a little disappointed too, because it was Uncle James who opened the meeting in prayer usually and led the hymn singing to put people in the right mood for the gospel. Also, Theo had said that he might witness for Christ and tell them the story of his life of sin in France under Wellington and how he had been brought out of darkness one day on the way back to Teignmouth from Exeter with Mama.

People were beginning to arrive. Every morning after breakfast for the past month, Papa had asked the Lord's blessing upon this special meeting, and had visited the local assemblies to ask for their support. Mama had called it going into the highways and byways to compel them to come in.

That was what they were doing now: they came clumping up the wooden stairs, each being handed a hymn book by brother Beer, the wizened stockman from Squire Murchington's estate. They were people of yeoman stock for the most part, though there were a few of the labouring class among them, and Miss Buckley, the governess to Lord Meldon's children, slipped in quietly and began reading her Bible in the back row. They sat down with sighs and grunts and barely audible whispers: women in tight, black Sunday best, and fiery-faced men with thick fingers and heavy boots.

As the benches and chairs filled up, Thamasine found the temptation to look round at them irresistible. Slowly, she began to move her head round, keeping a watchful eye on her father (who had a habit of opening his eyes without warning) but before she could achieve much more than a glimpse of old Mrs Jessop who lived alone below Yeo cornmill and kept goats, Mama had placed a hand gently on her knee to remind her to keep her eyes to the front.

Papa was getting to his feet. 'Let us approach the throne of grace,' he boomed, an exhortation which never failed to bring a holier-than-thou look to Grace's naturally prim expression. The Room was immediately filled with rustlings and creakings, sighings and clearings of throats, as the brethren and sisters adopted their customary attitudes for prayer, some of the men thrusting heads forward into open palms, some sitting back with closed eyes; and most of the women bending slightly forward and closing their eyes with trembling lids. Thus they remained, while brother Harvey gave thanks that so many had been led by the Spirit to come that evening to Brimstonedown, and besought the Lord, should it be His will, to yield the increase so that souls might be gathered safe into His barn. This prayer – which lasted almost five minutes – was punctuated by the occasional drawn out amen from some of the brethren, and marked by a series of affirmatory grunts from brother Beer.

When it was over, they sang hymns.

Thamasine enjoyed hymns because she liked to see if she could find the place before Bea, and to demonstrate that she could read although she was only five. The Room had never been so full before, and the sound of so many unaccompanied voices singing with that passion found only among those who believe themselves to be sole possessors of the truth soon had its effect. Although she was still in disgrace over dancing with Ruff three days before, and although she was afraid that Grace might yet report her for mentioning Sodom and Gomorrah, she still longed with all her heart to be *good*. She wanted, just for once, to be loved and accepted by her father – to be called his Treasure or his Darling or his Special One; so when the last hymn was over and it was time for the gospel, she climbed back onto her chair and folded her arms, determined to do as her Mama had told her and listen to every word her father said.

His text for the evening was 'Come unto me all ye that labour,' and he developed his theme with all the force of oratory at his command. Appealing directly to the emotions of his listeners – and particularly his women listeners – he delivered what they wished to hear: a message of atonement, of forgiveness and of ultimate glory that made compelling listening in those hungry days of shortages and low wages. Embellishing his address with little anecdotes and vignettes from his own experience, he showed how often life was made possible by death and perfection brought about through suffering. Comparing the taint of original sin found in every human being with the filth that caused diseases in cities, homes and dairies, he explained the need for the washing away, once and for all, of sin, which could only be achieved through the blood of the Saviour. Slowly, he expounded and made plain the choice that lay before each person listening to him that evening – between the gift of God, which is eternal life, and the wages of sin, which is death. He made word pictures of the Lamb seated upon the throne on the last day, and of the lake of fire, repeating those dread words of Christ Himself: 'I never knew you: depart from me, ye that work iniquity.'

Finally, moved by the solemnity of his own words so that the tears stood in his eyes, he rehearsed all those promises of the second coming which he believed so imminent.

'The Lord himself shall descend from heaven with a shout,' he declared, linking text to text for the maximum effect. 'With the voice of the archangel and the trump of God. The dead shall rise first, then we which are alive and remain – yea, even we ourselves in this Room tonight – we which are alive and remain shall be caught up together with them in the clouds, to meet the Lord in the air, and so shall we ever be with the Lord.'

He paused and in the silence the wind sighed in the eaves and sheep could be heard bleating on the moor. Had there been any one person unconverted among those present that evening, then surely he would have been won over; but though the benches and chairs were full almost to capacity, their occupants came from the assemblies of Chagford, Wonson, South Tawton and Drewsteignton, so that while Harvey's oratory was impressive, it was largely wasted.

'It may be,' he started again, beginning the final appeal, 'that there is one here this evening listening to my words who has not yet repented of his – or of her – sins, who has yet to approach the mercy seat to be washed whiter than snow. It may be that that person even now knows in his heart that he is in darkness and still earning the awful wages of sin. Let me speak to you directly, whoever you are. Let me say to you this: that however vile your sins may be, however deep you may be plunged in the mire of worldly iniquity, there is yet time – a little time – in which to open your heart to the Saviour, who stands outside knocking to come in. And it is not much that He is asking, for His yoke is easy and His burden is light, and all that

He asks of you is to believe in your heart and confess with your lips that He is Lord and Saviour . . .'

Here there was an interruption, for the sound of hooves and wheels came from the yard, followed a few moments later by footsteps on the stairs. The effect upon Harvey was apparent to all, and the effect upon the atmosphere he had carefully created disastrous. It was as if a violin string that was being tuned higher and higher had snapped. Within seconds, all interest in eternal things had evaporated, to give way to a new curiosity of a more temporal nature.

Heads turned. It was the Captain, accompanied by his new wife. They stood in the doorway, Endacott tall and military, and the woman beside him generously built with dark, laughing eyes and black hair that was uncovered – in flagrant disregard of I Corinthians xi.

Thamasine was one of the few who did not turn round, and perhaps she witnessed the more striking event, for the colour drained from her father's face, his eyes stared as if he were hypnotised, and a vein rose under the damp skin of his forehead, making a blue serpent above the bridge of his nose. His mouth opened and shut: he was like an actor who has forgotten his lines.

He made a supreme effort. In a changed voice – a voice that was little more than a whisper – he attempted to pick up the thread of his appeal.

'If there is one here tonight . . . only one . . . who is not saved, who does not know Jesus . . .'

He stumbled to a halt, and there was a terrible silence.

It was during that silence that Thamasine saw suddenly how she might at last win her father's approval.

Slipping off her chair, she ran to him and sought his hand. 'O Papa!' she cried, gazing up in love and pity. '*I* love Jesus, and *I* want to be saved!'

This brought forth a little murmur of emotion from the sisters of Brimstonedown, but Blair was able only to stare down at his daughter and shake his head.

Susannah stepped quickly forward and took Thamasine by the hand. She led her quickly from the Room, down the wooden staircase and out into the yard. There, she crouched before the child and explained gently that she was still too young to take up her cross, but that Jesus loved her every bit as much, all the same.

Thamasine's reaction was heard clearly by everyone in the converted hayloft. 'Why – why – why – can't – I – be – saved?' she sobbed, and her wails receded as she was led away into the house.

CHAPTER 16

She wouldn't have given him a second thought if he hadn't acted so strangely, but the way he looked everywhere except in her direction, the way he hardly said a word at supper when everyone else was bombarding her with questions, and the way he excused himself and went off to his study at the earliest possible moment convinced Molly that at some time in the past Mr Harvey must have been one of her clients.

It wasn't the first time she had encountered such a reaction in a man. Over the years, she had come to regard it as good business sense to recognise past customers so that she could encourage further attentions or keep well clear, as the case might be. She had seen before that look of terror in a man's eye on passing her in the street with a little wife hanging on his arm and had become a mistress of discretion in such matters, aware that it was greatly to her own advantage to perpetuate the fallacy that no gentleman ever stooped to tumble with a professional.

James had told her a great deal about Mr Harvey already. He had described him as the most learned, upright and godly man imaginable, and had praised his wife for her gentleness and sincerity. 'I'm not good enough for the likes of them,' she had said, but he had reassured her, saying that the Harveys lived with their delightful daughters in all simplicity, awaiting the coming of the Lord.

In her heart of hearts, Molly didn't really go along with

the religious side of things, but as James was out of funds and she didn't fancy going back on the streets, she didn't have much choice. Being essentially a pragmatist, and having spent most of her life so far doing anything for money, she decided that she might as well now do anything for security. She was a good actress – you had to be in her profession – and it wasn't difficult to convince James that she had made a genuine decision to repent of her sins. 'Who cares?' she had often asked herself in the past. 'I'll play their silly games provided the money's good.' Now, she used the same argument. After all, no harm could come of it, and no woman in her right mind would turn down an offer of marriage from a charmer like James Endacott.

So here she was in the back of nowhere and Mr god-almighty Harvey was looking at her as if he'd seen a ghost. Mrs Harvey had fitted James's description of her exactly, so much so that meeting her was like meeting a dear friend; but Mr Harvey – he was a fake, you could see it from the word go, and she was amazed that no one else had seen it too. But where had she seen him? And when? She watched him covertly throughout supper, becoming increasingly convinced that she had heard that booming voice and seen that lordly manner before, but racking her memory in vain.

After supper, Mrs Harvey took her along to the new wing where she and James would live as man and wife. Following her along the chilly back passage, Molly couldn't help feeling that she had become involved in some magnificent charade; and it was all she could do, when Susannah made an oblique reference to her wedding night, to prevent herself bursting out laughing.

'We rise at four-thirty,' Susannah said, 'but we shall not expect to see you tomorrow morning until breakfast, which is at seven. I shall have Peg put hot water outside your room half an hour before.'

She led the way into a small, neat parlour and lit

another candle. Molly looked round at her new quarters, mentally comparing the plain furniture and whitewashed walls to the cluttered, grubby boudoir she had left behind in Exeter.

'I hope you will not find our life here too spartan,' Mrs Harvey said, and regarded her with steady, intelligent eyes. 'I myself found it difficult at first, when we removed from Teignmouth five years ago.'

'Oh yes? You were at Teignmouth, were you?'

'Do you know it then?' Susannah asked, hopeful of a reminiscent chat.

'No. I never been there,' Molly replied, and as soon as the words were out of her mouth knew she had made a grammatical blunder. She saw Susannah's face and took a quick decision. 'You might as well know, Ma'am. I'm not – I'm not what you might call educated. I'm not a proper lady.'

Susannah laid a hand on her arm. 'All that matters, my dear, in this house, is that you belong to the Lord. We make no distinction of class or social standing here. So you must not call me "Ma'am" but Susannah, which is my name, and I hope you will allow me to call you Molly.'

She felt a little overcome by this earnest gentility, and allowed herself to be led up a narrow flight of stairs to the bedroom above. She didn't know why, but that act of mounting the stair and entering the bedroom set off a little mechanism of memory, rather in the same way as a clock that has been stopped for a long time may start ticking again if given a gentle shake.

There was a dressing table by the window and a bow fronted chest of drawers by the door. The bed covers had been turned back, and the linen sheets were freshly laundered and fragrant with lavender. On the windowsill, a bowl of nasturtiums threw an awkward shadow in the candlelight.

'You've gone to a lot of trouble, haven't you?' she said.

Susannah smiled, pleased to have her work appreciated. 'We want you to feel at home from the start, Molly.'

'I'm sure I shall,' she said awkwardly, quite unsure inside herself how she could ever accustom herself to this strange, Christian friendliness.

'My daughters have been most anxious to know what they may call you,' Susannah said, 'and with your permission I propose that you adopt the title of honorary aunt.'

'So I'll be their Aunt Molly?'

'I suppose you shall be, yes!' Susannah laughed, and took Molly's hands in her own. 'I do sincerely hope that you will be happy with us, my dear. I'm sure we shall get along famously, and I hope we can join forces as joint mistresses of the house to build a truly Christian home for our husbands and – dare I say it – our families.'

Molly suddenly found herself being kissed on the cheek.

'There. Welcome, sister in the Lord,' Susannah whispered, and when she had made sure that there was nothing else Molly needed for the night, left her to prepare herself for her new husband.

Molly looked at herself in the dressing table mirror, and taking out her tortoiseshell combs, shook out her hair, laughing aloud at the extraordinary situation she found herself in – and it was at that precise moment, as she lifted her hair and combed it with her fingers, that she remembered exactly when and where she had met Mr Harvey.

She gasped and bit her knuckle at the realisation. It was – yes, it must be the same person – that chump of a fellow who had been so severely attacked by his conscience after losing his virginity to her, and from whose purse she had extracted six important shillings which had bought her new shoes, a cotton dress and the confidence to set her sights on a better class of gentleman.

She went on laughing about it for some time, and when James eventually came upstairs to join her, he found her quite naked between the sheets, and more eager than ever for his attentions.

*

Her presence at Brimstonedown was to have more far-reaching effects than Blair Harvey could possibly have imagined. From the first morning when she arrived down late for breakfast, the household began to revolve round her; and just as each spoke in a wheel is subject to both centripetal and centrifugal forces, so each person at Brimstonedown was both attracted and repelled by the new Mrs Endacott.

Sal was afraid of her; Peg resented her; Susannah felt obliged, for James's sake, to make every allowance for her; Endacott himself found her demands exhausting, while the children – and Grace in particular – took a delight in reporting her unconventional remarks and behaviour.

It became quickly apparent that she could not take over as housekeeper, for Peg – who had by now grown quite colossal – saw Molly as a direct challenge to her authority in the kitchen. But she had to be given something to do: it was bad enough having her lying abed every morning until six-thirty, let alone getting in everyone's way and asking questions. So Susannah decided to teach her how to milk, and the cowshed was filled one afternoon with her husky laughter and exclamations as she learnt to manipulate Persephone's udders. Peg, Sal and the children gathered to watch, and the performance was turned into an entertainment, Molly laughing so much that the tears ran down her cheeks. But in spite of the fun, and several remarks with double meanings, Molly proved to be a natural milker, with gentle hands and a confidence with cattle which Sal was first to notice.

'You sure you never milked afore, Ma'am?' she asked.

Molly winked broadly. 'Not cows, no,' she said, and her laughter gurgled up again, so that the children bit their lips and giggled behind their hands.

Then there was an accident, and Molly made the first of several remarks that were to send shock waves through the family: 'Saints alive, the sinful beast's gone and shit all over me, look!'

In spite of her natural expertise at milking, Molly considered herself a cut above the domestics (who, in spite of Susannah's remarks about equality, were required to call the Captain's new wife 'Ma'am') and she declined to lower herself to the level of a mere milkmaid; so the only place for her was the dairy, which up to now had been Susannah's responsibility.

Over a period of several months, she was taught the art of skimming milk and churning butter, clotting cream and pressing cheeses, so that within a year she was able to take over command, and ruled among the fleeters and curd agitators. Beating the whey out of the butter, or rolling and packing it for market, she would sing songs she had once learnt in a Dublin slum: songs about wayward goats and sinful cows that had Bea and Thamasine listening at the door in suppressed giggles, and Grace running to her mother to report the latest outrage to fall from Aunt Molly's lips.

It was Sal who made the most shocking discovery about her. Once every three weeks, a big copper was filled with water from the tank and boiled up over a wood fire for Sal to do the family wash. Mounds of bed linen, shirts, skirts, aprons and underclothes were steamed and pummelled from dawn to dusk, and the following day Sal worked equally long hours with smoothing irons, laying out the laundry in neatly folded piles. This routine gave Sal a peculiar insight into the more intimate secrets of each member of the family, and it did not take her long to notice that although the Captain and his wife submitted two sets of night clothes every three weeks, such articles were seldom used.

'Look at that!' she remarked to Peg one morning. 'They've still the ironing creases in them from six weeks since!'

Peg jumped to the natural conclusion.

'The shameful hussy!' she whispered. 'She been making the poor Captain sleep naked with her!'

'Naked!' Sal repeated, quite aghast.

'They do, you know,' Peg said darkly. 'I heard it. In them foreign places like France and Spain. They sleep stark naked, like animals.'

'And the Captain too, I can't hardly believe it, with him a gentleman, an' all!'

Unfortunately this exchange was overhead by the omnipresent Grace, who had a knack of staying behind doors when others were having private conversations. That afternoon, she repeated the news to Thamasine, with whom she sat among the straw bales in the top barn; and when she had relieved herself of this juicy piece of scandal, she made Thamasine play babies, a game Thamasine didn't enjoy because it meant having your drawers removed and your bottom examined by Grace's pale blue eyes and probing fingers.

The summer following Molly's arrival, she allowed herself to be persuaded into baptism. Really she had little choice in the matter, for having assured her husband to be that he had won her over for the Lord, she could not now very well claim that no conversion had taken place. Accordingly, the brethren and sisters of the Brimstonedown assembly walked down to the Teign one afternoon in June, and Harvey found himself obliged to take Molly in his arms for the second time in his life, performing the rite of immersing her backwards into the brown waters of a rock pool while the others welcomed her into fellowship with a rousing hymn; and after that, at the breaking of bread on Lord's Day mornings, Molly was permitted to take the bread and wine when they were passed round, becoming a true sister in Christ, one of the saints, a member of God's elect.

Gradually, she made herself an integral part of the household. Confident that she had Harvey exactly where she wanted him (for although he could never be sure whether she recognised him, she was in no doubt that he knew her) she adjusted the rules of the house to suit herself, seldom rising before six-thirty, never lifting a finger to help in the kitchen, establishing an absolute authority in the dairy and making demands upon her husband that were to send him from his middle years into old age within the space of half a decade.

Blair wore her presence like a hair shirt. For the first time in his life, he had encountered a woman who not only displayed no trace of awe in his presence but even seemed to hold him in faint derision. To compensate for this attack on his self-esteem, he surrounded himself in an ever denser aura of ecclesiastic authority, withdrawing further from his family and deliberately making himself remote from his children. Conversation at table went on without his participation, and if he spoke it was usually to pronounce on some doctrinal question of faith or morals put to him by Susannah. He was particularly careful to avoid any occasion which might leave him alone in Molly's company, for he was continually afraid that she might make some oblique reference to their past encounter, or even seek to lead him once again into sin.

But Molly brought prosperity to the farm as well as shock, scandal, whisperings and unease. Now that the dairy was established, Endacott started experimenting with new types of fodder to improve the quality of the milk, and his wife had no qualms about putting carrot juice in the winter butter to improve its colour. Once a week, she went down to Chagford market with butter and cheese, and being a natural saleswoman she secured contracts to supply local hotels where anglers came for the famed trout fishing. An arrangement was made with a local carrier to collect the churns of milk that were set out on a raised platform outside the gate each morning, and within a few years demand had increased sufficiently to warrant Harvey enlarging his herd by a half and purchasing a massive bull with long, brass-tipped horns that sulked by himself in Break Field.

Quite suddenly, this strange little community found itself in clover: Susannah had more time to spend with the children; Endacott and Molly virtually ran the farm, while Blair, free at last to pursue his ecclesiastic interests, became increasingly involved in the contentions which had arisen in the Ebrington Street Meeting in Plymouth between brother Newton and brother Darby.

CHAPTER 17

If the cattle had eaten wild garlic or ox-eye daisies or fool's parsley, the milk was tainted and the taste came straight through into the butter, so you had to smell the milk first, when Sal brought it in warm in the pail. You had to put your nose right down over those creamy bubbles and inhale the milk-mist to make sure it was fit for setting and churning.

Everything had to be spotlessly clean, too. There was a saying down in Chagford that you could always tell butter from Batworthy Farm for the smell of Mrs Creaber's bodily odours in it, so Molly used that cautionary tale to insist on hot water for washing every morning and a weekly hot bath.

You poured the warm milk into wide, earthenware setting dishes for the cream to rise overnight, and first thing the next morning you fleeted it off and covered it with muslin to ripen. When it was ready, you rinsed out the churn with salt water so that the butter wouldn't stick, then you poured in the cream, added a drop of warm water, and started churning.

It was good exercise, churning butter, and an art in it too, because if it went to sleep on you you could spend your whole morning with the cream swishing in the churn and your arm muscles feeling like over-stretched leather, and never a sign of the swish-swish changing to swidge-swidge and later a splash and thump that meant the butter was coming.

'Story of my life!' Molly laughingly remarked to Thamasine one morning when the butter wouldn't come, but when Thamasine – who was now nearly ten, with dark hair and thick black eyebrows – asked what she meant, Molly only laughed more and said 'Never you mind, my little lover.'

When the butter started coming, it had to be frequently inspected to make sure that it was neither over-churned nor under-churned. The whey had to be drained off (and if Thamasine was lucky she would be given some for a refreshing drink on a summer's day) and the butter transferred to the scrubbed deal table, to be pummelled with wooden bats called butter-beaters. Then, when it was stiff and yellow with a nice grain to it and perhaps a few tiny beads of moisture standing on it like sweat on a milk maid's brow, you moulded it into rectangles, weighed it into quarters and halves and stamped it with the carved wooden butterstamp which announces that it was the finest produce of Harvey's Dairy (est. 1843).

Twice a week, she made butter: week in, week out, season by season, year on year – and she was sick to death of it.

She had taken it for granted that she would have children by James. When she had agreed to marry him she had seen that there at last was her chance to become a 'real' person – a wife and mother rather than an outcast whose very existence had to be kept secret. Giving up her precautions against childbirth had been one of the greatest joys of marriage: for the first time she felt that she truly belonged to James, and was able to give herself entirely to him.

When the months and years passed and no babies came, her yearnings for them turned by degrees from disappointment to incomprehension to smouldering resentment. James had said that they must lay it before the Lord, and they had done so, kneeling side by side every night before getting into bed. Then there had been a terrible argument between them, caused when James had repeated a remark Harvey had made to him which implied that the Lord might have rendered her barren as a punishment for past sin. She had flown at him, furious that he should condemn her when he had himself been involved in such sin and he, with characteristic humility, had hastened to explain that the guilt for such misdeeds need not necessarily be laid at her door.

Their relationship had been soured nevertheless, and the continual longing for children had produced an element of tension between them that had by now rendered James all but impotent. This in turn caused her to despise him, and planted a new idea in her mind that was as dangerous as it was titillating.

She began setting her cap at brother Harvey. She manufactured opportunities to encounter him during their daily round, lying in wait for him outside the cattle shed in order to bump into him when he came out, or taking a stroll on the moor when she knew he had already gone up that way to ponder the contents of a pamphlet received through the penny post. During the meetings in the Room, she took to fixing him with her dark, liquid eyes when he expounded the Scriptures, so that his fingers would sometimes shake as he separated the onion-skin pages of his Bible. At the end of his prayers, she took to saying her 'amen' separately from the majority, indicating by tone of voice and careful timing, a devotion that was temporal rather than spiritual.

The effect of these stratagems was satisfyingly obvious to her. He was visibly disturbed by her covert attentions, and she could see that he was becoming torn between returning her signals of affection and holding himself aloof.

One August afternoon soon after haymaking, she arranged a 'chance' meeting with him in the passage at the back of the house which led from the kitchen to his study and the extension where she and James lived. She was carrying a bundle of lavender-fresh linen in such a way as

350

to force up her bosom for maximum effect, and by occupying a little more of the corridor than was necessary, managed to achieve contact between this particular part of her anatomy and the sleeve of his shirt. The colour shot to his cheeks, the vein in his forehead swelled up as if it were about to burst – and Molly, begging his pardon demurely, went on her way, biting her lip to stop herself laughing, sure now that it was only a matter of time before the master of the house succumbed to her charms.

He went quickly back into his study, shut the door behind him and dropped to his knees. 'O Lord give me the strength to resist her,' he begged, feeling quite powerless in himself to overcome the surging excitement that momentary contact with her had caused.

He pressed his hands hard against his face, repeating the prayer, terrified already of his own weakness and the devilish attraction she held for him. He was sure, now, that she knew exactly who he was. For five years there had been a mute agreement between them to have as little to do with each other as possible. He had deliberately held himself aloof, had used his involvement with the affairs of the Brethren as an excuse not to indulge in table chatter at meals and had deliberately set himself far above the women folk. Now, within the space of a few weeks, Molly had changed everything, and the effect she was having upon him was even greater than she had intended.

He found it difficult to think of anything else now. While his relations with Susannah were cordial they were by no means passionate, and Molly's sudden advances had set off a physical reaction in him that sent him back into his early twenties. Troubled by the most lascivious dreams, there had been occasions recently when, half asleep and half awake, he had achieved sexual gratification in a way that was not entirely involuntary, and such emissions had always been accompanied by the most vivid impressions (they could not exactly be called dreams) that Molly herself was the cause of them.

What a strange irony it was that Susannah had often expressed a wish that he could act with a little more warmth towards Molly! A spark had fallen on him now and had started a blaze that was threatening to engulf him.

He rose from his knees and paced the room, peering out of the window at the moorside behind the house, trying to put the image of Molly from his mind. The only possible solution was to throw himself wholeheartedly into the affairs of the Brethren, and to this end he now sat down at his table and returned to the question of Bethesda.

The controversy between Newton and Darby had deepened seriously in recent weeks. After the separation of Darby from Ebrington Street, caused as much by personal rivalry as by the disagreements over the secret rapture or Newton's tendency towards clericalism, the Brethren had been thrown into confusion. There had been inquiries, confessions, judgements and accusations. For years, a war of pamphlets had been going on between the Darbyites and the Newtonites, and this war now developed into little short of a slanging match of calumny and character assassination. Running short of ammunition to hurl at the opposing camp, some of Darby's followers dredged up a new scandal based on notes taken by a lady at an address given by Newton some years before, in which he seemed to have suggested that Psalm vi referred to the sufferings of Christ and therefore cast doubt upon His true divinity. Leaping on this heresy as proof positive of all their worst fears, the Darbyites accused Newton of 'entire indifference to the truth and glory of Christ'. They called him a 'poisoner and a seducing spirit'; and Darby announced that as Newton was clearly no longer guided by the Holy Spirit, he must be guided by Satan, and that it was therefore essential for brethren to disassociate themselves not only from Newton himself, not only from his followers, but even from those who had chanced to worship at

Ebrington Street and had not since judged the errors there and condemned them.

The sheep separated from the goats and the goats, believing themselves to be sheep, separated from the sheep, whom they regarded as goats.

Blair Harvey, anxious to lead the saints of Brimstonedown along the path of light, had been careful to give his unqualified support to brother Darby from the start. But now events had taken a new turn. Two of the Ebrington Street brethren — Captain Woodfall and his brother — had sought communion at Bethesda Chapel, Müller's meeting in Bristol. Until now, Müller and Craik had kept themselves neutral in the controversy; but as Darby pointed out (and Blair could see very well) it was one thing to say they had no quarrel with either party, but quite another to receive into communion brethren who had continued to worship at Ebrington Street after Darby's secession.

Darby had — rightly in Blair's opinion — condemned the decision of Müller to accept the Woodfalls into fellowship, and at a large meeting of labouring brethren in Exeter, had announced publicly and without forewarning that as Bethesda had received friends of Newton's into fellowship, he could no longer take communion at Bethesda himself.

As a result of a further separation at Bethesda, Müller had felt obliged to take action. A meeting of elders had been convened, and 'The Letter of the Ten' published, in which Müller, Craik and eight others declared that they had no wish to become entangled in a controversy that was not of their making, and that they would therefore not comply with Darby's requirement that they judge the errors of Ebrington Street.

'The requirement that we should investigate and judge Mr Newton's tracts,' they wrote, 'appeared to some of us like the introduction of a fresh test of communion. It was demanded of us that, in addition to a sound confession and a corresponding walk, we should, as a body, come to a formal decision about what many of us might be quite unable to understand.'

Blair felt the dilemma particularly keenly. While he had been inspired by Darby's leadership at the Powerscourt conference sixteen years before and had maintained contact with Darby by post while he was labouring among the saints in Switzerland, he could not overlook the fact that Susannah was very friendly with Mary Müller and still exchanged letters with her frequently; and that not only had Müller been partially instrumental in bringing him to the Lord, but that he had been baptised by Newton himself off the beach at Teignmouth; so that while all his inclinations were to take Darby's side, he could see that doing so would inevitably involve him in some difficult decisions.

Sitting at his table, he brooded vacantly on the whole question, his line of thought interrupted repeatedly by visions of Molly. And it was those very visions that prompted a decision: ashamed of the sexual stirrings she was causing in him, and at the same time aware that brother Darby was already travelling the country to drum up support among the Brethren against Bethesda, he saw that there was one way in which he could defend himself against the wiles of the devil. Just as Darby had separated himself from evil by leaving the Ebrington Street meeting and refusing to enter into fellowship with the brethren at Bethesda, so must he resist the evil Molly presented by separating himself – even if only temporarily – from her.

He went briskly along the passage to the kitchen, where Susannah and Peg were busy bottling plums, and Thamasine was lost in concentration over a pencil drawing she was making of William the Conqueror's longship.

'My dear,' he said importantly. 'I have been led to see that I must take a short tour.'

'A tour?' she echoed, brushing back a wisp of hair with the back of her hand. 'What sort of tour?'

'I feel it is my place to meet with the brethren in

Plymouth and Exeter to lend my support in these sorry struggles, that they may be brought to a speedy conclusion.'

'I see,' she said carefully disguising the chink of pleasure she experienced at the thought of having him out of the house for a while. 'How long do you intend to be absent?'

'For two or three weeks. Perhaps more.'

'So you will be away for Thamasine's birthday.'

'Quite possibly,' he replied, lifting the weight off his heels. 'I don't think my absence will mar the celebrations, will it Thamasine?'

His daughter looked up from her drawing, aware that she should not speak to her father unless spoken to but that if spoken to she must be careful to make a suitable reply. 'No, Papa,' she said unguardedly.

He snorted. 'There. I think you will all be very glad to be rid of me, will you not?'

'Not at all, dear,' Susannah said, coming to the rescue. 'We shall miss you a great deal.'

'Then that is settled,' he said. 'I shall depart tomorrow.'

'For Exeter?'

'I shall follow where the Lord leads, Susannah. And – before you ask – I doubt if I shall see the Müllers, so you need not trouble yourself by writing a letter to Mary.'

'Will you see brother Darby, Papa?' Grace asked from the door, having arrived there unnoticed during the conversation.

For once he was short with his favourite daughter. 'Yes, I expect I shall,' he said, and left the kitchen abruptly to signal his disapproval at being questioned in this way upon his intentions.

In the space of a year, James Endacott had aged noticeably. For no apparent reason, he found himself perpetually tired, underconfident in his own decisions, and at a loss over Molly's coldness towards him.

Since Molly's arrival, he and Susannah had been careful to remain on strictly proper terms, and although each was aware of an inseverable bond between them, so finely tuned were they to one another's wishes that they had never once approached the borders of impropriety.

This fragile situation had already been set off balance by Molly's growing antagonism towards her husband, and the equilibrium was further distrubed by Blair's departure. From the moment he drove out of the yard and went down the lane to Chagford, it was as if an invisible cloud had suddenly lifted.

'Now you're *really* the Captain, Uncle James!' Thamasine remarked with that uncanny perception children sometimes show.

'That's right,' he laughed. 'Promotion at last!' He looked back at the other three, lanky girls in their early teens, with long fair hair and wide, innocent eyes. 'So mind you all behave yourselves, understand?'

They walked back into the yard. Sal was washing out milk pails at the water butt by the dairy, and Molly was shaking out a rug from her own front door.

'Mama,' said Theo, 'what are we going to do for Thamasine's birthday treat?'

As all their birthdays except Thamasine's occurred in the winter months, it had become a custom in the family to make Thamasine's birthday an occasion on which the three elder sisters also benefited. This year, her birthday coincided with the Chagford revel, an occasion Theodosia was anxious not to miss.

'Can we go to the revel?' she pleaded.

'I didn't know there was one,' Susannah admitted, bringing forth gasps from her children at her ignorance of local events.

'Mama, there have been notices in the village about it for weeks!'

'Aunt Molly said it would be an education,' Bea put in.

'Did she indeed?' Susannah said, and her glance coincided with James's for a fraction of a second.

'I don't want to go,' Grace said. 'Papa says that revels are occasions of darkness.'

'And your Papa is quite right,' Endacott said. 'Revels are no places for young ladies.'

'I didn't think we were young ladies,' Theodosia remarked, remembering something her mother had been saying about the equality of all people before God.

'Can we have a picnic instead?' Thamasine asked.

'I shall have to think about it,' Susannah told her. 'You'll just have to wait and see.'

'We always have to wait, and we never see!' Bea complained. 'We don't even have Christmas!'

'Christmas is a pagan festival,' Grace observed.

Endacott glanced at Susannah. 'I think we might make an exception this time, don't you? If they're very good?'

'But we are! We're always very good!' Bea insisted, and slipped her hand into her Uncle James's. 'Aren't we?'

'Fair to middling,' he granted. 'You could be worse.'

'So shall we definitely have a picnic then?' Thamasine pestered. 'Please?'

Susannah laughed, relenting. 'Very well, then, yes.'

'And can we go down to Dogmarsh and see the Logan Stone?'

'Oh – I expect so, Theodosia – if the weather's fine, yes!'

'*And* if the Lord tarry,' added Grace, and looked up at her mother with an air of unctuous superiority.

Two weeks later, when Thamasine came down to breakfast, she discovered a package by her place with a card on it that read, 'To Thamasine, on your tenth birthday, with love from Uncle James.'

She gazed at it, quite nonplussed at receiving a present on her birthday, and aware that her sisters must be envious at this departure from family custom.

'Well go on, open it!' Bea urged.

They watched her stubby fingers unknot the twine and unfold the brown paper, and there was a gasp of appreciation when the gift was revealed.

'A Bible!' Grace exclaimed.

'No, it's not a Bible,' Thamasine said. 'It's – it's the sonnets of William Shakespeare.'

'James!' Susannah breathed. 'You really should not have –'

'Is it for me to keep, Uncle James?'

'Of course it is. I want you to have it because I know you will look after it and appreciate it. If you look inside you will see –'

But Thamasine had already looked inside the cover, and had found the dedication made thirty years before. 'To Frances,' she read. 'Who is Frances, Uncle James?'

'It was his first wife,' Molly cut in rather sharply. 'The one that died.'

But even Molly could not spoil the moment: Thamasine appeared not to hear her. She went straight to James, and throwing her arms round his neck planted a kiss on the small expanse of pink cheek between his moustache and his sidewhiskers.

They set out for their family picnic in the early afternoon, riding down the hill in the four-wheel wagon: James, Susannah, the four girls and Sal – Molly having chosen to remain behind with Peg, to see to the afternoon milking. They went down past Yeo cornmill and Waye Barton and on through Chagford, where wagons and horses were cluttering the village centre and flags were draped from house to house in honour of the revel. But in spite of earnest pleadings on Theodosia's part to be allowed to stop 'just for a few minutes' to see what was going on, the grown-ups insisted on driving on down to Easton, where they turned left onto the turnpike to Dogmarsh Bridge.

There, they unloaded the covered baskets, the rugs and the churns of milk and whey, and proceeded along the

358

path that skirts the Piddledown escarpment. This path plunged into woods after half a mile, until a little further on a glade opened out where the river widened and flowed over smooth boulders, among which stood a large natural obelisk known locally as the Logan Stone; and it was here, with the shallow waters chuckling at their feet, that they spread out their rugs and made their picnic.

They paddled in the river, played hide-and-seek and watched as Uncle James made the Logan Stone rock back and forth.

'Has it always been like that do you suppose?' Thamasine asked, when they were eating fresh baked scones with clotted cream.

It was the sort of question which would normally have been referred to their father had he been present, but as he was not, they looked to James for an answer.

'It is quite possible that it has been, yes,' he answered. 'Though I suppose it might have lodged in that position as a result of a landslide.'

'And do you think it will always stand thus, Uncle James?'

'Just because you're ten you don't have to give yourself airs and ask complicated questions, Thamasine,' Theodosia remarked, and bit so self-indulgently into her scone that a blob of cream stuck to her nose.

'I was only asking,' Thamasine said. 'I wasn't giving myself airs at all.'

'Yes you were, you were!' Grace put in.

This exchange threatened to develop into a squabble, so Susannah put an end to it by suggesting that they all walk down to Fingle's Bridge. 'Off you go, all of you. Uncle James and I will stay here and look after the picnic.'

So the two grown-ups were left alone, whether by accident or design Endacott could not be sure, though he thought he detected a flush on Susannah's cheek as she despatched her four daughters in the care of Sal.

He rolled up his coat and made a pillow of it against a

young oak that grew a few feet from the water's edge. Sitting down, he let out an involuntary sigh, which caused Susannah to remark that he sounded tired. Both were aware that the occasions for private conversation were few and far between, and both were a little shy of each other as a result.

'No, not tired,' he said. 'Merely decrepit. When I think how I could spend all day in the saddle then go partying and dancing until all hours, I sometimes wonder if I am the same person.'

'I can assure you that you are the same person, nevertheless, James.'

'Old age,' he said. 'That's what it is.'

'Nonsense. You are not even sixty!'

'I will not contradict you, but I can't pretend to a vigour that has departed.'

She had been putting away the picnic, and when she had tucked a napkin over the basket, sat down a little way from him so that if he turned his head he could see her face in profile. This he now did, and was immediately certain that her downcast eyes and gentle dignity disguised an inner turmoil, for the colour was still in her cheek and her head moved in a way that told him she was frightened of the situation she appeared to have engineered.

For several moments he felt quite tongue-tied: he knew that the only alternatives to silence were either shallow chit-chat or an intimate sharing of their deepest thoughts, and he shrank from both.

She turned and looked back into his eyes, and he felt a great flood of love for her, together with a strange telepathy, so that when she spoke her words seemed no more than a confirmation of a message already transmitted.

'I wish life could have been kinder to us, James.'

He knew her too well to attempt any sort of optimistic pretence. 'We have to accept what life brings,' he said. 'I learnt a long time ago not to fight against what must be.'

She made no answer to that, and for some while sat staring out over the wide stretch of water, which eddied and gurgled over the boulders at their feet.

'I have sometimes wondered,' she said at length, 'about the true meaning of those words, "whom God hath joined, let no man put asunder". Do you think it is possible – ever – for a man and a woman to be married legally, and yet remain unjoined in the sight of God?'

He smiled. 'You ask as difficult a question as your youngest daughter.'

'But what is your opinion?'

He paused for so long that Susannah began to wonder if he would reply at all. But eventually he said, 'If I am to be entirely honest, I must answer yes.'

'So the corollary must also follow, and it must be possible for God to join two people who remain unjoined in the eyes of the law.'

'It is tempting to think so, Susannah.'

'Tempting? You make such a union sound sinful. But if it is made by God, how can it be?'

He struggled to think clearly. 'The difficulty is that if such a premise were to be accepted, then surely all sorts of evil would result. Divorce would necessarily become a commonplace. The family would be destroyed.'

'How do those lines of Shelley's go?' she asked, and answered her own question by quoting:

'I never was attached to that great sect
Whose doctrine is that each one should select
Out of the crowd a mistress or a friend,
And all the rest, though fair and wise, commend
To cold oblivion . . .'

'And do you identify yourself with those sentiments?'

She looked up at the tracery of leaves, through which the sun was sending a dappled pattern of light, and he saw her as a young woman again, undaunted by life, unaffected by tragedy and unoppressed by her husband.

'Not entirely, but I cannot help thinking that there is an element of wisdom in them.' She laughed sadly and seemed to speak her thoughts aloud: 'You only have to consider our respective marriage partners to see that.'

'I think we're on dangerous ground,' he said softly.

'Of course we are! But must we go through our whole lives on safe ground? Cannot even you and I, James, admit that our marriage vows are strained to the limit?'

He shook his head, unable to continue the conversation, but at the same time longing to confirm to her that his feelings coincided exactly with hers. So he spoke to her without words: he reached out his hand and laid it, palm upward, at her side; and after a moment she put her hand in his and they were joined in the very way Susannah had been at pains to explain.

For a long time, they were silent. Across the river, a kingfisher flashed, blue and green.

'Why did you marry her?' Susannah asked suddenly.

'Surely you know. I could not have remained at Brimstonedown –'

'I did not ask why you married, but why you married *her*.'

He hesitated, aware of the promises he had made Molly never to reveal her background.

'Was she your mistress?'

'She had . . . depended on me for many years. I was morally bound to support her. And . . . as my money was running out, and I felt obliged to marry for reasons we both know, it seemed the only proper thing to do.'

She laughed suddenly. 'It is an extraordinary world indeed, when a gentleman feels obliged to marry a woman who later deliberately sets about making his life as unpleasant as possible!'

'She does not do it deliberately, Susannah.'

'Of course she does! You are too gentle, too blind to see

it. She goes out of her way to belittle you. She rules you, can't you see that?'

He felt suddenly tired. 'Yes, of course I see it. But I have failed her, Susannah. She wanted children of her own, and I have been unable to give them to her. Besides, is not the pot calling the kettle black? How many times have I heard you accept Blair's castigation in humble silence?'

Her hand tightened suddenly on his, and he sensed immediately that he had caused her distress. Releasing him, she stood up and faced away from him, her head down at first, and then thrown back; and when he went to her he found that she was fighting for control.

'Susannah – please forgive me –'

'No, you are not at all to blame, James. I should not have started this conversation. I have led you . . . away from the path. Please, if you can, forgive *me*, and disregard entirely what I have said.'

'I could no more disregard what you have said than cease to love you,' he whispered, and when she turned to him the dam burst: he took her gently in his arms, and for a few moments shared with her a love that was far stronger than any forged by man-made certificates or rubricated forms of service.

Blair came slowly up the hill in his gig the following Saturday, his face the colour of a well-baked salmon, a small cloud of horseflies buzzing along behind him. Harvest was home now: to his left and right the fields of stubble were bare of sheaves and gleaners, and the countryside was having a few days' respite before autumn ploughing.

Grace ran down the hill to meet him and climbed into the gig to ride the last hundred yards.

'Papa,' she said, 'Uncle James has gone away to Teignmouth. Mama says he needed a holiday.' She looked at her father and was gratified to see that her news had caused a furrow in his brow. 'Did you know that he was going away?'

'No I did not,' Blair said with ill-concealed anger.

'I didn't think so,' Grace said, and folding her hands looked ahead as the gig approached the farm gate, which was being held open by Bea.

Molly came to the dairy door as the gig clattered into the yard, and Susannah appeared from behind the chicken run. Six geese approached noisily in V formation, waddling with military precision, and the remaining members of the household converged to welcome back the master.

Blair stepped down from the gig with more self-importance than usual. Having spent much of his time away in the company of John Nelson Darby, he now gave off a self-conscious after-glow, as a piece of dead cuttlefish that has been placed in a bright light will glow on after dark. He gave a formal little bow to Susannah and accepted the greetings and salutations of his children and domestics; and having instructed Peg to arrange hot water for his bath and Sal to stable the horse, he invited Susannah to accompany him into the house.

She followed him into the study. 'Now – what is this that Grace tells me about James?' he asked as soon as the door was closed.

'He has gone down to Teignmouth to stay with Lord Congleton,' she replied, having been well prepared for the question.

'Well, he is in for a disappointment. The noble Lord is in London with the brethren of Rawstorne Street, according to my latest information.'

'In that case I expect he will be staying with one of the brethren at Ebenezer.'

Harvey frowned and nodded to himself as if this were of considerable importance.

'And why the sudden departure? Could he not have waited until my return?'

'He has not been in the best of health, Blair, and as the

harvest was in he felt that now was the best time to take a few days away.'

'In my absence? I find that very surprising, Susannah, very surprising indeed.' He looked closely at her. 'Or was there perhaps another reason?'

She forced herself to stare directly back into his pale blue eyes. There had indeed been another reason: so powerful was the love she and James had discovered for each other, that he had felt obliged to leave at the earliest opportunity, saying that he must discover for himself whether he could stay on at Brimstonedown. So now it was necessary to tell Blair a direct lie.

'If there was any other reason, then I am not aware of it,' she said, and felt her heart thumping so hard in her rib cage that it seemed impossible that Blair should not hear it and suspect the truth.

But he did not hear it. He pursed his lips and puffed his cheeks; he lifted the weight off his heels and stuck his thumbs into his waistcoat – and, having taken a turn round the room, he peered out of the low window as if to make sure that Dartmoor was exactly as he had left it.

'There is a letter for you,' Susannah said behind him. 'It arrived this morning.'

He seized it from her, looked at the address, then turned it over to examine the sender's on the back.

'Have you seen who it is from?'

'No, I did not look at it further than to see that it was addressed to you, Blair.'

'Then I shall tell you. It is from J.N.D.' He tapped the letter against the palm of his left hand. 'I was with brother Darby in Leeds, Susannah. He showed me the first draft of this letter before sending it out.'

'Is it a circular then?'

'It is more than a circular. It is . . . an epistle. A letter to the churches.' He frowned and bit his lip. 'I suppose you have not been in correspondence with Mary Müller have you, Susannah?'

'No.'

'Good. Then see that you don't in the future without first consulting myself. Now – if you will kindly have Peg inform me when my bath is ready, I shall spend the intervening time in private prayer.'

She hesitated at the door. 'Have you had a disagreement with the Müllers, Blair? Is that why I must not write?'

His eyes narrowed. 'There is much darkness at Bethesda.' he told her cryptically.

'May I know the cause?'

'Certainly you may, but you must wait until after the breaking of bread tomorrow, when I shall make a full statement to the saints.'

She accepted this and departed; and as soon as the door had closed, Blair took out a paper-knife and slit open the letter from brother Darby, whose printed contents started simply: 'Beloved Brethren . . .'

They came up the hill in twos and threes and fours: the brethren and sisters of the Brimstonedown assembly, their sombre clothes contrasting with the pale golds and dusty greens of late summer, their unhurried pace made the more deliberate by contrast with the swallows that swooped and darted overhead.

They entered by the latchgate and made their way across the yard to the stables, going in single file up the open stairway to the Room. There, they sat down upon the upright chairs arranged in a rough circle round the Table, bowing their heads in prayer and maintaining a dead, black silence that turned the softest rustle of a woman's skirt or the most carefully suppressed cough into an outrageous interruption.

The Harvey girls sat in a row as they always did: their eyes down, their Bibles open, their lips closed. Glancing across at them, Blair was inwardly content at the docile and saintly deportment of the elder three but irritated – as always – at the way Thamasine managed to sit slightly askew on her chair, fidgeting and glancing about her instead of elevating her mind to the worship of the Lord.

It was several minutes after the last arrival that the meeting started. Brother Glebe rose to his feet, and having ensured that no other brother had also been led by the Spirit to speak (Brethren custom being that the first should always be last, and the last first) he tentatively suggested they sing hymn number 225; and a few moments later Blair Harvey led off in his confident baritone:

'We're not of the world which fadeth away;
We're not of the night, but children of day;
The chains that once bound us by Jesus are riven,
We're strangers on earth, and our home is in heaven . . .'

There was a long silence after this hymn, caused by the expectation that brother Harvey would lead the saints in prayer as was his normal custom; but when five minutes had passed and he still remained deep in silent prayer, brother Archer, an ex-member of the Wonson assembly, rose to his feet and approached the throne of grace.

Once again, when brother Archer had sat down, the saints were sure that brother Harvey would make a contribution. But extraordinarily, he did not: sitting at the head of the Room with his head thrown back and his eyes closed, he seemed to be intent on reminding the brethren that he exercised no form of pastorship over them.

As the meeting continued, this departure from a form of service for which no form was claimed but which had developed its own conventions over the years, created a peculiar tension. All present knew that brother Harvey had been away for three Lord's Days in a row, and no one had failed to note that brother Endacott was now absent. These mild and humble people who had been taught to regard themselves as members of God's elect were also aware that in the past year there had been separations and disagreements among the Brethren which were already threatening to tear the movement apart. The tension mounted gradually and turned into a sort of fear – a fear of the unknown, a fear of judgement, a fear of some great evil that might snatch them from the hand of their Saviour.

Humbly, brother Beer took it upon himself to break the bread and pour the wine, and when these had been passed among the saints, they settled back, confident that brother Harvey would now minister the Word and close the meeting in prayer.

But he did not: after a further lengthy pause, brother Withecombe felt moved by the Spirit to do so, and when he had stumbled through a muddled comparison of the sacrificial requirements to be found in Leviticus and the role of the high priest, Melchisedech, in the Book of the Hebrews, he closed up his Bible and led them for the final prayer, pointedly thanking the Lord for remaining within their midst and giving them the blessing of saintly fellowship.

During this last prayer, Thamasine experienced that ache of impatience known only among children who have had to sit motionless through nearly two hours of improvised turgidity, and who look forward to the escape into the fresh air and sunshine with a longing far more intense than that experienced by most religious persons during a lifetime's longing for the Parousia.

And now, the meeting really did seem to be over. The people began to collect together their Bibles and hymn books, and eyes turned once more to brother Harvey, whose custom was to rise first in order to signal the completion of the morning's worship.

But when he did rise, Blair held in his hands several sheets of printed lithograph, which he held at arms length in order to accommodate his longsightedness. 'My dear brethren and sisters in Christ,' he said, ignoring an audible sigh that came from Thamasine's direction. 'Before we depart, I have a letter which I feel bound in Christian duty to read to you. I will read it in full, and I beg you to give it your closest attention, for I am convinced that the words here written come not merely from our beloved brother Darby, but from the Holy Ghost acting through him as mouthpiece – and that they apply to each one of us here present in a way that will have an everlasting bearing upon the well-being of our souls.'

So saying, and having glanced round once more to ensure that he had the rapt attention of all, he launched into the letter which Darby had sent out to all assemblies, and in which he set out the principles of exclusivism upon which the Darbyite sect was to be founded.

'Beloved Brethren,' he read, 'I feel bound to present to you the case of Bethesda. It involves to my mind the whole question of association with brethren, and for this simple reason, that if there is incapacity to keep out that which has been recognised as the work and the power of Satan – if brethren are incapable of this service to Christ – then they ought not to be in any way owned as a body to whom such service is confided: their gatherings would really be a trap laid to ensnare the sheep . . .'

As he continued, Blair noticed that Molly was fixing him with dark, inviting eyes, just as she had done so often before his recent tour. She was sitting on the opposite side of the Room from him, so that the table with the carafe of wine, the goblets and the broken bread lay between them; but now, drawing strength and authority from Darby's words, he felt a new confidence in his ability to resist her.

'The object of Mr Newton and his friends is not now openly to propagate his doctrine in the offensive form in which it has roused the resistance of every godly conscience that cared for the glory and person of the blessed Lord, but to palliate and extenuate the evil of the doctrine and get a footing as Christians for those who hold it, so as to be able to spread it and put sincere souls off their guard.'

Blair paused for effect, and the stunned attention of his

listeners confirmed his belief that he was playing a vital role in the guidance of the saints. This in turn filled him with what he regarded as justifiable pride that it had fallen to his lot to perform such a service.

'In this way precisely Bethesda is helping them in the most effectual way they can: I shall now state how. They have received the members of Ebrington Street with a positive refusal to investigate the Plymouth errors. And at this moment the most active agents of Mr Newton are assiduously occupied amongst the members of Bethesda, in denying that Mr Newton holds errors . . .'

A little shiver went through the ranks of his audience. The words of a revered brother in Christ, read out with all the dramatic power at Blair Harvey's command, were beginning to have their effect. It was as if a hairy, horned beast were lurking somewhere just beyond the door, and that at any moment they might hear the satanic clatter of its hooves.

The reading went on and on. 'A solemn trifling of facts' was how it was later described, but to the saints of Brimstonedown, the issue of Craik's and Müller's acceptance into fellowship of certain brethren from the separated Plymouth meeting seemed to strike at the very heart of Christianity: having 'come out' of the world and set themselves apart; having made themselves strangers on earth and convinced themselves of the Lord's imminent return, it was now of truly infinite and eternal importance that they keep themselves free of any taint or error that might lure them back into the apostasy they saw all around.

'. . . I do call upon brethren,' Blair went on, turning at last to the final paragraphs of the letter, 'by their faithfulness to Christ, and love to the souls of those dear to Him in faithfulness, to set a barrier against this evil. Woe be to them if they love the brethren Müller and Craik or their own ease more than the souls of saints dear to Christ! And I plainly urge upon them that to receive any one from

Bethesda (unless in any exceptional case of ignorance of what has passed) is opening the door now to the infection of the abominable evil from which at so much painful cost we have been delivered.'

Here, the text changed to italics, and Blair slowed his delivery to give due emphasis and solemnity: 'It has been formally and deliberately admitted at Bethesda under the plea of not investigating it (itself a principle which refuses to watch against the roots of bitterness), and really palliated. And if this be admitted by receiving persons from Bethesda, THOSE doing so ARE MORALLY identified with the evil, for the body so acting is corporately responsible for the evil they admit. If brethren think they can admit those who subvert the person and glory of Christ, and principles which have led to so much untruth and dishonesty, it is well they should say so, that those who cannot may know what to do.'

The atmosphere in the Room now seemed quite electric, and Susannah experienced an unearthly sense of helplessness as the full import of Darby's message sank in; as if she, along with all the rest, was being forcibly rounded up and herded away into a separate enclosure.

Blair had reached the peroration: his voice now assumed a quiet reasonableness that added a new dimension to the insidious power of what had gone before. 'I only lay the matter before the consciences of brethren, urging it upon them by their fidelity to Christ. And I am clear in my conscience towards them. For my own part, I should neither go to Bethesda in its present state, nor while in that state go where persons from it were knowingly admitted. I do not wish to reason on it here, but lay it before brethren, and press it on their fidelity to Christ and their care of His beloved saints.

'Ever yours in His grace,
'J.N.D.'

Slowly, humbly, wordlessly, the saints of Brimstonedown departed. Though some were shocked and some bewildered at the boldness of Darby's edict, the majority only dimly understood its causes, and these gained a grim satisfaction and a heightened sense of their own importance from it, quite unaware that its contents were to bring about a sea change in the Brethren movement that would identify it with schism and hatred rather than unity and love.

Only Susannah saw anything like its full implications, for only she apart from Blair knew Müller and Craik personally, and only she appreciated that from then on she was required by brother Darby to disown them as brethren and refuse to break bread with them; so while the others filed out, she remained with her head bowed in prayer, her thoughts in a turmoil and her instincts shouting that she should have the courage to come out against this cruel act of excommunication.

But the years of wifely submission had taken their toll: it was unthinkable that she should pit herself against the authority of her husband; so when Blair, standing at her side, murmured, 'Come, Susannah,' she rose obediently and with a heavy heart allowed him to take her arm and escort her from the Room.

Endacott arrived back towards evening on the following Tuesday. As he dismounted in the yard, he caught a glimpse of Susannah's face at the kitchen window, and though their eyes met for only the briefest instant, that was enough to dispel any doubts he might have had about his feelings towards her.

During his short time away, he had thought long and hard about his attachment to Susannah, but even now, the arguments for and against staying on at Brimestonedown seemed quite irresolvable: the love he felt – and which he was quite sure was returned – was so strong that if he remained he knew that it would break out, however hard he tried to contain it, with disastrous results; but on the other hand, what possible reason could he give to Blair and Molly for a decision to remove? And where would he go? How might he provide for Molly?

He led the horse into the stables, whose rafters were hung with cobwebs and whose whitewashed walls were brightened by the diagonal rays of the evening sun. He was just removing the saddlebags when a shadow fell across the stall, and Sal entered.

She looked up at him with mournful eyes. Life had not used Sal as well as she had expected: she had become little more than a workhorse herself now, with nothing to look forward to but another day, another season, another year. 'We be just starting supper, sir,' she told him. 'The master says for you to be as quick as possible, like.'

He thanked her and gave her the saddlebags to take into the house, and when he had seen to the horse and hung up the tack, he crossed to the kitchen, where the family had already sat down to cheese and onion pie.

'So you're back!' Harvey said rather too jocularly. 'We thought you'd gone for good, didn't we, Susannah!'

He kissed Molly on the cheek before taking his place beside her, but she scarcely acknowledged the gesture. When he had bowed his head to give silent thanks, and Peg had ladled a helping onto his plate, Blair asked him: 'How was Teignmouth? Did you find Lord Congleton there?'

'I didn't go there,' he said between mouthfuls. 'I went first to Exeter, and hearing he was in London, travelled to Barnstaple instead.'

'To stay with brother Chapman?' Susannah asked.

'Yes, but I found him absent also. He had not yet returned from his preaching tour in Ulster.'

'I must admit I was a little surprised to find you absent on my return,' Blair said.

'Yes – I owe you an apology –'

'Absent from his place of duty!' Blair chortled, mock-military.

Endacott smiled faintly, and saw Thamasine regarding him kindly from across the table. 'And how is the birthday girl?' he asked her. 'Have you got all those sonnets by heart yet?'

'Sonnets?' said Harvey. 'What sonnets?'

'The Shakespearian sonnets James gave to Thamasine for her birthday, dear,' Susannah said. 'If you remember, I did tell you about it.'

Blair made a non-committal grunt. 'I can think of any number of passages in Holy Scripture that would be better worth getting by heart than any single line of Mr Shakespeare's work.'

Thamasine's eyes widened in admiration. 'Do you know all of Shakespeare's works then, Papa?'

Blair ignored this question totally, so that Thamasine was in no doubt that she had committed a grave error of tact.

'So where did you stay in Barnstaple?' Blair asked. 'As brother Chapman was absent?'

'I stayed only one night – with brother Heath. I went to Bristol the following day.'

'You went to Bristol? Where in Bristol?'

He could not understand why they were staring at him so, nor why Susannah looked so frightened. Molly was the only person who was at all relaxed, and she seemed to be gaining some sort of amusement at his expense.

'Why – with the Müllers, of course, who else?' He turned to Susannah. 'Mary sends you her love in Christ, and asks you to continue to remember the orphanage in your prayers.' He stopped, sensing their reaction. 'Is anything wrong?'

Harvey had laid down his knife and fork and was blinking rapidly; the three elder girls were staring at him as if he were an alien, and Peg, turning back from the hob where she was watching the apple stew, regarded him with

374

undisguised horror.

'You stayed with brother Müller?'

'Yes of course –'

'And you broke bread at Bethesda?'

'Certainly –'

Harvey stood up. 'In that case, we must speak in private, James. Immediately, if you please.'

They left the room. Their footsteps echoed on the flags as they went along the back corridor. A moment later, the study door closed with a slam.

Susannah, struggling to maintain an outward calm, returned to her cheese and onion pie, glancing at her daughters to ensure that they followed her example.

'What will happen to Uncle James, Mama?' Bea asked.

'That is not for you to ask,' Susannah said. 'Now finish what is on your plate.'

Grace's eyes slid from side to side, enjoying the crisis, and noting the gleam of triumph in Molly's eye. Then something of even greater importance took her attention.

'Mama,' she said. 'Look at Thamasine. She's playing with her food again.'

A wind had sprung up within the past hour, and as they entered the study, the door closed with a slam behind them.

'My dear James,' Blair said with surprising gentleness. 'I must apologise for cutting short your meal, but I know you will see that I was justified in doing so.' He picked up Darby's circular, which lay on his writing table among other papers. 'I presume you have not seen this letter?'

Endacott glanced at the sheets, and confirmed that he had not.

'I am relieved to hear it,' Blair said, and looked quizzically at the other, wondering what was his best course of action. 'What I propose, then, is that we go across to the Room – the two of us, in all humility, as brethren in the Lord – so that you can read brother

Darby's letter undisturbed and we can seek guidance upon it. Will you agree to that?'

Endacott was tired after his day's travelling, but knew Harvey well enough not to argue; so they took a lamp with them across the yard, and mounted the steps to the Room.

Placed on the table, the lamp cast an unsteady light so that the shadows of the worm-eaten rafters wavered back and forth and the silhouettes of the two men swayed on the wall. While Endacott sat and read the circular, Blair closed his eyes in prayer, and for several minutes the only sounds that could be heard were the sighing of the wind and the screeching of an owl.

'You have read it,' Harvey said, his voice booming in the empty hayloft.

'Yes.'

'So you see the predicament.'

'I see brother Darby's predicament, certainly.'

'It is ours also, James. I have read out that letter to the brethren this Sunday past.'

'I see.'

Harvey looked at him closely. 'Do I detect a note of disapproval?'

Endacott stroked his moustaches. 'I do not disapprove of your reading out the letter – but it seems to me that it was not necessary to do so, as this matter hardly touches us here at Brimstonedown.'

Harvey took a little breath – almost a gasp – of surprise. 'I am disturbed to hear you say that, James. We cannot ignore the Plymouth errors, however convenient it would be to our own ease. Nor can we identify ourselves with Ebrington Street by breaking bread at Bethesda or even allowing the notion of it. Fortunately – or perhaps I should say mercifully – it is clear to me that you went to Bristol and broke bread with George Müller in complete ignorance of what had transpired between him and dear brother Darby. Had it not been so –'

'I should tell you that it was not entirely in ignorance,'

Endacott interrupted. 'I was made aware, while staying with the Müllers, of some of the events which gave rise to that letter.'

This admission stunned Blair into silence for several seconds. 'So . . . you broke bread with them in the full knowledge of their disagreement with brother Darby?'

'Yes I did, and would do so again. I have no quarrel with any of the saints at Bethesda. Indeed, from what I have heard of the matter, brother Darby has in some respects acted quite shabbily.'

Harvey glistened with inner wrath. 'I have no doubt that is the story Müller is putting about,' he said. 'It is hardly to be expected that he would admit to truth while embracing error.'

'Have you heard both sides of the case then?'

'I have heard the *facts* of the case, James. From brother Darby and brother Wigram themselves. I do not need to hear what Müller has to say in self-justification, for I am led by my Lord to see that there can be no justification of his actions.' He stood up, and his footfalls on the bare boards resonated as he paced up and down. 'I sincerely hope that you can be one with me in that opinion, James, for I am sure you will appreciate what a stumbling-block we should present to the saints here if we are not seen to be of one mind over this matter.'

'I see that,' Endacott replied, and there was a quiet confidence in his manner which was in contrast with the heavily contained pressure of Blair's temper, 'but nevertheless, brother Müller and brother Craik have been cruelly used. What brother Darby has done, in effect, is to excommunicate them – and all those who break bread with them or who admit to fellowship saints who have done so – for nothing more than suspending their judgement on the so-called Plymouth errors.'

'So-called? Do you not therefore accept that they are errors?'

'I have not examined them in detail, nor do I intend to.

I do not believe it is the place of brethren to pick over each other's consciences in this way. Once we start that, we shall proceed quickly to a point where, instead of accepting all true Christians into fellowship, we shall find cause to exclude them.'

Harvey stopped pacing and put his head in his hands for several seconds. He was already becoming convinced that the Lord had hardened Endacott's heart, and that no amount of argument would win him over. In a way, he was glad, for although he felt it his duty to argue as forcefully as possible, he saw that there might be good reason now to separate from Endacott and be rid of Molly once and for all.

'See here,' he said. 'Have you not read what brother Darby has written?' He picked up the circular from the chair where Endacott had left it. ' "A paper was read, signed by Messrs Craik and Müller, and eight others, to the body at Bethesda, in which they diligently extenuate and palliate Mr Newton's doctrine, though refusing investigation of it, and blame as far as they can those who opposed it." And again: ". . . members of Ebrington Street, active and unceasing agents of Mr Newton, holding and justifying his views, *are received at Bethesda*." ' Harvey slapped the paper with the backs of his fingers to emphasise the words. 'Now what could be clearer than that, I ask? Can you not see that in breaking bread at Bethesda you are identifying yourself directly with the oldest and most pernicious heresy known to Christianity? Can you not see that you are, by condoning their unwillingness to judge this error, yourself becoming guilty of it? I can hardly credit that you can be so nonchalant about this! Why, man, we are speaking of the glory and divinity of Christ! Are you so completely in the grip of this evil that you cannot recognise it for what it is?'

Here, Endacott attempted to get a word in edgeways. 'But – but is brother Darby necessarily right when he –'

'There! That is exactly the nub of it! You question

"whether brother Darby is right". Can one who is fighting to protect the very cornerstone of our faith be wrong? Why, even questioning such a premise causes me to shrink from you, and to say, "Hence, Satan!" '

'I am not for one moment denying the divinity of Christ, nor any part of His glory,' Endacott replied with tired patience. 'All I am saying –'

'All you are saying, James, is that you refuse to disassociate yourself with the brethren at Bethesda, and as brother Darby so rightly points out, the body so acting is corporately responsible for the evil they admit. Thus, though you may attempt to disassociate yourself with the Newton errors, you are nevertheless chained to the evil of them through your association with brother Müller. It is as simple as that.'

'I find it difficult to put my case if words are to be placed in my mouth,' Endacott observed drily.

Harvey laughed without any trace of humour. 'You have no case to put, James, and what is more, words and ideas have already been placed in your mind – that you have made quite clear to me.' He sank unexpectedly to his knees. 'O Heavenly Father,' he prayed, clenching his fists together beneath his chin, 'do Thou shed the light of Thy grace upon this Thy wandering sheep. Do Thou make plain before him the darkness towards which his steps have been turned by the evil one, that he may turn back now, before it is too late.'

Endacott stood up and turned away at this, shaking his head in sorrow.

'James,' said Blair behind him, 'I beseech you: listen to the voice of your conscience. Do you think that I don't know how difficult it is to separate from brothers Müller and Craik? Why – I have known them fifteen years or more! But consider the cost – the awful cost – of putting human friendship before faithfulness to Christ!'

They argued on and on into the night, Blair crossing the same ground from every angle, exhausting every possible line of reason, every dark foreboding, every dire forecast of hell-fire; and Endacott replying quietly, briefly, firmly. Outside, the wind moaned and rain began to fall; a damp draught chilled the Room, and mice scuttled under the floorboards.

After an emotional appeal as from one old friend to another, Blair was left with tears standing in his eyes, and seeing these, Endacott made one more attempt at reconciliation.

'My dear brother in Christ,' he said, and not even Blair could fail to note the sincerity of his manner, 'can we not reason this out humbly before the Lord? I have not changed my beliefs one whit since we last broke bread together. And if brother Müller has been guilty in any respect, is it for us to judge him?'

But Harvey had already opened his Bible at the second epistle of John. ' "Whosoever transgresseth, and abideth not in the doctrine of Christ, hath not God," ' he read out solemnly. ' "He that abideth in the doctrine of Christ, he hath both the Father and the Son. If there come any unto you, and bring not this doctrine, receive him not into your house, neither bid him God speed: for he that biddeth him God speed is partaker of his evil deeds." ' He looked up. 'There is your answer, Captain Endacott, and though it grieves me to tell you this I must do so if I am to remain obedient to this clear directive of Scripture: while you remain in this state of wilful apostasy, I can neither receive you in my house, nor bid you God speed, nor break bread with you, nor even regard you as my brother in Christ. And if you refuse to separate yourself from this evil, then I am given no choice but to separate myself from you, along with your wife, who will no doubt follow your lead on the matter.'

For a long time, Endacott stood silent, his head bowed, and it seemed to Blair that perhaps this solemn declaration had at last won him over. But he was not won over: looking up at last, he spoke the only words that seemed possible: 'Forgive us our trespasses, as we forgive them that trespass against us'; and with that he turned, and went down the stairway, and out into the darkness.

He was not missed until breakfast the following morning. When Susannah asked Molly where he was, she said she had no idea: he had not come in the previous night, and she had naturally presumed that he and brother Harvey had had one of their all-night prayer sessions in the Room.

A search was started: Susannah and Molly went together and visited each of the outbuildings, while Blair strode off down the hill to find out if any of the cottagers of Teigncombe had seen him that morning. But it was Thamasine who found him. Aware that he sometimes took a solitary walk over Chagford Common, she went up the path to Castor Rock and discovered him huddled in an unnatural position with his face in the mud and his legs drawn up under him.

When she tried to move him, she found that his body had gone stiff and he toppled over – revealing a face so distorted in anguish that she was terrified, and came running and weeping down the hill, to fall into her mother's arms and break the awful news that her darling Uncle James was dead.

CHAPTER 18

As soon as the body had been brought down on an improvised stretcher and laid out in Endacott's own front parlour, Harvey went down to Chagford to inform Dr Thorn. He came up on a piebald mare, and after a two-minute inspection of the cadaver pronounced that an apoplectic fit had been the cause of death. This diagnosis was whispered round the household until it reached Peg, who pummelled dough with massive pink fists and observed that if anyone had cared to ask her opinion on the matter, which they hadn't, she would have told them that the poor Captain had died of a broken heart.

The following day, the undertakers came up to measure the body, and Harvey booked a place in the dissenters' burial ground. That night, Thamasine woke up in the small hours to hear her parents having an argument in the next-door room, and though she did not actually hear her mother accuse her father of having less compassion than would cover a cherry stone, or her father accuse her mother of loving Captain James too well, she heard enough to guess that her parents were deeply divided as a result of the death, and that this division in some complicated way affected them all. In the morning, she heard from Peg (who had heard it from Grace, who had overheard it from her father) that because of the disagreement between her father and Captain James, there could be no proper funeral service in the Room, and this in turn caused Molly to react strongly, saying that her husband had a right to a proper Christian burial. At supper, when the subject of the arrangements was touched on again, Beatrice had the temerity to ask her father if they were dissenters.

Harvey explained that as the State did not recognise the true church but only the so-called Church of England there was no choice, in certain matters, but to be classed as dissenters. But the real dissenters, he told her, were those who refused to follow New Testament teaching and introduced all manner of idolatry, clericalism and the belief in salvation through works. 'For by grace are ye saved, through faith,' he added, causing Grace to murmur, 'not of works, lest any man should boast,' and look demurely down at her plate.

'Are we in the church of God then?' Beatrice asked.

Now that his daughters were growing up, Harvey was frequently called upon to pronounce upon certain matters of doctrine and faith, and he was always careful to give well considered answers which were prompted by his inner voice, and the teachings of brother Darby.

'Not exactly,' he replied, 'for the true church of God cannot be defined by man. Nevertheless, it finds expression only through our beliefs and way of worship, Beatrice. Do you understand that? So while those who have believed in their hearts and confessed with their mouths – who are born of water and of the spirit – may be considered members of the church of God, that church remains invisible until the last days.'

The carpenters arrived the following day: a father and son of seventy and forty, and the shed below the stable was busy with the sound of sawings and planings. The result of their labours was a plain oak coffin, in which the late Captain lay for his last night at Brimstonedown.

Molly, intent upon observing the deepest possible mourning for her husband, played her part with all the passion and finesse of a Sarah Siddons, and there was no doubt that black suited her splendidly. She kept an all-night vigil in her front parlour with the open coffin, and in the morning the children were required to come in and pay their last respects.

'It wasn't really Uncle James,' Susannah explained quietly to Thamasine when they had returned to the kitchen. 'Just his shell.'

Neither the children nor the domestics attended the burial, and few of the saints of Brimstonedown could be spared from their work for it. Molly, Susannah and Blair travelled down to Chagford in the gig, and the interment took place during a heavy downpour, which swept suddenly off the moor. The trees swayed and creaked all around them, and the raindrops thudded on the coffin lid and made rivers in the red earth.

That night, when the family was at supper, the wind dropped and the rain ceased. Now that Captain James was buried, it seemed that the household had entered a new era in which nothing could ever be quite the same as before.

There was a long silence, towards the end of which Theo and Bea began glancing about to see who would be the first to speak, and in due course Bea let out a nervous giggle. This set her elder sister off, and for a few moments the kitchen was filled with the noises of ill-suppressed hysteria.

Since the first shock of discovering the captain dead on the moor, Thamasine had remained unnaturally composed, but now her sisters' behaviour released a new flood of emotion in her. She appeared to choke on her food, and without a word rushed from the table and up to her room.

Susannah went up after her and discovered her kneeling by her window, sobbing bitterly. She took her on her lap and searched her mind for words of comfort.

'Listen,' she said, rocking Thamasine back and forth in her arms, 'when a baby is born, it causes the mother great pain, and the birth is difficult for the baby, too, so it cries as well. But afterwards, when the birth is over, the mother and the father, the brothers and the sisters – sometimes the whole village or town or nation – rejoice, because a new person has been brought into the world. And while that person is alive, his soul grows in the same way as a baby's body grows inside the mother. When the person dies, the soul moves away, that's all. It goes out of the body, out of this world and into the next. The body remains behind, but the soul is delivered like a baby into a new sort of life. And just as the birth of the body is painful to the mother, so the birth of the soul is painful to the world.'

She knew that such an explanation was unscriptural and that Blair would have strongly disapproved; she knew that she should have explained again about death being the wages of sin and eternal life being the gift of God; but such doctrines seemed unsuited to the comfort of her ten-year-old daughter. So she took out her handkerchief and told Thamasine to have a good blow, and for some time afterwards they remained there at the window, content to be quiet together and to allow their thoughts to dwell on the love and happiness they had shared with James.

A new, furtive atmosphere now pervaded Brimstonedown, in which it was easy to see blame in others but difficult to recognise it in oneself. Something had sown deceit and pretence among them, so that facts that stared them in the face had to be smoothed over or deliberately ignored. Blair's disagreement with Endacott over Bethesda was known about by all, but was never referred to. Molly's treatment of her late husband had been noted, but now her pretence of mourning was accepted as genuine.

Before, their way of life had been brave, confident, daring. They were entering the last days, and God was gathering in his elect. Now, the flock had been scattered: neither Chagford, nor Wonson, nor Drewsteignton, nor even South Zeal or either of the Tawtons had separated from Bethesda. The saints at Brimstonedown had become like the Israelitic remnant: a handful of sheep, penned up on the moor, baa-ing and shivering in the wind, while satanic foxes lurked behind boulders and waited for the night.

Harvey was aware of the uneasy atmosphere, but was powerless to alter it. From whatever angle he considered the events leading up to Endacott's death, he could not see that he had at any stage acted against the dictates of his conscience. There was no doubt in his mind that Newton had been guilty of doctrinal error, and Darby was undeniably right to insist that brethren must separate themselves from the evil. Müller had refused to judge the question, and Endacott had refused to separate from Müller. 'Many are called, but *few* are chosen,' he quoted to the saints in one of his dissertations on the matter. 'Are we to side with Mr Müller simply because we believe his point of view is shared by the majority? God forbid!'

There were other causes of unease. Since his argument with Susannah over the funeral arrangements, they had become almost estranged from one another, and he felt increasingly that Susannah and Thamasine were drawing away from the rest of the family; and on top of that, there was the question of what was to become of Molly.

He had already made up his mind that she must go. He had not told her directly, but had mentioned in his breakfast prayers the difficulty he faced over running the farm without assistance, and had made it clear in remarks to the domestics and his daughters that he would have to seek a new stockman to take Endacott's place.

Molly was still playing her part as a heartbroken widow. She went about her duties in the dairy in bleak silence, and seemed very much more devout over her prayers. The sly looks of invitation she had given Blair only weeks before were now replaced by dewy-eyed glances that

386

shouted for his sympathy, and she was careful to inform each member of the household of her concern about the future.

'If your father sends me away, I'll end up in the workhouse,' she told Theodosia, who at fifteen was developing into a serious, responsible young lady who blushed easily and said little; but when Theodosia passed on Molly's apprehension to her mother, Susannah reassured her that Molly need have nothing to fear at all, and that she could stay on for as long as she liked.

She reported the conversation to Blair that evening and the question came quickly to a head.

'There is no question of her staying, and you are quite wrong to give her any such impression,' he said. 'We must give her notice as soon as a suitable interval has elapsed.'

Another argument developed, along the lines of many previous, in which Susannah again indicated to Blair that she found him lacking in compassion.

'I am not at all lacking in compassion, Susannah. I have Molly's well-being very much in mind. It will be far better for her if she removes immediately and finds alternative employment than if she hangs on and becomes dependent upon our charity. Indeed, if you wish to display a little compassion you will give her a month's notice now, so that she can be in no doubt of her position.'

'If you wish to give her notice, you can give her notice yourself,' Susannah answered. 'I do not like to disobey you, but I will not act as your mouthpiece for decisions with which I heartily disagree.'

He was determined to be rid of her. She had been a thorn in his flesh from the moment he laid eyes on her in Exeter. If he did not get rid of her now, he never would; so a few days later, he took the bull by the horns.

She was bandaging the cheeses when Grace came along to say that the master wished to speak with her in his study. Never once in all her time at Brimstonedown had he sent

387

for her like this, so she knew very well what it must be about.

She rinsed and dried her hands, and went up to the bedroom she had shared with Captain James at the end of the house, to make herself look respectable in front of the mirror.

She added a suspicion of rouge to her cheeks, and turned to one side to catch a glimpse of herself in profile. She tilted her head and gave herself a sidelong look, mentally rehearsing the part she would play; and having loosened her stays to give herself more freedom of movement, she went confidently down the stairs for her interview.

Susannah was giving the girls a singing lesson in the large parlour. Their voices rose in an arpeggio to something approaching a shriek. Molly tapped on the study door, and entered on command.

Harvey was sitting at his writing table, having pushed his chair slightly away. One leg was stretched out and the other tucked under; one hand rested on the table and the other resided in his jacket pocket. She was amused to see that he had obviously prepared himself for the interview as carefully as had she.

He indicated a wheelback, and she sat down, adjusting the pleats of her skirt in a sad, demure way before folding her hands together on her lap and looking up to await what he had to say.

He took a very long time to come to the point. He told her a great deal of what she already knew about the circumstances of her arrival at Brimstonedown and of the delicate condition of his finances. He acknowledged, in passing, the contribution she had made in the dairy, and used that observation to reassure her that she should have no difficulty in finding employment elsewhere – 'whether as a dairywoman, a housekeeper or a nurse.'

'I would not stoop to nursing for the riches of the Indies,' she said with considerable dignity.

'Perhaps not,' he replied, aware that he had made a gaffe. His eyes looked everywhere but back into hers. 'However, be that as it may,' he went on, making up in clichés what he lacked in courage, 'I must inform you that I shall shortly require your lodgings to accommodate the new stockman and his wife –'

'You've found a couple, have you?' Molly put in. 'That's news to me!'

'– so I must regretfully ask you to vacate by the end of the month.' He hurried on nervously: 'I have given the matter thought, and have decided that in the long run this will be fairest to you. I shall give you a good character reference, so that you have the best possible chance of making a new start. Have you given any thought as to where you will go?'

She tilted her head at him, looking him in the eye. 'Exeter,' she said. 'I'm known there.'

Harvey said 'of course' twice and took from his waistcoat pocket a gold hunter which had once belonged to Dr Brougham. He flipped it open and shut it again with a snap.

'I'd like the testimonial now,' she said. 'If it isn't too much trouble. I doubt if it'll be any use, but it may keep me out of the workhouse.'

'Come, come,' he said, regaining a grain of self-confidence. 'You're an able-bodied woman. You should have no difficulty at all in finding suitable employment.'

She stared at him with deliberate insolence. 'If you'll just write me the testimonial, I'd be grateful.'

He blinked very fast and sought pen and paper. She waited while he scratched away, and before he had finished said she would like to read it and that he need not bother to seal it. He added his signature, and handed it across.

James had taught her to read when she was sixteen. She scanned the testimonial, and having ascertained that she was suitably described as hard-working and honest, pocketed it.

Then she took a breath and burst into tears.

She gave him a good minute's worth, and only eased off when she was sure she had softened him up. She clutched her bosom and pretended to struggle for control. She begged him not to send her away, told him she was sure she'd end up in the poorhouse, pleaded with him, said that if he let her stay she would see that he never regretted it.

She had not expected an easy victory, and was unsurprised when she did not achieve it. Though Harvey managed to look sympathetic, he insisted that he could not accede, and that he was sure she would understand.

She sighed deeply and said, yes, in a way she did understand.

'But then in another way I don't, Mr Harvey. 'Cos although I been a bad woman in my time I have tried, haven't I? I mean – I never said anything about . . . about you and me. I didn't make any trouble, now did I?'

The window rattled in the wind. Harvey's mouth opened and shut.

Molly leant forward and put her hands under her bosom in a way that hardly suggested distress.

'You don't want to be rid of me really, now do you?' she said, and he noted that she had reverted to that low, husky voice she had once used to entice him. 'Not you. No, the only reason you're doing this is because you're frightened. That's the beginning and the end of it, right? You're frightened of what might . . . develop. Then you always were a bit shy and retiring, weren't you? Remember that afternoon? With you down on your knees, stark bollocky?'

He stared at her speechless.

'Now what if I was to make you a promise, Mr Harvey? What if I said I wouldn't be no trouble? Would that change your mind?'

'I've told you – you can't stay. My mind's made up.'

'Oh dear,' she said, mock-serious. 'Oh dear, oh dear. Now I really don't know what I'll do! I suppose . . . if you really insist I've got to go, I'll have to breathe a few words in a few ears, won't I? About a certain young gentleman who climbed a greasy pole and corrupted a young girl by asking her to take in his washing, right?'

'No one will believe you. It'll be your word against mine –'

She took out his letter from her pocket. 'Wouldn't they? With a good reference like this? I think I could persuade them, don't you?'

'This is unwarranted inducement! It's blackmail!'

She watched him squirm.

'Molly – be reasonable – please –'

'I am being reasonable. I'm not asking much. Just a roof over my head and a bit of security.' She considered. 'Of course if you'd prefer it you could set me up with a capital sum. But I'd want a thousand pounds, and I don't think you can run to that, can you, Mr Harvey?'

He pouted like a schoolboy.

'Come on, love,' she said gently. 'We can have an agreement if you like. I'll keep your secret, and you'll keep mine. We'll get on lovely, you see if we don't. And besides – you need someone to look after the dairy, and I know as much about them cattle as my James ever did.'

'I will not do it,' he muttered, shaking his head in impotent rage. 'I will not be intimidated in this way.'

Molly sighed. 'Well, I'd better show you something else in that case. A couple of things as a matter of fact. You'll have seen 'em before, but I know you'll be interested to see 'em again.'

There was no time to stop her: by the time he realised what she was doing, it was too late. She had unpicked the top buttons of her dress, and with a quick twisting movement of her white shoulders had slipped out of her stays.

'There you are, love,' she said quietly. 'A nice view of the hills for the gentleman. Now are you going to let me stay, or am I going to start screaming rape?'

CHAPTER 19

Molly took over because Father said that Mama needed a rest, which was true, but Mama never had the rest she needed. She should have gone right away for a change of air to Bristol or Exeter or Teignmouth, but all her friends were in darkness and she wasn't even allowed to write to Mary Müller in Bristol, whose husband Father called That Awful Man. Even if she had been able to go away there would have been no one to look after the kitchen garden and the poultry, or to see that they did their lessons properly, so she just had to stay at home and have what rest she could there. But it wasn't much of a rest because as soon as Molly took charge (Father made her the farm manager, the dairywoman *and* the housekeeper) she started making changes. Mama said that it was a blessing because she was a natural organiser and organisation was just what they all needed. She said that Molly was to be obeyed without question because a house divided against itself could not stand. So Molly set Theo to work in the dairy and taught Grace how to keep accounts; she directed Bea to help the domestics in the kitchen and about the house and Thamasine to assist in the kitchen garden and with the cleaning and marketing of the eggs. She made Sal start scouring the pots properly and stopped Peg burning the porridge and watering the broth. She bought herself new clothes with the money she was allowed to pay herself from the dairy profits and went about in full black skirts and buttoned boots, and at market she wore a hat with a brim and carried a stick. Even the cows obeyed her. When she called them in in the evening she made a yodelling noise from the back of her throat, and they all started lumbering across the field towards the gate like ships of the line, each one taking her time as she came unsteadily through the gateway, each one knowing her way into the milking shed and knowing her own stall, each one having her own personal likes and dislikes and foibles. Everyone had to take a share in the milking except Father. The winter mornings were the worst, when there was ice in the yard and sleet driving down off the moor and you had to milk by lamplight. There was a feeling that you were in a different world on those mornings – a world of swishing tails, chewing cud and splattering dung; of a warm flank against your cheek and the milk going ting-tang, ting-tang into the pail. All for one and one for all, that was Molly's motto, but although it was easy to see that all were working for her benefit, it was harder to see how she could be working for the benefit of all. What it came down to, Mama said, was that Molly was a natural leader, the sort of person who steps forward in time of crisis. When she told Papa to fell the oak for winter fuel, or got local labour to come and do the muck spreading and hedging and ditching, or sold the bull and bought in four prime Jersey heifers in his place, no one argued with her because if you argued she gave you what she called the edge of her tongue, which could be very rough indeed. But nobody could deny that she was working wonders. Peg said she had even Father where she wanted him, which was under her thumb.

Now that they were separate from Bethesda, they were separate from a lot of other meetings as well, and that meant that if you met one of the separated brethren or sisters in Chagford you had to look the other way. It meant there were some shops where you could no longer go, because Father said it was better to do business with the world than with brethren who had refused to judge the evil. It also meant that Father couldn't go on nearly so many speaking visits to neighbouring villages, so instead he started going up to London on the new railway train from Exeter, and brought back accounts of special meetings and conferences which he had attended, and at which brother Darby had spoken. There had been a feeling of bleak dread at first, after the separation, partly because of poor Uncle James, but also because the church was in ruins. Later, Father came to see that the church *had* to be in ruins before prophecy could be fulfilled, so that it was an occasion for rejoicing. They were not partakers of other men's sins, and all that mattered was that they keep themselves blameless unto the Lord, as living sacrifices. Nevertheless there was a difficulty, because Father said that it was good that brethren from different meetings should come together for fellowship, and the nearest assembly to have judged the question was at Okehampton, nearly ten miles away. There was nothing for it but to start exchanging visits with the brethren there, although this meant a two-hour journey each way just to break bread on a Lord's day or attend a Bible reading on the Thursday. That was how they came to know the Philpott family. Brother Philpott owned a mine near Sticklepath and was always very well turned out in well-pressed suits and shiny boots. Father said that he was a man of unusual intelligence. His wife was large and gentle and given to sighing audibly during the silences at the Lord's supper. They had several sons who were known as the Chinless Wonders, and not one single member of the family was capable of singing in tune. They were said to be wealthy, and lived in a mansion at Belstone Cleave, where the River Taw widens out below Cawsand Hill. The Chinless Wonders were earnest, pure young men who were destined for the professions. They sat apart from their parents and averted their eyes when the Misses Harvey entered the assembly hall. Grace made cruel little jokes about them. She said that Alexander always looked as though he was about to swallow his Adam's apple and that she was sure Simon had not even started to shave, though he must be at least twenty-two. But it was no good complaining about the Philpott boys being as wet as milksops because being separate meant that there weren't many opportunities for intercourse with young people and, as Mama so frequently pointed out, beggars couldn't be choosers.

Theo, Grace and Bea were baptised in the summers following their fifteenth birthdays, so that by the time she was thirteen, Thamasine was the only person who went to the Room for the breaking of bread on a Sunday who was not in fellowship with the saints. Having the bread and wine go past under her nose and sitting bolt upright with her eyes open while her parents and sisters bowed their heads in prayer made her feel self-conscious and embarrassed at first, but Mama said that was because she was reaching the awkward age. Thamasine thought every age she had known had been awkward. She was small and dark and obstinate, while her sisters were the right size, fair, and obedient. She knew she was supposed to have accepted the Lord Jesus with her heart and confessed Him with her mouth by now, but she still shrank from doing so. It was not that she didn't understand the message of the gospel, because that didn't take any great intelligence and she had been soaked in the doctrine of it as often as bread in milk for breakfast. Indeed she had listened to Father preach so many times – at church gates and village revels as well as on Sunday evenings in the Room – that she was quite sure she could preach the gospel quite adequately herself. She had even 'tried' to be saved – had knelt by her bed and surrendered herself to the Saviour. She had gone to sleep with a wet pillow over His abundant mercy and her miserable sinfulness, and had often made resolutions to read the Scriptures with greater attention, to eschew evil thoughts during the meeting and to keep silence when tempted to chatter or answer back. But it didn't work. Her conversions were contrived, they were an act. She preferred her book of sonnets to Isaiah, and sketching a tame sparrow on her windowsill to copying out yet another chapter of Ephesians; and although she knew she was supposed to join her hands under her nose if she woke in the night and was unable to sleep – although she had been told she was supposed to recite one of the psalms and ask God to quieten her thoughts and send her back into her slumbers – it was very much more comforting to suck your thumb with one hand and to pass the other very gently over the tips of your breasts, which were like two young roes that are twins, and asked to be stroked when they were lonely.

They never had Christmas because it was a pagan festival, along with Easter and every other feast day the so-called Church of England had inherited from the Whore of Rome. It was just another day of milking and mashing, cooking and cleaning, and going to the Room in the evening. Once they heard carol singers down in Teign-combe and saw their lanterns glimmering in the trees as they went singing down to Chagford, and Peg said it was a crying shame they couldn't even have so much as a plum pudding to mark the day. On another Christmas, she baked a few mince pies in secret. They came hot out of the oven and had to be bounced about in your hands and eaten as quickly as possible so that no one would find out, and the eating of them made you feel as if you had dallied with Lucifer. But that feeling was not new, because Thamasine was beginning to suspect that she was like Sal, and not numbered among the elect. Sal was convinced of it because she said she had committed the unforgivable sin, the sin against the Holy Ghost, and that not even the blood of the Saviour could prevent her being cast into the lake of fire on the last day. Mama spent whole afternoons and evenings with her, trying to reassure her of her salvation, but without success. Even Father had failed to persuade her back into confidence in the Lord. Once, almost losing his temper with her he had shouted, 'See here, you foolish child, I *know* I am going to heaven!' and had quoted a whole string of verses to her saying that salvation was irreversible, and that they were members of His body, of His flesh and of His bones – so that poor Sal had broken down, sobbing 'O sir – please don't go on at me! Please leave me be!' and Thamasine knew exactly how she felt because she was aware of a slowly mounting pressure to come forward and declare herself for the Lord. But only recently, dear brother Philpott had spoken on Matthew twenty-four verse forty and she was beginning to see that if you weren't one of the elect it must be quite impossible for you to be saved, because God was omniscient and had known – out of all eternity – which of His creatures would accept salvation and which would refuse it; if He hadn't known, He wouldn't be omniscient and wouldn't be God. So there was a possibility that she was not predestined to accept the Lord, and if that was so, there was nothing at all she could do about it.

But it was frightening nevertheless, and made the more frightening one night when she woke with a start to find Sal in her room with a lighted candle, peering down into her face. 'O Miss Thamasine!' she breathed, and there was a strong smell of cheese and onions about her, 'I come to see if 'ee was still here! I woke up an' it was so quiet like I thought the end had come! I thought the Lord had come down out of the clouds and snatched away His saints, and you and me was left to face the tribulation!'

Mama said there was no need to wait until she was fifteen before asking for baptism because she was an intelligent child and quite old enough to decide for Christ. But she had felt old enough for a long time already – ever since that night Uncle James arrived with his new wife, the night she had been told she was too young. How long ago that seemed, and how strange it was to try and imagine what you would be doing in ten years' time when you would be twenty-four! Grace said she didn't think the world would last that long because since the separation with Bethesda they had entered Laodicea; and the Lord might come any day now, like a thief in the night. Thamasine hoped very much that He wouldn't, because she wanted to be a proper grownup. Theo said they were to stop chattering and come and practice the gospel hymn. It was 'I have heard Him and observed Him, seen His beauty rich and rare.' They had to sing it before the gospel for the spiritual enrichment of the saints. Thamasine disliked having to sing in public, and she likened these performances to the songs of Zion required of the Children of Israel during the Babylonian captivity. 'I shall hang *my* harp upon the willows one of these days,' she said, but nobody thought that was at all funny. She was different and had always felt herself to be different. Even Mama was distressed when she tried to use a sore throat or a cold on the chest as an excuse not to attend the meetings. 'Dearest,' she said, 'He suffered the agony of the cross for you, can you not suffer an hour of slight discomfort for Him?'

But it was not an hour, it was your whole life that was required. Father was always saying it: that they had to die to the world and even hate it. They had to keep themselves separate from it, so that they could not be tainted by it, as milk could be tainted by the cattle eating buttercups. But she could not separate herself from it, nor did she believe could anyone else, however hard they tried. She was a human being: she had become a woman and suffered the affliction along with her sisters. They all had it at the same time each month, so that the house became full of sharp remarks, tears and tension. It was as futile to try to separate yourself from the world as it was to attempt to separate yourself from the affliction or to try to have it at a separate time or to pretend that it didn't happen. And besides, she loved the world. She enjoyed going over to Okehampton with Molly on market day. She adored the jostle and the noise, the lines of horses and wagons, the carcasses hanging outside the butchers' shops, the smoke and laughter coming from the alehouses and inns. She revelled in the crowds of country people in their smocks and low-crowned hats, and listened in delight to the sometimes ribald chatter among the women who kept the stalls. This was the world she was supposed to detest: these were the people – including that gentle apprentice boy who eyed her adoringly from the smithy door – who were 'in darkness'; this old Devon shepherd who chucked her under the chin and called her 'my flower' was yet one more soul that was destined to spend an eternity in the shriekings and wailings of perpetual torment.

And yet she was afraid. The thought of losing Mama for ever terrified her. She could not help wondering, when they were lifting potatoes side by side in the field, whether the Lord might come that moment and take Mama away, leaving her alone. She had a strange dream that she was actually in hell, and that a demon was cutting out her tongue with Mama's best pair of cutting-out scissors. At the breaking of bread, she no longer felt embarrassed or self-conscious, but simply remote: present in the flesh, but not in the spirit. The extraordinary pursuit of a theological theme through the pages of Scripture each week no longer involved her in any way. When, at meals, her sisters discussed with Father whether a speaker had been 'good' – which meant whether he had spoken well or not – she took no part at all in the conversation, preferring to observe the line of Grace's lower lip when she said 'sanctification', or the black hairs that were growing on

399

Sal's upper lip, or the fastidious way Father had of pressing his table napkin to his mouth. Nevertheless the terror of hell lingered on, and she was dogged by a drab awareness that she could not delay the announcement of her conversion for ever – that it might even become necessary to claim she was converted when she was not in order to release the pressure: to submit to a baptism in which she did not believe and to live like a spy, an infidel, in the bosom of her family.

Beatrice was the only one of her sisters she felt able to talk to. Grace was too intent upon pleasing her dear Papa and Theo was too frightened of walking disorderly. But Beatrice was a dear: she was comfortable and jolly and not very good at her lessons, so that Thamasine almost caught up with her. One winter afternoon, she asked Bea if she really did love God. It was during their French conversation hour, and usually they spoke of their likes and dislikes, their favourite colours, the weather or what each was wearing. Speaking of spiritual things in French was an oddly daring thing to do. 'Oui, certainement!' Bea said, putting her puppy-fat arms across her bosom and turning pink and white in surprise. 'Je l'aime plus que je ne pourrais vous dire!' Thamasine sat at the gateleg table and stared out of the window. The fields were white with frost, and the trees in South Park hung with lace. 'Et vous?' Beatrice asked, not having come to grips with the second person singular. Thamasine said that it was what she wanted, but that she found it impossible. Beatrice was appalled and wanted to know why. Thamasine said that she had tried to love Him, but that she could never escape the feeling that she was pretending. Beatrice's vocabulary did not extend to the verb *feindre*, so Thamasine broke into English to explain. 'Then listen,' Beatrice said, considering the subject of their conversation too important to continue in French. 'Can you say sincerely that you are still a little child? Can you say that?' Thamasine sighed impatiently, 'Yes, yes of course I can *say* it –' 'Then listen, listen to me! It is each little child whom He calls to Him, whom He wishes to embrace, for of such are the kingdom of heaven.' 'Well He doesn't call *me*,' Thamasine objected. 'Dearest sister – can you not ask Him to teach you to love Him?' 'I have already done so! I have asked Him into my heart a dozen times, but He does not stay. I do not enjoy reading the Scriptures, I hate going to the meetings. I hate everyone watching me and wondering when I shall take up my cross! Sometimes I want to run out in the middle of the breaking of bread and scream at the top of my voice! I have to hold on to my chair to prevent myself doing so!' Beatrice's eyes filled with tears: she reached out to her sister and held her hand tightly, as if to stop her falling away over a cliff. 'You should not say such things even if you think them,' she said, but Thamasine was unconvinced. 'Why should I not? Why must I stifle true feelings? Am I to pretend to beliefs I do not hold?' But their conversation was interrupted, for their father looked in and demanded to know why they had been speaking in English; he gave them no time to reply, and addressing himself exclusively to Thamasine, told her she must go up that minute to inform her Mama that she had been disobedient and had spoken in English during her French conversation hour. 'But Father, she is resting –' Thamasine put in. 'I know very well she is resting, and I know equally well that she will not be at all pleased to have her rest disturbed. Perhaps you should have considered that before chattering thus in English to your sister.' 'Papa –' began Beatrice, in an attempt at explanation, but her papa wished to hear no more excuses or explanations, and said so. He remained looking in at them for a few seconds more, his pale blue eyes flitting back and forth, his still thick hair going back in waves from his high, noble forehead; and having watched Thamasine rise from her place at table and go up the narrow stair to her mother's bedroom he returned to his study where he was engaged upon writing a pamphlet entitled 'Things Which Must Shortly Come To Pass' and which he hoped, in due course, to have printed by a publisher in Paternoster Row.

She tapped on the door and entered. Her mother was asleep in bed. She gazed down at her, saddened at her dear, careworn face, her greying hair and that look of tragedy that had never left her since the death of Captain James. Her eyes fluttered open and she asked 'What is it?' Crouching by her bed, Thamasine took her hand and told her that she had been speaking English during her hour of French conversation and that she was truly sorry to have disturbed her. 'But why have you come to tell me this?' her Mama asked, and she admitted that her father had sent her. 'Wait, don't go away, I was not asleep, you have not disturbed me,' said her mother. 'Sit on the bed and tell me why you have been wasting your time. What were you talking about to Bea?' But Thamasine did not wish to make excuses or to justify herself, so she said she had been telling Bea of her likes and dislikes. 'Then that is very foolish of you,' said her mother, and raised herself on one elbow, looking intently at her. 'You are too intelligent a child to fritter away your hours in empty chatter. You have a good mind, and that places a special responsibility on your shoulders to use your talents and not waste or bury them. Papa has not sent you to me as a punishment, but because he too knows that you must learn not to waste your time. He reproves you for your own good and is strict with you because he loves you.' She looked back into her mother's eyes and saw in them a longing which she had seen often before: she was old enough now to sense the estrangement between her parents and to know that had her mother felt entirely free to speak her mind she might have taken her side more forcefully. 'Listen,' she continued. 'You are fourteen years old. In less than four years you will be eighteen, and old enough to go out and use your talents for the benefit of others. Do you know what I

402

think you should do? I think you should work hard, now, to achieve the highest possible standards in your French, your English composition, your music and your drawing, so that one day you may find a position as a governess in a good family. And the harder you work, the better chance you will have of finding such independence. Now do you see how important it is not to waste your time?'

That was the year the books arrived. Her father did not want to allow her to have them, and as a result there was an argument between him and Mama that went on behind the closed door of their bedroom, so that you could hear his voice buzzing indistinctly through the plaster long after the candle had been snuffed and you were supposed to be asleep. She never discovered how or why Mama had gained the victory, but gain it she did, and a few weeks later they arrived in two boxes, by carrier from Exeter. Father stipulated that only she was to be allowed to read them, as he was not going to have any other of his daughters corrupted by worldly literature; so Mama (who was even more excited about it than herself) helped her to unpack them in the large parlour and showed her again how to hold a book and how to turn a page so that it would not tear and how to keep it away from the heat of the fire and to put away your pen and ink while you were reading so that there was no danger of a blot falling upon the page. There were works by Malory, Milton, Blake, Pope and Southey among them, and a precious early edition of Montaigne's essays whose lucid observations upon life and living she was to find particularly invigorating. At the same time, her mother gave her a sketchbook for her nature studies and a leatherbound notebook for her fair essays. 'Whatever you observe, try to record your observations with accuracy,' she said, 'for there is no finer discipline than that of precise observation.'

In the fly-leaf of each book, written in her grandfather's

black copperplate were the words '*Ex libris*, Percival Brougham'. Seeing his inscription, and knowing that diligent study now presented the first glimmer of hope that she might one day find her independence, gave her a strange, almost eerie feeling. Sometimes she felt that her grandfather was there in the room with her, watching to see that she handled his books properly and did not allow her attention to wander.

They called into Finch's foundry on the way back from Okehampton market. Molly was out of weeds now and smartly dressed in pleated brown, with a curly brimmed hat worn at a confident angle. Thamasine was in her sixteenth year: a small, dark young woman whose eyebrows threatened to join forces over her nose, and whose watchful manner gave the impression of one used to observing and noting rather than performing or taking part.

While she was sitting in the spring cart, waiting for Molly to collect a pair of gate hinges, Mr Philpott drew up in his carriage, along with his head gardener and his eldest son.

Mr Philpott was a dapper man with a florid complexion and smooth, white hair. He raised his hat to Thamasine and gave her good day. What brought her to the foundry? he wondered, and when she had explained, replied that he too had come to collect an article, and a rather important article at that. The Chinless Wonder hung about in the background fingering his collar and making apologetic grunting noises, and Thamasine had a sudden vision of him rolling on his back like a sloppy dog to have his tummy tickled. But he did not do that, and instead Mr Philpott invited her to descend from the trap and come to the door of the foundry.

It was like a glimpse into Hades: sparks flew up from one of the furnaces and a grimy artisan was using the massive tilt hammer to squash a piece of blue-hot iron.

Aloft, a boy lay full length, his nose inches from a fast revolving grindstone, against which he held the blade of a felling axe. Water sloshed along the launder, and another huge millwheel started turning, to power some other relentless piece of machinery.

They emerged again into the chill spring day, and were met by Mr Finch himself, an imposing man in a frock coat, with a fine head of iron grey hair. He snapped his fingers to an employee, and ordered him to bring out Mr Philpott's machine.

A complicated engine was wheeled out from the side of the building, and Mr Philpott handed his ebony stick to his son in order to explain to Thamasine how his new acquisition functioned. 'It is a machine for cutting grass – grass, mark you, not hay. It is a *lawn-mowing-machine*.' His complexion went a more dangerous pink as he bent to point out its various parts. 'The operator takes hold of these handles here, with which he propels and steers it, and his assistant pulls on this handle which swings to the front, so. Now: as this heavy roller revolves, literally ironing out the lawn as one might say, a chain, here, drives these blades round and round in a perpetual clipping action against this fixed blade here. And see! – the clippings fly upward into this box at the front. Now what could be more ingenious than that?'

He was like a child with a new toy, and insisted that the machine be wheeled over to a stretch of turf so that its marvels could be demonstrated, and while this was going on Molly, who had enjoyed a few minutes conversation with the foreman in the office, came out with the hinges and insisted that she and Miss Thamasine must be getting along.

They drove home through South Zeal and Whiddon Down and plodded slowly up the hill between fields beginning to turn green with young wheat. When eventually the wheels clattered onto the flagstones in the yard at Brimstonedown, Theo was herding the last of the cattle in for the afternoon milking, and the long, low shed was full of clangs and bellows. Sal came out with Bea to help unload the provisions bought at market, and they were joined later by Harvey himself, who wished to take delivery of his hinges.

'And what is this, may I ask?' he demanded suddenly from the back of the trap.

Molly and Thamasine stared. He was holding Mr Philpott's ebony walking stick.

In spite of her denials, Blair was convinced that Thamasine had stolen it. 'It cannot, as far as I am aware, fly of its own accord into the back of the spring cart, so it must have been put there by somebody's hand, and I intend to discover whose,' he said. 'In the meantime it must be returned immediately to its rightful owner and a full explanation and apology given.'

'It is a beautiful thing indeed,' Grace said, taking it from her father and passing the palm of her hand lovingly back and forth over its shiny black knob. 'Do you suppose it was put there on purpose Father, in the way Joseph put the silver cup in Benjamin's sack?'

'Of that I have no idea, though I very much doubt it,' said her father. 'In the meantime I intend to return it straight away. You must accompany me, Thamasine, in order to tend your apologies. We shall drive over to Belstone Cleave immediately.'

'My dear,' said Susannah, who had come out of the kitchen, 'if you go over to Belstone Cleave now, you will not be back until long after nightfall, and it would not surprise me if there were further snow showers tonight. Can we not return brother Philpott's stick to him on Thursday when we go for the Bible reading?'

But Blair was not to be put off by this, or by the fact that the pony was not up to making the journey, saying that he would go as far as the Ring o' Bells and change horses there. Then, just as they were about to set off, a horseman came into sight, coming carefully down the moor path from Batworthy, and when he arrived in the yard Rufus Philpott found himself surrounded by a bevy of females who gazed upon him as upon a messenger from the gods.

'Your father's stick, I believe!' said Blair, becoming suddenly jovial and holding up the article.

Young Mr Philpott's Adam's apple jumped up and down two or three times and he uttered more of those strange little cries Thamasine had heard from him outside the Sticklepath foundry.

'Yes indeed, sir,' he gargled awkwardly. 'I do believe I must have inadvertently placed it in the back of your – ah – Mrs Endacott's – ah – carriage.'

'A quite understandable error,' Blair said, and seeing the froth on Philpott's horse suggested he come inside and take supper when it was ready. 'You will stay over until morning, will you not? Your horse is in no fit state for any more miles. No – I insist. We shall enjoy your fellowship, and if my nostrils are not misleading me, I think you will enjoy Peg's leek and potato pie.'

So he stayed, and a bed was made up for him in the large parlour; the fire was lit, the piano opened up and hymns sung; Blair gave him the benefit of his views on the place of the tabernacle in Old Testament prophecy, and the Misses Harvey gathered round the hearth, exchanging sly looks with one another, each beginning to think to herself that perhaps this Chinless Wonder was not quite such a milksop as she had thought. As for Blair, Thamasine had never seen her father looking so warm and welcoming, and she even began to wonder if the placing of the stick might have been the result of some conspiracy. Rufus himself, on the few occasions when Blair gave him the opportunity to reply, tended to swallow his words rather, which sent Bea into private convulsions and earned her a sharp elbow from Theo. Behind the scenes, Molly, scenting romance in the air, prodded Peg into putting on the best supper they had had in years, and the unexpected arrival of this blushing, hesitant young man turned into something of a celebration, with such gales of laughter from the young ladies at matters of very little consequence that it brought a sparkle back into Susannah's eyes and even succeeded in making poor dark Sal look more cheerful.

The following week, Mr and Mrs Harvey and the four Misses Harvey were invited to take tea with the Philpotts. It was the first time the young ladies had met the young gentlemen other than under the roof of the Okehampton assembly hall, and the occasion proved a rather formal one, with Rufus, Alexander and Simon balancing china teacups on their knees and stuttering about the weather. But that was only the beginning of an acquaintance between the families that was to develop rapidly as spring gave way to summer. The route from Brimstonedown to Belstone Cleave became well worn by the Harveys and the Philpotts, though there was a tendency for the Misses Harvey to spend more time on Mr Philpott's neatly mown lawn than the boys spent among the ancient circles of stone above Harvey's farm. Several afternoons were spent playing croquet, and a solemn group they made too, with the Mamas sitting under black parasols on the garden seat, the Papas discoursing earnestly about spiritual matters and the young people cavorting decorously in long full dresses or waistcoats and shirtsleeves. Suddenly it seemed that a new goal had been set before them, and matters of eternal importance temporarily set aside. Blair and Susannah had agreed with Lewis and Elizabeth that the budding friendships between their respective offspring were the best possible outcome of a misplaced ebony stick; and when the predictable conclusion occurred, it was as astonishing as such predictable conclusions often are: a week before Thamasine's sixteenth birthday, Rufus – who had heard a call from the Lord to go and serve Him in Africa – asked little Bea to be his life's partner.

Of course she had to consult her Mama and her Papa, because she was only nineteen, but the height of her colour and the fluttering of her hand upon her heart proved that she was the happiest possible young person, and her father had no hesitation in giving the proposed union his blessing. Mother and daughter fell upon each other's necks. Grace and Theo looked on with green eyes, and Thamasine decided that she might attempt a descriptive vignette of the scene instead of an essay on *Paradise Regained*.

The wedding was fixed for mid-September and the arrangements were undertaken by Molly, who planned a sit-down feast at trestle tables under the rowan trees after the ceremony in the Room. The large parlour was turned into a sewing room, and quantities of tulle and white cambric purchased for the wedding dress. Susannah and Bea set about the task of dressmaking, having great difficulty with the sleeves which 'wouldn't come right'; and in the middle of this shemozzle of pricked thumbs, maternal advice and premarital tension, Theo and Grace dropped a further bombshell by announcing that Alexander and Simon had decided to jump on the bandwagon.

'I am amazed,' said Blair, 'that you should take this attitude. I should have thought you would be only too delighted to see your daughters making such sensible, suitable matches.'

They were taking a walk, at Susannah's urgent request, to discuss the latest development, and were now topping the rise of Park Field, which overlooked the thickly wooded gorge of the North Teign.

'I *am* delighted,' said Susannah, watching a buzzard soaring on the far side of the cleave, 'but I would like to be more certain that my Theo and Grace are not marrying simply because they are afraid that this is their last chance.'

Blair made a scornful explosion with his lips. 'Last chance! You make them sound like old maids, Susannah!'

'Nevertheless, the opportunities for meeting suitable marriage partners are not very frequent for them. I cannot help thinking that if we were in the world, my daughters would not be in such a hurry to accept the first offers that came along – nor, for that matter, would brother Philpott's sons be quite so anxious to make them.'

Blair poured scorn on this view at some length. They strolled solemnly up and down, while around them a profusion of bees attended the wild flowers in the grey stone walls and yellow brimstones flapped along in steady procession, taken away by the southerly breeze so that they streamed up over the conifers in South Park.

'What do you propose then? That I forbid the union?'

'No, simply advise caution. They do not have to be married all on the same day, and it would be no bad thing for them to be better acquainted.'

'But you did not raise any objection to Bea's proposed marriage! Why should you object to Theo's and Grace's?'

Susannah became distressed: she was thinking of her own hurried decision to marry, but did not dare cite it as an example.

'There is no doubt in my mind,' Blair went on, adopting his pontifical manner, 'that this union – or, I should say, these unions – are in accord with God's wishes. Have not events conspired to bring us into contact with the Philpotts? Have we not frequently besought our Lord for his blessings upon our family – and has not this betrothal come about as a result of blessed, happy fellowship between our two families? No, my dear, I cannot take it upon myself to put a brake upon the wheels and workings of the Holy Ghost. Who am I to interfere with what is so clearly in accordance with His plan? We must give our permission, our approval and our blessing to this proposal, and accept it as an overflowing cup of riches and goodness.'

As they went back to the house, Blair decided to try and cheer Susannah up a bit. He rubbed his hands together and laughed. 'Come come, look on the bright side! The Philpott boys are splendid fellows. Their father informed me that Alexander will take over the mine within a decade, if the Lord tarry, and that Simon plans to qualify as an apothecary! And think! Within a few years we shall be grandparents! We are not losing a family but gaining three!'

She wished she could feel as enthusiastic, but could not escape a feeling of dread that her daughters were about to make the same sort of mistake as she herself had made: that they would marry in haste and regret at leisure, that they would discover their dreams turned into drudgery and their romance into a soul-stifling routine. Watching her daughters in those last days before their marriages she could not help remembering her own youth, and was forcibly reminded of how much enthusiasm and energy she had once had, and how little remained. But there was nothing whatever she could do now: Blair had given his wholehearted approval; the three brides-to-be spent hours together in their rooms, chattering and giggling and whispering; there were episodes of almost hysterical gaiety followed quickly by sudden tears; and from time to time Susannah would catch Thamasine's eye and would know with relief that at least she saw events for what they were and was unlikely to follow her elder sisters' example by rushing so precipitately into wedlock.

The day approached; the day arrived. Equinotial gales brought heavy rain that lashed down with unmitigated fury. The Philpotts' carriage became stuck half way up Waye Hill and two extra horses had to be sent down to pull them up; plans for a wedding breakfast outside had to be hastily changed to a crowded gathering in the large parlour; brother Beer placed the leg of his chair on the hem of Grace's dress, so that it ripped when she tried to move away, and Molly was distinctly heard swearing at Pandora (the cow) for kicking over a milk pail.

Otherwise, it was a success. After weak tea and heavy pastries, the three couples departed by carriage for Belstone Cleave; the guests departed, the parents embraced and shook hands and took their leave.

The rain had stopped, and under the dark clouds a yellow sunset bathed the Teign valley in a strange light, so that the forests looked black and the fields an unnaturally brilliant green.

The remaining members of the household supped in almost total silence, Blair keeping his head down over his plate, Susannah looking tired and red-eyed and Molly making brisk little attempts at conversation about the weather or the new arrangements that would now be necessary for the running of the farm.

'We'll all have to work the harder,' she said, and looked at Thamasine.

Thamasine excused herself, saying that she had some reading to do, and having kissed her father dutifully on the cheek went to embrace her mother.

Susannah pressed her hand. 'Never mind, dearest,' she murmured. 'Your time will come.'

She lit a candle and mounted the stair, her full grey skirts brushing the plaster as she went; and as she was about to enter her room she heard her father make a remark downstairs that caused her to stop and listen.

'If she thinks I can spare her to go off and be a governess, my dear, she'll have to think again. We shall need every pair of hands we've got to keep this place afloat now – am I not right, Molly?'

Thamasine went into her room and closed the door. The wind moaned in the chimney, sending in chill draughts that were like advance messengers of the winter to come. She stood for a moment looking back at herself in the mirror. As the candle flame moved in the draught, her own shadow swayed back and forth on the wall behind her, as if it were desperately seeking to escape.

CHAPTER 20

Winter came. Westerly gales gave way to days of frozen fog that hung on the larch trees in South Park like white lace; icy rain turned to sleet and slush that splattered under the wheels of the spring cart on the way down to Chagford, and in the new year blizzards swept down over the moor, sending ten-foot snow drifts that completely blocked the lane and left Brimstonedown isolated, a tiny, throbbing island of life in a white wilderness.

February was the cruellest month. Just when spring was encouraging daffodils and crocuses up through the melting snow, there was a further cold snap: the slush and snow re-froze and turned the yard into an ice-rink and decorated the grey stone walls with heavy, pointed icicles.

What bitterly cold mornings those were, when you woke up and could not see through the hoar frost on the windows; when milk froze over in the pail on the way from the cow-house to the dairy; when Sal, gathering an armful of sticks for kindling, would weep to herself, breathing on her nails.

Poor Sal: she was almost demented now. She was still capable of fetching and carrying, laying fires, scrubbing floors and scouring pots, but the love of life had gone out of her, and she spent more time talking to herself in a rapid undertone than in communicating with anyone else. Sometimes at meal times she would weep quietly, sniffing and spluttering, but as any attempts at comfort were inclined to produce hysteria, such miniature breakdowns were ignored. If she was working alone in the kitchen when someone entered she would never fail to give a little scream of surprise; she seemed perpetually frightened that she would be found to have committed some error, and her roamings about the house in the middle of the night to ensure that she had not been left behind became a commonplace, occasioning a sleepy, 'Go back to bed, you silly girl!' from Blair.

The departure of the three elder girls had lightened the communal work load in some ways. The mounds of darning and mending had diminished; there were smaller meals to prepare and clear away, and the weekly wash had reduced to more reasonable proportions. But their absence left Susannah feeling as though her life's purpose was all but fulfilled: she missed their chatter and laughter, their hymns round the piano in the evenings, their bright faces at the breaking of bread on Sunday mornings.

Blair was taking a greater interest in the management of the farm, and seemed to be transferring his affections from his daughters to his cattle. He and Molly were devising plans to build up a prize herd, and every Saturday afternoon he spent an hour or so in her parlour to discuss agricultural subjects. Exactly why they required so much time for these discussions, Susannah didn't bother to enquire: she was content that her husband had found an interest that had nothing to do with spiritual matters, and that in spite of his earlier objections, he and Molly were able to work amicably together. Besides, the arrangement improved his temper noticeably, especially on Saturday evenings, when his company became quite enjoyable.

It was Thamasine's behaviour that worried her now. Since her sisters' departure, she had neglected her studies and had left her books on the shelf. She went about in a sullen silence that was quite unlike her, and often went on long walks by herself, returning only just in time for the afternoon milking, a duty mother and daughter shared between them.

414

Cows like routine, they are reassured by it: they like to be milked by the same hands night and morning, to use the same stalls, to be spoken to by the same voices. To milk a cow well, you must become one with the animal; you must sense her mood and adjust for it; you must transmit, by your own tranquillity, a spirit of peace and cooperation, so that the milk comes down readily and quickly. For those who have never milked cows night and morning all the year round, the idea of it may seem attractive in a rustic sort of way, but for Thamasine it quickly became a drudgery she detested.

Nor was she hesitant about explaining why. She told her mother that she felt completely enslaved by these smelly brown creatures and that if she had her way she would never look on another set of udders in her life. Susannah tried to reassure her with optimistic ideas of a future life of independence.

'I shall never leave Brimstonedown, Mama!' she exclaimed one afternoon when they were milking. 'I know it for a fact.'

Susannah's cheek rested against the warm brown flank of Antigone, and her hands were sending white jets of milk down into the froth.

'All the same I am sure you would be happier if you were to recommence your studies, dear.'

'But there is no reason to continue them!'

'I think there is a very good reason, Thamasine. I thought you had hopes of becoming a governess one day.'

'I am as likely to be Empress of China,' said Thamasine, and took her pail briskly to the large upright churn to empty it.

'But is not study worthwhile for its own sake?' Susannah asked when her daughter was seated again on the milking stool. 'You have talent, you know that. So should you not develop it?'

'You do not study, Mama. And yet you used to. So you must have reached the conclusion that a time comes when study is no longer worthwhile for its own sake.'

Susannah sighed, thinking of her own enthusiasm for Greek and Hebrew, and afternoons spent in the Exeter city library with Mary Groves when they were nineteen. 'I do not suggest you follow the example I have set, dear – just that you learn from the mistakes I have made.'

They looked at each other across the stalls. 'Mama!' Thamasine whispered. 'You have not made mistakes! You are the best and the dearest possible mother in the world!'

Though it was kind of Thamasine to say so, Susannah was painfully aware that she had fallen far short of the high aspirations of her youth. How ridiculous it seemed now that she had literally panted for Blair's embrace! That she had sent for him and pushed him quickly into a proposal of marriage! And how easily she had let slip her own studies, how readily she had embraced the life of conventional triviality – both in Exeter and later at West Lawn! What rubbed salt further into this open sore was the fact that Blair himself was now attempting to carve a reputation as a letter writer and author of religious tracts, so that her own history seemed to be repeating itself and she was once again enslaved by a man who spent most of his time in his study and who flattered himself upon his literary ability. She had seen his attempts at spiritual literature and evangelical pamphlets, and they had appalled her by their blatant appeal to emotionalism, pseudo-academicism and fear. But because she had wished her father dead she felt inexorably bound to love, honour and obey her husband, so that she was caught between two shadows: one, the shadow of her past wilfulness and the other that of her marriage vow.

Between these two shadows lay the path of light, and it was in this light alone that she was secure. Here, in the simple message of the gospel, Susannah felt herself to be on firm ground. There was no doubt in her mind that all – and she in particular – had sinned and were in need of salvation; that refusal to accept the Saviour necessarily resulted – through the infinite justice of almighty God – in eternal damnation, and that she, having put her trust in the Lord, could be certain to have a place in the heavenly mansions. These three concepts, of original sin, free salvation and the prospect of eternal bliss were the sure pillars upon which rested her sanity and which maintained her equilibrium, and what distressed her most of all about Thamasine was that she had not yet made them her own.

For a long time, Susannah and Thamasine had been virtually in telepathic communication with each other. Each could tell immediately if the other were concerned about something, and it was common for one to raise a subject that was already uppermost in the other's thoughts. So although Susannah seldom spoke of spiritual things to her daughter, Thamasine was well aware that her mother longed for her conversion. As the winter gave way to spring this longing seemed to intensify. It was transmitted without words: by little pressures of the hand as they went up the wooden stairs to the Room on Sunday mornings, by tender glances during the gospel address in the evenings and by prolonged embraces at night before retiring to bed.

Blair, who seemed to be taking pains to be on better terms with his daughter these days, was altogether less sensitive about such matters. He called Thamasine his 'little doubter', and made no bones at all about praying for his ewe lamb that was lost and still in danger of hell fire. But he also had cause for concern over the fall-off of attendance in the Room. Since the separation from Bethesda, some of the saints had chosen either to worship with the brethren at Chagford, or to leave the assembly altogether and join the Methodists or Bible Christians. Blair saw such backsliding as the worst possible evil, regarding it as one more sign of the approaching end, along with the much vaunted strength of the new Oxford Movement and the rapid upsurge of interest in Catholicism since J.H. Newman's conversion – an event which he hinted, darkly, might constitute the arrival of the anti-christ.

'We must redouble our efforts,' he told the saints of Brimstonedown one evening when the winter had abated and the Bible readings had been resumed. 'We must go out into the highways and byways, and compel them to come in.' He looked down at Thamasine, who was required to sit beside him these days. 'And I am confident that certain of our number will come forward this year to approach the mercy seat.'

This pointed remark caused Thamasine intense embarrassment. She sat staring straight in front of her, her cheeks and neck flushed, her heart pounding in her chest.

Susannah saw her discomfort and mentioned it to Blair that night when they were undressing. 'It may be that she will be more readily persuaded if we do not make such frequent mention of it in public,' she said as tactfully as possible, and to her surprise Blair agreed quite mildly. 'Nevertheless it is high time she decided for Christ,' he said. 'She cannot remain indefinitely in darkness. I think you might do well, Susannah, to point out to her that if she hesitates too long, we should feel obliged to consider her position here at Brimstonedown.'

'Her position? In what way?'

'Isn't it obvious? It is all very well for a child to be present at the Lord's table and not receive the bread and the wine, but for a grown woman to remain obstinately separate within the body of the saints is surely a stumbling-block.'

This veiled threat was not lost upon Susannah, and although it pained her to raise the subject so directly with Thamasine, she felt obliged to do so. 'It may be,' she said a few evenings later, sitting on Thamasine's bed before snuffing the candle, 'that you are prevented from accepting Him through your own pride, dear. I myself suffered – and still suffer – from pride, and I fear you may have inherited it from me. It is the most difficult thing to do, to cast yourself at His feet and admit that you are a poor sinner, but when you do, you will feel that an immense burden has been lifted from your shoulders. You will no longer be the slave of your own pride, your own self-will: you will be set free.' She took Thamasine's hand lovingly between her own. 'Oh, my dear – do you know that I pray almost constantly that you will approach the throne of grace? Do you not realise that nothing – nothing at all – will make me happier than to hear from your own lips that you have accepted the Saviour? Do you not see that my dearest wish – my only wish now – is to know that you are safe, and that one day we shall be together in glory?'

A week or so later, on a Saturday afternoon, Thamasine descended the steep path that goes down beside South Park to the North Teign. The first spring flowers were blooming now, and over the steady roar of the torrent could be heard a chorus of birdsong. Hastening down-hill, the brown waters leapt and swirled over smooth boulders, and the afternoon sun slanted through the trees onto brilliant banks of moss and scarcely opened daffodils.

This was the part of the river where her sisters had been baptised. A pool of slower-moving water could be found just a little way up stream, and Thamasine could never look upon it without wondering whether she might some day submit herself to that symbolic burial with Christ. For as long as she could remember she had lived within the sound of these rushing waters – 'the waters of Babylon' as she and her sisters had called them – when they had been younger. Their changing moods and colours held a fascination for her, and upon reading the Greek myths she had had no difficulty in believing in river nymphs, for her own mood seemed influenced by the mood of these tumbling waters.

She wandered up-hill following the river's course, pausing from time to time to observe the wildlife or to gaze upward at the sunlight filtering down through the branches.

Eventually she sat down on a fallen tree, and putting her chin on her hands stared for a long time as if hypnotized by the river, allowing her thoughts to tumble without any contrived sequence or logic.

Today, this afternoon, marked the end of the struggle. She had argued the case back and forth in her mind, had fought bravely against the sure knowledge that there was no real choice. It might just have been possible to go against the wishes of her father – in spite of her mother's warnings about that – but to turn her back on her mother's loving entreaties was too much. She simply could not do it.

And yet . . .

The trouble was, she understood the implications all too clearly. She had already delayed too long, she was already past that state of childlike submission which Bea had said was required if a sinner was to repent.

'And I don't *feel* like a sinner!' she announced to the roaring waters.

She felt tears starting in her eyes and blinked them away, determined not to allow emotion to play any part in the decision that must be taken.

She whispered her thoughts to herself, and they sounded strangely facile and childish to her. Did she really claim to be without sin? No, of course not. Then . . . she was a sinner. And if a sinner, in need of salvation; and if in need of salvation . . . .

She shook her head, as if by doing so her thoughts might be rearranged into an easier pattern, like spillikins. But they were not rearranged. Her immediate dilemma was like a miniature of her ultimate fate. Either she repent and confess her Lord in baptism here in these waters, or she must face the future as a castaway from her family, an infidel, a black sheep. Either she identify herself with God's family, or she must willingly walk away from the free gift of eternal life and down into the horrors of eternal punishment.

Really there was no decision to take, and the final victory (or was it a defeat?) came quickly and without any outward sign on her part of its occurrence.

One moment she was sitting on the fallen oak; the next she was making her way back along the river path, and up the side of the gorge to the field behind the house.

When she reached the top she paused a moment, and because of a forcible awareness that if she looked back she might change her mind, she went forward again almost immediately, and down the hill to the yard, where the cows were already lumbering slowly in through the gate for the afternoon milking.

She washed her hands at the water butt and went in to join her mother, who had already rinsed the pails and was wiping Persephone's udders with a damp cloth to prepare her for milking. Mother and daughter greeted each other, and Thamasine collected a milking stool and pail from the end of the cowhouse, setting about her work in silence.

There were eight cows to milk, two having recently calved. Now that spring had come, the yields were increasing, and it was important that each cow was milked right out in order to maintain or increase her production.

For some time they milked in silence, and Thamasine struggled inwardly to say what she was determined to say. But it was not easy: her mother seemed lost in her own thoughts, her grey head bent against the cow, her hands swinging rhythmically, her eyes occasionally closing for seconds at a time.

She promised herself that as soon as this pail was full, and as soon as she had emptied it into the churn, she would say it.

She worked steadily on. The level of milk rose slowly.

It was full. She took it to the end of the shed and emptied it into the churn. Then, turning back to her mother she spoke the formula: 'Mother – I accepted the

Lord Jesus as my Saviour today.'

Susannah stopped milking immediately and came rapidly along the central aisle, her face radiant. Thamasine found herself hugged tight, and was unable to prevent herself shedding tears of happiness.

'I must go and tell your father,' Susannah said, and ran out, leaving Thamasine a little dazed at the suddeness of it all, and relieved that the occasion had proved far easier and happier than she had expected.

Susannah ran across the yard and along the front of the house to the kitchen door. Inside, Peg was snoring by the hob and a tabby cat was curled up on the windowsill. She went through the kitchen to the passage, and finding Blair's study empty continued to the end of the house to Molly's parlour.

She tapped on the door and entered. There were papers on the oak table and some copies of a farming magazine. While she stood at the door looking in, she heard a movement upstairs, and then – quite clearly – Blair's voice.

'What was that?' he asked, and was immediately silenced by a sudden, 'Shhh!'

She looked up the back stairs which ran from the small parlour to Molly's bedroom. 'Hello?' she called. 'Are you upstairs, Molly?'

There was a movement, then, 'Just a moment!'

She waited just a moment, and several moments more. From the room above, she heard rustlings and half-stifled breathings.

Molly came downstairs, looking flushed.

'I was looking for my husband.'

'He was here just a minute ago. He's just this minute gone out of my door to visit you in the shed!' Molly was breathing rather fast and fingering an ivory brooch at her neck.

'Is there anything wrong?' Susannah asked.

'No – no – it was nothing. Just a little dizzy fit!' Molly went to her door and opened it. 'I'm sure you'll find him outside somewhere. He said he was looking for you.'

It was easier to believe her than to argue. Just as the natives of Pacific islands had failed to 'see' the presence of a British sailing ship on its first arrival among them, so Susannah preferred to ignore what was fearfully obvious. She wanted to believe Molly, wanted to be saved from having to admit to herself a situation which she had known subconsciously for some time; so she went out by Molly's door and took her time going back to the cowhouse, and as she reached the door, heard Blair's shout behind her.

He came striding up, looking very jolly. 'My dear!' he said, 'we have been playing Cox and Box! I have been in search of you, and you have been in search of me!' He laughed over-loudly, and his pale blue eyes went quickly from side to side, as if something had passed by at great speed.

'Why were you looking for me?'

'Why? Why? Why – because Molly and I have – have been going through the accounts and have discovered a small surplus! Now isn't that good news? We shall be able to afford a few little luxuries for ourselves. New clothes for yourself, my dear – perhaps even a holiday by the sea!'

She turned away from him.

'I too have good news,' she said. 'Thamasine has come to the Lord.'

He accompanied her to the cowhouse, and embraced his daughter. Listening to the booming echo of his voice, seeing the swollen vein in his forehead, watching him rock on his heels and stick his thumbs in his waistcoat, Susannah could not help recalling past scenes: scenes with Zilla, with Miss Cox and a host of other young women who had caught his eye; and the recollection of these scenes was like a dull thud in the pit of her stomach, a thud of awareness that he had never truly loved her, that she was no more than an appendage to him, and that now that she had provided him with children and he had found a woman more attractive and younger than herself to keep him company and tell him what to do, she might just as well cease to exist.

CHAPTER 21

Thamasine had presumed that her conversion would bring about a marked change for the better. She had expected happiness, celebration, laughter. She had believed she would at last find the heartfelt approval of her father, and that though life might be difficult at times, she would never again feel unloved or unwanted.

For half an hour, more or less, these expectations were fulfilled; but she had been trained from an early age to think and observe objectively, and soon became uneasy at her father's unctuous blessings. She did not enjoy being told, for instance, that his soul would bubble over with joy on that day when he saw her buried with Christ.

He announced her conversion to the brethren and sisters after the breaking of bread the following day. Clasping his Bible to his chest, he informed them that a little ewe lamb, dear to his soul, had at last approached the mercy seat. This revelation brought forth a flurry of damp handkerchiefs, and when brother Glebe stood up to give thanks 'for the little sapling planted in our midst' his words were echoed by a series of amens the like of which can only be heard in the House of Commons when the lobby fodder groan their approval.

What caused more serious misgivings was the change Thamasine noticed in her mother. Almost from the moment she returned with Blair to the cowhouse, she began to look preoccupied by some new inner trouble, and her valiant attempts at cheerfulness only emphasised the signs of strain her daughter detected in her.

It was as if the household had needed at least one dissident among its members to preserve a finely balanced equilibrium. Now that she had crossed the deck to join the others, the ship seemed in danger of capsizing.

In spite of these misgivings, she felt unable to turn back. Her father had already written to brother Darby to invite him to officiate at the baptism in July – if the Lord tarry – and had made arrangements for her to be examined on the essential doctrines by brothers Glebe and Fowler.

They came up the hill one Monday evening, Glebe in his best white corduroys and fustian jacket, Fowler, who was in service at Meldon Hall, wearing his livery. They were shown into the large parlour and invited to sit at the table, which was covered by a heavy cloth that reached within inches of the floor so that its legs might be hidden from view. Thamasine was sent for: she had been reading in her room, and looked small and gentle among these men, who gasped and grunted and repeated themselves.

Blair had decided to sit in on the interview, and took a chair directly behind his brethren, so that Thamasine found herself confronted by all three of them across the table.

Brother Glebe did most of the talking. He was a dairyman, with abominable halitosis, a nasal delivery and quick, chestnut eyes that seemed unusually attracted to Thamasine's neck and bosom.

He wanted to know how it was that she had come to repent and how she knew she was saved; she told them in a quiet, well modulated voice of her inward struggle and final decision. She quoted John iii 16 and I Corinthians xv 22, but brother Fowler was not content with that. He had strong ideas about being washed in the Blood, and wanted to hear Thamasine admit to having undergone the process.

Half way through the examination, she felt herself splitting in two. Part of her remained sitting in her chair, answering the questions as gravely as they were put, while the other half seemed to fly up into the corner of the room and look down on this extraordinary unrehearsed charade they were playing out.

'Yes, I have been washed in the Blood,' she heard herself say, and at the same time knew that such a statement was ridiculous, for she had never been washed in any blood, and had no desire to be.

'And what of Bethesda?' brother Fowler asked suddenly.

She had been well prepared for this question, and was aware that it was crucial to her acceptance into fellowship. Her father had instructed her upon the scriptural basis for brother Darby's withdrawal from Plymouth and his excommunication of Bethesda. She knew 2 John 10 & 11 by heart, and understood that it was necessary to act upon it with regard to all those who failed to interpret Scripture correctly. She knew, too, that by judging the question of Bethesda she would identify herself, once and for all, with the last remnant of believers whose privilege it was to hold the slim stem of truth while the world plunged on, downward into darkness.

'Will you now judge the question so that we may be sure of your position?' Glebe asked.

She felt her heart thudding in her chest, and for a moment saw Captain James huddled in his death agony on the moorside. He had failed to judge the question and had been struck down. Did she believe it? Or rather, could she dare *not* to believe it?

'Yes, I will judge it,' she whispered.

There was a silence. Outside, one of the trees behind the house was creaking in the wind.

'Let us hear you do so then, Thamasine,' her father said.

So she recited the words she knew must be recited. She took a breath and said: 'Bethesda refused to separate from the teachings of Mr Newton. They refused to judge

427

his teachings concerning the atonement and divinity of our Lord. I – I judge them to have been in error, and I acknowledge that we must, as long as they persist in their error, remain separate from them.'

Glebe and Fowler exchanged a few whispers, and turned back to consult Blair, who had folded his hands on his chest, closed his eyes and thrown his head back in prayer. When he had been extracted from this semi-trance and informed that Thamasine had made satisfactory answers, he rose, and invited the other three to bow their heads while he gave thanks. Afterwards, brother Glebe took Thamasine's hand and held on to it for longer than was necessary.

'Welcome, sister in the Lord!' he murmured.

But she did not feel like a sister in the Lord. She was frightened by the new element of tension between her parents and believed herself to be to blame for it. She began to have recurring nightmares. One was of being condemned to death by stoning, and another – far more terrifying – of descending through innumerable halls, each one smaller than the last, until she found herself alone in a dark room with no door, and she knew she had been damned for all eternity.

While Blair rejoiced over his daughter's spiritual rebirth, Susannah felt herself sinking into an ever deeper depression. Having longed and prayed for Thamasine's conversion, she now regretted it, realising too late that it had been through Thamasine that she had been able to keep alive her interest in literature and the outside world, and that of all her daughter's qualities, the one she had treasured most was her independence of mind.

The unexplained presence of Blair in Molly's room was at the root of her unhappiness. No matter how hard she tried, she could not prevent Thamasine from being aware that something had gone seriously wrong, and yet she was unable to explain what. This in turn damaged the special trust mother and daughter had always had in each other, so that just when they should have been at their happiest and closest, they were forced apart into virtual estrangement.

That Molly and Blair were on intimate terms, Susannah was convinced. In the first days after the shock of discovery, she had tried to believe that she had been mistaken, and that some trick of sound had enabled Blair's voice to come from Molly's bedroom; now, she could no longer ignore what seemed to her wifely intuition almost unbearably obvious. They positively glowed for one another, and though they were always careful, in her presence, to address each other in formal terms, she sometimes felt that she could actually smell their bodily lust. So powerfully was she aware of it that she had difficulty remaining in the same room with them, and found herself avoiding them for fear of making some further discovery. On emerging from the cowhouse in the afternoons, she was always careful to make plenty of noise with the pails to warn them. What she feared above all was that she might come upon them unawares and discover them *in flagrante*.

The strain began to tell. Her depression led to a loss of appetite and an inclination to talk to herself when she was alone. She became agoraphobic and experienced the greatest difficulty in leaving her room. On waking up each morning, it was as if she had to lift a heavy load in order to get out of bed. She spent hours in her room, emerging in the afternoons for milking looking hollow cheeked, with bruise-like marks under her eyes from prolonged weeping; and though she never rebuffed Thamasine, she made it clear to her that she wished no comfort, no consolation.

She did not blame Molly or Blair. If she despised anyone, it was herself. She saw now that she had never been a good wife. Looking back on the lascivious yearnings of her youth, her wilful behaviour towards her father, her shrewish treatment of Blair and – above all – the secret passion she had nursed for James, she regarded her present situation as a judgement and a just reward. Was it so surprising that Blair had turned to Molly for comfort and company? Of course not! Molly was nearly ten years younger, and unfatigued by childbirth. She was still in possession of that glow of youth, that musky sensuality, which attracts men to a woman like ants to molasses.

No, she could not blame them. Had she not herself almost panted for the embrace of James? Had she not, by her own romantic inclinations, paved the way that Blair was now following?

Thamasine stood at the door. 'Mama,' she said. 'You should not stay indoors so long. It is a beautiful day. We should be outside.'

She came into the room and took Susannah's arm. 'I will fetch your coat and gloves, and we shall take a walk, the two of us. Please!'

So she consented, though the sight of the rolling moors, stretching away as if into eternity, terrified her. She clung to her daughter's arm, leaning on her, and they battled their way up to Castor Rock.

Standing together on its summit, they looked out over Devon. The moor was putting on its summer coat of soft greens and heather purples. It was one of those brilliantly clear days, with not a trace of haze in any direction. Little clouds raced overhead, and their shadows were like phantom ships that sailed swiftly over a petrified sea.

Molly had relished practising her powers of seduction again. She had enjoyed engineering the first touching of fingers, and had taken a delight in his stumbling advances. He seemed to have forgotten the profession she had once followed, and treated her as a lady, which was immensely flattering. He had pressed her fingertips to his lips, had gazed soulfully into her eyes; and she, with unerring accuracy of judgement, had flattered his spiritual vanity by seeking reassurances as to the wellbeing of her soul. She had admitted with well-feigned timidity that her needs

430

as a woman extended to physical as well as moral comfort, and in doing so provided him with an opportunity to explain away his own misgivings at the same time as he soothed away hers.

He made much of the doctrine that they were dead to the law: he said that having been buried with Christ they were no longer under the 'schoolmaster' referred to in Galatians iii. He read her Genesis xxxviii and Deuteronomy xxv and cited the laws of Chalitza as a precedent for the intimacy that was becoming theirs. 'It is not good that man should be alone,' he said, and quoted Matthew xix 29. He told her that although he might be married in the eyes of the State, he was alone in spirit because his wife no longer bore the part of a wife. Thus, he said, the provisions of Romans vii were valid: the Lord had raised up Molly to be his help-meet, and their conduct was beyond reproach.

'So it isn't sin, then?' she whispered.

No, he told her, it was not sin, for to regard that height of pleasurable anticipation to which he had been so obviously raised as anything but pure would be to deny Genesis i 31, and would relegate creation to the level of a Satanic paradox.

She lay milky white on the bed, and he went in unto her. 'Oh, Mr Harvey!' she sighed. 'You're a lovely man!'

There was a clatter of hooves in the yard. He looked obliquely out of Molly's window, taking care that he could not be seen.

'The post boy,' he announced, and having buttoned his waistcoat and fastened his necktie, he threw on his coat and was gone.

It was a letter from brother Darby himself, written in his usual hasty scrawl and with his customary disregard for the niceties of grammatical construction:

20th May 1856

Beloved Brother in Christ,

What joy filled my heart on receiving your letter regarding the safe gathering in of your beloved daughter's soul! Truly He has poured forth the abundance of His tender mercies upon us! May she grow in Grace to love and serve Him. As to the question of my attendance at her baptism, I have been led to see that it is not in His mind for me at this time to bend my footsteps to Devon as I have much labour elsewhere while He tarry. However I thank you from my heart for your invitation and will most certainly take it up if ever I should be led to tour your locality. I was indeed saddened to hear from you of the darkness with which you are surrounded and was led to Hosea iv 17 – 'Ephraim is joined to idols; let him alone.' It is well that we should for ever bear the Saviour's awful declaration in mind: 'He that is unjust, let him be unjust still; and he which is filthy, let him be filthy still.' (Rev. xxii 11) Terrible punishment! Harder than the most severe outward chastising! (Read Heb. x: we need the perfect, settled assurance that there is no sin upon us before Him – AND WE HAVE THIS ASSURANCE!) Not for us the snares of mysticism which, while boasting much of its feelings, never gets beyond desire, for with simple Christianity, giving the KNOWLEDGE of salvation, we are in full possession of the love of God; thus can we delight in the nature of God and our intimacy with Him; thus we can enjoy the blessedness of being with the Son before the Father; thus can we rejoice in His being a man, with whom we are at one, *yet divinely perfect*. What joyful certainty! What blessed assurance to know that He is glorified in the saints and that just as Eve was of Adam we are of Christ! That when He has possession of our hearts there is power to silence what is not of God and to guide every act of our lives and of our work!

I send greeting to the brethren and sisters.

Yours in Christ, until He come –

J.N.D.

Blair had just finished reading this letter for the second time when he heard Susannah and Thamasine return from their walk. He went to the door of the study and called them in.

'I propose to hold the baptism without delay,' he told them when he had explained that brother Darby would not be able to officiate. 'We could go over to Okehampton for it and use their tank, I suppose, but I think I know my daughter well enough to be certain that she will much prefer the more traditional way, of being dipped like her sisters in the Teign – isn't that so, Thamasine?'

A week before the event, he entered Hermione at the Moreton show and won first prize, which put him in an exceedingly good mood. The farm was running at a profit; his household was in good, godly order, and Darby's letter had reassured him in his belief that having died to the world he was dead to the law and untouched by it. He was above such things: his heart was sprinkled from an evil conscience; his salvation was irreversible, and his new-found intimacy with Molly was part of God's plan.

Riding on this wavecrest of confidence, he announced that a special day of prayer and ministry would be held to mark the eve of his daughter's baptism. Accordingly, the brethren and sisters of Brimstonedown, together with several visitors from the Okehampton assembly, gathered one hot afternoon to hear Brother Harvey speak.

The title of the afternoon address was 'prophecy in relation to the Jews', and from two until five, Blair

433

expounded his chronological interpretation of the seventh book of Daniel. He explained the meaning of the four beasts and the ten horns. He suggested that the dispute between Russia and Great Britain over the holy places in Palestine being fought out in the Crimea might signal the fulfilment of Ezekiel xxxvii, and that in spite of the world's scorn of the idea, the Jews would soon return to Israel.

After a break for refreshments in the large parlour, during which Susannah and Thamasine milked the cows, the saints returned to the hard seats in the Room for another three hours of apocalyptic interpretations.

Turning to the book of Amos, Blair spoke of the transgressions of Damascus, Gilead, Gaza and Moab, and warned that nations as well as individuals would be held responsible for their actions at the last judgement.

'This England of ours is the nation we call the nation of Bibles, of religious activities, of missionary societies and professed Christianity. We boast of its being the land from whence the light of God's truth shines out to the whole world. But so did Israel of old, in the abundance of their sacrifices and their solemn assemblies. Yet God says in Isaiah i, "My soul hateth them, they are trouble to me; I am weary to bear them."

'My dear brethren and sisters, it is not likely that England will be either the abode or birthplace of anti-christ, for we know from Scripture that the place of his rising will be in the east of Europe. But there are many antichrists even now, and everything that is against God and His truth, whether openly or covertly, is the spirit of antichrist . . .'

As the evening wore on, he proceeded to explain the symbolic meaning of Babylon in the Book of Revelations; he expanded (interminably, Thamasine began to think) on that much loved subject, the Last Days; he pondered aloud upon the question of who would go when the Lord came, and returned once more to the book of Isaiah:

'Is it not enough to make us tremble when we think what we who are saved have escaped from? Listen again to the prophet in connection with the punishment of nations: "Woe to the multitude of many people, which make a noise like the noise of the seas; and to the rushing of nations, that make a rushing like the rushing of mighty waters! God shall rebuke them and they shall flee far off, and shall be chased as the chaff of the mountains before the whirlwind." '

On and on he boomed; the midsummer sun slanted in through the small high windows of the Room and his listeners struggled to maintain their attention. Finally, Harvey closed up his Bible, and after a short prayer of thanks, invited the saints to join him in a hymn whose words never fail to reassure the frightened heart:

> Swift to its close ebbs out life's little day!
> Earth's joys grow dim, its glories pass away;
> Change and decay in all around I see;
> O Thou who changest not, abide with me.

Later, when the saints were departing with lanterns carried inches from the ground to guide their footsteps, Blair felt an urge to give some sign of his reconciliation with Thamasine, whose recent repentance had softened his heart.

'My dear,' he said as they stood between the Room and Molly's front door, 'I would like you to have my notes for the two addresses you have heard today, as a reminder to you of your baptism and as a sure foundation for your spiritual life in the time that remains.'

He took five sheets of notepaper from the flyleaf of his Bible and handed them to her. 'I suggest it will be no bad thing if you spend an hour reading them and meditating on them before your burial with Christ tomorrow,' he added, and in a rare gesture of affection, patted her shoulder before going on into the house.

That night, she sat up late reading his notes and thinking about his two addresses; and strangely she felt that she would have been more reassured and certain in her mind if she had not attended his ministry that day. The apocalyptic content of the notes and the sense of urgency and of time running out, were not at all new to her, but seeing them set down in her father's hurried scrawl put them in a new perspective. Not for the first time, she fell to thinking about the chasm of eternity, and in particular the meaning of eternal punishment. Perhaps it was the lateness of the hour and the hypnotic effect her father's address had had on her that evening – or perhaps the imminence of her own baptism – but whatever it was, she began to see that the whole system of belief which her father and other brethren had constructed seemed to be flawed. This flaw was like a hairline crack that she had glimpsed from the corner of her eye before but had never quite managed to examine fully.

Feeling a little frightened, for the hour was late and the candle guttering as the wick burned down, she tried to fix certain beliefs in her mind which she could hold without any doubt at all. The first of these was Cartesian in its simplicity: creation existed, and was infinite, and if infinite could be termed The Infinite, or God. All things were made by Him, and without Him was not anything made that was made – yes, she could believe that wholeheartedly. But here the hairline crack suddenly widened, for if nothing was made except by the infinite God, hell, if it existed, had also been created by Him; and if so much as a single soul was to suffer infinite pain for all eternity, then that all-enclosing Being, that omniscient God, must have known it from time out of mind – indeed, He must have created beings which He knew must be punished.

Was this the nature of an Infinite God? Was this the way the Judge of all the earth did right? Trembling, she realised that she could not believe it, for no just creator could be a just creator if He created beings knowing they

436

would be tormented for all eternity.

She blew out the candle and got into bed without bothering to kneel and say her prayers. She lay in the darkness and watched the moonlight creep across the wall, and quite suddenly it occurred to her that the term 'eternal punishment' was itself meaningless.

She struck a match and lit a new candle. Taking down her grandfather's dictionary, she looked up the word 'eternal' and discovered the definition 'without beginning or end'. She experienced a thrill of relief. I am not undergoing torment at this moment, she reflected, and as I have no recollection of any perpetual punishment in the past, any torment that I may undergo must have a beginning, and – *ergo* – cannot be eternal!

It was not so much the relief at finding she would not undergo eternal torment that cheered her however, as the discovery that her instinctive rejection of this important part of her father's doctrine was well founded.

But that was not the end of it. Slowly, but with gradually increasing clarity, she began to see – not into the mind of the Lord, but into her own mind, and to discover more of what she could sincerely believe.

I do not believe that souls are saved or lost, she thought, nor do I believe in the elect and the damned, the sheep and the goats. I believe in an infinite Being, a God who is present equally in all His creatures, and who does not punish any soul for existing in the way its creator knew it was always bound to exist.

She stood trembling by the casement, and looked out at the valley of the Teign, which was bathed in a pale light. She listened to the steady roar of the river and reflected that up on the moor water droplets were already seeping down into rivulets and streams, the coming together of which would fill the pool in which she would be baptised. And then . . . then they would go on down the hill; they would join with the waters of the South Teign at Leigh Bridge, and the enlarged river would later be joined by many more rills, brooks and tributaries until the whole flowed out to the sea, losing all identity, becoming salt, and perhaps, one day, falling as rain upon some other high ground in a distant land, to become part of another confluence with another name.

Perhaps I am part of a river, she mused, a river of thought which flows down to the sea of knowledge and experience.

She blew out the candle and got back into bed, but thoughts still bombarded her mind, and she found herself being forced further and further back towards an inevitability which was as uncomfortable as it was inescapable.

If, first, she could not accept the concept of eternal punishment, then by denying it she was denying the teachings of Christ and the apostles, as recorded in the New Testament. It was no good picking out those parts of Scripture which you liked and discarding the rest: if you once divided it up in that way, you devalued the whole of it, put it all into the realm of doubt and rendered it almost worthless. Either she must accept it or reject it, and if she rejected eternal punishment she effectively denied Christ, and ceased to be a Christian.

And even if I do accept the whole of it, I am still faced with the problem of interpretation – whether my father's, the Archbishop of Canterbury's or even the Pope's, all of whom insist that they are guided by the Holy Spirit and all of whom disagree among themselves, to the misery and distress of their followers.

Really she felt quite grateful to her father for speaking at such length that day, and for making her a present of his notes, for if he had not, she might have blundered into the pool and got caught up in an eddy, to remain there for the rest of her life, while braver spirits found their way out to the sea.

Her mind was unchanged the following morning. She called the cows in from Middle Field: they came lumbering slowly through the lush grass like ships of the line, their hips swaying, the mud oozing between their cloven hooves, their milk veins swollen. She was joined by her mother a few minutes later, and they sat down to milk in silence. Once again, Thamasine found herself trying to summon her courage to tell her mother something, but this time her courage failed her. When he had been alive, Uncle James had told her stories of army discipline, and how the foot soldier was made courageous in the face of the enemy through a greater fear of the sergeant-major. She felt her situation to be similar. It would be easier now to say nothing, to allow the fear of her father's displeasure to have sway over the voice of her conscience.

She tried to put her doubts behind her, tried to cling simply to the barest essentials of the gospel; but having progressed so far in her thinking she could not stop: it even occurred to her that these very thoughts had been known to God from time out of mind, and that deliberately to suppress the natural urge to reason and to question would be to bury the talents she had been given at birth. The question was a ghastly paradox, a foolish-to-be-wise merry-go-round.

They had finished milking, and she had given no hint of her misgivings. They went back into the house for breakfast; there was some light conversation from her father about the coming events of the afternoon. He smiled upon her, pleased with her. Kneeling at her chair afterwards, she watched him covertly as he prayed, and wondered whether he could genuinely believe it all, or whether his doctrines were the result of a self-deception, exercised over many years.

She attended the breaking of bread, and after lunch her mother and Peg helped her dress. The old domestic squatted down to bunch up her stockings for her, and her mother brushed her hair vigorously and tied it in a white ribbon. And still she was unable to say that she could not go through with it.

The longer she left it, the more difficult it became. She began to be terrified that she would not have the courage to refuse, and felt panic rising like vomit in her gullet.

They descended the narrow stairs and went out into the sunshine. The saints had gathered in the yard. She saw them for what they were: humble, well-meaning country folk, ordinary human beings, dressed up in their Sunday best. She began to feel quite detached from the proceedings, as if it were not herself walking along between her parents, not Thamasine at all, but some other young woman, some person untroubled in her mind, whose serene smile disguised no feelings of terror.

The steady roar of the Teign – that roar that had lulled her to sleep every night and had greeted her every awakening for as long as she could remember – grew louder as they descended into the ravine. Knuckles whitened as sisters clung to their menfolk for support. Her father helped her over a fallen tree, though she needed no help. Taking his hand, she felt like a traitor already. She did not know how she could stop what was happening; she had left it too late.

And here was the river, its brown waters cascading and bubbling, whirling and eddying, sliding smoothly over boulders and making a rainbow-shot mist where it fell into a pool.

They gathered at the edge of this pool and sang a hymn, though their voices were scarcely audible even to themselves above the roar. Her father bade them bow their heads while he led them in prayer, and for the first time in her life she disobeyed: she kept her head up and her eyes open, and while he prayed she heard another voice, one that asked her how many millions of souls had gone and were going unbaptised to their graves.

Her father finished praying. She glanced at her mother, tried to transmit some warning to her, but was unable.

Clad in waders, he went down into the water. He turned and beckoned her. She felt her mother's hand at her back, pushing her gently forward – and at that moment it was as if two relentless forces met inside her, and she broke down, sobbing and shaking her head.

She felt hands supporting her, heard voices speaking in her ear. They said there was nothing to be afraid of, she wouldn't drown. Hands patted her and arms encircled her. It would all be over quickly, they said, and think! what blessed assurance to be born again of water and the Word!

She heard a shriek, and was aware, dimly, that it had come from her own lips. She shook herself free, glimpsed her mother's face, and broke away from the group. She ran a few steps and turned back to face them. They stared at her with upturned faces and open mouths. Her father shouted to her to come back.

But she did not go back, she could never go back. She scrambled upward over boulders and fallen trees, through bracken and brambles to the moor.

She walked for a long time. She went round Batworthy to the Teignclapper bridge, and up over Scorhill Down. She stared at the ancient circles of stone, wondering at the eternal destiny of those souls who had lived and died before Christ, who had known nothing of original sin, or salvation, or the fear of hell. For a while, she felt persuaded to run away and never to return; she was tempted to walk south over the moor and seek her fortune on the other side, in Tavistock or Plymouth. But the thought of her mother and an instinctive knowledge that her presence was needed eventually drove her back to Brimstonedown.

Towards sunset, when the pines in South Park were black against a glowering sky, she summoned her courage and went down the hill towards the grey slate roof that nestled below the ridge. She walked among her father's cattle in Middle Field, ignoring their stupid stares and bellows of recognition.

It was that dull time just before dark when candles are

lit and shadows creep about. The upper windows reflected a dull, metallic light. Hens, locked up for the night, were clucking sleepily in the coop, and a blackbird was panicking in the hedgerow by the lane.

She entered the kitchen. A cat jumped down from the sill and ran out of the house. Sal was laying the breakfast table before going to bed. She stared at Thamasine as if she were the devil incarnate.

Her father came to the door of the kitchen. 'So you're back,' he said, and looked her up and down. Her dress was torn and her hair undone.

'Yes, father.'

'Go to your room then. We have no wish to speak to you.'

She went to her room and sat on her bed. Except for the continuous roar of the Teign, there was an unnerving silence. Not a sound. The light went from the sky: she had no candle or matches. She heard her father's study door close, and then his footsteps coming upstairs. A few minutes later, Sal came up also. The yellow candlelight slipped in through the door like an uninvited guest. It paused a while, and slipped out again. After it was gone, the darkness seemed all the more intense.

CHAPTER 22

Blair woke early. He had the bed to himself: some weeks before, Susannah had moved out to sleep in the spare room, with the result that these days he was sleeping better and feeling considerably more energetic.

It was another brilliant summer morning. Outside his window, house martins chattered under the eaves.

He was not at all perturbed by the débâcle of the previous afternoon. He did not fear any loss of face in the eyes of the saints, or that he might become a laughing-stock; rather, he delighted in being able to offer up this set-back to the Lord, that it might win for him a further jewel in his heavenly crown. What Thamasine had done was to present him, unwittingly, with an opportunity to give witness to the wise counsels of the Holy Ghost, and an object lesson to the brethren. There could be no question, for instance, of making an exception of her because she was his daughter. He must treat her as he would advise any one of the brethren to treat a daughter or domestic who walked disorderly; he must invoke 2 John 10 & 11, and refuse to be a partaker of her evil deeds.

A separation – that was what was required. The thought of it intrigued and fascinated him so much that for a moment he was worried that Thamasine might give in too easily, and bow to his authority before he had had sufficient time to wield it.

He threw the covers aside, and his legs out of bed. He

sat in his nightshirt, his knees apart and his hands joined. 'Lord, we have weighty matters to deal with this day,' he muttered. 'Let not Thy servant flinch from carrying out the dictates of Thy holy will.'

He dispensed with prayers that morning, and instead ordered Susannah to accompany him to his study. Pale and hollow-eyed, she had been weeping for most of the night. It annoyed him that she should wallow in her misery so; but at the same time he could not help seeing that there was an element of justice in this low state to which she had been brought: here at last was her reward for so many years of obstinacy and superiority. Here was the result of her attempts to give Thamasine a worldly education.

'My mind has been much exercised on the question of my daughter,' he said, waving her to take a seat, 'and I have been led to the conclusion that we have no choice but to do as the Lord directs, however painful that may be to ourselves.'

He waited for some reaction, but received none. Really, he was beginning to have doubts as to Susannah's sanity. She had spoken scarcely more than a dozen words to him in the past month.

'Do you understand what I am saying?' he asked distinctly, as if addressing a child.

Her eyelids lifted: she regarded him steadily. 'Yes, I understand.'

He smiled – or rather, parted his lips and showed his teeth. 'What am I saying then, Susannah?'

She glanced to one side, considering.

'You are saying that you will decide what action you will take, what will be most likely to increase your stature among the brethren, and that you will then choose a scriptural text to support your decision, and wield it like a club if I try to oppose you.'

It was as if she were standing before a fire, and the light of it was reflected in her eyes. She blazed at him silently.

He felt a brief uncertainty, but it quickly passed, for she was only a woman, and a broken one at that. She was merely hitting out in the way she had hit out so often before. It was nothing more than reflex action, like the jerkings of a fowl after its neck has been wrung.

'What I am saying,' he said, enjoying the control he had over himself, 'is that we shall have to enforce a separation. Thamasine has chosen to separate herself from us, so we must separate ourselves from her.'

'It doesn't occur to you, I suppose, that that is an abominably cruel thing to do?'

'Cruel?' he echoed, 'Why so? Do you suppose that we do not have her well-being in mind? Would you prefer to see her remain obstinately in darkness?'

She tilted her head back defiantly, her nostrils flared. 'Thamasine is a thinking, intelligent child. She is not a person who can obey blindly, like her sisters. She needs time – and we have not given her enough. We have rushed her into baptism, and if there was any doubt in her mind about it then surely not even you can deny that she was right to refuse it.'

'I see, I see,' he said, and his anger was like a hot animal inside him. 'So you take her side, is that it? You condone a deliberate refusal to identify herself with our Lord's death and resurrection? Is that your position?'

'I will not have you place words in my mouth, Blair. I will say what I have to say and stand by it. And I tell you this, if you send Thamasine out of this house –'

'When did I say that? When did I say anything about sending her away?'

She was checked: he had taken the wind out of her sails.

'I presumed that by a separation you meant it.'

'In that case you presumed wrong, Susannah, as you have presumed wrong so often in the past. No, I shall not send Thamasine out of this house. She may remain under my roof. But while she remains in disobedience, I am led by my Lord to see that she cannot be regarded as our sister in Christ. Do you disagree with that?'

She faltered again, and seeing he had her on the run, he pursued her.

'No, of course not. You cannot, for to do so would be to deny Him, just as she is denying Him. You would be walking as disorderly as she – or more so, for her error is at least mitigated somewhat by her youth. Do you think I have not prayed earnestly for guidance on the matter? Do you think that I have not submitted myself entirely to His will? And how can I, having been led to see into His mind, disregard what I find there? Should I, because Thamasine is our daughter, seek a course that is comfortable rather than the one He directs? God forbid, Susannah! God forbid! What a stumbling-block to the saints that would be! What a blot in the Book of Life against my name!

'No,' he continued, and seeing that he had subdued her, adopted a gentler manner. 'We must act boldly, and we must act as one. The child must see that we are undivided. She must be made aware that her action was not of the Lord, and that until she has judged her own error, she must be separate. She must neither eat nor speak with us. She can stay in her room and meditate upon her actions, and as soon as she has judged them and confessed them before the brethren in accordance with James v 16, we shall welcome her back into our bosom with joy and thanksgiving in the Lord.'

Susannah stared at the worm-eaten floorboards. Inside her head, a high pitched note was ringing louder and louder, like an unending scream.

The separation began. Blair gave orders that Thamasine was to remain in her room and was to be allowed to leave it only in order to obey the calls of nature. Sal was to take her her meals, but apart from that, she was to be approached by no member of the household without his permission.

He informed her of his decisions personally. 'Make no mistake,' he said, standing at the door of her room, 'I have your mother's full support and concurrence. We shall not keep you under lock and key, but if you leave your room without permission, then that shall be a sign that you no longer regard yourself as our daughter, and we shall be absolved thereby of our temporal as well as our spiritual responsibilities for you.'

A week passed, and then another. Every afternoon before milking, Blair mounted the stairs and visited his daughter to ask her if she was ready to judge her error, and every afternoon he received the same silent refusal. To concentrate her mind a little further, he directed that Susannah should no longer receive assistance with the milking from Sal. In this way he was able to inform Thamasine that her obstinacy was the cause of a further burden upon her mother's shoulders. At the prayer meetings, Bible readings and breakings of bread, he kept the saints informed of the situation rather as a general briefs his staff officers on his strategy. Walking about his farm, leading the household in prayer or taking his ease with Molly, he believed himself to be acting under divine guidance. The issue seemed to him of eternal importance, and he was sure that the decisions which he had been led to take would one day serve as an example to the brethren. He started writing a journal again, anxious to make a record for posterity, and turning a conveniently blinded eye to the part of his doctrine which held that very little posterity remained.

In her room, Thamasine spent the first few days struggling with her conscience, and was particularly distressed to learn that her mother was being made to suffer for the decision she had taken; but having progressed so far, she could not turn back. She had climbed out of the ravine, she had abandoned it. The wind of independent thought was bitterly cold, but invigorating nevertheless, and though there were moments when the emotional appeal of the gospel tempted her back, such moments were short-lived.

One afternoon when he visited, he found her reading Montaigne. It was now nearly three weeks since she had been separated, and she seemed, if anything, more resolved to defy him. Seeing her sitting demurely there by her window, her dark hair tied neatly in a bun, her slippers just visible beneath her skirt of russet brown, he experienced a whiplash of anger, and striding across the room snatched the book from her hands and tore it apart. His anger choked him. He felt blood surging in his ears. What infuriated him the more was that, apart from the faintest flush in her cheeks, Thamasine gave no sign of discomposure.

He stamped out of her room and down to the kitchen, where he found Peg sitting in her customary place by the hob. 'Go upstairs to Miss Thamasine's room,' he told her, 'collect every last book on her shelf, and bring them down to me here.'

The old domestic got painfully to her feet and waddled out of the kitchen to obey. She made three journeys, returning each time with her arms full. He ordered her to throw the books down in the yard, and then he set them alight. The act of doing so gave him a deep, spiritual satisfaction. When they were well ablaze, he went upstairs to Thamasine's room. He grasped her by the neck and marched her to the window. 'Now,' he said. 'Behold your false gods. Where your treasure is, there will your heart be also.'

While they were at the window, he saw Susannah running back from the cowhouse. She began screaming hysterically, and beating at the flames with her bare hands. He went quickly downstairs to control her.

She came into the kitchen as he entered from the back corridor. Seeing him, she grabbed a pile of dinner plates, and threw them to the floor with every ounce of her strength. He called to the servants to assist him and seized her by the arm; but she fought him off, her arms flailing wildly, her eyes red like a mad dog's, her hair undone, her dress rent so that her bosom was partially uncovered. It took the combined efforts of himself, Molly and Peg to restrain her, and even then she struggled and screamed and spat at them.

He received a sudden revelation of the Lord.

'I command you in the name of God to come out of her!' he roared; and she was immediately docile.

'I am not possessed,' she said, breathing fast and deep, a trickle of blood coming from her nose.

'No, Susannah,' he said gently. 'Not any more.'

They released her: she held the top of her dress up against her neck to preserve her modesty.

'I shall be with Thamasine,' she said, and went quickly upstairs.

He stood in his study and bent to peer out of the window. Yellow butterflies were fluttering about on the cabbage patch, and a lark was singing overhead. It seemed strange that such brilliant summer weather should be accompanied by such demonic, spiritual darkness.

He reflected on his actions, and was content that he had acted entirely in accordance with his conscience.

'If I have erred at all,' he said aloud to himself, 'it has been in destroying those infidel books too late.'

There was the cause of it – he saw it all now. By allowing Susannah to bring them into the house, he had admitted evil under his roof, and by finally burning them, that evil had entered their owner. The realisation of it gave him a heady feeling that he was walking with destiny, that his every action was being guided by the Holy Spirit, and that the Lord was providing positive proof of the spiritual causes and their effects.

He began pacing his study, one arm bent behind his back, the other hand stroking his lips and whiskers.

Molly appeared at the door. He stopped pacing.

'Well?'

'When did you last look at the cattle?'

He frowned. 'Yesterday – the day before. Why do you ask?'

'You better have a look at them now,' she said simply, but the way she said it commanded his obedience.

He strode out of the house and along to the cattleshed. On entering, he was struck immediately by a putrid smell of rotting flesh. The cattle stood in their stalls in silence, as if something had come upon them to which they were totally resigned.

He examined the first one. Her eyes were dull, and she was drooling. He forced open her mouth: the tongue lolled out. It was covered in small, watery blisters.

He moved on to the next stall, and the next. Nearly all were showing symptoms of the disease, and in some the symptoms were already advanced. He was attacked by a fit of shivering, and felt himself to be in the presence of a great evil.

He fell to his knees, aware suddenly that the time of testing had come – the time for which the whole of his past life had been but a preparation. Making a comparison between these poor drooling creatures and the swine of Gadarene, he saw that the powers of good and evil were meeting head on, here at Brimstonedown. This was his personal Armageddon.

'Lord . . .' he began. 'Lord . . .'

'You can save your breath,' Molly said behind him. 'Praying won't cure this lot. They've got the epidemic.'

They did not have the epidemic. They were possessed. The devil had gone out of Susannah and into his cattle, and to believe anything else would be to deny the existence of divine intervention and undermine the very foundations of his most treasured beliefs. The knowledge of what had happened had illuminated his mind like a brilliant comet travelling across a dark sky. Here in this humble cowshed, he was to be tested: his faith 'as to a grain of mustard' would be used to move the great mountain of doubt and disbelief that had come among his womenfolk; through him, the Lord would show His mighty hand. He would be tested, and he would not be found wanting.

'Lord, make them whole,' he prayed aloud, so that Molly would hear and would be a witness in later times to the miraculous answer to his prayer, 'that the power and majesty of Thy Name may be made manifest.'

She walked briskly out of the shed, and returned ten minutes later. He was still on his knees in prayer.

'I've looked it up,' she said. 'It says we ought to put the healthy ones out in the field and keep the rest under shelter. We give them a good dose of Glauber salts and plenty of bran mash.'

When he made no reply, she set about examining each cow in turn. They shifted uneasily, coughing and lowing. Drools of saliva slipped silently down onto the stone floor.

She clicked her tongue. 'This one's foul in the foot already. Look at this muck and pus! We could bathe it, I suppose, and give it a dressing of hot tar.'

She came back along the aisle that ran down between the stalls. She stood in front of him, her fists on her hips. He looked down at the hem of her dress. It was covered with mud and muck.

'There's work to do, and I'll be obliged for some help, love. They were talking about this down at Moreton only a few weeks back. Even if a beast survives, she's never the same again. Some folk say the best thing to do is slaughter straight off to stop it spreading.'

She paced to the doorway and back. Her shadow was framed by a bright trapezium of sunlight on the whitewash.

'They won't be made better by praying, mark my words they won't. If you ask me, we might as well slaughter most of this lot. They're too far gone to save, that's my opinion.

We'll have to build a proper fire-ditch, mind, and that'll mean you rolling up your sleeves for a start. A good long ditch, that's what we want, with plenty of kindling and split logs. There's an old iron gate in the stable we can use to take the weight of the carcasses. They say you can eat the meat, though I doubt we'll have much taste for roast beef by the time we've had the smell of it hanging round this place for a few days.'

She went to the door. He heard her snort in exasperation.

'Look – no one's going to blame you for not performing a miracle. If you get off your knees, we can get a move on. We can get the digging under way, and if we all pitch in and work through the night, we'll have them slaughtered and blazing by midmorning. We'll have that daughter of yours making herself useful for a change. We'll forget what's in the past and make a fresh start. So what do you say? Are you going to do something about it, or are you going to kneel there and watch them drop?'

After she had gone, the cows began to bellow mournfully. It seemed that Susannah had not milked them. Having remained on his knees for over an hour, he welcomed the chance to do something positive.

He collected a pail and stool from the end of the shed and set about it. Moving from animal to animal, he was stirred by admiration for their dignity in distress. He patted them and murmured to them, and they rewarded him with stomach rumblings, twitchings of the tail and an occasional, half-apologetic moo.

'My beasts, my poor beasts!' he murmured and Hermione swung her head heavily and regarded him with huge, sorrowful eyes.

Each time the pail was full, he emptied it down the drain, and each time he completed milking a cow he offered up a prayer: 'Lord, let this Thy creature be cleansed and purified to the glory of Thy holy name.'

The task completed, he went down on his knees once more. The evening dwindled slowly away: the birds fell silent, and only the unceasing roar of the Teign remained. As the sun went down, the shed was filled for a few minutes with a faint, reddish glow, which faded rapidly, leaving him in deepening shadows and final darkness.

When he had been keeping his vigil for some hours (though he had no idea of the time) he heard footsteps approaching. As the lamplight entered the shed, his own shadow leapt down between the stalls, then swung over to one side. It was Molly again.

She stood in silence behind him. He remained on his knees, his head bowed, his hands clasped.

'Why don't you come in now?' she asked gently, and hearing her husky voice he saw her in his mind's eye as a girl of fourteen, soliciting strangers at the Exeter fair. 'They won't get any better for being prayed over, and you'll only catch your death staying out in your shirt-sleeves.'

She went past him, carrying the lamp. He watched her examining the cattle. Down at the end of the shed she looked back at him and said: 'They're no better. In fact they're a sight worse.'

Her words echoed briefly. He pressed his hands against his face, trying not to listen to her.

She came back to him. He sensed that she was standing over him. Suddenly she was whispering in his ear: 'They be all gone to bed, love. So why don't you come inside?' She paused, then added, 'You can come in with me if you fancy it. Isn't that what you always wanted? All night! Well, isn't it?'

He felt her fingers, gentle on his neck. He bent forward, shaking his head.

She had moved away. She was standing behind him, in the doorway.

'You're more of a fool than I took you for, Blair Harvey,' she said, and a moment later he was alone again

453

with his cattle, and the bats that whirred in and out overhead.

The night was very dark now, and he became aware of a wavering of confidence. What if Molly were right, and no amount of prayer would cure them? The thought of it filled him with dread, but it was this very dread that drove him back into the conviction that his request must be granted. It was impossible for him to believe otherwise: the thought of the saints coming up the hill in the morning for the breaking of bread and discovering his cattle dead or dying and his wife and daughter separated was too much. God did not reward His faithful servants in this way, he was sure of it.

And besides: if he followed Molly's advice, he would be abandoning spiritual faith for mere human commonsense. Could that be the Lord's will?

Another possibility arose. If Molly was now tempting him away from his path, should she not now be judged to be in error? And if in error, was there not also a possibility that his behaviour with her had not been of the Lord?

'How can these things be, O Lord?' he cried out, feeling angry to have been driven into this corner. How could he have been misled so, he who had prayed so earnestly before finally responding to Molly's advances and granting her the physical comfort she sought?

As the hours dragged by, he became assailed by ever more tortuous possibilities and arguments. He felt himself being driven down a dark tunnel at the end of which he could see no light. His joints ached and there were shooting pains in his knees. He tried to pray, but found himself simply muttering, 'Lord, Lord,' repeatedly. His mind began to present him with a succession of memories, a montage of half-forgotten faces and voices. He saw his father, a fierce gentleman in knee breeches of whom he had been mightily afraid. He had died when Blair was six, and the widowed Mrs Harvey had taken her son into bed every night for her own comfort, a practice he had looked back on nostalgically throughout his later life, remembering how much he had enjoyed the sense of being protected and safe in her arms. He recalled his chattering sisters and his devoted aunts. What carefree days those had been when he was little, when money was plentiful and the summer days were long! He had been the centre of attention then, the 'little man' who could do no wrong, and for whom great things were confidently predicted. How steadily, how inevitably had the Lord directed his footsteps from those days to this! He recalled afternoons of choir practice in Oxford as a child of ten and heard again his own soaring treble echoing beneath high, ancient ceilings. He recalled early days with Dr Watling, struggling over syntax and grammar and knowing inwardly that his ability was no match for that of his contemporaries. Blinking in the darkness, he remembered his arrival in Exeter and the first glimpse of his room in Idle Lane.

Had he achieved the great things that had been expected of him? Had he fulfilled the promise he had once shown? There had been times, along the years, when his confidence had faltered; but God had moved in a mysterious way, and in recent years – especially since the withdrawal from Bethesda – he had been mercifully strengthened, and he was sure, even now, that though his wordly circumstances might be lowly, spiritual riches awaited him in glory.

A bat swooped low over his head and out of the door. At the far end of the shed, one of the beasts relieved herself lengthily. He became lightheaded with fatigue, and his spirit seemed to jump about in time and space. He saw an old hag playing hopscotch in a prison yard; a little child, his only son, lifted on a pole – and the pale fingers of Dr Brougham as he waved the sign of the cross in absolution.

He was suddenly jerked awake. In the stall next to him, a cow had collapsed heavily on the stone floor. He felt sick, cramped, thirsty – all at the same time. He stood up and relieved himself into the drain. The stench of disease and ordure was overpowering. He stumbled to the door, and leaning against the jamb, looked upward at the silent stars.

The first insidious doubts slipped into his mind. A quiet voice was speaking to him. 'It is not working,' the voice said, 'and it will not work. They are diseased, not possessed, and they will continue to be diseased until they die, one by one. However long you stay here, whatever promises you make to Almighty God, however fiercely you rage against Him, you will not get your way . . .'

He ran inside again, unable any longer to look upward to the heavens, for the sense of his own insignificance was settling upon him as surely as the summer dew. Softly at first, but then louder and louder, he heard the voices of women: women laughing, women whispering, women chattering, arguing, weeping. He heard the deep throated lust-groans of Lavinia Pendlebury and the whimperings of Susannah disturbed by her dreams. He heard his daughters singing and giggling, and the voice of Molly, laughing in the cowshed as she milked her first cow; and over these voices he heard a new voice, a muttering, masculine voice that went on and on, louder and louder, saying whosoever looketh on a woman to lust after her hath committed adultery in his heart be not deceived neither fornicators nor idolaters nor effeminates nor abusers of themselves with mankind nor thieves nor the covetous nor drunkards nor revilers nor extortioners shall inherit the kingdom of God and if thy right eye offend thee pluck it out and cast it from thee for it is profitable for thee that one of thy members should perish and not that thy whole body should be cast down into hell many will say to me in that day Lord Lord have we not prophesied in thy name and in thy name have cast out devils and in thy name done many wonderful works and then I will profess unto them I never knew you depart from me ye that work iniquity for I am come to set a man at variance against his father and the daughter against her mother and the daughter-in-law against her mother-in-law and a man's foes shall be they of his own household hear and understand not that which goeth into the mouth defileth a man but that which cometh out of the mouth this defileth a man for nation shall rise against nation and kingdom against kingdom and there shall be famines and pestilence and earthquakes in divers places all these are the beginning of sorrows then shall they deliver you up to be afflicted and shall kill you and ye shall be hated of all nations for my sake and then shall many be offended and shall betray one another and shall hate one another and many false prophets shall rise and shall deceive many then let them which be in Judaea flee into the mountains let him which is on the housetop not come down neither let him which is in the field return back to take his clothes and woe unto them that are with child and to them that give suck in those days but pray ye that your flight be not in winter neither on the sabbath day for then shall be great tribulation such as was not since the beginning of the world to this time no nor ever shall be and except those days should be shortened there should no flesh be saved for as the lightning cometh out of the east and shineth even unto the west so shall also the coming of the Son of man be for wheresoever the carcase is there will the eagles be gathered together and he shall send his angels with a great sound of a trumpet and they shall gather together his elect from the four winds from one end of heaven to the other and I saw an angel standing in the sun and he cried out with a loud voice saying to all the fowls that fly in the midst of heaven come and gather yourselves together unto the supper of the great god that ye may eat the flesh of kings and the flesh of captains and the flesh of mighty men and the flesh of horses and of them that sit on them and the flesh of all men both free and bond both small and great and the beast was taken and with him the false prophet that wrought miracles before him with which he deceived them that received the mark of the beast and them that worshipped his image these both were cast alive into the lake of fire . . . .

He dreamt he heard the horses of the Apocalypse, and awoke shaking and panting with fear to the sound of his own horse whinnying in the yard.

He got up from his knees and went to the doorway. A veil of mist hung over the valley; the fields were laced with grey gossamer. Going to the corner of the shed, he saw that Susannah and Thamasine were backing the horse between the shafts of the spring cart.

My wife, my daughter, he thought, and watched as Thamasine went back into the house and emerged with two heavy bundles which she lifted into the back of the cart. That done, she mounted to take the reins and reached down to help her mother.

But Susannah did not accept her daughter's hand: they appeared to converse for a few moments, and Blair could see Susannah's distress in the way she was shaking her head. Suddenly she had turned, and was hurrying towards the cattleshed in whose shadow he stood. She was like a graceful, grey phantom, floating towards him in the gloom.

He presumed immediately that she was coming to beg his forgiveness before taking her leave, and he was filled with a grim fury, a determination that she should not have it. He would not even speak with her. He would not even grant her the privilege of seeing him for the last time.

He went quickly inside the shed and hid himself in the stall with Hermione, one of the few of his cattle still standing. He crouched under her belly: she shifted uneasily, and a globule of saliva plopped down on the stone floor beside him.

Susannah was in the doorway.

'Blair?' she whispered softly. 'Blair?'

He froze, holding his breath. Seconds passed, and he became aware that she was weeping. Though he heard only the whisper of her breath, a stifled sob, the sound of it unexpectedly tore open some deeply hidden pocket of tenderness and love and he was suddenly conscious of a yearning for what might have been.

But it was already too late: he heard her footsteps receding, and then a clatter of hooves and the grinding sound of iron rims on stone as the spring cart turned and went away out of the yard and down the hill.

He remained in the stall with Hermione for some time, aware of a bleak, inner silence. A hush. It was as if the whole of his past life had been a dream, and that Susannah's departure had brought him to consciousness.

Dawn was coming: he could see the shapes of his cattle emerging from the darkness. But he had no wish to face the new day. He dreaded it: how could he hold up his head before the brethren when they came up for the breaking of bread?

He tried to pray, but was unable. He found himself in a new, stark reality, one in which he could no longer turn to Susannah, or Molly – or even the memory of his mother – for comfort or reassurance. He tried to see into the mind of the Lord, but all he saw was his own inadequate mind. Had it been that misconception, that misguided conviction of divine guidance and inspiration which had led him along a road of hubris and dogma to this stenching cowhouse?

And it did indeed stench – he recognised the fact for the first time. His stomach heaved, and he gagged on vomit.

'God?' he whispered. 'God?'

A cock began crowing in the hen coop. Pushing himself stiffly to his feet, Blair leant heavily upon Hermione and she, with a groan, collapsed.

Nothing remained: no hope, no certainty, no self-assurance. He was afraid even of being found there by Molly: the prospect of living on with her as mistress of his house and his bed chamber was like a glimpse of hell on earth.

He stumbled out of the shed, sobbing. All he wanted was an end to it all: not heaven or hell; not judgement or rapture – just an end, a final oblivion.

Was that too much to ask?

The sun came up; the cobwebbed fields sparkled; the forest echoed with birdsong. When Molly and the domestics came down, they found not only the mistress and Thamasine gone, but the master also.

"E's not in the cowhouse,' Sal said. 'I been and looked. I heard horses in the night an' all. I reckon they be caught up, I do. Caught up they be, and us poor souls left for the tribulation.'

Molly told her not to be so daft, and went along to the cattleshed to see for herself. She had heard the trap depart as well and had been unsurprised to find Mrs Harvey and Thamasine gone; but she had not expected 'Himself' to do a flit.

She entered the shed. The disease had made shockingly rapid progress among the herd: the smell of putrefaction was overpowering. She went up the aisle, shaking her head at the carnage, and was glad to get out into the fresh air again.

'He'll be back,' she told Peg and Sal. 'You mark my words.'

After breakfast, she went down to Chagford to report the epidemic, and she returned two hours later in the company of farmer Bennett from Teigncombe, who brought a couple of labourers and a carthorse with him to lend a hand with the slaughtering.

The burning of carcasses took nearly a fortnight. Day after day, a pall of smoke rose from Brimstonedown, and a notice hung on the gate forbidding entrance and informing the saints that no further meetings would be held in the Room.

Molly was already confident that the farm would become hers, and was playing her cards extremely carefully. Peg seemed quite unmoved by the whole catastrophe. As for Sal, she was much more her old cheerful self, now that the worst had happened. She thought the smell of roasting beef quite tantalising at first; but later she confided to Peg that perhaps you could have too much of a good thing, after all.

They never found Blair Harvey, and although most people were sure he had wandered off over the moor to his death, there were a few who clung to the hope that he was alive and would return one day to Brimstonedown; and in the Ring-o'-Bells at Chagford, the story is still told that he may sometimes be seen late on a summer evening, kneeling in prayer by the waters of the Teign.

EPILOGUE

Susannah and Thamasine had travelled to Exeter, where they took lodgings in Northernhay, close to Rougemont Castle. Hearing of their plight, the alderman who had been instrumental in rescuing Dr Brougham's books from destruction, and who had since served as mayor of the city, was quick to offer assistance. Through him, Thamasine was found a position in the library of the Devon and Exeter Institute, which now contained over six thousand volumes, and she was just able to support herself and her mother on her earnings.

For a few years, they lived peaceably together. Susannah's health had been seriously affected by the trials and hardship of her life at Brimstonedown, however, and she was far more dependent upon her daughter than she would have wished. But in one way even that was a blessing: Thamasine was thrust immediately into the rough and tumble of the world, and had no time to dwell upon past unhappiness.

Sometimes they would take a stroll together in the cathedral grounds, and Susannah, glancing back at the neat sash windows of Broad Gate House, would reminisce about old times. Often, she referred to the city by its motto, *semper fidelis*: she used to speak of the days when the town was full of markets; when there were no railways, no gas lamps, no telegraph.

'. . . and when we went out at night, we used to take a maid, to walk ahead with a lamp held a few inches from the ground to light our footsteps,' she would say.

She spoke a great deal of her childhood in those last years, but although she appeared to achieve a certain contentment and peace of mind, she never truly forgave herself for certain mistakes she felt she had made in her life, so that death, when it came in the frosty autumn of '62, was a blessed release.

A few years later, when she was still working at the Institute, Thamasine had a stroke of luck. Her flair for cataloguing books and her capacity for hard work and meticulous accuracy won her the offer of a post as a junior librarian in the Reading Room of the British Museum, which she accepted immediately.

She moved to London, and lived in Bloomsbury for the rest of her life. She never married, though there was a whisper that she had an unsatisfactory affair with Gosse, who was ten years younger than herself. In the eighties she published a slim volume of essays inspired by the works of Sainte-Beuve, and as she moved on into old age she came to be regarded by her wide circle of friends as a lovable eccentric, whose sharp wit and rigorously defended views they relished.

Her sitting room overlooked the pillared entrance to the Museum, and it was there, surrounded by her books, that she used to entertain guests to literary tea.

Miss Harvey always gave as good as she got. She had yellow-white hair pinned untidily into a sausage at the back, and usually wore a black velvet band with a locket round her neck. She had jet dark eyes and thick eyebrows. Her voice was rather mannish (she smoked cigarettes!) but her delivery precise and fluent.

One afternoon just after the coronation of the new King, one of her relations brought their nine-year-old son to visit her. He was a good-looking child with thick, wavy hair and very blue eyes. Thamasine asked him if he could parse the line from Horace, '*et militavi non sine gloria*' and gave him sixpence for doing so. Then she raised the question of his religious education.

His name was Ben. For a while, he stared out of the window at the pigeons strutting on the sill, uninterested in what the grown-ups were talking about. But then Cousin Thamasine made one of her provocative remarks – a remark that was to stick in his memory and be passed on to his own children and grandchildren. She declared that she regarded all forms of organised religion in the same way as a game of football.

There was a shocked little silence.

'I have no objection to others taking part or looking on,' she said, 'providing they do not make too much noise about it, and I am not obliged to join in.'

And then, according to my grandfather, she winked at him, and his elders and betters laughed uncertainly.